- **ISBN-10:** 1505212847
- **ISBN-13:** 978-1505212846

Cover photo courtesy of Houmas House Plantation, Darrow, La.

For my daddy, the boy who grew to be the man who saw that the emperor had no clothes and could not keep silent about it, and for my mama, the woman who loved him.

And for Catherine, any roof that you're under is home.

The Saints of Lost Things

C. H. Lawler

SAN JUAN

BULLETIN 2 PM EST FRIDAY AUGUST 27, 1965

INFORMATION FROM RECONNAISSANCE AIRCRAFT INDICATES MODERATE TROPICAL DEPRESSION CENTERED NEAR 11.5 N 54.5 W AT 2PM EST. MAXIMUM WINDS ARE ABOUT 35 KNOTS IN A BAND OF SQUALLS JUST TO THE NORTH OF THE CENTER AND WINDS OF 25 TO 30 KNOTS EXTEND 200 MILES TO THE NORTH. THE WINDS TO THE SOUTH OF THE CENTER ARE RATHER WEAK.

THE DEPRESSION WILL MOVE IN A WEST TO WEST/NORTHWEST DIRECTION AT 15 MPH. PEOPLE IN BARBADOS THE GRENADINE ISLANDS DOMINICA AND MARTINIQUE SHOULD TAKE IMMEDIATE PRECAUTIONS AGAINST MAXIMUM WINDS OF 40 TO 50 MPH IN A FEW SCTD SQUALLS OCCURRING LATE TONIGHT AND SATURDAY MORNING AND STAND A WATCH FOR POTENTIAL CHANGE IN INTENSITY OF THE SYSTEM.

THIS DEPRESSION IS BEING WATCHED FOR POSSIBLE DEVELOPMENT AND FURTHER INFORMATION WILL BE RELEASED LATER THIS AFTERNOON.

Chapter 1

St. Matthew Parish, Louisiana, September 9, 1965

The big house was quiet except for the tapping of the clock and a lone voice upstairs. Downstairs, an empty silence took the place of everything else.

It crept up the worn wooden stairs under the cut glass chandelier, the one that was converted to electricity some fifty years before. It oozed around the legs of the ancient mahogany furniture and up past the portraits of ancestors frozen as they were a century ago when the itinerant portraitist had the subjects sit still on a series of sunny afternoons. Upstairs, a thick breeze pushed through the doors of the balcony past everything and met the silence.

The young man was stretched out on one of the red brocade settees in the front parlor upstairs. His socked feet hung off one end, and his shirttail was out and over his jeans. His hand held a phone as a lazy plume of pale smoke curled into the air from a cigarette. Everyone else was gone, and now he could smoke indoors. Outside the door to the balcony, the vast fields of sugarcane rippled in shades of green to white to green again all the way to the distant tree line that marked the Twelve Arpent Canal.

"Don't worry, daddy. I'll watch the place," he said into the phone, and his lower lip blew out a cloud of blue-white smoke. He flipped a silver cigarette lighter, embossed with a fancy T, over and over in his hand, and then clicked out a flame and stared into it with one eye closed. His daddy's voice was just a distant murmur in the phone.

The place was Mount Teague Plantation, a misnomer because there wasn't a rise of land higher than the levee within one hundred miles of it. At this time of year with the cane tall, it stretched in feathery green over ten thousand acres, hemmed by tree lines, the bayou and the highway. His family had farmed it for more than a century, or more exactly, the people they hired had farmed it and before that the people they owned had farmed it.

A storm was in the Gulf and where it went was anybody's guess. The mere threat of it had scattered the people of St. Matthew Parish northward and inland. The inhabitants of neighboring parishes were directly on their heels, filling up motels and the spare rooms of family as far north as Arkansas and as far west as Texas. Sammy Teague was staying, but the rest of the Teague household was evacuating to Jackson, Mississippi, where his older sister Charlotte lived with her family. It was either there or Atlanta, where his other sister Marilyn and her family lived, but time had gotten away from them and the closer choice was the better choice. His daddy was evacuating his own daddy, Sammy's grandpappy, and Sammy's mama, the former Miss Ewell County Mississippi. Due to proximity, Charlotte had once again drawn the short straw.

Sammy's grandpappy slept in a corner bedroom in the upstairs of the house. He had been a firm man when he was young and then a hard man and now in old age he was a brittle man. A thin white widow's peak sharpened his chin and nose, and made him look like an animal that might rob eggs from a henhouse, a fox or a possum maybe. His grandpappy's crumpled form only came out for meals and to dispense unsolicited advice. Junior Teague had a low tolerance for foolishness, except for his own.

"We Teagues built this up from nothin', nothin' I tell you, by sweat and hard work," his grandpappy would argue as if someone was trying to contradict him. Never mind that the sweat and hard work had been supplied by others, owned and hired by the Teagues, and that the Teagues had only strategically offered guile and, when needed, deceit.

"And we not lettin' anybody wrench it way from us eitha." His scrawny fist would wag in the air, threatening whoever it might be.

Sammy's mother was a woman whose youth was ebbing like a moonless tide. It was hard to look at her and not think of a withered camellia dropping petals, and it was hard to hear her voice and not think of a sweet wine lapsed into vinegar. The curves of the bags under her eyes were the only thing on her face that smiled spontaneously, though she could force a counterfeit one when needed for social effect. Her voice was smoky from years of cigarettes and drunken shouting. When she and Sammy's daddy had met at Ole Miss, it was a sweet southern drawl that called every other person 'shuga' and 'precious', but now it was closer to a growl.

Rather than stay at Mount Teague and ride out the storm, she was going to Jackson, too, citing her daily headaches and the very real possibility of a post-storm gin shortage. And a potential shortage of meat, bread, and milk, too, of course.

Sammy and his daddy had loaded the big white Lincoln with essentials and nonessentials. The car in the circular drive sagged with his grandpappy and his mama, her ill-tempered Chihuahua, Sugarboy, eight suitcases, two garment bags, a hat box, a steamer trunk with something heavy in it, a paper bag with who-knows-what in it, and a case of gin. His mama sat in the front passenger seat with her head covered by a scarf and her eyes made big by dark sunglasses. Sugarboy trembled in her lap.

Just before the Lincoln pulled away, his grandpappy sniffed Sammy through the window, made a face, and said, "You smell like a French whorehouse. There's some Aqua Velva on my nightstand. Use it." In the driver seat, Sammy's daddy raised his eyebrows and laughed silently. Then he shook his head and winked at Sammy.

Sammy wore the sweet smelling cologne because a girlfriend had given it to him, though he was thinking of breaking up with her when he returned to school. He was attending Ole Miss, like his father and grandfather and great-grandfather had. For a Louisiana boy, attending Ole Miss was like espousing Communism or Integration. There was something perverse about it.

The windows of the Lincoln rolled up. Sammy waved and put his hands in his pockets as the enormous car crunched over the crushed white shells, through the lane of live oaks to the highway. He saw the silhouette of his grandpappy saying something with his finger in the air, and he knew his daddy was in for a long ride. The car bottomed out as it lifted onto the pavement of the two lane that paralleled Bayou Lafourche. It turned and then labored up Highway 308.

Sammy lit a cigarette and looked up to the sky. Gray and white clouds were racing east to west, but only the very tops of the trees were swaying slightly in the wind. The breeze picked up the smoke from his cigarette and carried it off with the clouds.

The impending storm, named Betsy by the National Weather Service, had just plowed into and through south Florida and was prowling the Gulf for its next victim. The timing couldn't have been worse. Sammy was set to leave for college that week, his red and white Tbird convertible packed and ready. Then his daddy had asked him to postpone leaving to keep an eye on 'the Place,' as he called it.

Sammy had just finished his second year, using the same formula he had used for his first year. Drink, make merry, chase skirts, do just enough to get by. Plod along on course to graduate with a degree in Agriculture & Economics, and fall into the lap of the job he had been born for anyway, running Mount Teague.

Miss Della Mae, the black woman who had cooked and cleaned for them and had almost single-handedly raised him used to say, "Oh, he show a purty chile, but he gone be an eben purter man." Her shining black face, kind and fat and furrowed, broke into a proud smile when she said it. When she died last year, Sammy's face was the only white one in the weathered gray cypress church full of cardboard fans and ill-fitting clothes. Miss Della Mae's face looked up to heaven from the coffin, still kind and fat. She had crossed over into Canaan, the preacher said, mopping his brow with a handkerchief and shaking his head. Fans fluttered and heads nodded to a disjointed chorus of 'Praise Gawd,' 'Yussuh,' and 'Das right.'

After going back and forth to Oxford for two years, Sammy knew every titty bar, roadhouse, and barmaid between Lafourche Parish and the Tennessee line, and could describe the birthmarks, hidden and unhidden, of half a dozen sorority girls at Ole Miss. He was smooth, persistent and had a well-tuned sense of timing. His sandy brown hair fell in a wave to his eyes, which were the size and color of nickels. As he tore down the highway in his convertible, heads in the small towns turned, and for days talk in the diners and beauty shops would be about the movie star who came through town in his red Thunderbird. They just weren't sure which movie star it was, on account of the dark glasses he was wearing.

On his eighteenth birthday, he lost his virginity. His fraternity brothers took him to New Orleans, put their money together, and then waited outside the grimy red brick building on Iberville Street, where a fire escape clung to the mildewed brick like rusty black ivy. Upstairs, Sammy braced himself above the hooker, a lumpy, middle-aged woman with heavy makeup and large false eyelashes. She stroked his upper arm with one hand while she smoked with the other.   Above the squeaky wrought iron bed was an amateurishly drawn nude.

"Oh baby," she croaked indifferently, "You really know what you doin'." She exhaled a thin cloud of smoke out of the side of her mouth. He opened his eyes to see her watching in amusement as two pigeons fought on the window ledge over a scrap of bread. He felt like he was someone else.

She took his hand and put it on her floppy breast and said, "Feel summa dat." The bedsprings squeaked evenly. After a few minutes more, she looked to an alarm clock on the bedside table, pulled him down to her and licked his nipple. He was done then. The springs squeaked one last time as he got up and eased his member, limp and wet, into his underwear. Its head hung low.

"Money onna dressa, baby," her flea-bitten voice rasped through her cigarette as she pulled up her stockings. Sammy produced a pocketful of ones and fives that his frat brothers had put up, and he left them there along with an irretrievable bit of himself. The breasts of the nude on the wall seemed like eyes that were looking at him.

His footsteps were hollow going down the stairs. A chorus of hoots and cheers greeted him at the bottom, as his frat brothers patted him on the back and ruffled his hair and one of them crowed like a rooster, "Cock'll do the dooooo." Sammy was a little sick to his stomach and had to force a smile. The group started down the street swarming around each other like a litter of puppies. Hands were clapped on each others' shoulders and elbows were wrapped around each others' necks, ready for a night of laughter and drunken promises. They staggered down toward Bourbon Street and into the carnival of neon.

But that was two years ago, and the start of his third year was now postponed. He watched the tops of the live oaks wander left and then right in the capricious breeze. The branches twitched like fingers beckoning the wind. The air was thick and light like cotton candy and as volatile as gasoline, rushing about briskly and gusting occasionally. He sank back into the couch, wondering how things would look later, when and if the full force of the storm passed over.

Just then he heard a rifle shot, and then its collapsing echo above the trees. Then another and its echo. He mashed the cigarette into the ashtray, and then fell off the couch and onto his feet. Scrambling

9

onto the balcony, he braced himself on the railing as the screen door slapped behind him.

Across the field, in the yard of the house of their tenants, a young woman had her arm stretched out to the side and the dark gray length of a snake dangled from her hand like a strip of old tire tread. It was so long its head bounced against the ground as the girl picked her way through the yard in white rubber boots and a red and white shift dress. A rifle was balanced in her other hand. She approached the tree line and reached back and flung the limp snake. It wheeled end over end, glanced off a tree, and made a distant splash in the bayou. She watched the splash and turned back to the house, wiping the hand that had held the snake on her dress.

Sammy leaned into the balcony rail and shouted, "What the hell was that?"

She looked up at him, shielded her eyes with her hand, and shouted back, "Moccasin. On the porch." Leaning the rifle against a post, she tapped her white rubber boots on the wooden planks to knock off the mud, and then sat in an aluminum chair to wrestle them off. The screen door squeaked open and she disappeared inside.

He turned from the balcony and went back inside. In black and white, WWL in New Orleans was showing the possible track of the hurricane, anywhere from the Florida panhandle to Galveston. Governor McKeithen had the Louisiana National Guard standing by, and President Johnson was already promising federal aid. The television showed the satellite view of the storm, the puffy white blade of a buzz saw.

Downstairs, there was a knock on the door. He padded down the main stairs and opened it. The young woman was there, her eyes round and dark like an animal's. Her face was smooth and tanned, with a light scattering of freckles on her cheeks.

"Use your phone?" she greeted him.

"Yours out?" he asked and he blew a mouthful of smoke up and out to the side with his lower lip.

"Don't have one. Never have."

He opened the door and made a sweeping gesture. "There's one in the hall past the stairs. Or one upstairs in the parlor. Oh, and one in that front bedroom."

"Thank you," she said, and she probed around the corner of the stairs.

He heard the rattle of the dial and then her voice. His cigarette had almost burned down to the filter, and he smashed it into the ashtray.

"Operator, Eunice, Louisiana. Lorena Soileau. Collect from Betsy, thank you." A pause. "Hey Tante Na, how you? Speak to mama?" A pause. "Hi mama. Fine, fine. No, the roof's still on, yeah, no water more than usual. Wind just now pickin' up. We all okay." She listened for a moment. "Put her on the phone, then." She changed to French and spoke louder. "*Comme ça va, Mimi? Ça va bien ici. Je vais bien, tracasse-toi pas. Et toi, Mimi.*" She continued on for a minute and then switched back to English before hanging up.

"Thanks again," she told Sammy.

"Where's your folks?" he asked her as he reached in his shirt pocket for a pack of cigarettes.

"Mama and my Mimi are in Eunice for the storm. Daddy's in Labadieville."

He shook a cigarette out of the pack. He raised his eyebrows and pointed the red and white pack of Marlboros at her. She declined with a raised palm.

"He comin' back later?" he mumbled with the cigarette between his lips, his brow furrowed as he clicked out a flame from the lighter.

"No, 'fraid not."

With the flame poised at the tip of the cigarette, Sammy pondered whether or not to ask why.

"He's in the cemetery in Labadieville," she continued, and then she added, "*Defan.* Dead."

"Hmmp," Sammy grunted into his cigarette as he lit it. He nodded and exhaled a mouthful of smoke as he stowed the lighter in his pocket. He thought for a moment and then said, "You stayin' for the storm?"

She was half in the front door and half out. "Gotta take care the animals and the house. Not gonna leave my babies, no." She left him on the front porch and walked barefoot over the field to her house. A little orange dog of no particular breed met her half way and followed her home, trotting at her heels. She whistled a quick

11

burst and called to the dog, *Allons, Chanceux.* The dog's bushy tail curled over onto his back. He paused to mark one more clump of grass and ambled to catch up with her.

Later that afternoon, Sammy watched her from the upstairs balcony as she worked in the garden patch behind the little shotgun house. The dingy white and faded red of her dress disappeared in and out of the head-high okra. She cut off the pods with a knife and put them in a pocket of her apron. The tops of the okra swayed in the ocean-blown wind, but shook with the cut of each pod. At the end of a row, she emptied her apron into a chipped enameled basin. Crude wind chimes hanging in a tree in her yard tinkled like cowbells, and he thought he could hear her singing softly in French.

The people across the way were always an enigma to Sammy. He would watch them from the catwalk of Mount Teague's water tower, sitting with his forearms and chin resting on the galvanized metal railing high above the ground, watching happiness and joy happen across the field. Behind him, 'MT' was emblazoned in big black letters across the enormous gray tank. The hired hands of Mount Teague liked to joke that MT meant the tank was 'emp-ty.'

He dangled his legs and studied the neighbors from his perch on the embossed metal walkway, partially obscured by the spring green leaves, as the aroma of boiled crawfish tickled his nose from across the field. The family came together in the backyard and ate off a rickety table. Hands and mouths were busy as they gathered around it, peeling, eating and tossing shells, talking and laughing all the while. When the red-orange mound flecked with yellow ears of corn dwindled, they adjourned to the shade of the new green leaves. They sat in a semicircle and the French language, or a French language, floated on the spring breeze. Women laughed so hard they leaned out from their lawn chairs and into each other, touching foreheads and grasping each others' hands. Children raced and tagged in circles over the lime green grass. Instruments were brought out. An accordion wheezed, a triangle dinged, and a fiddle squealed low as couples paired in every possible combination, young and old, to shuffle and twirl in the vivid spring light.

And in the fall it was repeated, this time with blue crabs, boiled orange and white in a big aluminum pot. Sometimes it was a pig

12

who was the guest of honor. But there was always laughter that flared and diminished and flared again. Always.

He had always been aware of her presence next door. When he was little, he saw her in a First Communion dress with relatives gathered around her in the yard of the little house, her jet black hair and eyes half hidden by a veil, a bride in miniature. Her little hands, gloved in white lace, held a small book as aunts and uncles knelt to hug and kiss her. He had wanted to go next door to play with the little girl in the white dress. His mother said no.

"They're not cut from the same cloth as us," his mother told him. He was a boy then who took things literally, and was unaware that people were made from cloth. He had even felt his own skin to see what cloth he was made of. The memory of the girl in the lacy white dress stayed with him for a long time, until it was pushed aside by other memories, and then it was forgotten and not a memory at all. When he got older, he went to boarding school in Tennessee. The girl went to public school, if she went at all.

But the girl had noticed him, too.

At her First Communion, she had seen him high up on the catwalk of the water tower, crouching and peering down at them from under the handrail. Between hugs and kisses and exclamations of *oh sha te belle,* she studied him and began to imagine him as a prince on the parapet of a castle. As another old aunt knelt and kissed her cheek, leaving a lipstick pucker print, the girl looked up and hoped he would descend and come play with her. She imagined the mule would be a good substitute for a horse, and that she and the boy could ride the mule like a steed. She could sit behind him with her little girl arms around his little boy waist, and they could look for a dragon to slay. One of the tractors could play the part of the dragon. Looking back, she saw it as her awakening to the ideas of love and romance.

Then, as she got older, she was awakened to the idea of sex. She would spy on him from the green leaves of the okra and corn under a bonnet of the type that her Mimi called a *garde-soleil.* Under its brim, the sun had freckled her face and puberty had pimpled it. Her body was growing and straining on itself, beset with menstruation and moodiness and an abstract longing. The black eyes in her not-quite-a-woman face watched him as he washed his car in just a swimsuit, and she could feel herself tingle and swell. She felt exhilarated and guilty.

In the confessional, she mumbled what she had felt, at last including the urge to touch herself. She closed her eyes and waited for the wrath of God and the church.

"*Quoi d'autre?*" the priest yawned from the other side of the partition. *Anything else?*

She opened her eyes slowly in the darkness of the booth. The lattice threw diamond shapes of light over her face.

"No, Father."

He gave her a friendly reprimand and a meager Act of Contrition. As she left the confessional, she thought she heard the priest chuckle.

Then her daddy died and her mother withdrew. Just as the girl's awkwardness was being replaced with loveliness, her mother's happy, outgoing, garrulous demeanor was replaced with distrust and resentment of the world and especially the wealthy neighbors. None more than that lazy son who slept in on weekday summer mornings, beginning the day at noon or after with a cigarette on the balcony and hosting loud, late parties on the weekends when his parents went to New Orleans.

Life was not fair; it was hard. Betsy bought into her mother's bitterness as circumstances forced the girl to be a woman, while across the field the boy prince had stunted into just a boy.

Sammy sat on the balcony of the big house and put his feet on the railing. The wind was picking up, sweeping green and silver-white waves through the sugarcane. The failing light was blue-gray, and sunset wouldn't be long. He went inside and clicked on the television again, and it now appeared that the storm was definitely going to strike the central Gulf Coast, probably Louisiana.

The cloud-hidden sun threw a sepia light over the fields and the houses. Over at the tenant house, the laundry on the line fluttered and snapped in the wind. The girl balanced a wicker basket on her hip while her hands took down clothes with the same quick, restless industry they used in picking okra. A white blouse, still tethered to the line by clothespins, reached out its sleeves, which rolled and trembled a frantic warning. The little orange dog yipped as the girl brought the basket in the back door, and the wind slammed the door

14

behind her. The air felt combustible, and, in the fields, the cane bent and whispered a desperate sigh.

Night fell hard in a matter of minutes, and the wind picked up another step. Out in the fields, the sugarcane bowed and swayed to the coming wind god. The shutters on the balcony slapped against the boards, and Sammy went to secure them. Something metallic clattered to the ground across the way, and he saw an aluminum pot rolling on its side in a semicircle on the concrete slab in the back of the tenant house.

He spent the evening watching television and getting updates on the storm. The television said that the Beatles would be on Ed Sullivan again later that week. He would most certainly watch it, if he was safely back in Oxford by then. He was a big fan and had gone to see them in City Park in New Orleans the year before and then driven back all night to Oxford. He had even grown his sandy hair from a crew cut to the band's signature mop top, developing the habit of sweeping it out of his eyes for the girls.

When he tired of the television, he sat at the upright piano in the wide central hallway and played. His mother had made him take lessons, and he had been a reluctant student, but now he was glad he had done it. It had made him a favorite with his fraternity brothers, and it was one more attribute that made the girls weak in the knees over him. He ran through "Love Me Do" three times until he had it mostly right.

Outside, the storm was slowly tuning up. Rain fell diagonally and then sideways in the glow from the yellow light on the utility pole. The live oaks were tossing, the barrel sized limbs swaying up and down, veering wildly. The lights flickered, but then stayed on. He went to bed but couldn't sleep, embarrassed to be frightened by the storm. He curled up on the settee and watched the wind and rain, peering from under a blanket like he had done during bad weather when he was ten years old.

He dozed for a moment and woke up two hours later. The lights were still on, and the air conditioner in his window was still humming cold air into his room. He looked at the clock. Ten-thirty. Outside the window and across the field, the lights were still on at the tenant house.

The wind was howling now with gusts that came in a high pitched harmonic whine. It lifted up shingles, pried them loose, and then tossed them into the air and out into the cane. Across the field, it picked up the edges of the tin roof of the tenant house and beat the wood frame with it. The water tower groaned against the force of the wind, singing a sorrowful, metallic lament. The shadows of objects tumbled through the yard on their way from wherever they had been to wherever the wind would have them go. The wind plucked at the gray moss beards in the trees and then snatched them away one by one. The trees were lopsided against the push of the storm, and it looked like the scenery had been tilted ninety degrees and everything was falling from right to left. The world roared sideways.

Suddenly, there was a crash, a pop, and then with an abrupt click the lights went out. The air conditioner in the window stopped humming. The television screen collapsed to a dot and then disappeared. The hurricane had eliminated all other competition for his attention. He closed his eyes and listened to the maelstrom. The shrill wind shrieked as it rocketed through the trees, ripping away leaves and snapping branches. It moved as if there were a larger, more violent wind chasing it. The rush cancelled all other sounds.

Sometime in the night he heard a loud crash, the sound of metal twisting suddenly and glass shattering, but he was too scared to get up to see what it was. The old house moaned in pain, its ancient bones twisting and bending as the wind howled excitedly at its suffering. Exhaustion finally closed his eyelids like an undertaker.

Chapter 2

At daybreak, very little light filtered in, but he could see that Bayou Lafourche was flowing backwards and threatening its banks. Half an hour later, water was in the tenants' yard, and the aluminum pot was bobbing in an eddy. Fifteen minutes later, the water was at the porch.

The hot breath of the wind still squalled, and it took an effort to open and close the doors. But after a night of listening to the howling, his ears were getting used to it.

And then in the matter of a few minutes, the wind slackened and the sun came out. He looked over to the girl's house. Water was over the porch and sliding next to the front door like a cat brushing against it. Sammy put on an old pair of pants and fastened his belt as he went down the stairs. He ran across the field and down the slope until his feet hit water, and then he waded up to the little house. By the time he got to the porch, it was up to his knees. He remembered the snake from the day before, and he shuddered. Rafts of fire ants drifted by, the red and black specks on them nervously searching for the earth.

He knocked on the door and found the girl in the process of deciding what was necessary and what was not. For a family of such meager means, there wasn't much to choose from. She opened the door and Sammy came in as if he always dropped in at this time of day. On the simple kitchen table, dried leaves from the previous year's Palm Sunday had been burned in an aluminum pie tin.

The little orange dog was up to his belly in the water. The movements of the three of them in the water made hollow liquid echoes off the walls. A wooden chest bobbed along, turning slightly as it floated past them toward the back of the house. They exited the front door, not bothering with the pointless act of closing it. The girl carried an old cardboard suitcase with her as she waded. She scooped the little dog in one arm and handed him to Sammy. The dog blinked at him and shivered in terror.

They waded away from the little house. The water was waist high and then knee high, and then they were on the dry land of the slope that led to the big house. She dropped the suitcase ten yards or so from the waterline. The faux red-brown leather surface was cracked down to the gray cardboard underneath.

She turned and waded through the water to a small outbuilding. The swirling brown water was almost up to her chest now. She struggled with the door of the barn and led out an old gray-whiskered brown mule. The girl's steps were big and sweeping against the current. The mule lurched up and down like a carousel horse, lifting his head and snorting and hawing.

As she emerged from the water, Sammy saw the outline of the inner woman through the wet dress she wore. At any other time he would have been titillated by the dark distant outlines of points and triangle under her dress, but he was too terrified and too exhausted.

17

If the girl was terrified or exhausted, she didn't show it. She moved purposefully as if she had planned for this.

Chickens roosted in the trees above the water that the little house sat in, and a yellow tabby cat roosted with them in a truce called by the storm. It washed its paw and scrubbed its head with it, trying to look nonchalant. Coffee brown water flowed in the front door of the house and out the back. The aluminum pot was wedged into the knees of a cypress tree.

"Stay in your barn?" she panted. Her arm was draped over the withers of the mule. Her hair was plastered wet and black against her head.

"No," he said. "The mule can. But you stay in the house. Plenty of room. I insist." He would be relieved to have the company.

She eyed him suspiciously for a moment and then said, "Awright."

She was grateful for his help but still wary of the boy who was once a prince, but had been demonized by her mother.

He held the door for her. The little orange dog shook himself and rushed in with her at her heels. Sammy began to say something about his mother not liking animals inside, other than Sugarboy, but, then again, she didn't like for him to smoke inside either. And who would know?

Her dress was still wet, and she shivered almost imperceptibly like someone who didn't like to display her own discomfort. He took her suitcase and showed her to his sister Charlotte's old bedroom, and then he brought her some towels and told her where she could bathe and change clothes. In about half an hour, she emerged from the back of the house with her wet hair framing her face. She wore a dress that had been faded to a pale blue by years, maybe decades, of washing and rewashing. The wreath of hair seemed blacker when it was wet and made her eyes shine like polished onyx, dark and bright.

"Hungry?" he asked her. She nodded yes.

He went into the kitchen and got two bowls. From the pantry he pulled down a big box of cornflakes and from the refrigerator he got a glass bottle of milk. The light in the refrigerator stayed dark, and he remembered that the power was out. He touched the bottle of milk with the back of his fingers. It was still cold.

At the dining room table, he poured them both a bowl of cereal, and they took turns with the milk bottle. They sat and crunched mechanically while they looked off into something unseeable that was out there at some unknown distance. Nature had made a serious attempt to kill them both in the last twenty four hours. Finally he spoke.

"I don't know your name," he said.

"It's Betsy Duplechain."

"Oh, Betsy, like the storm."

"Storm name Betsy like me?" she asked.

"Yeah. They're callin' it Betsy." He waited for her to ask him his name and when she didn't he said. "Mine's Sammy Teague."

"Oh, I know your name. Everybody know Sammy Teague. That boy that looks like a moobie star. The bon vivant. The rish boy."

Sammy was silent. He could have been flattered, but he was embarrassed, self-conscious, ashamed even. In the economy of a few words she had diagnosed him. She had given him a split second flash of what he was. A self-absorbed golden child. The rish boy. It was an appalling truth.

"Your car got crushed," she continued. She took another spoonful of cornflakes and chewed indifferently.

"What?" He asked.

"Your car. Gotta big limb on it. Outside this window." She motioned her head to the far side of the house.

He seemed to move in slow motion out of his chair. He walked hurriedly, his heels beating out bass notes on the wood floor. He got to the window in a downstairs bedroom and pulled the heavy, braid-trimmed curtain back. The red Tbird had a huge live oak limb resting squarely across it. The white canvas top was ripped, and the metal of the doors sagged under the weight of the limb.

He sat down on the side of the bed and was too emotionally winded to say anything. He got up and returned to the dining room. Chanceux was under the table and Betsy was giving him pinches of cereal. He gingerly took them from her fingers and then ate them with a relishing crunch.

"So it has," Sammy said. "Fu….crushed."

Without a word, she collected their bowls and took them into the kitchen. He heard the water run, and then the click of them on the tiled counter top. She came back into the dining room, waving her hands dry.

"Storm not done with us yet. Now we gonna get the other half. Me, I'm gonna lie down." She disappeared into her room. The little orange dog with the curled-over tail followed her.

Sammy went to the front parlor and lay back on the settee. He ran his fingers through his hair and fumed an exasperated sigh. The air was just as heavy and wet as before.

It darkened and the wind resumed from the opposite direction, stampeding across the flattened cane, lifting up the tops, pretending to help them up and then flattening them again. He closed his eyes and the monotony of rushing wind in the trees sang him into an exhausted sleep. An unlit cigarette protruded from under his upper lip like a solitary fang.

When he woke, the wind was fading and the sunlight with it. He smelled something from the kitchen, a good smell, and, for a moment, he thought he might find Della Mae there. What he found was Betsy's face illuminated by the blue light of the gas burner.

She saw him and said, "Can't eat cornflakes every meal. Found some shrimps in the freezer. Gonna go to waste if we don't eat 'em." She tapped a wooden spoon on the side of the skillet and wiped her hands on her apron. Chanceux sat on his haunches, looking up in admiration. If Sammy could have seen the look on his own face, it would have been the same as the dog's.

She clutched a ribbon in her teeth while she twisted her black hair into a ponytail. She took the ribbon and doubled it around the cable of hair. The wooden spoon resumed its scraping on the skillet.

"At least the gas still works," she said. She tapped the wooden spoon again.

The little dog turned and went to the dining room, his claws clicking as he walked. Just inside the doorway to the kitchen, he laid down on the floor where generations of food scraps had fallen and their aromas had permeated the wood. A spot on the floor and the table leg bore the charred marks of a previous fire.

The tale that Sammy's mother packaged up for the Spring Pilgrimage of Homes Tour was that Yankee soldiers were preparing to ignite the house when they were stopped by a Union officer who had once stayed as a guest at Mount Teague. The tourists would ooh and aah at the story and take pictures of the table leg and the black smudge on the floor.

In actuality, it was Mamie Teague herself who had almost burned down the house. She had had a few more gin and tonics than usual one afternoon and suddenly had to take a nap. Her cigarette fell into a cardboard box filled with old society page clippings. Miss Della Mae smelled the smoke and came running in to put it out with a broom. When his mother woke up, bleary eyed and hoarse, she banned smoking in the house.

Sammy and Betsy sat and ate by candlelight in the big dining room with the mahogany sideboard and the paintings of hunt scenes on either side. In the dim light, she studied him with furtive glances. She hadn't seen him close up in a long, long time before today, not since they were small children and then only in passing. Her mother always said he was a little devil, but what she didn't say was that he was a *handsome* little devil.

She watched him eat hurriedly, hungrily. His appetite had returned suddenly and he could scarcely make conversation. She had smothered okra to go with the shrimp.

"'S good," he mumbled between bites.

A faint smile rose and fell on her lips.

After dinner, he retired to the piano bench. Under the yellow-orange light of a hurricane lamp, he played everything he knew, some things twice. He realized how much he had neglected to play during the summer break. Then he remembered one of his favorite things to play, the Beatles' "I Wanna Hold Your Hand." He enjoyed the bass riff played with the left hand between the lines of the song. He had practiced it over and over again until his grandpappy had snarled, "Do you know anything else besides that claptrap?"

Sammy realized that Betsy was sitting down behind him in a chair across the hall and was listening. He stopped for a moment and looked over his shoulder. She smiled at him, and for the briefest moment it seemed like the electricity was back on. He moved over on the bench and patted it. She hesitated for a moment and then got up and sat beside him. Her hands were tight to her sides on the bench. She smelled like his sister's lilac soap.

He played some more, going around a second and third time on his repertoire. The music would stop and restart, tracing over itself as he worked the rust off his playing. Finally, he ran out of things he knew how to play and instead just softly picked out notes and chords. He felt a weight on his shoulder and in the corner of his eye saw the top of Betsy's head. Her eyes were closed, and a thin tide of air passed back and forth between her slightly parted lips. He quietly eased the lid over the keys and gently touched her knee. She jumped and raised her cheek from his shoulder. Rubbing her eyes, she murmured, "Tied I guess." She tottered off to her bedroom, putting a hand on the door jamb to guide herself through the doorway. Sammy sat for a few minutes and then went to his room.

Chapter Three

In the morning, he woke and rambled through the house. Betsy's door was open, and the four poster bed was neatly made. He went to the kitchen and found coffee was made, but otherwise there was no sign of her. He heard the dog bark next door.

Across the field, the water had abandoned its attempts to take the house and had crawled back to the bayou. The back door was propped open. Sammy saw her throw an armload of something out the door and then turn and disappear back inside. Mud drifts and puddles were scattered across the field.

When Sammy arrived at the edge of the yard, Chanceux greeted him with a sniff of his leg and escorted him with a grin and a jaunty step to the back door. She was sitting on a kitchen chair and sobbing quietly. The floor was a sheet of mud studded with the tracks of her rubber boots. In her lap she held the white lace of a wedding dress, stained brown by the flood water.

He eased up the steps and through the door. When she realized he was there, she stifled her sobs and wiped her face and red eyes with the back of her hand. But she couldn't help frowning down at the dress in her lap like it was something that had just taken its last breath.

"I was gonna get married in this dress one day. It was my mama's. Her mama made it." She looked down at it vacantly. Then she forced a smile and stood up as she put the dress back in the wet cardboard box. "Well, that's that," she said with resignation. The smile faded from her face but she forced it back again.

Sammy started to sit down on a kitchen chair, but the seat was wet and muddy, so he leaned against a door frame, his hands behind his backside.

"Our lady Miss Dutchie might be able to clean it," he offered. To see this strong girl cry hurt his heart. He wanted to touch her lightly, to put a hand on her shoulder, to push the hair out of her weeping face. But he knew better. He could sense her distrust.

She looked up, and her face softened. She looked at him like he was someone completely new, a new arrival, a new neighbor.

"No, but thank you. Once bayou mud gets in somethin', it don't come out."

Sammy got two shovels and a wheelbarrow from the barn, and they spent the day shoveling mud out of the house, working silently side by side. They hosed off furniture in the yard, one handling the hose, the other turning the furniture in the spray. They stripped wallpaper where it had separated from the wall at the baseboards. They pulled up wet linoleum and hauled it outside.

"You really don't have to do this," she kept saying.

"No, I want to," he said as he kept working.

Other than that, they didn't say twenty words all morning.

They paused at lunch. A portrait of St. Francis with animals gathered around him looked down on them beatifically from halfway up the kitchen wall, just above the gray mark where the water had crested. They ate peanut butter and jelly on white bread and drank the last of the milk, managing small talk like two people who had been set up on a date.

In the afternoon, they went through closets. On a high shelf, Betsy found a box, and her black eyes lit up. She reverently placed the box on a chair. It contained a collection of old 78s. They sat next to each other on the bed and looked at the records. *The Balfa Brothers. The Hackberry Ramblers. Nathan Abshire. The Lafayette Playboys.*

She held the records to her chest like they were a lost child that she had just been reunited with. She looked at Sammy and said, "Tonight we listen to these, awright?"

"Sure," Sammy said. Then he remembered. "Wait, no electricity."

She got up, and from the top of a crude cypress armoire she gathered a small case. "Don't need none. We got this." It was an old victrola that worked on a crank. The speaker emerged from the case like a large blossom. "That's what we do," she asserted.

She put a record on the turntable and cranked the handle. She eased the needle on to the shining black disk. There was a scratch, then another scratch, then another. The music began, a song sung through the nose, "*Cher tout tout....*" When the song was halfway through, she pulled up the needle and turned off the victrola.

A smile slid onto her face with an idea. "Maybe I teach you to two step." She put the records back into the box like a stack of black plates and brought them into the kitchen. They spent the rest of the afternoon cleaning the little house. From time to time, Betsy sang the same few lines from the song in French, over and over. Sammy found himself looking forward to the dance lessons. As the last of the daylight faded, they finished the last room.

They were both dead tired. After they cleaned up, they cooked side by side in the kitchen, enjoying the intimacy of comfortable silence. Her motions were second nature, rhythmic, concise. She wiped her hands quickly on an apron in between movements of the ballet. His were inefficient, haphazard, disorganized. He clumsily chopped a bell pepper and an onion, while she did several things at once. She smiled and took the knife from him and finished the chopping in a matter of seconds. Her hands gathered the green and white cubes from the cutting board and dropped them sizzling into the black skillet. She rubbed the ones that clung to her hands into it.

With a fork she lifted the meat and turned the pieces sizzling into the skillet. Sammy studied her body and judged that it must be plain and featureless under her dress. There was little conversation, just the sound of the meal being prepared. A lantern gave them a grudging yellow brown light.

They set a table and sat and ate round steak, rice and gravy, which was even better than Della Mae's. Afterwards, they did the dishes side by side in the dim kitchen. When the dishes were all stacked on the drain above the sink, they retired to the central hall. They sat on a couch before the portrait of the original Samuel Teague.

"That your grandfather?" she asked, pointing to it.

"Great-grandfather," Sammy said.

"He looks mean."

"I've heard he ran a tight ship."

"Did you know him?"

"Oh, no. He was dead way before I was born."

"My grandpere worked for him. Cut cane, managed the place. Grandpere ran a tight ship too, my daddy say."

They sat for a minute and looked at the man on the canvas, listening to the clock inside the hall of the house and the crickets outside. The big front doors were open. Outside, the airless night was almost palpably black. The amber light of the lantern pushed out warmly. The clock ticked in the silent hallway.

"Ready to dance?" Sammy asked.

Betsy's face illuminated into a smile. "Okay."

She studied the records and then chose one for the turntable. The needle made a brushing sound that repeated itself and then the music started. The song was nasal and plaintive.

"Now, this the basic waltz step," she said. They looked at their feet, as he tried to follow hers. Her hand was rough in his, as if their sexes were reversed. She patiently explained the dances to him, guiding him through the steps, until he began to follow her and then lead her.

They moved through the steps of a waltz. The singer crooned a song in a voice that was flat and endearing around the wheeze and whine of the accordion and the fiddle:

"J'ai un bonne idée..."

"What's he saying?" Sammy asked. Betsy's mouth and eyes smiled.

"He tellin' his girl he got a good idea."

"And what's his good idea?"

She grinned and swatted his shoulder and then turned away as her smile broadened. "Just guess. You know." The fiddle wandered around the tune as the accordion kept it on task. The song ended, and she clapped her hands. She rushed to the victrola, shuffled through the records, and put on another. She ran and faced him again. She put out her arms, and he took them. This one, "Allons Dancer, Colinda," was more up-tempo. She patiently worked with

25

him, and eventually he got the hang of it, even venturing to twirl her now and then.

He showed her the swing dance moves he had learned at Cotillion, and they danced those. The clock in the hall chimed eleven. Sammy wondered if it was correct. Surely it couldn't already be eleven.

Chapter 4

In the morning he woke and checked the house. He found himself alone again. The pendulum of the clock in the central hall tapped back and forth in the stillness. Motes of dust floated like snowflakes in the sunbeams. He looked in her room. The bed was made, and there were no clothes on the floor. From the back porch, he looked to the little house across the way, but the quiet was there too.

He sat on the balcony with a cup of coffee and a cigarette. Presently, a dog barked down the road, and Sammy got up and leaned over the railing of the balcony. Chanceux trotted at Betsy's heels, stopping and sniffing the bases of trees, gauging the subtleties of the scents there. His nose pushed low over the ground like he was reading Braille with it. Now and again he would clear the palate with a snort. Or he would turn and flick soil with his hind legs at a scent he either found offensive or wanted to hide for later.

Betsy had a lace handkerchief bobby pinned to her head. She had returned not an hour after leaving for Mass with news that the bridge into Labadieville was out. She ascended the stairs. The door to her room shut, and Sammy heard the murmur of the Rosary in French.

In the afternoon, Betsy went to feed the mule, and Sammy went with her. The yellow cat jumped from the tall grass and then walked with them to the barn. It paused at the door in a patch of sunlight, sitting and rearing its head back to lick the white tuft of fur on its chest. The afternoon heat blurred the line of trees at the far end of the fields into watery images like reflections on rippled water. Betsy swung the big door around and latched it to prevent it from closing.

Inside the barn a red wasp drifted silently around the rafters under the tin. The earthy smell of hay and manure floated in the air with the wasp. Long unused tack hung from pegs on the vertical planks of the gray cypress wall. It was a little cooler inside the barn but not much.

In a small corral that opened into the ground floor of the barn, the sorrel mule stood working his gray jaw side to side. His big ears were low to his head.

"This the last of the Mount Teague mules," Betsy said, scratching the mule's ear. Inside the ear was tattooed, MT182, which was also branded in charred black letters on his left flank. "Your daddy was gonna put him down when they switched to tractors. But he let my daddy buy him."

"He have a name? Other than MT182?" Sammy ran his hand over the letters and numbers in his hide and looked at her.

"Balthasar." She smiled back at Sammy at such a wonderful name.

"Quite a name for just a mule."

"Oh, he's not just any mule, no. He's smart. Smart as a whip."

It was true. The mule could recognize every curse word and every possible combination of curse words in both French and English, as well as which ones were likely to be followed by a lash and which ones weren't. He knew how many circles around the grinding wheel he would have to trudge before there would be feed and a scratch of his ear, about five hundred. He could look at a cane wagon, gauge its fullness, and know how hard he would have to pull to move it, or, being a mule, whether he wanted to pull it at all.

The mule's brown hide flinched away a fly. He stamped his foot and shook his head, then stood chewing the feed Betsy was giving him from her hand. She turned to look in the stalls that now were empty. The mule nudged her hand. She gave him another handful of feed and stroked the long narrow front on his head. His thick lips extended out from his big teeth, reaching for the feed. His eyes were large and black.

Sammy looked at the harnesses on the wall and thought of all the generations of mules and plow horses that had wore them, all the whipping and swearing in English and in French that had urged the wearers on. Those men and beasts were gone, and only this old gentleman remained.   The tractors and cane trucks were the workhorses now.

She watched how he moved, looking to see the boy or the prince atop the tower she had once idolized, and she saw neither. Neither did she see a man or a king. He seemed to be in transit between one and another of those things. His hands examined the leather traces, turning them over, trying to imagine how they would work together, where they would fit on the animal. Chanceux sniffed around at his heels. Betsy smiled, and thought that they reminded her of two old men in a hardware store, caught up in the quiet reverie of figuring out things. The dog put his paws on Sammy's leg and stretched, and without looking, Sammy reached down to scratch the dog's head.

The dog dropped onto his front paws and ambled back over to Betsy. She knelt down to pet him, and he rolled onto his side. She cooed to him, "*Te boo, te chien, sha be-bee.*"

Sammy noticed how her dress followed her body. He could see a hint of curves below the neckline, where the sun-browned skin became smooth and white. Her body wasn't as featureless as he had thought. He didn't want to get caught looking and knelt down with her.

The little dog rolled onto his back. His ears were extended and the tiny white pebbles of his front teeth were exposed behind his black lips. Sammy reached down and scratched the dog's extended belly, and the dog pushed the tip of his wide pink tongue in and out and blinked in sincere appreciation. He and his littermates were members of a breed so rare that they were the only members of it. There would likely never be dogs like them again.

They walked back to the house under the afternoon shade of the oaks. The ground was littered with leaves and branches, green from the oaks, and purple, white, and red from the crape myrtles.

"Maybe we can get this yard picked up tomorrow," she said, kicking at a fallen oak bough.

"Yeah," he said. He picked up the branch and threw it off the path. "Place is a mess. Hard to see it in shambles like this. I guess we ought to call our folks, but the phones are out along with the electricity."

"Maybe ol' Aucoin gotta phone."

They each got a glass of lukewarm tap water and drank it down. Then they ascended the stairs together. After a brief, awkward pause

28

at the top, they separated, retiring to their rooms to wait out the afternoon heat, which had reached its peak. There was no breeze. Not a molecule moved anywhere. It was dead still and hot, a vacuum world.

Sammy lay on his bed and studied the molding, how it cascaded down from the ceiling and wrapped itself around the mantel. He found himself thinking about her. Then he had an idea.

He slipped a piece of paper under her door. On it was the best penmanship a boarding school education could buy:

Mister Samuel Teague, IV, Requests the Honour of Your Presence at a Ball to be Held at his Residence, Mount Teague Plantation, St. Matthew Parish, Louisiana, September 12, 1965, at Seven pm. Attire: Anything in his Sister's Armoire.

Added at the bottom,

Regrets only.

He slipped the note under her door and knocked and scurried across the hall. He shut his door, smiling nervously to himself. Then a stray thought troubled him. Can she read?

She could most certainly read, though spelling was always a problem for her. Her forte had been math and science, and she had a love of nature and the mechanical world that was fostered by following her daddy in the fields and machine shop of Mount Teague. She had developed a keen insight into how things worked, and her grades were among the top in her class in the sciences, though not quite as good in the liberal arts. But by her eighth grade year, her daddy was sick, and her shortened ninth grade year was marred by long absences as she tended to him and her mama and her Mimi. There was no tenth grade year.

Mrs. Landry, the math teacher who could spot genius when it was still in seed form and then figure out how to make it to germinate, flower, and flourish, had even paid a visit to the tenant house to persuade Betsy to return to school, certainly something could be worked out. She had found the atmosphere in the house hopelessly oppressive and Betsy's spirit flickering like a candle

29

starving for oxygen. In the end, Betsy couldn't be cajoled into leaving the house and returning to school. She had inherited her daddy's strong sense of loyalty and duty.

So Sammy waited in his room, hoping he hadn't humiliated her and mentally preparing an apology in case he had. A few moments later, the note slipped under his door. Written in loopy script at the bottom was a reply:

I asept

He smiled.

Despite the evening heat, he waited in a tuxedo. His sweat gathered the pungent tang of the Aqua Velva and pushed it into the room. He slouched in a chair with his leg draped over the armrest and studied the portrait of his great-grandfather. Ever since Sammy was a kid, he marveled at how the man's facial expression changed depending on what angle he looked at it. From this chair, it was a thin smile. From the front door, it was a scowl. From the back of the hall, it was a smirk. Sammy would study the portrait and then his own reflection in the hall mirror and see that his great-grandfather's face was the same as his. The same chin, the same forehead, the same nickel-gray eyes.

At seven o'clock, the door to her room swung open with a prolonged squeak. She emerged in a dark green taffeta gown and a green hair ribbon that matched. Her country-strong hands were encased in white cotton evening length gloves. Sammy remembered the gown from his sister's prom, but he didn't remember her looking this good in it. Betsy's legs showed the marks where she had nicked herself, and it occurred to Sammy that she was probably unaccustomed to shaving her legs.

Sammy rose, like they taught you to do in Cotillion, whenever a lady came into the room. He took her hand in his and kept his other hand behind his back, and he bowed. She didn't know to curtsy.

"You look..." He paused before saying it because for some reason he didn't want to use the word, but it emerged anyway, "Fantastic." She looked down. Her lips stretched over her teeth and met as she looked down and blushed.

He reached for a cut glass decanter and turned over a glass. As he poured, he asked her, "Scotch?"

"That like whiskey?"

"Like whiskey, except better," he bragged. He honestly couldn't tell the difference. He had developed a taste not for scotch, but for the sound of the name, 'scotch.' It sounded regal and sophisticated. It was what his daddy drank.

She sipped it and fought hard not to make a face. Looking at her empty glass, she said, "Mais, that's nasty." She handed him the glass, and he refilled it.

"I used to see you at Aucoin's when we were kids," she said. "You always got a Mountain Dew."

"Yeah," he said as he remembered it for the first time in years. "It was my favorite. You always got a Pop Rouge."

"Yeah. That's right," she said in wonder.

"And a banana moon pie," they said together and laughed, and then she said, "You noticed. How you remember all that?"

"I just do." He didn't want to say that he had noticed everything she did back then.

"You used to come in with your sister, the real pretty one. Well, they both real pretty."

"Charlotte," Sammy said. "I'm closer with her than I am with Marilyn, I guess because we're closer in age. You don't have brothers or sisters?"

"No. My mama almost died havin' me. My daddy picked her up and put her in his truck and drove her to Thibodaux, and left little newborn baby me with my Mimi. They had to give mama blood and an operation and she couldn't have no more kids."

"I never knew your daddy," Sammy said. "I mean, I knew him when I saw him. Always had a smile with a cigarette in it. I just knew my daddy thought a lot of him."

She had always thought of them as adversaries, the Taker and the Taken, but she had always heard it described by her mama. That they could have ever admired each other was a revelation to her.

They danced in the wide central hallway, while his great grandfather's portrait looked on. The victrola was set on the mahogany sideboard, the record spinning under the amber light of a hurricane lamp. The shadows of furniture lurked in the hall. They

31

swing danced, they two stepped, they did *la valse de Mamou*. As soon as one song had finished, Sammy cranked the victrola and Betsy selected another record. Then they each took a quick sip of scotch and grabbed each other's hand as the next song began. They only stopped dancing to change records and crank the victrola. They danced and laughed and danced some more, until they tired.

A slower song played and they swayed together. White lights reflected in her black pupils.

"I can't believe you were right next door, all this time," he said.

"Ever since the day I was born, right in that house," she said and smiled at him. They continued to sway together.

"When was that? Your birthday?"

"August the Fit, 1945."

"No kidding? Mine's August the fourth, the day before."

"For true? We a day apart, then," she beamed. A day and a world, she thought as her excitement lessened a little.

He held her gaze in his, and she found it too powerful and too wonderful and she looked away. He continued to look at the graceful lines of her face, the angle of her jaw where her hair was swept up, and her eyelashes, enough to make any girl envious. She looked back to him, and he was still looking at her.

"You're beautiful," he blurted out. "Not just from far away, but close up, too. Especially close up."

The bluntness, the suddenness was uncharacteristically clumsy for him. She looked at him, but didn't smile. It was an expression more like someone trying to tell the truth from a lie. The song ended, but it took them a moment to realize it. They moved apart.

Instead of chatting and quickly changing the record this time, she took her time looking distractedly through the disks, and he looked out the window into the night. She wound the victrola herself, and Sammy turned from the blackness beyond the window.

"Tes Yeux Noirs" played, *little black eyes* in English, her daddy's nickname for her. They approached each other and waltzed slowly to it.

And then they were swaying from one foot to the other, floating in a circle facing each other like they were in an eddy. Sammy's tuxedo jacket was off and draped over an arm of the settee. His bow tie was undone and the ends dangled around his neck over his shirt front. She had long since abandoned her heels and danced in bare feet on the worn wooden floors. The cuffs of the white gloves gathered at her wrists.

Her hand was on his shoulder, his hand on the small of her back. They exchanged a look, their faces an inch apart. Then a kiss, a peck. Another peck. Another. Then fuller. Her head on his shoulder. Swaying. His hand migrated forward from the small of her back to her waist, glacially slow. When it reached her hipbone, it began an arduous trek north. It reached the round contour of her breast and then slowly swept over it. Despite the thick green taffeta, he got a sense of its loveliness. She shuddered and sighed, struggling with her body as it strained against her will. She felt herself melting.

He had almost figured out its topography when her hand clinched his wrist and pulled it down. He felt ashamed.

"I'm sorry," he said quietly. "It's just that..."

"Shhh," she whispered, and she put her head on his shoulder again.

They continued to sway, even after the needle reached the center of the waxy black disk. It scratched and popped rhythmically. They floated around the hallway, rotating slowly in the unseen current and the dim flicker of the lamp. Circumstances could not pull them downstream. Time was not passing. Time was like the disk of black wax, circular, and rotating on itself.

She broke their embrace, kissed his cheek, and went into her room. The door closed, and he was left standing there. For the first time since the midst of the storm, he felt lost. He waited for a minute or two or five or ten, the candle moving his shadow over the wall, over the portrait of his great-grandfather. The dancing light made his great-grandfather's smile move, and it looked like a chuckle. Sammy blew out the candle, turned, and went to his room. He took off his clothes and laid there in his underwear in the moonlight, gray and silver and blue.

In her room, she sat on the edge of the bed in the green taffeta gown and looked at her candle-lit reflection in the mirror. He told her she was beautiful, and in such a way that she could believe it. She peered into herself, there in the mirror. Was she? Or was it idle flattery, smooth and crafty? Or was it sincere? Her mama would have told her it was sweet talk, the favorite tool of a playboy, the snare of the *canaille*. But right now, Betsy felt like the princess she had always wanted to be, and he seemed like the prince from the water tower, all grown up and come down to earth.

She put her hand on her breast and closed her eyes and imagined it was his hand there, cupping the soft fullness through the taffeta. Her mind wandered in a trance of scotch and desire, and she tried to remember the patroness of Purity and the patroness of Chastity and she couldn't think of them, though she thought that maybe if she sat for a while she might.

She stood up and unzipped the taffeta gown, and it fell from her. As she plucked away the fingers of her gloves and pulled them off, she looked at herself in the mirror, and she saw herself lovely and she felt herself ready and aching and wet and she tried to think of the patronesses of Purity and Chastity again and she couldn't. There were at least a dozen she could call on, but she couldn't think of a single one, so she closed her eyes and whispered, *heaven help me.*

She reached behind her head and let her hair down and shook it out, keeping her eyes on herself in the mirror. Her hands ran over her breasts, down her front, over her hips and she exhaled and closed her eyes and lifted her chin. Her eyes opened to the girl in the mirror and they looked at each other in the flickering candlelight. They each pulled their thin cotton gowns over their smooth bare skin and beautiful, sloping breasts and flipped their hair out of their collars, and plopped down on the edge of their beds again.

She sat there trembling in the shadow of impending and inevitable ecstasy, a sensation like the stretching of an elastic band. Outside the open window, night noises flourished drowsily and the earth scented the air with readiness and purpose. As her mind wandered, she tried humming a few passing lines of songs to distract herself, and she fell into humming the line that felt most fitting, over and over. She mumbled it to the girl in the mirror, the girl who was now beautiful and it was true because a prince had told her so.

J'ai fait mon idée.

I've made up my mind.

She stood up and opened her door and walked into the hall. A glass tumbler was there on the sideboard with a small amount of scotch in it, either hers or his, it didn't matter now. She brought it to her lips and downed it to keep the patronesses forgotten and silent.

Like an apparition, she appeared in the doorway in her gown, swaying slightly from the scotch. "Isso hot," she muttered. Her fists clutched handfuls of the thin white cotton at her mid thigh, and she pulled up. Her gown came over her head, and then she held it in one hand before letting it fall to the floor. She wore the clumsy, loose fitting cotton drawers of country folk. Her arms, neck, and ankles were tanned, the rest pale. Not like the college girls who sunbathed between classes in bikinis.

She pushed the panties to the floor and stood there. Sammy's scotch-thickened tongue was tied into a knot. It was like finding the statue of a Roman goddess under an old quilt at a flea market, or the actual goddess herself, or like opening a door you thought was to a broom closet and finding a palace.

Her pale outline glowed in the moonlight. The tips of her breasts were dark atop the slopes of them. Her shapely hips framed the dark patch between them.

"Is jess so hot," she repeated quietly, and she crawled to him on the bed in the moonlight. Her lips found his, and they pulled soft and wet on each other. She kissed his neck and then gave him hers to kiss. Her skin was salty and soft and it made him think of the warm water of the Gulf. Her breasts hung down to cone-shaped nipples. Pale, full-yet-slender breasts with nipples hard and rugged like the contour of a pecan half. He kissed them and she rolled onto the bed beside him.

From above her he looked into the darkness of her eyes and felt something of himself fall there. He waited for the splash, but it never came, and he knew whatever part of him it was, it would never be able to get out, it was there for good. It was in a space as wide and deep as the ocean.

Her hands pressed into his chest, and her lips rose up to kiss him again. Then her hands were behind his neck. They broke their kiss, and they looked at each other.

It was not like it was with the others, cheap and meaningless, partially enjoyed. She made small sounds, almost like crying. "Am I hurting you?" he whispered.

She smiled and exhaled, "Shhh. No, no, no." Her fingertip, as light as the fall of a wisp of cotton, traced over his cheek and then his lips. "Shhh," she whispered again, "Don' stop."

Her movements on him resumed. Slowly pushing into him, her innermost parts asking for him, begging for him to push back. And he did. When he came, he collapsed on her, like a traveler collapsing on his own doorstep after a long odyssey, home, home at last. They slept with the windows open and a mosquito net over the bed, and the crickets sang to them.

Chapter 5

St. Agnes. One of them was St. Agnes.

Betsy awoke with the name on her lips, the name of one of the patron saints called upon to resist sexual temptation. Betsy's eyes hurt, and she was thirsty and a little nauseated. And she was alone, and for a moment, she thought that he had left her, that she had been toyed with, used and abandoned.

But then she heard him on the stairs, his steps heavy and ponderous as he shared the same hangover. He entered the room with a tray. On it was a plate of scrambled eggs with two forks, toast, four aspirins, a bottle of ginger ale and two glasses.

"Time tested hangover relief," he said, and he smiled. "Part of any good college education."

He was bare-chested with only pajama bottoms on. His chest was tanned and smooth with only sparse hair. She sat up and pulled the sheet around her nakedness. They nestled into bed together, sitting up and sipping ginger ale slowly, cautiously, and eating toast and scrambled eggs from the tray that spanned their legs.

The light of day was on them, and she was even more beautiful than she had been in the dim light. Her hair fell carelessly around her face, unintentionally stylish and he thought that was one of the things he liked about her.

"I make some coffee for us later," she said. She took a bite of eggs. "Ooh they salty."

"That's part of it," he said. "Believe me, it helps. And it helps if the ginger ale is warm."

He poured them each a glass of golden, bubbly ginger ale and they took a sip, and then another. Soon they were belching and giggling like two ten year olds, leaning into each other's shoulders with laughter.

"You right, it helps," she said as she put her hand to her chest where her other hand was holding the sheets next to her body.

After they had eaten all they dared, Betsy said, "I gotta go to the bathroom."

"Okay, go ahead. You know where it is."

She held the sheet to herself. "Look away," she said, "so I can put my gown on."

"Seriously?" he asked.

"Yes!" she said.

He smiled and looked away.

She toyed with the idea of standing before him without it and enjoying his eyes on her. The gown was so thin that it honestly made little difference if it was on her or not. But finally she slipped it over her head.

"Okay," she said, and he turned back.

"Miss Duplechain?"

"Yeah?"

"You're still beautiful."

He scrambled to his knees on the edge of the bed, kissed her cheek and she blushed.

"Come on, boy." She took his hand. "I make us some coffee and then we get dressed. We gonna need to make us some groceries."

The telephone poles along the highway tilted halfway to the ground, as if they were bracing themselves for yet another wind. It was hot now, with no breeze whatsoever. In the ditches by the road, insects moaned out a chorus like the dull shake of maracas. Sammy and Betsy walked silently, listening to the sound of their footsteps on the pavement of Highway 308. There were no cars on this side of the bayou. The highway was blocked by a succession of fallen trees and telephone poles and the closed bridge over the Bayou St. Julien. Across the bayou, on the Highway One side, the rush and recession of traffic sounded from time to time. Sammy wondered how they would cross when they got to Napoleonville.

The traffic across the bayou picked up as they approached the little town. The tower of the church was the first thing they saw, then the cluster of two story buildings on the main street facing

Bayou Lafourche. The flat, green water flowed lazily between them and the town. Betsy saw something in the weeds by the washed out bridge.

"Looka here," she said. "It's my daddy's bateau. The flood musta brought it up."

The wooden boat was square at the bow and the stern. "My daddy made this boat." Written inside the gunnels was, *'faite par Alcide Duplechain, 15 Fevrier 1958.'* The paddles and a long pole were still inside it. They used a stick to fetch the painter at the bow and pulled the boat onto the shore. Then they got in and crossed to the other side.

Mr. Aucoin was a wisp of a man with a head that was a shining pink dome, flecked with brown-black scaly moles and rimmed with thin white hair. His glasses were so thick that it was impossible to tell where he was looking. He wore a white shirt buttoned up to the top button, where it strained against his Adam's apple. Underneath the shirt were the outline of a sleeveless undershirt and the advancing stains of perspiration. Mr. Aucoin walked the fine line between the adorable and the grotesque. He said hello to Sammy and bonjour to Betsy, calling each by their name.

"Got no powa, so no code stuff," he said with his head tilted back and looking under the black rims of the thick lenses. Tiny thick tangles of hair protruded from each nostril.

"Mind if we use your phone?" Sammy asked.

"Now dat, I got," and Mr. Aucoin gave him the same sweeping gesture Sammy had used on Betsy. The phone was on the wall next to the counter, next to an advertisement for Mellow Joy coffee. *'C'est bon!'* the bright yellow letters said. Sammy went first.

"Jackson. Mississippi, not Louisiana. Martin Pettigrew," he told the operator. There was a pause.

"Charlotte?" he said to his sister.

"This is Sammy. Good to hear you, too. No, power still out. Phone too. I'm at Aucoin's. That's right, he's still alive. Very much so." He looked to Mr. Aucoin who was perched on a stool reading the *Thibodaux Daily Comet*. On the front page were pictures of submerged cars in New Orleans.

"Mama and daddy there? Okay, put her on." A pause. "Hi mama. What's that? I'm fine. Mama, I can't understand you.

Okay. Okay. Just give the phone to daddy. Phone to daddy. Okay."

"Daddy? Yessir, everything's okay. Lost a few shingles. Cane's flattened. The tenant house flooded. Oh, I wouldn't do that, I think it'll be salvageable, and where would they live?" A pause as his father spoke at length about something.

"Well …well…well…okay…" Sammy seemed to stammer as he tried to wedge a word into one of his father's lengthy sentences. He finally succeeded.

"Well, anyway, we don't have lights or telephone. I'm calling from Mr. Aucoin's, on the Donaldsonville highway." Sammy listened for a moment, then a look of relief came over his face, and his voice relaxed. "I agree, daddy, stay there until we get power back. I'll call you when we do. What's that?" He looked over to the shelves filled with bottles of spirits both amber and clear. "No, looks like they're all sold out. You and mom were wise to leave." The voice in the phone laughed and Sammy laughed with him. "You too, daddy," and he hung up the phone.

Betsy got on the phone. After getting through the operator to her mama, she spoke entirely in French. Her lip quivered at one point, and Sammy thought he heard the French word for dress. Betsy hung up with a muted *au revoir*.

"They gonna stay 'til the power and the phones are back," she said. "Mimi can't take the heat like she use to."

They bought two bags of groceries and walked down the shoulder of Highway One, each with a paper bag. Sammy felt Betsy put her hand in his. He hoped the power never came back on again.

Holding her hand, he eased her down the bank to where the skiff was tied to a cypress knee. She got in first, and he handed the bags to her. The brown water wandered in and out and around the weeds near the bank. She sat in the bow and he poled the boat down the bayou. The heat was steamy, and their clothes stuck to them as if they were trying to get inside their skin.

They floated down the bayou pulled imperceptibly by the current that was now flowing in the usual direction, toward the Gulf. An alligator bellowed rhythmically, a frog splashed.

Saut, crapaud, she said quietly to herself.

The thumb-sized heads of turtles broke through blackwater holes in the speckled green carpet of duckweed, yellow and black stripes

39

with red gashes and small upturned noses. Cars rushed by infrequently on Highway One, only their tops visible from down at water level. The pole dipped into and out of the water with a mellow, succulent sound. The tip of it picked up mud from the bottom and was then washed cleaned with the next stabbing plunge.

Betsy turned on her stomach and peered into the water, positioned like the ornament at the prow of a ship. Her legs were pulled under her, and Sammy admired how her dress fell over her hips and around her bare calves and feet. She trailed her finger in the water and rested her cheek on the back of her hand.

She turned on her back, closed her eyes, and ran her fingers back through her hair. Now every time she turned around she was more beautiful, something more than beautiful, something so light and magical and nameless that calling it something would only diminish it. Her thin dress stretched over her breasts, sloping and full, perfectly outlined, unfettered by a bra. Her hands rested on the wooden gunnels as she watched the blue sky and listened to the sounds of the pole and the boat and the bayou.

Sammy was watching her, the light scatter of freckles under her eyes and over the bridge of her nose, the eyelashes, the clear smoothness of her forehead. The top two buttons of her dress were undone, and the light blue cotton was draped over her thighs. Her calves were shapely, and her feet were bare, the sole of one on the top of the other.

The boat bumped into a log and jarred both of them. She turned and pushed against it, and they floated back into the middle of the bayou. Then she turned back, and they smiled at each other.

"You awake?" he grinned.

"Boy, you betta watch where you goin'." She smiled and closed her eyes again, giving him the license to keep looking at her. Ahead on the left, the roof of Mount Teague appeared and then the lower roof of the tenant house before it.

They tied the boat to a cypress tree, and each took a bag of groceries. Hand in hand, they walked across the field to the big house and went in the back door.

After they put up the groceries, they went out to the barn and found an old buck saw, a *pas de deux*, Betsy called it. Sammy put it over his shoulder like a lumberjack, the saw bowing and singing with each step. At the car, they took positions on either side of the log. The saw jumped out of the kerf at first, then as it found its way into the log, Betsy and Sammy alternated pushing and pulling, leaning back and leaning forward.

"My daddy used to say, I don't mind ya ridin' the saw, no." She breathlessly blew a strand of hair off her forehead. "Just don't let your feet drag."

The saw pulled out plumes of flaky wet dust that collected in drifts on the ground beside the car. The two of them fell into a rhythm, like the rhythm of lovemaking, back and forth. The saw sank into the flesh of the limb, halfway, three-quarters. The rigid blade passed between them, in to one of them while out to the other and then back. They felt the friction of the teeth. The log halves were barely tethered, hanging by a splinter, then the limb gave way and shifted. They bent over with their hands on their knees, panting, sweaty. The saw had passed through to the bottom, and she passed her handle under the limb to Sammy. They moved to the other side of the car and began cutting there.

When the second cut was made, they rolled the limb off the back of the Tbird where it fell onto the white shell drive. Shoulder to shoulder, they stooped to roll it to the side. The midday sun reached through the live oaks into dappled shadow.

Chanceux writhed on his back, a comma shape that kept reversing itself as he muttered to the itch along his spine. He jumped to his feet and leaned against Betsy's leg, and she and Sammy scratched his back together. He lifted his chin in pleasure. When they stopped, he pawed the air, and they resumed scratching him.

That night, they ate sweet potatoes with ham from the freezer, and fresh greens from the garden, though it took a bit of washing to get the bayou mud off them.

When they were finished, they did the dishes side by side in the dim light of the lantern. The big house was quiet except for the sounds of water and clinking dishes in the kitchen. When the last dish was dried and put away, she took his hand and put it on her breast. He felt the details of it under her dress as she reached up and kissed him. Taking the lantern in one hand, she led him with the other. They drifted upstairs to the bedroom.

She kissed him again at the side of the bed, as she unbuttoned his shirt. Her lips stayed on his as her hands worked unseen down,

down, button by button. Then his belt and then the button of his pants. She pulled his shirt back, down and off. Her fingers slid over his buttocks, inside his boxers. He was naked before her. She pulled her dress over her head, and they faced each other naked and without pretense.

With her fingertips, she pushed him onto the bed. She crawled onto it, her knees on either side of him, and she walked up on them. He slid into her and she fell forward onto him. Her breasts swayed in his face, but his eyes were closed and he was oblivious to them. She leaned back and felt his legs. Hair and muscle. Her hips slid back and forth in small, quickening movements. She pushed into him, the sweat began to bead on her brow and when she leaned forward again a drop fell on his cheek. Her fingers weaved into his hair as she clutched the back of his head and sang her climax into his forehead. He lifted his hips to meet hers, pulling them up to her as he released with a series of powerful throbs. They panted together as the hall clock tapped outside the door. Her body was draped over his.

Chapter 6

Sammy got up early the next morning. He woke from a dream in which Ole Miss was playing St. Matthew Parish High School, and he was at a tailgate party in the Grove. Betsy was there, too, and they were holding hands. As the dream progressed, they were both naked, and then he couldn't find her. In the dream, he wandered from party to party under the trees asking everyone if they had seen her. They all ignored his question or said they hadn't seen her. The people seemed not to notice his nakedness. Then he woke up.

He left Betsy sleeping, and went downstairs and made coffee. He walked out to the barn, pausing as he walked to take a sip from the fancy china coffee cup of his mother's. Chanceux was following him with a merry grin on his face. He advanced ahead of Sammy, then fell back and then advanced again. The dog's nose was taking inventory of everything.

The sunrise was on the verge of backlighting the eastern sky where it perched above the swamp. The brilliant orange pushed up a vivid light blue haze that wore the stud of a solitary speck. Venus, the morning star.

Sammy opened the barn door. The dog peered inside and then went in. Sammy stood for a moment and remembered being younger, when the barn was so much bigger to him. How his cousin Mary Louise had tricked him into going up to the loft with the promise of a kiss, and then taken away the ladder. She had taunted him from below, and when he had refused to cry or beg, she simply left and didn't come back for him. The loft was higher to him then, and he had almost panicked. Finally, his Uncle Teddy had come out and rescued him.

"Careful of women who offer you a kiss or anything else, son," his uncle had said as he set the ladder against the loft.

Sammy sorted through the tack on the barn wall and dressed out Balthasar the best he could. It was in the half hour of a late summer early morning when the weather was cool, or at least, not hot. He led the mule out of the barn and threw himself over him. The mule hawed and took off at a trot.

Along the path between cane rows was the old straightaway where the Parris and Teague men would race horses in the days before the feud. They were days of good natured boasts and wagering and camaraderie, men in trousers and waistcoats and top hats with money in their fists shouting at galloping horses as they passed or as one family's hired man champion boxed another, bare-knuckled.

But at some point there was a divide, and the amiable competition turned mean. A minor infraction of a inconsequential rule, or an unintentional snub, or a misunderstood look, perhaps, no one remembered exactly, but everyone reveled in the new sport, hatred of the other. Things were done and said that could not be taken back, not in a hundred years. One dynasty waited for a crack to develop in the other so that ultimate victory could be taken. It was Verona and the Parrises that cracked, fell, and burned, and Mount Teague consumed the carrion.

On either side of the path, the cane lay flattened like green leafy soldiers mowed down by gunfire from the east. At the margin of the place stood the columns of Verona. The chimney and the steps were there with the columns as if they were standing around wondering what had happened to the house. The dark green cedars and vivid pink oleander continued to grow, oblivious to the fact that the house they had ornamented was gone. On the grassy embankment of the Twelve Arpent Canal, flies swarmed in a buzz around a bloated animal that Sammy judged to be a possum, though he couldn't tell for sure. It might have been a raccoon.

They picked their way down the bank of the canal. The black nodular surface of an alligator patrolled the green water. The ridges of his back writhed ripples into the surface. He came to rest with his snout near the bank, looking very much like a log. Frogs croaked down the bayou and insects tumbled in clouds above the water, disturbed by fish that made a plunk as they broke the surface to grab at the cloud. The smooth round gray-green backs of turtles were lined up on a log like pearls on a string. On another log, a white heron with a thin orange beak, a big yellow eye and a wispy plume of thin white feathers arising from the back of its head stood on one spindly leg and scratched its neck with the other

A row of pecan trees extended down the edge of the canal. Windblown limbs sagged from the trunks and littered the ground, and the remaining limbs were stripped almost bare of leaves. Sammy tied the mule up to the trunk of one of them and picked through the carpet of green windfall. Pecans were everywhere in the downed foliage. Sammy picked a handful, and when his hands were full, he put them on the ground and took off his shirt. He knotted the arms and neck to make a sack and put the pecans in it. He continued to pick up pecans, peeling away the pungent green husks as he went. He almost had a shirt-full when he heard a squeak.

His ears tuned to find the direction of the noise, as he probed through the leaves. Under a pecan bough was a nest with two squirrel pups, one was dead, but one squealed behind sightless eyes. Its tiny tail was curled and just beginning to bush out. Sammy gently scooped up the live pup and put it on top of the pecans. He untied Balthasar and mounted him with his shirt of pecans and the squirrel pup atop them.

He turned and saw the distant white columns and black roof of Mount Teague and reined the mule around. He wondered how they would get the cane up with so much of it flattened. His thoughts had never been about practical things like that before. Before they had been esoteric and juvenile. His inner thighs slapped the brown hide of the mule as it cantered back the way they had come. The pecans rustled and clicked with the bouncing, while the pup clung to the top of the stack inside the shirt. The heat was intensifying already. The breeze of forward motion was little help against it.

When Sammy returned, he found her at the sink scrubbing the faucet with an SOS pad. He put the shirt of pecans in a chair at the table. The morning light in the window highlighted Betsy's figure through her thin gown like the breasts and hips of a ghost. She stood on a cloth mat in front of the sink, rubbing the sole of one foot on top of the other and humming. He came up behind her and scooped her breasts through the thin fabric, feeling the pleasant weight of them in his hands. He kissed her neck. She closed her eyes and leaned her head back and smiled. His hand traveled down to her lower stomach and he felt the hair there through the cotton of the gown. She turned to him, wiped her hands on a kitchen towel, and put them around his neck. They kissed, lips pulling wet and soft.

He meant to carry her up to their bedroom but got only as far as the dining room table. He lifted the gown over her head, and she was naked before him, perched on the edge of the table. She watched her hands tremble as she undid his jeans, and they fell to the floor. Her fingers were on his back, following his movements. She could feel herself building, and suddenly she surged, pushing her face into his neck, sobbing and laughing. He stopped, his back arched, panting, panting. He fell backward into the chair, and she put her hand on herself and ran to the bathroom.

Afterwards, when she emerged from the bathroom, Sammy was holding the squirrel pup in both hands against his bare chest.

"Ooh, sha be-bee!" she exclaimed, and she put her hands out to take the pup from Sammy. She held it and fussed over it and put her nose to the little creature. Its tiny pink hands draped over her fingers. Sammy went and found a box to put him in. Chanceux sat on his haunches and twisted his head at the squeaking of the little

45

thing, all head with rounded nose and tiny ears, as much a puppy or a kitten as a squirrel.

"You name him?" Betsy asked, holding him in her hand and looking at him closely.

"No. How about 'squirrel'?"

She gave Sammy an incredulous grin and examined the creature again.

"How about 'Lucky'?"

"Lucky?"

"Yeah. Chanceux in English."

Chapter 7

They sat on the front balcony in the wicker settee. Sammy's leg was draped over the arm of the settee, and Betsy's head was nestled on his shoulder and under his chin. She wore a red and blue Ole Miss T-shirt that came down to her upper-thigh. Sammy wore jeans without a shirt. Their bare feet were layered one on top of the other.

The metallic smell of approaching rain hung in the air. In the distance, a towering gray cloud floated above the fields with a gray skirt under it where the rain was already falling. When he was a boy, Sammy called them rain-beams, and his mother had laughed. That was in the days when she used to laugh.

A cool breeze stirred. There was a short preamble of a few plinking drops, and then the rain began suddenly, striking the roof with the sound of applause. It roared passionately as they watched it and listened to it and breathed it. The live oaks and crape myrtles bore it patiently. Rain leaped up from the ground and fell again.

And then it was over just as fast as it started, leaving the eaves dripping. It was cool for about fifteen minutes before the sun came out again and steam rose from the highway at the end of the tunnel of oaks, the vapor drifting aimlessly in the aftermath of the rain.

The dog lifted his head from his paws and cocked his ears sideways. He rose and went inside the house, his claws clicking on the wood planks. And then they saw the police cruiser appear from the mist on the highway and pull into the drive between the oaks. They went inside, too, and shut the door to the balcony.

Downstairs through one of the sidelights beside the great cypress front door, a face appeared, kept away a small distance by the brim of a hat. The hat was removed, and the face pressed up close to the window, the same square shape as the window pane. A hand shaded the eyes that peered in and scanned the hallway. The face disappeared, and there was a knock on the door.

Sammy and Betsy sat at the top of the stairs and waited for him to go away. They huddled together, their arms around each other, their eyes listening, their ears looking.

Deputy Parris was a massive man, wide and hard and solid with a square jaw that jutted out in a prominent underbite. His wavy red hair was plastered close to his square head by near constant sweating. His khaki deputy sheriff's uniform was perpetually two-toned tan and brown, except for the coldest of winter days.

His real name was Percy, but a grade school classmate with a lisp had mispronounced it and it came out Puthy. The rest of his classmates began to amuse themselves by holding the tips of their tongues and saying his name. It was soon corrupted into Pussy, a nickname no boy wanted, so he planted seeds of a new nickname that he had chosen for himself, Bulldog. He was bigger than them and easily enforced the change. Boys who still called him Pussy paid the price.

His family had owned the neighboring place, Verona, until the crash in 1929 began to take its feet out from under it. Percy's father was a man who was always looking for a new magic trick to amplify money and had placed a large amount in the market. After the Crash, the whole place hung by a thread, and then a fire on a cold night in 1931 took the house to the ground, leaving only the steps, the chimney, and the columns.

Parris was a little boy when the house went up. His earliest memory was watching from the front yard in his nightshirt, clutching a stuffed tiger while his parents and siblings shivered under blankets in the cold. The fire crackled in their glowing faces as the house's roof fell in, the massive flame-coated cypress beams crashing down.

Sammy's grandpappy saw the opportunity, the yin and yang of fortune and misfortune, and bought everything, doubling the size of Mount Teague overnight. No Parris would ever forget it. They were

47

raised on hatred of the Teagues and a hunger for retribution that only grew through not being sated.

The Parris family moved to New Orleans to get regular jobs and regular lives. Percy-Puthy-Bulldog stayed behind and was raised by his grandmother in a small house on a tiny plot that had been carved out of the sale. His driving force, his reason for being, was to one day buy back Verona and add Mount Teague as interest. It burned in him like a locomotive's fire.

The army sent PFC Percy Parris to postwar Germany, and then he returned home and got on as a deputy with the sheriff's department. He began amassing money through the "supervision" of dog fights, card games, whorehouses, anything he could hone in on, which was most things. The sheriff had little idea of what was going on, if indeed there even was a sheriff.

The sheriff was reelected easily every election day. The youthful campaign poster that was nailed to trees and telephone poles had not changed in thirty years. No one had actually seen the sheriff in at least ten years, but that didn't keep the people from voting for the youthful face on the flyers. His was a face that was at once friendly and resolute like the face of a faithful guard dog. *Vote for Me, Votre Ami, Sheriff Alphonse 'Alf' Lebeau*, the poster said and then under it in English, *Your Friend.*

Parris knocked one more series of knocks and tried the door. The rattle of the lock made Betsy cling to Sammy. Then there was one more look through the sidelight into the hallway. They heard his footsteps on the porch and waited for his cruiser to fire up like the sound of a flame leaping.

Instead, the deputy walked around the house, looking up to the rear balcony where a clothesline was strung. His eyes took interest in the fact that there were dresses and women's drawers hung up there as well as men's pants and shirts. He stepped over a small fallen oak limb as his eyes scanned the upper and then lower windows, looking for shadows or reflections.

On the far side of the house, a bigger limb that had been sawed up rested next to the car it had obviously fallen on. There were piles of sawdust on either side of the car, the red Tbird that spoiled playboy drove. He thought he heard a noise in the house, upstairs, the sound of a footstep on a wood floor. He shot a glance up, hoping to see someone in the window. It was empty.

He thought of going out to the barn, where the spare key to the house was kept. He knew where every spare house key in St. Matthew Parish was kept, every doormat and every flower pot. But there was really no need. He could come back and get in any time he wanted.

When he got to the front, he took one last look at the house, scanning it from column to column. He smiled and said to himself, Yours someday, Bulldog old boy.

Inside, Sammy and Betsy heard the cruiser ignite. Sammy tiptoed to the balcony door and saw Parris pull onto 308.

Chapter 8

In the morning he held her while she slept in the shaded light of early day. The smell of her hair was becoming comfortable and familiar to him. It fell sleep-tousled over her face, where her eyes were tiny curved brushes of long black lashes. Sammy and Betsy were becoming two interlocking pieces of the same two piece puzzle.

He propped himself on his elbow, his bare chest draped in white bedsheets. She slept and he watched her. He pulled the sheet down and admired her body, naked and prone. He touched the small of her back and ran his hand to the rise of her buttocks. She smiled, opened one eye, and shut it again.

"Boy, why you look at my butt?" She stretched and faced away.

He kissed the small of her back.

"What we gonna do today?" she murmured into a handful of sheets.

"Stay in bed," he said. "All day."

She smiled. "All day?" she giggled into her pillow.

He traced his finger along her back, drawing something.

She closed one eye in thought, pursed her lips, and asked, "A house?"

"Very good," he said. "What's this?"

She squenched up her cheek on one side.

"A…cat."

"Close. A dog. Chanceux, in fact."

"Do another."

He drew a heart.

She smiled and rolled over. Her eyes opened, and she said, "Awww."

She threw her arms straight up and out, and he eased into them. They kissed a long kiss and then looked at each other, and then they kissed again. She put her heels on the small of his back and pulled him down to her.

Afterwards, they took a long bath together in the claw foot tub, the luke warm tap water the perfect temperature, the smell of lilac soap floating invisibly, small waves lapping in the water every time they moved a little. They napped there, she reclining back into his chest, her wet black hair on his shoulder. Finally, she awoke and looked back. The quality of the light had changed, and it was well into the afternoon. Her fingertips were wrinkled.

"Sammy?" she whispered.

"Hm?" His eyes were closed.

"You hungry?"

"Yeah. Yeah I am." He said it like the idea hadn't crossed his mind until then.

"Me too."

The water sloshed as they stood up. They embraced again, Sammy's hands resting comfortably on the small of her back. She kissed him a peck and reached for a towel on the wicker rack by the bathtub.

She handed him a towel and said, "How bout chicken, then?"

The cruiser appeared in the yard of the tenant house as silently as if it had floated there. The door slammed, and there was the squeaky, juicy sound of tobacco spit. Parris hitched up his pants to meet his gut. The brown circles under his arms narrowed and lengthened as his arms moved.

"Aftanoon," he called.

"Help you?" Betsy asked, whisking away a strand of hair from her face with her forearm.

"Ain't been out this way in a while. Came to check on ya."

Betsy held the bird. Its eyes bulged, and it stabbed its beak in different directions, small thrusts that made its red comb quiver. She shushed it and stroked it and whispered to it.

"You gatherin' suppa for you 'n that playboy?" Parris sat on a stump with his legs open.

Betsy answered with a glare.

"Yo mama'll be quite interested to find that path beat 'tween these two houses, now won't she? She is comin' back, ain't she?"

"Yessa."

"You know when?" Parris asked as he examined his fingernails.

"Soon, prolly."

Parris' finger scooped a ragged wad of dark brown tobacco out of his cheek and flung it on the ground. The chickens that had been gleaning the bare earth swarmed it. They pecked at it, judged it inedible, and strutted away.

"You know," the deputy said as he stood up and brushed his backside. "Ain't nothing like seein' a pretty girl holdin' a grit big cock." He smiled and touched the brim of his hat as he turned to leave. The door of the cruiser slammed, and it roared to life. It left as silently as it had appeared.

She gathered up the chicken's legs and laid its head on the flat wood face of the stump. The brown and tan wings splayed out and beat a couple of helpless beats. The hatchet made a clop onto the surface, and there was a flurry of feathers and blood. After a few seconds, both stopped. The blade of the hatchet swept away the head and neck.

*   *   *

They woke early in the morning. If they were to get anything done outside, they would have to get up before the sun got a good head start on them. Not a leafy-rayed, friendly sun, a sunflower sun that might wear dark glasses and a benevolent smile, but a pale white-hot disc, an intense, indifferent orb that never let up.

Sammy had never driven a tractor at Mount Teague. In fact, he had never even sat in one and didn't know where the keys were, so they pulled limbs by hand to the highway where eventually the parish would pick them up. Sammy looked over to the tenant house.

"Who lives in there? With you?" he asked as he squinted into the distance. Chanceux trotted along, sniffing in the bases of the shoulder-high azaleas and marking them with a lift of his leg.

"Me, mama and my Mimi."

"How old is your Mimi?"

"Nobody know, she don't even know. Least ninety. She's my mama's grandmother. She's old, she remembers the blue soldiers, she calls 'em, the Yankees when they were down here after the Civil War. The blue Americans, sometime she say. She call anybody don't speak French an American. She was just a lil girl then. She stop goin' to school when she was ten when they told her she couldn't speak French no more."

"What about your mama?" Sammy looked over to Betsy as they neared the highway with their burden of limbs. The limbs scraped along the shell drive behind them, brushing in time with their footsteps. "She's not real friendly."

"No, she ain't," Betsy shook her head. "But she used to be, though. Before my daddy passed."

"You must've had boyfriends, huh? Pretty girl like you."

She smiled and blushed like someone who was pretty but not used to being called pretty.

"Not really. Ain't never had time. Gotta take care the house and mama and Mimi."

They piled their burden of limbs together by the highway and turned to the house. Their hands found each other and clasped, and they walked down the alley of oaks.

The rain boiled up almost every afternoon. They would sit in the cloud of tousled sheets in the middle of the bed. Their naked laps faced each other as they clung together like they were drowning in a vast ocean. Their lips pressing into each other, then into necks, chests, then onto lips again. Her breasts pressed into his chest, her nipples misaligned with his. She breathed through an open mouth, her closed eyes seeing the reckoning of her ecstasy as it approached, awaited and welcomed. She buried her face in his neck as it washed over her, and she smelled the sharp edges of the Aqua Velva he had put there.

The moon was subtracting itself a little more every night, an arc, a crescent, a sliver of yellowed ivory. Then, there was no moon, and no lights from traffic, and outside was an opaque void as airless and dark as deep space, as ancient and dark as the tombs of Egypt. The silence was enormous, and they enjoyed the comfortable intimacy of it.

Sammy knew that his daddy and, for that matter, his sister Charlotte couldn't hold out much longer in the house in Jackson. He wondered how many times in the last few days his grandpappy had addressed Sammy's father as 'Goddammit Trey.' Sammy knew that his grandpappy would hold court every afternoon with a reading of the gospel according to Junior Teague.

He blew out the candle at their bedside, and they settled in next to each other in the dark. They were content in the thick gray night air.

Chapter 9

Across the way a rooster crowed as the soft morning light found them again. Their naked bodies were entwined. Her black hair spilled over his chest where his heart beat sang into her ear soft and steady. The light through the window was just an unheeded suggestion for them to get up. There was a rapping next door that was remote but resolute.

Five knocks. "Betsy! Betsy Duplechain!" Another set of five knocks.

Betsy sat up at the distant call of her name as if it were in her ear. She got up, her forearm covering her breasts, and looked through a crack in the curtains. "It's my Nonc Claude."

She grabbed her light blue shift dress from the back of a chair and threw it over her head. It fell like a curtain over her nakedness. Her feet toed into her shoes and drummed down the stairs. Sammy threw on a pair of pants and headed downstairs after her. At the base of the stairs, his shirt came over his head in time for him to see her pour half a cup of yesterday's cold coffee and head out the back door with it. Sammy watched her walk solemnly across the field to talk with the men who were in the yard of the little house.

"Bonjour, Nonc." He heard the salutation through the door. A conversation ensued distant and in French. He heard her say, "*Oh merci, merci.*"

Men scrambled out of two trucks parked out front. Some of the younger men wore welder's caps backwards on their heads. They took ladders out of the back of the truck, propped them against the house, and climbed onto the roof. The wind god had picked up a corner of the roof of the little house and peered inside, but had neglected to replace it.

Within minutes, the sheet of tin was flung off the roof. It hit the ground in a sound like theatrical backstage thunder, and a new sheet went up in its place. On top, three other men hammered it into place, and another caulked over the nail holes. Their hammers worked briskly, each with a different cadence. The echoes of the hammer blows took off over the bayou.

She walked back. Halfway over, she slung her arm and emptied the cup out into the field. The coffee leaped out in honey-brown tendrils and splattered in the weeds.

"So what's up?" Sammy asked. The squirrel looked like a squirrel now, climbing over and through Sammy's hands.

"It's a crew of men from the church in Labadieville, one of 'em my Nonc Claude, my daddy's brother. They say the highway's open now 'tween here and there. They heard about the house and come to fix the roof and the linoleum. They been talkin' to my mama."

"What else they say?"

She sat down in a kitchen chair. "They wanna know what I'm doin' over here. I told 'em I was just over here havin' coffee. They all say be careful that boy. They all say he's *canaille.*"

"Canaille?"

"Clever. Sneaky."

For such a young man, Sammy Teague had a ball and chain of a past that would not let him move on. A reputation like an anchor. He wondered how long he would have to drag it.

He sat in a chair next to her. "What do you think?" he asked her. She put her hand over his.

"The truth? I think you only got raised halfway."

He kissed the top of her head. Across the way, two men carried a roll of linoleum into the house.

Time advanced namelessly. The days were airy and gossamer, bright mornings, blazing hot middays, thunderous and rainy afternoons, cricket-sung nights. Neither one of them knew what day it was. It could have been Wednesday, Friday, the Fourth of July, Christmas, Judgment Day. They had no idea and no desire for an idea. They watched the sunset every evening and then went to bed and loved and slept.

Then one day the mail was delivered. The day after that, the paper. Cars began to roam the highway in front of the house; it was open now. There was news that line crews were spotted in Donaldsonville and Thibodaux, and electricity could be expected within a week.

In the gray light of a warm dawn, the lights came on suddenly. The television snapped like a spark and then began speaking. The air conditioner in the window cracked on without warning and began spilling cold air into the room. The phones rang once and not again. Mount Teague was like an abandoned amusement park coming to life. As the chill settled on them in their half-sleep, they pulled the covers over their naked bodies and pillows over their heads, and nestled in close to each other.

They stayed like that, bunkered in against the world until they grew hungry around midday. Then they sat up and stretched. Betsy put on one of Sammy's button downs and went downstairs to make them a breakfast which had sagged into the time slot of lunch. Sammy slipped on a pair of jeans with no shirt. They looked like they were sharing an outfit.

Betsy crumbled the last of the cornbread for couche-couche and poured Pet milk and a little sugar over it, and they sat at the table. The shirt barely covered the dark tangle of black hair at the top of her thighs. They ate silently.

When they were done, he pulled back from the table and motioned for her to sit in his lap. She straddled him and put her head on his shoulder. Sammy felt her nipples on his chest through the soft cotton of his shirt she was wearing. He began to stir. He carried her through the dining room to the downstairs parlor, and then placed her on the couch and pulled down his jeans. He was ready, but he leisurely undid the buttons of the blue shirt and pulled it open. He kissed her breasts, one and then the other, slowly, reverently and then moved inside her. They went slowly. Slowly so that their

55

memories would etch it deep and indelibly. Slowly in case it was the last time. Slowly so they could remember it all their lives.

Afterwards, his head was in her lap, and he was almost asleep. She was playing with his hair, changing the part in it from one side to the other. She said something to him in French, so softly that it was almost a lullaby. He tried to piece together what she had said, but he drifted away having only understood his name.

What she had said was, "What we gonna do, Sammy? When the world comes back?"

The pendulum clicked in the mahogany case of the long clock in the hall. Sammy woke and looked up into her face. He smiled a forced, dutiful smile.

From the phone in the hall they each called their parents and spoke the news like a death sentence.

The power is back on.

Chapter 10

For the elite, marriages were not so much arranged as they were cultivated, carefully nurtured like a botanist would grow plants in a hothouse. Nothing was left to chance. Brides had pedigrees, grooms had résumés. Lineages were studied, almost as if they were racehorses or hunting dogs. Mamie Teague believed that most of the Mount Teague mules had had better pedigrees than that tenant girl.

And Betsy knew it. She knew that for Sammy or anyone else of his class to choose the wrong mate would, with rare exceptions, subject them to monetary exile. From the little house across the field, she had seen the courtship ritual at the big house. The spectacles of garden parties, engagement showers for Sammy's sisters, cotillion socials, debutante balls. String quartets in tuxedos under the green lacquered leaves of magnolia trees shared the dappled shade with white table cloths and white gloves. Fine china was filled from chafing dishes by handsomely dressed attendants. The big house loomed with expectations that demanded to be met.

Betsy had been raised Catholic and raised to believe in her own essential unworthiness. Her mother's greatest fear for her was that she would marry someone non-Catholic and that the priest would refuse to marry her and that she would be refused the other sacraments as well. Her mother was a woman who could imagine calamities like that, calamities that came in rapid succession, falling like dominos. Getting married outside of the church was one of the first dominos in the line.

In the dim light, the force of circumstance pulled Betsy out of their bed. It would be just his bed again. She studied him one last time as he slept clutching a pillow. She quietly packed the flimsy little suitcase and eased out the door. She hoped he would understand.

She paused at the top of the stairs, her hand on the banister, and then crept down them, stepping lightly on each old cypress tread. At the backdoor, she twisted the doorknob slowly, slipped through, and pulled it shut behind her. The morning was already hazy gray and humid. She turned away from the big house and the boy sleeping upstairs, and then she ran, her hand clutching the handle of the tattered valise, tears in her eyes, her feet beating across the ground, her free arm flailing, the wind rushing in her ears, running like she was trying to escape gravity.

Chapter 11

He woke up in the wee hours of the morning. Across the field, a light burned again in the window of the tenant house. His bed seemed prairie-vast and empty, the sheets were cotton white clouds in an airless sky. He put his nose to the pillow and tried to find the scent of her hair. It was there but just a little less than before, and he knew it was just a matter of time before it would be undetectable. But he knew the weight of expectations, too.

It was hard to get out of bed. He kept thinking that he would find her there, that if he drifted off to sleep and woke up again, she would be there next to him, sleeping with her hair fanned out over her eyes and cheek. Or that if he got up, and she wasn't somewhere in the house, she would really be gone.

He sat on the porch for a few moments and was about to go over to the tenant house when the Lincoln pulled onto the crushed shells of the driveway. A cloud passed under the sun and cast everything a shade darker for a moment. Sugarboy was yipping inside the car, one bark beginning as soon as the one before it ended.

Sammy opened the door for his mama.

"Hi mama."

"Hi son," she said flatly behind her sunglasses. Sugarboy jumped from her lap and ran around the yard, sniffing and lifting his leg daintily trying to mask the mark of that other dog. Sammy helped his mama out, and she stumbled up the steps into the house.

"I have some things in the trunk," she mumbled over her shoulder.

Grandpappy wore a hat, a white fedora with a brown band, low over his head. He slowly extricated himself from the backseat and stretched, his joints popping and creaking. His stiff legs tottered up the steps as he grumbled, "Thank God, I've had to piss since Amite."

Sammy and his daddy unpacked the trunk. There were two empty cardboard gin boxes of dirty clothes, as well as all the baggage they had taken up to Jackson. The amount of boxes and suitcases in the trunk of the Lincoln defied the laws of Physics and Geometry.

Sugarboy skittered around the house, sniffing out a map of where the intruder dog had been. He snapped out high pitched barks and growled with each new discovery of the scent. In the dining room, the smell under the table especially infuriated him. He lifted up his leg and urinated to override the scent of the interloper.

Mamie trundled past Sugarboy on her way to her room and her nap.

"Christ," she muttered, and then yelled, "Dutchie!" as she went into her room.

Sammy and his daddy walked around the grounds, pausing to look at his car. The top was crumpled down into the car, and the doors had two semicircular depressions in them.

"My goodness," his daddy said when he saw it.

They moved out to the fields where the cane lay flat and matted. Sammy and his daddy surveyed the downed stalks, pulling them

58

upright and pressing their feet to gauge how wet the soil was. At one point, his daddy produced a pocket knife, cut a cane stalk in half, and sucked the juice from it.

Sammy asked several pertinent questions about the upcoming harvest. How much is sugar per ton, currently? How many tons per acre can we expect? Do you think the ground would support the weight of the cane harvesters? How long before it dries out, would you imagine? His daddy raised his eyebrows in appreciation of his son's insight. As the sun began to sink, they returned to the house.

Miss Della Mae's daughter Dutchie cooked for them now. As short and fat as Della Mae had been, Dutchie was just as tall and skinny. She put the last dish, a terrine of lima beans on the table, and turned back to the kitchen.

"Some storm we had," Sammy's daddy said.

Sammy's mama used her teeth to slowly slide a bite off her fork. It was what a lady did to keep lipstick off her food and more importantly, food off her lipstick. She took the last sip of her cocktail and held up the tumbler with the waxy, rose colored stain on the rim. Dutchie knew better than to ask her if she needed a refill. Of course she did.

"Said it was bigger than Audrey was," Sammy said, stirring his tea. He clacked the spoon on the edge of the glass, and it gave a short ring.

"When was Audrey?" his mama asked. She was pushing the tines of her fork through her rice, waiting for Dutchie and her refill.

"What was it?" Grandpappy asked. "Fifty six?"

"Fifty seven, I believe, daddy, though I might be wrong on that," Sammy's daddy said. He knew for a fact it was 1957, but he also knew from a lifetime of experience that you never directly contradicted Junior Teague, only indirectly if you even dared that.

"Did I ever tell you about the storm of 1915?" Grandpappy asked.

They all knew that the right answer, *yes*, was also the wrong answer.

"No, daddy," Trey said. "Tell us about that." He put a bite in his mouth. The rest of the family braced themselves like they would for the first blast of cold water from a showerhead.

"The hurricane of 1915. Now that," Grandpappy tapped the air with his fork, "That was a real ass kicka. Ya mama and I were in New Orleans, s'pose to sail for Havana the next day. Naturally, that was delayed. The power was knocked out at the Hotel Monteleone, so they fed us sandwiches for three straight days. Three. Straight. Days." His fork tapped out each word.

What unspeakable hardship, Sammy thought, but he knew from experience that this was also a wrong answer.

"Havana was somethin' in those days. You could get anything you wanted. And they loved Americans back then. We brought in all the money, y'see. Bushel baskets of it. Different now, now that the commonists took over."

They all waited for grandpappy to rather clumsily translate this into a talk on the evils of integration or that damn civil rights bill but Sammy's mama spoke up.

"Charlotte and Hank are expecting again. February, most likely." Her teeth slid another bite off her fork. She dotted the corner of her mouth with her napkin leaving a rose-colored stain on the white linen.

"Really? That's good news," Sammy said as he chewed. "She feelin' well?"

"Well enough. They say if it's a girl they'll name her Sophia after my mother," Mamie said.

"Oh, that's real nice," Sammy said.

The click and clank of utensils and china carried the conversation for a while. Then his daddy spoke.

"Tomorrow I'll take you in to Thibodaux," he said. "Get you a new car."

"Thanks, daddy." Sammy looked up and nodded. He chewed and swallowed, and said again, "Thank you." Sammy's daddy looked at his son as if he had learned a foreign language in his absence.

"I'm curious, son. How'd you get that limb off the Tbird by yourself?" His daddy spoke while his eyes followed a dish.

Sammy took a sip of iced tea and swallowed. He watched his knife and fork work as he said with a trace of pride, "Betsy and I did it. Sawed it up and rolled it right off."

There was a pause, even the utensils, except for Sammy's.

"The tenant girl Betsy?" his mama asked. The look on her face was one of a queen who's just discovered a plot to overthrow the throne. Sammy didn't see it; he was looking at his plate, cutting another bite of meat. They were all looking at Sammy.

"That girl was over here?" his mama persisted. "Well, I just don't know how I feel about that."

"Why?" Sammy asked. He looked up from his plate as his chewing slowed, and he looked her in the eye. "Well, why don't you know how you feel about it?" As soon as he asked it, he realized that it was a question he wished he had asked ten years earlier.

Mount Grandpappy erupted. "Those coonasses? If ya ask me, they'h just two pegs better'n a nagga."

A rogue wave of anger rose up in Sammy, and he slapped the table so hard he could feel the lace of the tablecloth dig into his palms. Gin sloshed out of his mama's cut glass tumbler. Silverware jumped up from the table and landed askew. Dutchie put her head into the doorway, took one look, and quickly withdrew it.

"Nobody. Asked. You." Sammy seethed at his grandpappy. A second wave of anger followed the first. Sammy's mouth tried to hold back the next words, but it was no use. "Goddammit...grandpappy...sir."

Sammy continued like a runaway train. His finger stabbed the air between them emphatically. "They work hard and they play hard, while over here we live high and die slow. Truth be told, you probably think we're two pegs better'n everybody else. Goddamn your pegs. Goddamn. Your. Pegs." His fists banged the table, softer this time.

Silence settled on them like a shroud as everyone concentrated on their plate. The last time someone had stood up to Junior Teague, Roosevelt was president. Theodore Roosevelt.

Grandpappy's caterpillar eyebrows arched their fuzzy white backs high over his steely eyes.

"This is what I'm talkin' about with kids these days!" he said indignantly, this time his own finger stabbing the air. "This is it exactly. Ungrateful."

Dutchie looked through the door from the kitchen. Sammy's blank gaze caught hers, his chest rising and falling. She looked away and resumed drying the plate she had almost dropped. Sammy's daddy abruptly changed the subject.

"Another few days of dry weather, we can get in the field and try to salvage some product." After Sammy's daddy had come home from Ole Miss with his degree in Agriculture & Economics, he called sugarcane 'product.'

Sammy took his napkin from his lap and got up. "Excuse me, but I'm not hungry." He went upstairs and sat on the balcony in a wicker chair. The fingers of one hand were in his hair, while the fingers of his other hand held a cigarette. He and the cigarette fumed.

Later that night, Dutchie came up to his room with a plate. On it was a big piece of chocolate cake and a fork. Sammy thanked her and took a bite. It was rich and deep as a well of chocolate and heavily laced with cinnamon, still warm. He recognized it as Della Mae's recipe. Dutchie winked at him and whispered, "You a good man, Mist' Sammy."

Sammy had been called handsome, pretty, dreamy, cute, good looking, and attractive. But no one had ever called him good before.

Later that night, Sammy's parents appeared on the landing outside their bedroom and met Sammy at the top of the stairs. His father had on trousers and an undershirt, and his mother had on a ecru silk nightgown under her open robe. Her hair had fallen from its careful perch and hung limply around her face. The glass in her hand was almost empty, so she emptied it completely. Her breasts nudged against the silk, the outline of them clearly apparent, deflating mounds and defiant nipples. Sammy cast his eyes away, up to the door jamb.

"Cover yourself, Mamie," Trey said. She rocked backward a bit and yanked her robe over her front.

"Son," Trey said, "we believe you owe your grandfather an apology. You don't talk to a man his age that way."

Sammy didn't say anything, but his mother did.

"And you don't bring..."

A hiccup.

"...hired people or the children..."

A small belch.

"...of hired people into this house for anything other than work," his mama said. Her tongue was thick, and her eyes wandered aimlessly as she forced a fake smile. Her breath was gin-sweet as she waited for Sammy's capitulation on the subject, a contrite *yes ma'am.*

But instead, Sammy laid the trump card on the table.

"I'm in love," he said.

"Love?" his mama said.

"Love!" she shouted. "You'll love who we tell you to love!"

She tottered and swayed, her finger cutting a zigzag in the air between them. Her eyelids were at half mast, and she began pulling at his daddy's belt.

"Re-Speck. Thas what your boy needs a lesson in, Trey. Ree SPECK," She said it so forcefully that 'speck' seemed to pull her head forward, like she was spitting it out.

His daddy gently pushed her hands away from his midsection without looking, like a parent involved in a conversation with another adult would do to an interrupting child. She continued to fumble for his belt.

"Reee-Speck," she muttered petulantly. She belched a small mouthful of vomit that her rose colored lips and her jeweled fingers sealed in. She stumbled to the bathroom.

"What's got into you, son?" Trey said quietly. He really wanted to know. They stood and looked at each other for a while.

"Whip him, Trey," Mamie slurred from the other room, on the bed where she had collapsed. Her robe had fallen open and her breasts were pressing against the silk gown again. Blue and red spider veins were scattered on her thin pale legs, long ago shapely but spindly now.

"A man can't whip his grown son, Mamie," Trey said quietly over his shoulder.

"Whip him, whip the little son of a bitch," she muttered blank-eyed to the ceiling. "Use your belt..." and then her voice trailed into a snore.

His daddy turned from her, back to his son. His daddy didn't seem angry now, he seemed more in awe.

"You don't seem like the boy we left."

"No sir," Sammy said.

His daddy had hit the nail right on the head.

The big house at Mount Teague was like a prison to Sammy now, and the tenant shotgun house was like a temple. Now when he watched her in the garden behind the house, she would look up at him from under her wide brimmed hat, and without exchanging a greeting, go back to work, hands flitting among the branches of the okra like two birds. The tops of the okra jiggled as the knife worked. Chanceux sat in the shade, an orange sphinx panting and curling his tongue when he yawned. When she went inside her house, the screen door made a distant slap, and Sammy went inside his.

The following day he and his daddy rode to Thibodaux. The air outside was hot, but inside the Lincoln the quiet was icy. The clipped voice on the radio gave the news. His daddy turned the volume down.

"We're gonna have to get you back in school. I talked to an old friend in the Dean's office in Oxford. Says you're gonna have to come on soon to get credit for the semester." Sammy's daddy took his eyes off the road for a moment and looked at his son. "You know the government's got this place now called Viet-Nam. I hear that if you're not in college, they could send you there." He looked back on the winding highway.

"That right?" Sammy said as he looked out on the cane that passed by. It was all a flattened weave of green stalks that the intense sunshine was trying to resurrect.

He knew about Vietnam. Two of his boarding school classmates were there now. One of his fraternity brothers had flunked out and was at Fort Leonard Wood in Missouri getting ready to go. All three of them figured they wouldn't be there long, it being such a grab ass little country that just needed its ass kicked. Like Korea, Sammy had told them.

In Thibodaux they pulled into the Ford dealership, where the salesman came out of the office and greeted Mr. Teague like he was the governor or the pope. Sammy wanted something used and simple, but his daddy insisted on a brand new Mustang convertible, dark blue. He wrote the man a check, and Sammy followed the Lincoln home in the new car. The next day the Mustang was packed and ready for the trip back to Oxford.

That night Sammy smoked on the balcony and watched the orange squares of lights in the windows of the shotgun house next door. His heart was breaking with an intensity that was almost audible.

She was the kind of girl who knew that she was meant to be a woman, not perpetually a child. The kind that knew how to do a lot of things, most importantly, how to be content. He had a feeling that she could be content with or without him. The only thing that he knew for sure was that he could never be content without her.

His mother was right. Those people were cut from a different cloth. A cloth that was strong and vibrant. A cloth that kept you warm on the coldest night of the year. A cloth that felt soft and good against your bare skin. No matter how well dressed he would ever be, he would always feel naked without it.

Chapter 12

He sat on the hood of the new car and smoked, waiting for the return of the ferry from the other side, so he could cross and continue north. Traffic on the river was held up. During the storm, a barge full of chlorine had sunk in the river at Baton Rouge, and officials were trying to find it so they could decide what to do with it. He thought about taking the new Sunshine Bridge, but habit or maybe preoccupation brought him to the ferry landing.

A breeze off the river lifted the hair away from his eyes as he thought. The ferry swung around in the current, riding it downstream to avoid a tanker. The squat little wheelhouse was getting larger and larger as it approached, and his cigarette was getting shorter and shorter. He looked at the approaching ferry and then at the cigarette. He threw the butt to the ground and got behind the wheel.

The ferry docked at the landing, and the ferrymen lashed the boat to the pilings. The parade of vehicles drove off the deck and crunched over the crushed white shells of the road that led up to the landing. The inbound cars began loading. Sammy looked back one more time. He turned the key, and the Mustang rumbled to life. He drove onto the corrugated metal of the deck and the tires hummed.

When the other cars were loaded around him and the ferry shoved off, he felt he had made a mistake.

On the other side, they unloaded, and Sammy pulled off and parked under a scrawny live oak tree with a political sign nailed to it. He sat behind the wheel feeling like the rope in the tug of war between what was expected of him and what he wanted. He was grist between the two cold hard grindstones of social tradition and free will. He merged onto the highway and headed north.

The trip he used to make at a breakneck pace in seven hours took him ten. He stopped several times to smoke and talk himself into and out of going back. At sunset he was back at the fraternity house.

"Sam-mee!" they cried, shaking his hand and patting him on the back. His smile was feeble, and he felt like a stranger as he walked in the house. He was an upperclassman now and had a room to himself. He went upstairs to it, shut the door, and didn't come out. His fraternity brothers exchanged glances.

His suitcase sat on the floor of his new room and stayed unopened, with the rest of his belongings in cardboard boxes in his car. He thought writing Betsy a letter might help, but as he sat with a piece of paper and a pen, waiting for his heart to burst and flood the sheets of paper with words, nothing happened. What would he say? They were right, I am a playboy? Canaille? Da rish boy? He couldn't even get started.

Sometime in the night, he drove across the state line to Collierville, in Tennessee, to get beer and then sat in the dark of his room drinking it and smoking. In the morning, he didn't go straight to the registrar's office like his daddy had told him to. Instead he sat in the dark drinking beer and chain smoking. In the next few days, he didn't even think about going to class one time and rarely left the frat house.

On Saturday, Ole Miss hosted Florida for Homecoming. He sat there, alone in the midst of fifty thousand people. The stadium sloped back from the field and seethed with humanity, much like the Coliseum must have looked in Roman times, but instead of a flurry of white togas, the stadium was red and blue, with scattered spots of Florida Gator orange. Looking across the way, Sammy caught the familiar flip of silky blonde hair of Tina, his girlfriend during the spring semester. She was sitting with the Pikes, holding hands, exchanging glances, and pecking kisses with one of them, a boy named Freddy. Six months earlier it would have inspired intense jealousy, but now Sammy couldn't care less.

A flask was passed up and down the row between Sammy's fraternity brothers who added splashes and dollops to their soft drinks. Sammy Teague just let it pass.

The band played Dixie, and everyone got to their feet, and Sammy Teague just sat there and stared. The crowd chanted, "Hoddy-toddy-gosh-a-mighty-who the hell are we-hey?" and Sammy Teague just sat there and stared. The Rebels made a first down on a hopeless third and long, a back shifting through a hole behind a push of rooting, surging red jerseys, and the crowd leaped up, and Sammy Teague just sat there and stared. The homecoming court was presented, and everyone stood and clapped for the King and Queen, and Sammy Teague just sat there and stared. The band played Dixie again, and everyone sang along, and Sammy Teague just sat there and stared. The Rebels were shut out by Florida, and everyone filed out of the stadium and formulated reasons for the loss, and Sammy Teague just sat there and stared.

"Come on," one of his frat brothers said, snapping his fingers in Sammy's face. "Game's over."

He bumped shoulders in the egress of the crowd, pulled along in the current of people.

At the frat house, the guys all cleaned up for the Homecoming dance to be held after the game. They primped in front of mirrors, splashed on generous aliquots of cologne, and joked about their prospects of getting laid, Sammy's old life, his old pastime.

They tried to persuade him to come along; certainly there would be multiple girls who would want to dance with him, and certainly he could get lucky if he would only shave and put on a clean shirt and a smile for Christ' sake. And comb your hair, what's eating you, man?

Finally, they threw up their hands and left, and he was alone in the shell of a life he no longer cared for, a life he had outgrown, an empty husk. His fraternity brothers were boys, just boys. He put out his cigarette as the sun fell into the western sky, and he packed for the trip home. He didn't belong here anymore.

The trip home took the customary seven hours as he raced through the night with a cup of black coffee on the center console. He stopped only to go to the bathroom and then refresh his coffee.

As he drove, he wondered if Dutchie knew anyone who could restore an old wedding dress.

In McComb, Sammy stopped at a convenience store. A bus had also stopped to let passengers refresh themselves, and it waited panting out front. The driver leaned against the door with the bill of his cap tilted back. His foot was propped against the blue of the bus as he smoked a cigarette.

A man in a suit and hair slick with grease stepped out of a red Chevy Impala. They got to the wooden porch at the same time, and he held the door for Sammy and said, "Evenin', young feller." Sammy eased in the door and said "Thanks." The store had a dozen or more people in it, but the cashiers called to the man, "Hey Mr. Tibbit. Hey now."

"Hey there, ladies," the salesman gushed. He spread his arms to them and said, "Now this' the main reason fer takin' the south Mississippi territory. Seein' you ladies. I guess they got all the pretty gals a-workin' tonight."

"Aw, you such a card, Mist' Cap."

Sammy went to find the restroom, but there was a line of passengers already there. He decided to go around the side of the building, but heard someone back there in the weeds, so he left, deciding to go in the next town or on the side of the road. He didn't want to lose any time.

As he got in his car, he thought he heard someone heave and retch. He looked around but didn't see anyone. He listened again, holding his ear to the night air, but the bus rumbled to noisy life and pulled onto the highway. He got in his car and sped south.

The sun was breaking on the river as he passed over the Sunshine Bridge. He cursed the cane trucks that lumbered in front of him, shaggy with yellowing green cane stalks. He passed them maniacally, narrowly avoiding oncoming traffic. When he got to the familiar bend in the highway, he stopped not at Mount Teague, but at the tenant house. He hopped out of the Mustang without opening the door and then realized he hadn't shut off the engine, but he went to the door anyway with the motor running. He knocked, and Betsy's mama answered the door. She was a large lady with a potato body and a smaller potato head with slit-like eyes sunk in it. As big as she was, her redundant skin seemed to be the size of an even larger woman.

"Is Betsy home?" Sammy asked breathlessly. He looked past her shoulder, and she looked over it too and then turned to him. .

Then the woman studied him for what seemed like a full minute and said curtly, "Betsy don't live here no more."

Behind her an old woman with a big nose slowly pitched forward and back in a rocker. Her hands were draped over the head of a cane that met the floor between her fleshy knees. Her rolled down stockings sagged just below them. She was as deaf as a post and stared straight ahead as she rocked. The house smelled of rubber like new linoleum.

"Can you tell me where she is?" he asked again.

Her answer was instant this time, but the same. "Betsy don't live here no more."

She shut the door.

Chapter 13

His honest, brown eyes looked up to her through the window. Inside the bus was the goddess he had worshipped since he was a puppy. She looked away, turning the expression that he knew was the sad one, and putting it somewhere else. He yipped to get her attention, and she turned back to him. Through the glass he saw that she had water on her face. He knew this meant sad.

She was in a big metal animal that was nursing from a long black teat. The little dog snorted. Any creature that big should be weaned by now. A man pulled the teat away, and the animal belched after its meal from the pump. It lurched forward on round black-rubber paws, and then it carried her off.

The dog ran alongside it, but it was too fast for him and then he stopped in the ditch. He panted and sighed with a long curling tongue and watched it get smaller in the distance. He turned and ambled back to Mr. Aucoin's.

Mr. Aucoin was standing by the door of his store. He liked the dog; they were both curs. He pulled the top of a can of Vienna sausages, plucked one out and flipped it to the dog. The dog caught it in midair with a slap of his jaws and then sat on his haunches for

69

the next. The setting sun made his shadow long, and it crept up the side of the whitewashed planks of the store like a silhouette of the inner wolf.

When the can was empty, Mr. Aucoin scratched the dog's head and tottered back inside. The little man's dark trousers were hitched halfway up his chest, and the white shirt was wet under the arms. The screen door popped against the jamb. The dog walked to the gas pump and lifted his leg to mark a request for the big animal to bring her back. He snorted and flicked dirt on the message with his hind legs. It was important. He leaped onto the porch and curled up by the cold drink machine and waited.

Chapter 14

At a roadside store in McComb, the bus stopped in the middle of the night for the passengers to stretch their legs and get refreshments. The young woman in the faded red and white dress stepped off the bus and went inside with the rest of the passengers.

"Five minutes, folks," the bus driver called to their backs. The sole of his foot rested by the door of the idling bus as he lit a cigarette.

A wave of nausea gripped her when she smelled the greasy food inside. She ran to the restroom, but it was occupied. She looked around frantically with her hand over her mouth, and finally ran out the door and to the side of the building. She belched, and her stomach spattered on the white clapboard and in the weeds. She paused and rocked back from her knees. She squatted as another wave rung her like a rag, and she heaved again, but there was less this time. She wiped her mouth on the back of her hand and tried to stand up, but retched again. There was nothing left. Her hand was wet, and she looked around, but there was nothing there, so she wiped it on the inside hem of her dress.

She emerged from around the corner, shaky, to see the red taillights of the bus pull onto the highway. A glance told her running was no use. She walked to the front of the store and sat on the bench outside.

A man in a gray suit with the necktie pulled loose emerged from the diner and lit a cigarette. His graying black hair was slick with sweet smelling grease. He saw Betsy there and said, "Hey."

"Hey," Betsy said.

"You look sad," the man said. "You feelin' well?"

"A little sick in the stomach."

"You waitin' fer somebody?"

"I missed the bus. It left me."

"Well then, need a ride?"

"Where you goin'? she asked.

"Fer is Jackson." He pushed back his jacket and put his hand in his pocket while the other one put the cigarette to his lips.

"That on the way to Oxford, Missippi?"

"Shore is. You a collitch gal?"

"No sir, goin' to see my boyfriend."

"I can take ya's fer's Jackson. You got a bag?"

"The bus took it."

He went in and got her a green glass bottle of 7Up and a pack of saltines and opened the passenger door for her. As she got in, she felt his hand slide over her backside. When the door closed, she wished she hadn't gotten in.

"Cap Tibbit." He gave her his hand.

"Be'sy." She just smiled, and he withdrew it.

"Did you say Betsy? Well I'll be! Just like the hurrikin. Now, do I detect a bit of an accent?" he asked as if it were the most interesting thing possible. He had a salesman's voice and a salesman's cadence. Everything that came out of his mouth led up to a sales pitch, a fishing line with a hook attached. "Where you from, Miss Betsy?"

"Louisiana."

"Loozy-anna? Don't say! Y'all have any trouble with the hurrikin?"

They drove into the night. The first front of an approaching winter was sending a headwind of cold air right at them. Betsy drew her sweater around her shoulders. The radio played Buck Owens, "I've Got a Tiger by the Tail."

"So yer boyfriend's a collitch boy. What's he studyin' on?"

"Farmin'."

"Oh, I see. An Agger-culture type boy, then."

71

"I guess so." Betsy looked out the passenger window at the galloping night landscape and saw Mr. Tibbit's reflection superimposed on it. The reflection removed the ring from his right hand and dropped it in his shirt pocket. Then he took one last drag on his cigarette, cracked his window, and flicked the butt out into the cold night air. He switched hands on the steering wheel and put his right hand on the vinyl seat between them.

"So what do you do?" He pretended to look in the rearview mirror, but stole a glance at Betsy's breasts.

"I help my mama around the house." Her words were mumbled. She was struggled to wring them out of herself.

"That so? Y'all got a big place?"

"Kinda."

The man's hand slid across the seat, and the backs of his fingers stroked the outside of Betsy's thigh. She looked at his hand and pulled her leg away. The salesman's hand retreated. He seemed not to notice the rebuff and kept talking.

"So you'n yer boyfriend serious?"

She didn't know how to answer, and even if she did, it was none of his business.

His hand crept over the seat again, this time slithering over her thigh to between her legs. She snatched it and pushed it back at him. The car careened across the centerline, and they narrowly missed a truck in the oncoming lane. It gave a long, low, scolding horn blast that receded past them.

"Come on, baby, hows about a little feel? That's all. Ain't you Cajun gals spose t'be hot blooded?" His hand fumbled for her breast, and she smacked it. He went to slap her, and she bit his hand. It was bleeding, and he looked at it in disbelief. The car came to a halt in the night on the side of the road.

"Git out. *Git out*!" He bawled, holding his hand. She got out, and he yelled at her through the open door.

"Nobody rides for free in this world, hear me? Nobody!"

She slammed the door. Through the driver's window, his hand flipped the pack of saltines over the roof. The car accelerated through the gravel on the shoulder of the road. She threw the green glass 7Up bottle, and it glanced off the bumper and landed in the ditch. The taillights disappeared to pinpoints. The pinpoints sank below a rise in the road.

The wind was cold, colder than she had imagined it would be. She gathered the brown sweater around her shoulders and hugged herself as she walked along the side of the highway. The wind played with the lower edge of her sweater, lifting it up as if it wanted a peek. She passed a sign that said US Hwy 51, then half an hour later, one that said, Bogue Chitto 4, Jackson 68. A light rain fell and then stopped. She counted five cars that passed.

The sixth passed but then slowed down and stopped. It was an old car with the rounded fenders and bulbous top of the last decade or maybe the one before that. A black woman of about sixty got out on the passenger side and called to her, "Baby, what you doin' out on a night like dis?" She came toward Betsy and made a rolling gesture with her hands and said, "Come ride with us. Way you goin' Missy?"

"Oxford, Missippi."

"Oxfud? Das a long ways to travel on foot. We gone back home to Pelahatchie. Come wittus. We take you far is Jackson."

Betsy got in the back seat. The lady wore dark rimmed glasses and a print dress with puff sleeves. "My name Rosaline, dis my husband, Deacon John Laurence." Deacon Laurence smiled in the rearview. He wore the same type of black horn rimmed glasses as his wife. A black suit jacket struggled to contain his massive barrel chest, a chest which made his narrow black tie seem pencil thin. A porkpie hat perched atop his large melon head like a nesting bird.

Rosaline continued, "We been at a revival and church supper down Osyka. My John was da guess speaka. He spoke on 'I am da way, da trufe, and da light!' "

Deacon John nodded his head and said, "Das right." His square-toothed smile was broad and robust. It was so wide Betsy could imagine his head hinging on it and the top flipping back.

"If you code, they's some table cloffs back dey on da back seat. You can wrap up in 'em, iffin ya don' mind da bobbaQ stains."

"Gibber ma coat, Rosaline," the deacon said. He wrestled himself out of it, changing hands on the steering wheel. It was enormous and smelled sweaty like the coat of a man who had recently exerted himself. But it was warm.

The radio played gospel music, whole choirs of large women with large voices and large clapping hands compressed into the dash board radio dial. Oncoming headlights would illuminate the couple's faces, faces that looked serenely forward, side by side and listening obediently to the word of Gawd as it was preached and sung. Then the lights would pass on by and the backs of their heads would be illuminated red. A preacher's voice exploded from the tiny speaker in an almost hysterical voice, "Gitaway, debbil! Gitaway! Praise Gawd! Praise Jees! I say, Praise Gawd!" The choir resumed its rollicking singing, the music stumbling forward like a blind man in a hurry.

Betsy woke in the lights of a city. She pulled a barbecue stained table cloth around her shoulders and over the deacon's coat and asked, "Where we at?"

"Outskirts a Jackson," Deacon Laurence's voice resounded rich and buttery. "Up here's as far's we go for we turn for Pelahatchie." He motioned to an intersection that bristled with road signs.

At an all night diner in Jackson, they bought her a sandwich and let her keep a table cloth. Rosaline said, "We gone pray for you, chile. We gone pray real hard."

Deacon John put on his coat, whirling it over his burly shoulders like a matador and slipping his arms in the sleeves as he said, "Show will."

Betsy sat at the booth and watched Deacon Laurence open the door for Rosaline. The car pulled onto the highway and disappeared like a rounded fish into the ocean of the night. Betsy ate the sandwich slowly, more out of obligation to their kindness than hunger.

In the booth across the way were three girls. One of them wore her blonde hair in a flip. She was stretched out in the booth and sipped a soda. The straw went from white to black to white again. The girls were picking from a plate of French fries, mopping them in a puddle of ketchup and then dangling them over their mouths. The flip-haired girl was holding court, and the other two girls, a mousy girl in a pixie cut of black hair and a heavy set girl with spherical auburn hair, would burst into shrieking laughter almost every thirty seconds.

As Betsy ate slowly, she studied them and saw Colonel Reb, the squatty little white-mustached mascot of Ole Miss, on a button on the front of the auburn-haired girl's blue and white plaid dress. She recognized him from one of Sammy's T-Shirts. Betsy had worn the shirt without a bra, and he liked it. Honestly, she did too, especially when she sweated, and the faded blue cotton clung to her. The shadows of her nipples nudged through the O in Ole and the top of the final S in Miss. It smelled like him and was a treasure to her like something stolen from a sleeping giant. But it was in her suitcase, and the bus had carried it off.

"Scuse me, y'all go to school Ole Miss?" she called across the diner.

"Why yes we do," the blonde said. Her eyelids were heavy, and the whites of them were blood shot. All three smelled like liquor. The flip-haired girl said, "Flim flam bim bam," and the other two joined in, "Ooole Miss, by damn," and then they all whooped and hooted.

"Y'all goin' back?"

"Fixin' to. Why, you need a ride?"

"If you don't mind."

They introduced themselves, but Betsy didn't catch any of their names. One of them was Mary Something.

They asked Betsy her name, and they thought she said Bessie.

"Awrrrrrright, Bessie. Less make tracks." The pixie haired girl pointed forward somewhere, and the blonde twirled her around.

"It's that way," she corrected, and they stumbled into the car. The big auburn-haired girl, Loretta, drove.

The three girls chattered like Betsy wasn't there, which was fine with her. She leaned her head against the cold hard glass of the window and watched the rain. The ragged black silhouette of the tree line scrolled by. Above it the seamlessly fitted midnight blue sky, clouded and starless, scrolled by in perfect step. To a girl who had rarely been out of the parish, this was like a trip around the world.

She missed her dog. She missed all her animals. But most of all she missed Sammy. She thought of the way the sunlight played on his hair and made it look even lighter, the way he swept it out of his face, the way he put his leg over the arm of a chair when he sat. The way he clutched her like he was falling when his moment came.

The radio played the Beatles' "I Wanna Hold Your Hand," and a tear ran down her cheek. The tear reflected in the window where hundreds of other tears of rain had beaded up. The lights of other cars illuminated them in red and yellow. The jabber of the girls dimmed, and she drifted into a sleep.

She dreamed she was wandering in head high cane and pushing open paths. Chanceux was there, too, at her heels. They rambled through the green jungle, and she was unable to see where she was going. In the dream she realized that she was looking for something. They reached a clearing, and there stood someone dressed in a Mardi Gras costume. It was the kind the men wore, purple, gold and green with a small kepi and a flap of a mask with eye holes. The eyes looked at her, blinking in the openings of the mask. "Sammy, dat you?" she asked the person. The figure pulled up the mask, and it was her Nonc Claude. The cane washed over her again, and she was in the middle of it. She looked down, and the dog was gone and she was alone, and she could see the yellow slitted eyes of a moccasin. "Sammy?" she called in her dream. "Sammy Teague?" And then she woke.

The girls' faces luminesced in the dashboard lights.

"So Tina, how's it going with you and Sammy Teague?" the driver, Loretta, asked the girl in the back seat.

"Sammy Teague!" the girl in the front passenger seat cooed. "So dreamy."

Tina, the blonde girl in the back seat next to Betsy, said, "Haven't heard from him in over a month. He's been home with the hurricane. He may not come back to school, is what I've heard."

There was a click as the pixie girl opened her clutch purse. She pulled out a pack of cigarettes, tilted one out, and put it to her lips. She lit it and exhaled.

Loretta took her eyes off the road for a second. "Mary Nell! Not in mama's new Caddie! She'll be some pissed off."

"Jees Chrahst, don't have a cow, Loretta," Mary Nell said as she rolled the window down an inch. It made a whump like a blow on a cardboard box, and the bustling air rushed loudly past it. She held the cigarette to the crack, and the smoke escaped out into the chilly night.

"Gimme wunna those," Tina slurred. Mary Nell tapped the pack on the back of the seat, and Tina pinched one out. Mary Nell leaned over the seat with her cigarette in her lips, and Tina lit hers from it. Tina cracked the window, and the breeze lightly lifted her blonde flip curls. Her lips pulled on the cigarette, and the orange tip glowed intensely in the dark.

"So, Tina," Mary Nell turned again toward the backseat with a bounce and asked impishly, "Did you and Sammy ever…butter the muffin?" Loretta's hands held the wheel at two and ten, but her eyes looked up into the rearview mirror and waited for the answer. Mary Nell's pixie face was half lit by the dashboard. Her eyes were on Tina, too.

Betsy's ears and sideways glance were on her as well.

"Just maybe we did," Tina said coyly, "and just maybe we didn't." She blew smoke out of the side of her mouth, and the air current carried it off out the window. Betsy felt the two headed monster of envy and anger break the surface of a lake deep inside her.

"Ooooooooh!" Mary Nell and Loretta exclaimed.

Loretta turned the dial, and the receiver oscillated between stations, sputtering and spitting like a stutterer as it crossed each one. She found a Memphis station and a song that was clearly a favorite:

Stop! In the naaame of love,
Be-fore you break…my heart,
Thinkit o-o-over…

The girls made stop signs with their hands, broke imaginary sticks with 'break,' put their hands to their chests with 'heart,' and rolled their hands with 'o-o-o-ver.' The cigarettes in Tina and Mary Nell's hands made curly cues of smoke.

Air spilled in through the open windows and made the car colder, but the girls didn't seem to feel it. Betsy felt it and pulled the church table cloth over her and smelled the vinegar from the barbecue sauce. On the radio the Dixie Cups were going to the Chapel of Love. The girls finished their cigarettes and rolled up the window, and then they sang along to each other.

A sign approached and loomed large and passed. Oxford 5. The girls fell silent. Tina yawned, looked over to Betsy, and said, "Hey, you okay?"

Betsy nodded though she wasn't sure.

Chapter 15

Betsy don't live here no more. The words stuck him, and his soul felt like it had been bled white. He felt blanched and lethargic.

He sat in the barn loft, the same one that Mary Louise had lured him into when he was a boy. It smelled of ancient sweat and old leather, and recent hay and manure. An afternoon shower pelted the tin roof, and Sammy watched it streak the door opening.

Balthasar stood below him chewing sideways. His ears twitched, which gave him the appearance of thinking.

Tell me Mr. Mule, where is she? Sammy thought. If you're so smart, where is she?

A small shadow entered the crack in the barn door. The shadow yipped. Sammy scrambled down the ladder, and Chanceux raised his wet paws and put them on Sammy's leg. Sammy scratched the dog's ears, and he gave Sammy his neck, and Sammy scratched under the dog's chin.

Why would she leave her dog behind? Sammy thought.

When the rain stopped, Sammy waded through his aimlessness toward the house. The dog followed him for a while, but then peeled off and scampered down the muddy trail to the tenant house. Sammy ascended the wooden stairs at the back of the house and walked past Dutchie who was rinsing a colander of green beans in the sink. She turned her head just as he exited into the dining room.

Upstairs, he sat in a wicker rocker on the balcony. The parish mosquito truck crawled down 308, the motor in its bed chugging, churning out a bitter fog. Beyond it, the sun was setting in a fireball across the bayou. The silhouettes of cane harvesters scrambled across it in the yearly race to cut the cane and get it out of the field. There was a knock on the jamb, hollow and far away. Dutchie's face appeared, and then she came onto the balcony.

"Mist' Sammy, I know way she is," she said in a voice just above a whisper.

Sammy looked up. His leg was draped over the arm of the rocker. Smoke from the end of his cigarette twirled languidly in the air.

"I know way she is," Dutchie repeated.

There was no need to ask whom she meant.

"Where? Where is she?"

"I's at Mist' Aucoin's tutha day and I seen dat dawg, dat ernge dawg, da one she call shon-soo. I ast Mist' Aucoin I say way dat girl got dat dawg and he say she done got on da bus fup nawf. And I say wuffo and he say he speck she gone see dat Teague boy up deh All Miss."

"When?"

"Day fo yesty."

Sammy threw his cigarette over the balcony and looked down the road. A gratitude-fueled impulse spurred him to hug Dutchie and kiss her on the forehead.

"Ooh, Mist' Sammy." She put her hand to her forehead as if she thought she could feel the outline of the kiss. He moved past her into the house, and she called to him.

"Mist' Sammy, be cafful."

Inside his room the latches on his suitcase popped and rattled. He was packed again in five minutes. His feet drummed on the stairs. At the bottom there was a challenge from Sammy's mama whose gin-scorched voice gave an incoherent lecture on respect and then another lecture from his daddy.

Your mother's right son. How can you establish yourself as the head of Mount Teague if you can't learn to respect your elders that forged all this out of the goddam...the god....dammed mosquito infested swamp and sent you to school, the best schools, so that you can have the tools to make this....

"Enough!" Sammy's voice rose like an ember in a firework display. It rose again like a second, trailing ember. "I've had enough!"

The fireworks of his voice brought about no ooh and no aah. His parents' faces were quiet. He threw the door open and went out of it.

Nothing punctuates a sentence like slamming a door. As soon as the big front door shut with a gust of wind at his back, Sammy wondered if he would ever enter back through it again. So be it, he thought. Wherever Betsy was would be his home from now on.

He threw his suitcase in the back, and the Mustang tore down the white shelled drive under the oaks and pulled onto 308. He took one last look back. In one of the front windows of the big house, his daddy stood close against the panes and watched his only son disappear. Behind the house, the water tower rose in the sunset light. Written boldly across the tank were the block letters MT. Empty.

The machines and the fields were sleeping now, but in the morning both would be awake again, the machines trying to cut the cane and get it to the mill. Within a month or two, the cane stubble would be burned, and the air would be murky with smoke. And the mill would begin grinding and racing to beat Christmas.

The Mustang pulled up to the pump at Aucoin's. A round orange and blue Gulf sign beamed cheerfully from on top. He got out and began to fill up for the long trip north. The sun had disappeared, and the western sky was bleeding an orange and magenta film.

Chanceux padded silently around from behind the car. The little dog trotted over, and Sammy scratched his ears. The pink tip of the dog's tongue pushed and pulled across his thin black lips. He whined softly and rolled over on his back.

Let's go find her, the dog said. I saw the big animal take her, take her off that way. It fed from this same teat and it carried her away. Take me and I'll show you, we'll find her, please.

Sammy replaced the nozzle and went in to pay, wondering if this would be the last time he would ever see Mr. Aucoin. The old man had been a fixture in Sammy's childhood, in all of their childhoods. From the time that they had been allowed to ride their bicycles to town, Mr. Aucoin learned their names. He kept up with them, spotted them a dime or a nickel for candy or a Pop Rouge when they needed it and bantered with them in French or in English.

Sammy slid a ten across the worn cypress counter. Aucoin took it and punched in numbers on the cash register. It whirred and rang like a slot machine, and the old man gave Sammy his change. In an advertisement by the register, the Marlboro man stared into some western distance from under the brim of his cowboy hat.

"Where you headed, Sammy?" Mr. Aucoin asked. The old man was propped on his forearms. Smoky blue tattoos of anchors adorned them.

"Up north to Oxford."

"Kinda late for school, ain't it? We done got all way true September."

"Yessir." Sammy was itching to go, but he didn't want to leave Mr. Aucoin in a rush. This may be it, their last meeting.

"You gone fine dat girl, no?" Mr. Aucoin's head was tilted back as he looked through the bottom of the thick lenses of his glasses.

"Yessir. Yessir, I am." The old man had watched people come in and out of this place for sixty years. He knew what they were up to even before they knew it themselves. There was no reason or use in avoiding the truth with him.

"She got on da bus it make now…two, tree days or so. Had dat little brown valise witta."

"Two or three days?"

"Yeah, bout dat." Aucoin paused. Somewhere in the back a radio played a song in French, soft and low like the hum of a mosquito. He pushed a button on the cash register, and it rumbled and opened with a ding. "Take dis, Sammy. Gaz on da house today. Jess take car yoself, hey?"

"Yessir. Thank you. Thank you." Sammy turned to the door. When he went through it, Chanceux was there wagging the curl of his tail from one side to the other. He scratched the dog's head again, and the dog followed him to the blue Mustang. When Sammy opened the door, the dog tried to jump in. Sammy shielded him away and slipped in a narrow crack in the door. The car roared to life, and the dog yipped frantically, desperately trying to find language. The car pulled onto the highway and left the dog and the old man and the town behind.

Mr. Aucoin opened the door to the store a crack and whistled. The little dog's tongue curled in an exasperated yawn, and he got up from his haunches. He trotted over and slipped inside the store as the old man flipped the sign from Open to Closed. Through the screen door the man and the dog watched the red taillights fade down the road.

It was full blown night now.

Part II: Oxford, Mississippi

Chapter 16

It was late.

The halls were covered with gray-toned pictures of pledge classes back to the 1890s, daughters of Civil War veterans. Betsy stood and studied them, comparing their hair and their clothes. The pictures were a study in the evolution of ladies' fashion. High white lace collars receded south, and hair length ascended north as the pictures advanced through the old century and turned into the new. If the daughters of the veterans could look down the wall and see the great-granddaughters' low necklines, they would be scandalized.

Betsy felt drained and dream encased. From a large common room adjacent to the stairs, a radio blared to the half dozen or so girls who studied around it. No two of their postures were alike: prone and splay-legged, curled up on a couch, backwards in an armchair with legs over the back. Tina presented Betsy to the girls.

"Ladies, this is Bessie," Tina said, gesturing to Betsy with an upturned palm. They looked up from books and notepads. Their voices rose together.

"Hello, Bessie. Hey-hey-ho-hi, gotta say it's great! *Clap!* To be a Kappa Chi!"

"The pledges have to say that whenever they meet somebody new," Tina whispered behind her hand. Alcohol lingered on her breath, sour and sweet.

Tina took Betsy's hand and guided her up the stairs. Tina's hand was small and soft in Betsy's hand. Betsy lifted her legs from one step to the next. She felt twice her weight.

A girl in a housecoat with pink foam curlers in her hair was talking on the black rotary phone on the landing of the stairs. She saw Tina and Betsy, smiled, and waved with her fingertips. Then she turned to the wall.

"No you say it first," the girl murmured. She blushed and repeated, "No you say it, Jerry."

Tina and Betsy proceeded down the hallway. Behind a closed door were the dull puffy slaps and muted giggles of a pillow fight. Tina knocked lightly on the door, and there was a sudden silence behind it. The door cracked open, and a face of cold cream greeted her.

"Shhh," Tina drew a finger over her lips and said in a whisper. "Sylvia, this is Bessie. Bessie, Sylvia."

Sylvia smiled a cold cream encrusted smile, then put her pillow under her arm and whispered, "Hey-hey-ho-hi, gotta-say-it's-great-*clap*-to-be-a-Kappa-Chi." She said it quickly, almost as one word, rambling through it by second nature. Then she said, 'Bye!' and shut the door.

"You stay in my room tonight." Tina told Betsy. It was a statement, not a question.

At the end of the hall, Tina leaned against her door, twisted the knob, and fell through it. It was an upperclassman's room, larger and with a bathroom and shower connected. On the door was a poster of the Beatles. A blue pennant with red cursive *Ole Miss Rebels* was on one wall, on another a red pennant with gold *Laurel Golden Tornadoes* and a whirlwind with fists and a belligerent face.

"Need the shower?" Tina asked.

"No, thanks."

"I have nightgowns in the second drawer," Tina said. "Help yourself. I'm gettin' in the shower." She was shedding her clothes there in front of Betsy. Blouse, skirt, bra with pointed cups. She wondered if Tina had done the same for Sammy, and then Betsy felt green. She bolted past Tina and knelt in front of the toilet. The sandwich that the Laurences had bought her came up.

She felt a cold rag on the back of her neck and glanced up to see Tina kneeling on the floor beside her. Tina's breasts swayed down to pink points. Betsy thought about Sammy's hands on them and heaved again.

"You been drinkin' too?" Tina asked, and Betsy shook her head no and pulled a loose strand of hair back out of the line of fire. Her mouth opened wide, but only a honking sound came out.

They waited together on the floor. The squalls of nausea seemed to have passed, and Tina helped Betsy up and into the bedroom.

"Just wait here, I'll be out of the shower in just a little bit." The door to the bathroom shut, and the shower curtain jingled. A dull rush of water pounded on porcelain.

Betsy floated around the room, feeling like an intruder. She looked around and found pictures of Sammy here and there. There were also two bouquets of flowers. A card with one read, *To Tina, from Freddy*. The other one, the flowers faded and frayed, had no card.

Betsy looked through all of the pictures with Sammy in them. He seemed like someone else, not the boy she knew. There was a bitter taste in her mouth.

Tina emerged from the mist of the bathroom with a towel around her torso and drying her hair with another. She looked completely different without the flip in her hair, no longer beautiful but merely pretty.

Tina dropped her towels as she rummaged through the chest of drawers. Her tan was expansive and spared only two pale triangles over her breasts and a swath across her hips. She held up a pair of panties to see which side was front and tried to step into them. They were small, little more fabric than a man's handkerchief. Her foot stabbed into them for an opening and kept catching in them, and after a few drunken attempts she threw them across the room and simply slipped a gown over her head.

Tina glanced at Betsy and then pulled a gown out of the drawer and tossed it to her. It landed in Betsy's lap, and she got up and went into the misty bathroom to change.

When she came out, Tina was on one side of the full size bed. Betsy hesitated, but Tina said, "Would you rather this side?"

Betsy pulled back the covers and slipped in. The light in the bathroom was still on and threw a yellow cast on one side of their faces. Tina tossed to her side and propped herself on an elbow. Her voice was still laden with alcohol and wandered out of her.

"You have an accent. Where you from, sweetheart?"

"Louisiana."

"What, may I ask, are you doing in Mississippi?"

"My mama threw me out."

"That's horrible. Why?"

"Long story."

"With no bags or anything?"

"I had a suitcase, but the bus took it when we stopped."

Tina stroked Betsy's hair. Betsy felt herself about to cry and turned away to the light of the bathroom. She didn't know if she could sleep with the light on, but she was too tired to get up and turn it off and didn't want to provoke the nausea that perched awkwardly inside her. Besides, she didn't know if Tina preferred it on.

Tina continued to stroke Betsy's back and her hair. "Do you have anywhere to stay? Besides here?" Tina asked.

Betsy's head shook no on the pillow. Tina couldn't see it, but in the bathroom light Betsy's lip quivered and tears dripped onto the sheets. Tina rolled on her back and spoke to the ceiling with her arms to her sides.

"Well, don't you worry. We'll figure out something for you. In the morning we'll get some breakfast and get on it. Now, we'll have to get our own breakfast. Our housekeeper's got some female trouble and is gonna be out for a while."

Betsy's voice rose from the pillow.

"I can cook. Clean, too."

"Can you?" Tina fell silent as her drunken mind worked on the problem. "Well, as the new Chapter President of Kappa Chi, I hereby hire you to be our temporary housekeeper."

Betsy sank into the bed, wondering if Sammy had sunk there too.

They woke to a crystal clear morning. The stabbing sunlight of what was so far the coldest morning of the year overpowered the sheer curtains and flooded the room with chilly light. The long lump in the sheets that was Tina groaned and pulled a pillow over her head. She peeked from under it and saw Betsy, who was quietly praying the Rosary on her fingers. It was Sunday morning, and Betsy doubted there was a Catholic church nearby. Even if there was, she had no way to know when Mass was.

"Christ," Tina mumbled. "You tie one on, and you never know who you'll wind up in bed with." Tina's eye disappeared under the pillow, and her voice wrestled against it.

"Good morning…Bessie, that's right, Bessie," Tina reassured herself.

Betsy was halfway through the Sorrowful Mysteries but managed to break in with a good morning. When she got to the end of the decade, she asked Tina, "You show me the kitchen so I can make breakfast?"

"Oh yeah, you're our fill in housekeeper. I remember now." Tina flipped over the covers but kept the pillow over her head. Her hands rubbed her stomach then pulled up the edge of her gown. She patted for the edge of her panties, realized there weren't any and then scratched herself. The pillow came off her face, and her eyes squinted out the sunlight. She put her hand over them.

"You okay?" Betsy asked.

"I'm fine. Just a little headache, just a little dry." Tina sat on the side of the bed and scratched her head with both hands. She leaned over, got a headband, and pulled her hair back with it. Her feet toed into a pair of fuzzy pink slippers as she took her housecoat from a peg and slipped it on. She stretched, slowly pushing her fists in the air as her neck contorted.

"Come on, I'll show you the kitchen," she yawned.

Chapter 17

The midnight blue sky was speckled with the pinpoints of stars that were white like jagged pebbles of broken glass. The highway was deserted except for the blue Mustang. The black rubber of tires hummed monotonously against the black pavement. The dashboard light outlined the resolute face in green tinted yellow.

In the wee hours of the morning he pulled into the Oxford bus station. On the oil-stained concrete floor of the loading bay was Betsy's beat up suitcase sitting by itself under the window of the ticket agent.

Sammy parked and walked over to examine it. The man at the ticket counter looked up from his paper for a minute and then looked back down. Sammy knelt and opened it. On top was the faded Ole Miss T-shirt. He held it to his nose, and he knew it was hers. He put it back and closed the suitcase.

"Excuse me, sir," he asked the ticket man. "Did you see the woman who this belongs to?"

"They let that'n off. No name and no passenger with it."

"Nobody claimed it?"

"No sir. You know who it belongs to?"

"Yeah. I'll see to it they get it."

"Awright, then. Just sign here fer it, ya hear?"

Sammy signed on a ledger and took it. He put it on the passenger seat and drove to The College Hill Diner for breakfast.

Sammy sat in the diner. In his cup of coffee he saw his face in the shimmering black surface, and then it seemed to be his daddy's face, the diminishing face of the man in the window, a man trying to wish away unkind words. Then he saw his mother when she was a queen, taking joy in him, singing with him while he played the piano.

Every May on Memorial Day weekend they came to Parents' Day at the boarding school in Tennessee, his daddy in a light blue seersucker suit, his mother tall and imperial in heels and a perfectly tailored dress with pearls around her neck and glittering rings on her fingers. Each year it seemed her good looks had faded a little, but she was still recognizable as a former Lambda Sweetheart at Ole Miss. His daddy always shook his son's hand, and his mother hugged him lightly, almost politely, and held him at arm's length with her hands on his shoulders. She looked him over, the blue blazer with the crest on the pocket, the handsome young face.

"Just look at him, Trey," she said. "A real credit to us."

At first, it made Sammy feel good to be a credit to them, but with time he began to feel he was simply a credit to her, an appendage, an accessory that she was delighted with. And if she was happy, then his daddy was happy.

He checked the clock on the wall of the diner and then drained the coffee cup and set it next to his empty plate. It was almost nine, and the banks should be open.

Sammy was there when the teller twisted the lock open. His footsteps echoed through the marble lobby as he approached the metal bars of the window. Portraits of men in moustaches and paper collars lined the walls.

"I'd like to make a withdrawal."

"Name please?"

"Samuel Teague," he said, and then he added, "The fourth."

"Here it is," the teller said. "Says here, Mamie Teague just called. Put a hold on it. I'm sorry Mr. Teague, I can't give you any money."

Sammy's head whirred, and he drifted away from the window, through the door an entering customer opened for him, and staggered through it without a thank you. His mind was groping for a next step.

Chapter 18

Tina drove Betsy down to the bus station to see if she could get her suitcase. The ticket man was working on a line of people buying tickets for the Memphis bus. Tina waited patiently in the car.

"Where to?" The man asked through the hole in the glass.

"Scuse me?" Betsy asked back through the hole.

"Where you wanna go?" The man asked. He chewed gum lazily like a cow working on a wad of grass.

"I'm lookin' for my suitcase. The bus left me last night."

"Little brown, red-brown suitcase? Kinda beat up?"

"Yeah, that's it."

"Somebody done claimed it. Feller with hair in his eyes." The man looked over to his right and traced the names in the ledger. "Feller name a Sam-Mule Teague, I-V."

Betsy's heart leaped. "When? When he was here?"

"This mornin'. Real early. Looked like he'd driven all night. Looked pretty rough."

"Did he say where he would be?"

"Didn't say. Took it and left. Had a...had a blue Ford. Yeah, that's right. Blue Mustang."

She put her head to the glass. She was glad that Tina had waited in the car. The man tapped on the glass, and Betsy lifted her head from it like it was suddenly hot.

"Any thin else?" he asked through the hole. "Don't wanna go no wheres?"

"No sir. Thanks."

Betsy went back to the car. She was vaguely hopeful. He was here, in north Mississippi, somewhere. Right here, in Oxford.

"Any luck?" Tina asked. She had painted beautiful facial features back over the pretty ones. Her eyes were hidden by dark sunglasses, but her lips were rose red.

"No, they don't have it," Betsy said. But she turned and looked out the window and couldn't help but smile.

Chapter 19

The long hall was dark and echoed with footsteps and the droning whispers of conversation in unseen offices. In one of the rooms a telephone rang and was answered by a woman's voice. The corridor was brown tiled and waxed to a luminous shine.

At the end was a room with a sign indicating the Office of the Dean, and under it, Agriculture & Economics, Dr. T. C. Bice. A typewriter clattered inside the door, and though it was open, Sammy knocked on it anyway. A middle aged woman typed, looking from a piece of handwritten paper and then back to the paper under the cylinder of the typewriter. Her dark rimmed glasses made her look feline. She stopped typing and looked up to Sammy.

"Help you sir?"

"Sammy Teague. Here to see Dr. Bice?"

"Have seat. He'll bay with ya shartly."

Sammy sat on the dark green vinyl of the steel armed sofa, and the cat woman resumed typing. Dr. Bice's voice muttered from within his office. The conversation terminated with an "awright," and the phone made a clunking sound.

"Riddy, Dr. Bice?" She looked into Dr. Bice's office and then at Sammy. "Dr. Bice'll see yew now," she meowed.

Dr. Bice seldom wore a tie, and more frequently wore overalls. Today he was in plain trousers and a plaid shirt. He stood up to shake Sammy's hand and then slumped back in his chair. An ashtray with several angled butts was on his desk next to the current copy of *Mississippi Farm Country Magazine*. On the front a smiling young beauty in blue jeans, an orange plaid shirt with the sleeves rolled a turn, and a straw hat posed between two Guernsey cows. The lead story, however, was an article on turning 'spent hens' into fryers.

Dr. Bice gestured to a chair across the desk from him, a variation of the same green vinyl and steel chair in the secretary's office. Sammy sat on the edge of it. On the wall were pictures of President Lyndon B. Johnson and Governor Paul B. Johnson, LBJ and PBJ the joke was.

"Well, Mr. Teague, good to see ya. Understand y'all had quite a time with the hurrikin down yonder Loozy-Anna."

"Yessir, we did."

"Yore diddy called me and asked if we could let you start late on count uvvit. But I'm 'fraid too much time's passed. You'll have to sit out till the spring."

Sammy was afraid of that, too. There were no other options now. He was pretty sure that at his mama's insistence, his daddy would decide not to pay for anymore college anyway. He was set adrift in an ocean of pine forests and cotton fields. Regret flared, as he suddenly wished he had been a better student, that he had been worthy of an education and maybe even a scholarship, that he had been a young man rather than an old boy. The note had come due on the old lifestyle.

Dr. Bice reached behind himself and turned a knob on a fan. The blades within the black metal cage whirred to life, and the air nudged the cover of *Mississippi Farm Country*. The girl and the cows trembled in the breeze.

"Only thing I kin offer ya's a job round here. Man name a Finley over Pontotoc got a sawmill, and he's lookin' fer a hand to hep out. Innerstid?"

"Yessir," Sammy said. There were no other options. Dr. Bice stood up with a scrape of his chair on the floor and shook Sammy's hand. He spoke through the door to his secretary.

"Mavis, you got Mr. Finley's number?"

"Yessir, here somewheres."

"Will you get it fer this gentleman?"

Sammy left through the secretary's office. The clack of the typewriter stopped for a moment. Mavis got up and her heels clicked over to a file cabinet, enameled smooth and gray, and opened a drawer. She riffled through the edges of paper and pulled one out.

Her feline glasses clung to the end of her nose as she copied the name and number and gave it to Sammy.

"Have a nahce day, now," she purred.

Sammy wandered into the hall, looking at the paper. Behind him the typewriter resumed.

Chapter 20

Back off the main highway in St. Matthew Parish, a dome of light was pushed up by the headlights of cars. Insects swarmed in it, suspended between the darkness of the night above them and the spectacle below. Two dogs lurched at leashes and were released. They set on each other in a cloud of garbled barking, as men clutched fistfuls of money and exhorted one animal or the other.

Within a minute, one dog began to assert himself. The other dog tried to escape the ring of cars, but boot heels met his big eyes at every turn. The other dog came for him and took a jawful of his back. His jaws held firm as he stared into the crowd. His slobbering mouth squeezed and his head shook in small snapping movements. One man conceded, and the dogs were separated with poles that had loops of rope at the ends.

A new set of headlights pulled up. The vanquished dog lay on his side as his chest rose and fell. The hubbub of the ring of men quieted until all that was heard was the hiss of air in and out of the punctures on the losing dog's chest. His face stared up blankly. His owner reached down to stroke his ear, and the dog yelped and snapped at him.

The door of the police cruiser slammed, and a man in khakis and a cowboy hat moved into the ring of light. The glint of light from his badge stabbed the men in the eyes. Locks of greasy hair clung to foreheads, sweat darkened shirts clung to torsos, and the piss-warm air clung to everything. There was quiet except for the shrill trembling whistle of insects in the live oak boughs.

"I bleeve yo dog's done f' good," Deputy Parris said, and he took a bite of the link of boudin he was holding. He turned to the man who stood over his dying dog.

"You a me?" the deputy asked the man.

"I can't, can't do it," the man said. The dog lay on its side, its chest rising and falling rapidly, its tongue draped velvety and pink onto the dirt. Its gaze was vacant, past the circle and out into the thousand mile night.

"All right then," Parris said. He drew his revolver and fired. The dog's body bounced with the impact, and several of the spectators jumped with it. The dog's chest was still, and his owner scooped him up. Parris put his revolver in its holster and took another bite of boudin.

He turned to the crowd drawn up around the pit and took off his hat. His red hair was sweat-matted against his big cube of a head. He said, "Just come to pass the hat so's y'all can keep havin y'all dawg show. We'll keep it out the big man's hands thataway." The hat bumped around the crowd from hand to hand, changing altitude from high to low and low to high like a collection plate. Parris' gaze kept it tethered in the circle as he made sure everyone made a contribution.

When it had made its way back to him he announced to the crowd, "Well I thank you so very kindly, gennelmen. Mare-see boo-coo, mare-see. If you'll scuse me now, thay's a ho-house back a Paincourtville needs a little supervision. And to pay they dues. Bleeve I may even sample the wares," he said, and he turned his head and winked like some kind of malignant Santa Claus.

The men laughed knowingly and nervously. Parris shoved the last of the boudin in his mouth and wiped his greasy fingers on his khaki trousers. He leaned into his cruiser and opened a cardboard box, then emptied his hat into it and shut the lid. He put his hat back on and got in his patrol car. It cranked up, and the lights pulled away from the illuminated circle.

As he drove off, two more dogs were brought in from the darkness of the perimeter.

Chapter 21

The sign said simply Finley's Mill. Sammy's blue Mustang pulled up in the clearing and parked next to the rusted cars and pickup trucks already there. The mill yard was bounded by stacks of logs, cast off heavy equipment sitting on a nest of yellow weeds, and collections of gargantuan I-Beam girders, orange and rusting into patches of brown. A flurry of mice scurried under one of them. Old fifty-five gallon drums wore low grass skirts.

Mr. Finley had a jaw full of tobacco that pushed out his cheek and made him look like a feeding rodent. He stood on the porch in front of the office with his thumbs in the bib of his overalls and a weather beaten fedora covering a gray shock of hair. Sammy reached out his hand, and Mr. Finley took it and smiled. His teeth crowded together, resting on each other like drunken sailors coming in from shore leave, no two teeth occupying the same axis. His nose was leathery and reddened, flanked by thick gray eyebrows like wings.

"Mr. Finley?" Sammy asked at the end of the shake.

"Sammy Teague?" he asked back.

"Yessir. I appreciate you takin' me on," Sammy said.

"Get ready to do a little work, there then, boy," Finley said as he turned. "Come with me."

They entered the front office of the mill. In one corner was a desk where Mr. Finley kept a ledger and a coffee cup that served as a spittoon. Over the desk was a 1965 calendar of the Mississippi Foresters Association. A wooden bank of file cabinets occupied the wall by the desk and in an adjoining room there was a long table and a small kitchen. Sammy and Mr. Finley passed through it.

"I bleeve in feedin' you boys. Get more work ouch y'all." Mr. Finley said.

In the kitchen was a large dark skinned woman, a Choctaw named Tillie. She was close to six feet tall, with billowy features, a giant mound of a woman. The bottom of her face was almost twice the size of the top, where there was a crude bowl cut of crow black hair. Her eyes were nestled down in a face that was brown and doughy like the top of a dinner roll. Hers was an expressionless face, flat and blank, neither happy nor sad. She moved lethargically around the kitchen, wiping her hands on the apron tied around her large waist. A long wooden spoon disappeared into a deep pot where it stirred something. It smelled aromatic like turnip greens.

"Tillie, this Sammy. Say hello, Tillie," Mr. Finley said without slowing.

"Hello," she monotoned without looking up from a cutting board of onions.

Mr. Finley opened a back door from the kitchen-lunchroom, and an avalanche of noise fell on them. The humming and snarling of machines from different corners of the yard weighed down the air with the smell of Christmas and the sound of Dante's Inferno. They made their way around a pallet of cut lumber to an area where logs were being fed into a saw. A man in dingy blue overalls with a blue bandana hanging from his back pocket shoveled sawdust into bins and mounds where it accumulated like sand dunes in the desert.

"Storm from down south passed through here too and left a lotta down trees, windfall. We gonna be busy here fer a while tryin' t' make is much lumber as we can of it." Finley shouted into Sammy's ear as they walked the dirt path between two immense piles of logs that looked like the hearth fires of giants.

The big hurricane shaped blade snarled through the wood and when it was finished gave a rattling metallic chuckle. A man barely five feet tall wandered along the carriage above it. He gathered a lever in the elbow of a stump of an arm and cradled it against his flank, then gave it a shove forward with his body. He had curly blonde hair and a five o'clock shadow of whiskers. He returned to his perch, squatting on the high walkway like a gargoyle. The air smelled like engine oil and pine resin.

"Jude Hawkins! Git down here! New man, name a Sammy!" Mr. Finley shouted, and the thick noise made it sound like a murmur.

Hawkins pulled the lever back with his remaining hand. The saw whirred down to a stop, and the little man vaulted down with the easy step of a wood sprite and offered the stump of his arm to Sammy. Sammy hesitated, and shook it. There was a callus at the end of it as if the hand was trying to grow back, and he could feel the bones in it shift under the skin. Other engines rattled in the rest of the yard, and Mr. Finley yelled even though the saw had stopped.

"We cut upperds a couple ten thousand er so board feet a day, sometimes more, sometimes less, giver take. Mostly yeller pine. Some cypress, some hardwood." He spat an amber ribbon out to the side.

"Yer job's to keep them logs a movin' in, an' at lumber yonder a movin' out, keep yerself out from under 'em. And stay out the blade. Ain't that right, Jude Hawkins?"

"That ain't no shit," Jude said dryly. He raised the stump of his arm to display the missing evidence.

"Awright, Jude. Take this young feller round and show him ever thang." Mr. Finley spat again and turned to the shed that served as the office.

Jude Hawkins looked like a fairy tale creature come to life. He was small and light brown, with eyebrows that curled upward at the outer edges and green eyes that were ringed in brown. Sammy judged he couldn't be more than five years older than himself.

The little man stepped jauntily down between the machines and the sheds, gesturing with his stump at this and with the cigarette in his hand at that, and shouting above the howl and whine of the operation.

"Mr. Finley says there's two ways to do a job around here. One of 'em is First Rate." Jude made an okay sign with his lone hand and pushed out with First and Rate. "That means good. The other's Slap Ass. An' that's bad."

Sammy was taller than Jude, but still struggled to keep up with the little man, leaning in to hear him over the noise and the cigarette perched in Jude's lips. His stump pushed his shirttail back into the side gap of his overalls. They turned a corner behind one of the larger sheds where the noise abated a little, an eddy in the river of sound. Jude continued to point at things.

"Planer shed, storage sheds, one, two and three. Over there, order pick up shed." They stopped, and Jude threw out the stub of his cigarette and stomped on it. He leaned over an enormous stack of white wood and ran his hand over it.

"This wood here is poplar. It's a real poplar wood round here, heh heh. Now over yonder we got....stand still."

"What?" Sammy said.

"Stand still. Don't make a move." Jude was staring at the ground just ahead of Sammy's feet. A bronze and brown copperhead was coiled there, its yellow-eyed head moving back. Sammy froze.

"Hold still," Jude said again. He slid a board, a six footer, slowly off the pile to a vertical, and then using his stump and his hand he quickly jammed it down behind the snake's head. Behind the board the body of the snake straightened, undulated and straightened again.

"Look in that shed there, just inside the door," Jude said, still eyeing the snake. "There's a short handle shovel."

Sammy's gaze stayed fixated on the trapped snake for a moment, and then he stepped to the shed and found the shovel.

"Take the board," Jude said. "Firm, now. Keep 'im pinned down."

Sammy pressed down hard on the board, harder than he needed to. The snake continued to struggle, its body flipping and squirming. Jude took the shovel and placed it against the board. The copperhead opened his mouth wide, an empty threat.

"I hate to do this, they keep the mice and the rats down, but this time of year with the cold comin' on they get so dang aggressive." The shovel made a gritty, crunching sound as it separated the head. Jude scooped up head and body in the shovel and walked over to the edge of the woods where the grass was high. He tossed it back beyond the edge.

"Coon'll get that tonight, I betcha," Jude said as he walked over and set the shovel inside the shed again. "Be lookin' out 'cause where there's one copperhead, there's usually two or three more." He leaned back against the stack of poplar. "Anyways, you'll learn one wood from another. Differnt leaves, bark, grain, what have ya, differnt smell of the sawdust, all that."

The little caramel man never knew his daddy or his mama. He knew that one of them was colored, and one was white, that was as plain as his face and hair. What he didn't know was that his daddy was a handsome young black serviceman from Chicago who was stationed at Camp Cheatham in Tennessee, preparing for the war in Europe. On leave one night he met Jude's mother, a tiny dragon-faced white woman whose set of morals was the source of whispered entertainment in the town. They became an item, the two of them, sneaking around for a few weeks together, trysting in the woods, in deserted cabins, in barn lofts. Then her period went missing, and she couldn't find it anywhere.

She panicked, and said she was raped, and went to Memphis to see a woman who could change the thing. But there were complications, and the girl almost died then. Somehow, she and the thing continued on anyway.

Word got out in the little town. She was quickly elevated from the town harlot to a petal-less, defiled flower of southern womanhood. It was an outrage. Something had to be done, things like this could not be tolerated.

So on a steamy, moonless night Jude's daddy claimed the distinction of being the last person ever lynched in Mayfair County.

The morning after the hanging, the whole town turned out to have their pictures taken with him. They posed with their hands behind their backs, just like the victim, who was tethered by his neck to a white oak limb, his face bloated. Faces smiled on the sweaty heads of the men who had rendered the service, some of whom had brought their families so they could enjoy the day. They would all remember it forever, especially the children.

The army apparently never saw the photographs and listed him as AWOL. Some men from Camp Cheatham came down to investigate, but no one had seen anything, including the sheriff whose squad car had been driven out from under the man. No one had joked that when the rope went taut the man looked like he was riding a bicycle in the air. No sir, nobody saw anything like that. The sheriff reckoned that the colored feller had just gotten cold feet about all that war business and walked off. You know how them people are, he said.

Six months later the thing happened and Jude Hawkins was born at the Good Shepherd's Home for Unwed Mothers in Memphis. His mother, the little dragon faced girl, exited the world in the fog of a searing fever just as he made his entry. He never knew either of his parents, though he often wondered about them. All he knew was that one of them was white, and one of them wasn't. The nuns would only say that he was simply a child of God.

They named him after the patron saint of Lost Causes, and raised him until they saw that they'd done all they could. Realizing that they had named him correctly, they washed their hands of him. He was turned over to the will of God and the streets of Memphis.

"Archie!" Jude yelled to one of the men. A gray headed black man with powerful arms looked up briefly and raised a hand, then turned his attention back to his task. He and his co-worker on the platform, a balding white man, were using cant hooks to roll the big logs onto the carriages that fed logs into the saws.

"Careful you don't get downhill from them lawgs. They git loose, then that's yer ass," Jude yelled over the machinery. The blade sent another crescendoed blast through a log, ending with the vibration of whirring steel. The carriage lurched backward with the rest of the log like the recoiling bolt of a rifle. The two men repositioned it, and the carriage sent the log forward again.

Jude nudged Sammy and pointed away, and they resumed their tour.

"Onced I seen a man get hit in the head with a pine knot. Came off the saw like a fastball, hit him right here." Jude touched his forehead with his stump as he stalked through the mill yard. Sammy was still trying to keep up.

"Kill im?" Sammy shouted.

Jude shook his head. "Naw. Knocked him out, though. Woke up with a helluva headache and a bump the size 'n color of a peach." His hand palmed an imaginary peach on his forehead. "Looked like a horn. We called him Ol' Horny for a while. Pissed him off. Heh heh."

They arrived back at the office and stepped up on the porch. Jude opened the door and motioned for Sammy to go in first. Mr. Finley was sitting at his desk in front of a fan, his face right in it. There was an envelope on his desk. When Jude and Sammy came in, Mr. Finley looked startled and put the envelope back into his desk drawer.

"One more thang, son," the old man said to Sammy. "You oughta think about gettin' yerself a haircut. You gotta nuff hair to stuff a mattress. Awright, Jude Hawkins, put him to it."

Sammy shoveled sawdust for part of the morning, raising blisters on his hands, and then stacked lumber with those blistered hands. His clothes were sopped in sweat and stained deep with dirt and sawdust. His body ached with the rush of pain that the very first day of honest, manly work brings.

At noon, Tillie wiped her hands on her apron and rang the bell atop the post in the weedy yard in front of the office. As usual, only the man closest to it could hear it above the ear-splitting, skull-trembling noise. He went to the next man, whose machine stopped, and then that man went to the next man and waved at him and made eating motions. That man went in turn to the next man and gradually the clearing in the woods fell silent.

White men and colored men gathered at a sink made out of a horse trough and washed the sawdust and sweat off their faces and hands and forearms. Then together they sat at the same table where Tillie put down pails of simple, hearty food. There was no segregation at this table. Mr. Finley believed that equal work made equal men and that a colored man was as good as a white man, as long as he worked.

Mr. Finley also believed that your work was your prayer, and the men passed the pails around the table without saying grace. White hands passed the pails to black hands which passed them to white hands. The fingers of some of those hands wore simple nickel wedding bands; some had fingers missing or permanently bent. The whir of a fan cooled them; when you work in the heat, a fan is plenty cool enough.

They ate mostly in silence, the saws and planers and chippers still ringing in their ears. The men were an odd collection of skin tones, face shapes, hair colors. Gray, blonde, black, red, kinky, straight, bald. Of the dozen or so men, some were young, some were old, but exhaustion made them all feel equally ancient. The room was filled wall to wall with the smell of sweat, sawdust, and food, and with the sound of utensils scratching on plates and the smacking of big mouthfuls. Under the table Jude's knee bounced with nervous energy, oscillating while he ate thoughtfully like the rest.

After they ate, they took quick naps in the shade of a tree or the porch, while some just sat as they took a thoughtful smoke. One of the men farted a loud bass note, and none of the rest of them chuckled or even stirred. How different from the frat house, Sammy thought. The sound of steel on wood reverberated in their heads until the bell summoned them back.

At the end of the day, Mr. Finley appeared where Sammy had been stacking lumber. The old man limped down the row of pallets and pointed at each with a cigar.

"First Rate. All right. First Rate. First Rate." He paused at the next pallet and made a clicking noise.

"Wait a minute, this'n here's Slap Ass. See how them narra boards are at the bottom? Need them at the top. And there's too much empty space in there. Restack it."

He moved on down the line pointing with his cigar and saying, "First Rate, ok, First Rate." Jude looked down and snickered until Mr. Finley said over his shoulder, "Hep 'im, Jude Hawkins."

At noon on Saturdays, the end of the work week, Mr. Finley had Tillie set out a number two washtub on the porch. Amber brown necks of bottles of beer protruded from ice, the reward of a week of First Rate work. Mr. Finley looked on proudly but never had a beer himself. He claimed it gave him 'die-rear.'

The men each took one when the bell rang at the end of the work week. They gathered in the shade and talked about their Sunday plans and their families. Silently and almost subconsciously each gave thanks to the God who had made them, as much for toil as for any other reason, that they were still whole. With a final pull on the neck of the brown glass they finished their beers and put the bottles in an empty ten gallon bucket before dispersing to the most cherished seventh of their lives.

Sammy left with them, heading back into Oxford again to scour the town looking for Betsy. His blistered hands gripped the wheel of the Mustang as he drove slowly looking left and right in the green glow. And after yet another night that his search ended fruitlessly, he returned to the parking lot of the saw mill and slept in his car.

"You gotta hand it to that Teague feller," Mr. Finley said as he launched a ribbon of tobacco juice. "Always the first here in the mornin's."

Chapter 22

The wind billowed out the sheets hung on the line in back of the Kappa Chi house. Betsy stood in sandalled feet, pulling down dry sheets, snapping the wrinkles out of them, and then folding them double until they fit with the others in the basket at her feet. The cut edges of the grass of the manicured lawn brushed against the sides of her feet. The breeze carried the sound of a chorus singing off in the Music Building, the same section of song sung through several times on its way to being perfected. The notes were distant and pastel as the wind rushed in the pine tops.

The back door of the house opened and then closed, but it was just as distant to Betsy as she enjoyed the monotonous revelry of busy hands, busy hands that helped the mind clear.

"Bessie, we have a dryer," Tina said as she stepped carefully through the back yard of the sorority house. She wore pink pants that ended snugly at her ankles, and tan skin showed between the knotted tail of her white blouse and the brass button of her pants. Her hand clutched a tumbler of iced tea that she held up like a torch as she walked gingerly. Her feet were bare, and she watched every step.

"You can use the dryer, you know." Tina repeated.

Betsy snapped a sheet and matched the corners, then folded it in half and then half again. She laid it in a wicker basket and took the wooden clothespins from her mouth and put them in the basket too. A mockingbird chased a blue jay across the yard in a tumbling flurry of blue and gray feathers and then landed in a crape myrtle. The colorful blossoms were holding on even though it was October, and half of the petite green leaves had either turned a reddish orange or turned loose. The ground below was littered magenta and pink.

"Thanks, but I like the fresh air." She pulled down another dry bed sheet, matched the corners, and snapped out the wrinkles.

She had found the spool of clothesline in the laundry room and decided to hang it from the oaks in the back of the house. In the week of doing the house laundry, she had come to know who was on her period, who was still homesick, and who had buttered the muffin.

Tina paused as she weighed her words. "It's just that...the girls don't like their underwear hung out where everyone can see it, see. It's embarrassing to them." Tina took a sip of her tea and ice clattered in the tumbler. Past the sheets, there was a line of pink, yellow, blue and white underwear like a semaphore message on a ship's rigging. Tina's tiny pair at the end was like the punctuation mark.

"Here," Tina said, as she set her tea in the grass. She picked up the basket and began removing the wet underwear from the line, beginning with her own. "We'll take these indoors and run them through the dryer."

"You sure?"

"Sure I'm sure."

They lugged laundry baskets through the downstairs parlor, Tina's glass of tea rattling ice with each step. On the big wood consoled television, Ricky was asking Lucy, *splain sometheeng to me Lucy.* A couple of the girls laughed along with the canned laughter.

Tina emptied the wet sheets and underwear into the dryer and shut the lid. She turned two dials and then pushed a button, and the dryer began sighing and mumbling.

"Now isn't that easier?" Tina gestured with her palms up.

"But they gonna be fresh?" Betsy asked.

"Fresh enough. They'll be clean and dry, the whole point, right?"

Betsy gave a resigned look. They listened to the dryer for a moment. Betsy's eyes were mesmerized by the whirlwind of tumbling clothes behind the glass.

"We gonna need to make groceries," she said into the vortex.

"Make groceries?"

"Sure! These girls can eat, yeah!"

The other housekeeper had her own car and would get groceries on her own. For Tina and the rest of the Kappas, food would just magically appear in the pantry and the refrigerator. Elves could have brought it for all they knew.

Tina and Betsy passed back through the parlor. On the television, Lucy bawled with her big black-and-white lips squashed together like a duck's as the canned laughter erupted. All but two of the girls had left, and the remaining two napped on the couch with textbooks in their laps. Tina grabbed her keys off the hall table.

They drove through campus under the overpass on Jackson Avenue, past the spire of St. Peter's Episcopal Church, and toward the square. Tina's hair was covered with a scarf, her eyes hidden by sunglasses. Betsy's black hair whipped in the breeze, and she closed her eyes and smiled at the feel of it. She opened them suddenly when she realized she was missing an opportunity to look for Sammy.

102

"Show me the town," she said. "I ain't seen it good."

Tina took her up and down the streets, up every numbered street, down every street named for a president, past old churches and old houses, including the one where that man who wrote all those books had lived, oh I should know it, Tina said. They saw the Circle, the Lyceum, Steve and Angelo's Drive-In, Dee's Drive In, Home of the Deeburger, The Kream Kup, Pettis Cigar Company, and Shaw and Sneed Hardware, and then J. E. Neilson Co. and Leslie's Drug Store on the square,

But no sign of Sammy Teague.

"What's down this street?" Betsy kept saying, her eyes searching, until Tina finally said, "Don't you think we should go *make* our groceries?

The Jitney Jungle was just off the square in Oxford. They stepped inside to the polished floors and the soft music and the immaculate shelves. Battalions of canned goods stood at attention, waiting for inspection. Rows and columns of chickens, whole fryers already prepared, waited next to packages of beef and pork, deep red and trimmed in white fat. Towers of bread loaves rose like Aztec temples. Fields of apples, minus the trees, stretched up and back to mirrored backdrops of still more apples. Clerks in white shirts, aprons, and ties attended to everything. To Betsy, it wasn't a grocery store, it was a grocery palace. A voice overhead called for a Mr. Sheffield to come to produce, *playze*.

An old black woman with gray hair pushed two white children in a basket, a boy and a girl who pleaded for one thing after another. The woman was unmoved.

"Baby, yo mama don't allow such. Put dat back, now, an' keep yo hans to yoselves," she said placidly as her eyes moved between the shelves and the list in her white gloved hand.

There was a rack of more magazines than Betsy had ever seen in one place. Tina selected a copy of *Cosmopolitan*, the lead stories, "Choose the Perfect Father and the Sex of Your Baby" and "'Who's afraid of Virginia Wolf'-Inside the Next Burton-Taylor Movie." Betsy picked up a copy of *Good Housekeeping*, "Ten Quick and Easy Suppers" and "Banish Those Pesky Stains-For Good!"

The boy bagging the groceries made small talk with the girls about Ole Miss football and music and where the best hamburger in

103

town was, clumsily letting slip the fact that he went to Memphis 'onced a month.'

Betsy continued to scan the grocery store, half in awe of it and half in a search for Sammy, expecting him to stroll down an aisle so they could come face to face. Meanwhile, Tina teased the grocery boy, smiling and softly biting her lower lip with her even, white teeth. She made eyes at him, pursed her lips in a brief kiss, and then bent forward to slyly arrange items and give him a fleeting glimpse of her cleavage. He stammered and then stopped talking altogether.

When the total came up, Tina wrote the check on the Kappa account, dotting the 'I' in Tina and Sullivan with a friendly little circle. The boy, still tongue tied, took their bags out to the car and put them in the trunk while Tina stood by and watched him. She yawned theatrically and stretched her arms high, and the tanned and toned skin of her midsection tantalized the boy, whose gawking made him hit his head on the trunk cover. He stood up, feeling for a bump on his head as Tina slid a dollar into his hand, her fingertips raking lightly, seductively over his palm. She wiggled her fingertips goodbye, and then she got in the car with Betsy and they pulled out of the parking lot. The boy in the red apron and tie stood motionless, receding in the rearview mirror.

Chapter 23

The shadows of the mill yard sheds loomed in the moonlight to the accompaniment of drowsy night noises, insects and birds and other creatures, all hidden by the night and only suggested by the moonlight. Sammy had just put out the last cigarette of the day in the ashtray of the Mustang. The smoke of it faded and was lost against the white sky. The faint distant roar of a train's diesel engine and the repetitive ding of a crossing bell floated on the night air from far, far away, through miles and miles of woods. It was the perfect temperature for sleeping out with the top down, and would have been something to be enjoyed if it had been optional and not necessary.

The first evening of looking had been fruitless. He had searched randomly, without a plan, finally returning to the mill yard well after ten. He had thought it would have been simple; Oxford wasn't that big, but today it had seemed an immense, endless horde of people.

Now, night had taken the world and sapped all the color out of it and put it on a gray scale. The mill yard was just a collection of shapes and outlines, indistinct with a tendency toward the sinister and the macabre. A night breeze came up and whispered in the treetops, and the black silhouette of the tree line swayed, rolling in a sinuous wave against the gray heavens. The shadows of falling leaves fluttered like ticker tape.

The profile in the moonlight appeared suddenly and startled him. One moment it wasn't there, and then the next it was, like the flash on a screen. His eyes narrowed in the dimness as his eyes tried to elucidate the shape. At first he thought it was a bobcat, ears flattened down, but the shape was shoulderless, backlit by the night sky. Sammy sat very still in the backseat, shivering not from cold but from fear. A mosquito hummed in his ear, and he let it, rather than move. Finally, his hand eased into his shirt pocket, next to his pounding heart, and fumbled for the lighter. He held it out at arm's length like a weapon and clicked it, but it only produced a spark. The second click produced a flame and illuminated a small sphere.

The owl sat perched on the windshield peering into the dome of light. In its mouth it held a snake, a copperhead half the size of the one Jude had killed. The snake hung from the narrow hooked beak like a long scaly tongue that ended in a pointed tip near the Mustang's rearview mirror. The owl's eyes, perfectly round yellow and black concentric circles blinked as if astonished. Its throat pulsed, the finely striped feathers rippling, its head bobbing and weaving as it looked at Sammy, and Sammy looked at it.

The flame became too hot for Sammy's thumb, and he released it. The halo of light collapsed and the owl was a profile again. The tufts of feathers on the bird's head stuck out like ears, and Sammy understood why he had thought it was a bobcat. The shadow of the snake hung down slender and twisted. The owl pivoted its head, which moved like the turret on a gun. The snake shadow wriggled with the turn.

Sammy clicked the lighter again, this time not out of fear but instead out of fascination, awe. The light pulsed out, and it appeared that the owl had no face. It rotated its head again, and the surprised eyes and hooked beak returned. It held the snake in one of its talons now, and panted in and out of its beak like a dog, its eyes flashing yellow and black circles. The snake had a small bloody gash in its throat. Sammy let the flame go again, and as soon as he did the owl flew away in a feathery beat of wings, each flap diminishing. Sammy's eyes strained to follow the shadow. The owl nestled on a limb with the disk of the full moon behind it. Sammy heard the owl hoot, cooing in a downy cadence like the old secret knock without the counter knock. On the limb in the silvery moonlight, the tail of the snake dangled in a thin shadow. It shook as the owl pecked at its scaly flesh.

Chapter 24

The needle popped and scratched as the United Artists label rotated right side up to upside down to right side up and around and around the spindle and into a blur. The music started, and then the Exciters sang:

I know
Somethin'
About love

Girls squealed, and Tina backed away from the stereo with her arms extended high over her head and the backs of her wrists together. They were running around barefoot, in curlers and in different states of dress and undress. The chatter rivaled the stereo, which blared as the girls got ready.

They danced and shimmied as they put on eyeliner, compared outfits, and sprayed hairspray. When the Exciters were finished, Tina took them off the turntable and put on Chubby Checker's "Pony Time." Several of the girls threw up their hands and jumped up and started prancing, a couple of them still in curlers.

"The Pony! Show me how, show me!" one of the younger girls shouted as she hopped up. She watched the prancing feet of the others and then fell in. Their hands went from side to side like they were holding reins.

Betsy looked up and smiled around the pins in her mouth. She was doing some last minute alterations for a girl named Frances, a pledge from Jackson who was sweet and had a lovely figure and beautiful straw colored hair but an unfortunately long, equine face. Betsy took the extra pins from her lips and stuck them in a pin cushion, and took a needle and thread from it and stitched in the changes. Frances wiggled with the music, and Betsy said, "Be steel, now."

"There," she said as she snapped the wrinkles out of Frances' dress. As soon as she said it, a girl handed her a brush and sat on the sofa with her back to Betsy. Betsy brushed out the girl's thick red hair and smiled as the girls danced to "Let's Twist Again." She kept brushing and brushing, the bristles pulling furrows in the copper strands, thinking about dancing in the central hallway with Sammy, furrows streaking down through copper, again, again, again. Dancing, swaying against Sammy. Streaks in copper, more brown than red in the depths of the furrows, his hands on the small of her back, the brush pulling through the sleek copper.

She felt hands on hers stop the brush, and the red haired girl smiled, "That's good, thanks. You're about to put me to sleep doin' that!"

Different combinations of girls went upstairs and came downstairs, all gradually becoming completely dressed and ready. "He's So Fine" by the Chiffons played and they all danced. Tina pulled Betsy up, and she danced too.

"You're sure you don't want to go?" Tina asked over the music. "I could tell the boys you're my cousin from France. Drive 'em crazy." Tina raised Betsy's hand and twirled herself.

"No, yaw go. I stay with the girls don't feel good." Two of the girls were staying home to nurse cramps.

When the door closed on the last girl, Betsy went upstairs and watched them walk down sorority row, laughing and dancing in small snippets as they walked. Then she changed into her gown, pausing to admire her breasts, fuller now more than ever, the nipples large and dark. The gown fell over them, and she shook out her hair.

Across the street someone in a dark Mustang sat parked. She studied the driver but couldn't see who it was because of the shadow of the streetlight. As the last of the girls made the corner, the Mustang started. The dashboard light illuminated the interior, and she saw the driver. She tried to get the window open, but in her haste it wouldn't budge. She ran down the stairs and out the front door in time to see the taillights disappear around the corner. Her bare feet pattered down the sidewalk past the Phi Mu house where she halted in her gown to see the Mustang evaporate into the night.

She sat down in the cool grass in her nightgown and looked up into the black sky. The white dots of stars were scattered with no order whatsoever, a random dispersion. From across campus the young laughter of carefree people trickled. She listened to it and felt tiny as she looked up at the immense sky.

It was Friday night, and Sammy drove through campus like a ghost haunting a past life. The lights were on in Hemingway Stadium as the grounds crew prepared the field for tomorrow's game. Insects swarmed in flurries high up in the white glow of the light standards. People walked around campus going to and from parties. They were all his own age but seemed much, much younger now.

He turned off West Jackson onto Sorority Row. A long irregular line of happy, laughing girls walked along toward the Grove, and Sammy knew that they were on their way to a party on Fraternity Row. He parked in front of the Kappa Chi house as the Memphis radio station quietly played Smokey Robinson and the Miracles, "Tracks of My Tears."

In the line of girls, Sammy saw a figure from the past, the silky blonde flip and headband of someone from a former life, like a character in a movie. Tina laughed, snapped her fingers, and watched her feet dance as the ragged line of girls walked toward the Grove. He watched her go, like someone in the beyond would watch someone in the world of the living, detached and cut off.

In the upstairs window in the Kappa house, he saw the silhouette of a girl who had stayed behind, which usually meant she was ill or was on probation for grades. The shadow undressed and put a gown over her head in a manner that was familiar to him, the motion of her hands, the way she shook out her hair. It looked so much like Betsy, but after dozens of hopeful sightings that turned out to be mistaken, he dismissed it. What would she be doing in the Kappa Chi house, anyway?

He shook his head at his irrational optimism and cranked the Mustang to life. Its acceleration was becoming the sound of hope deflating. The headlights pulled him back through town and out into the country toward the mill yard. When he arrived to the outcrop of night time shadows, he pulled the top down and reclined in the back seat. The sky was black and speckled sparsely with white stars. He tried to put them into constellations but they didn't seem to belong together.

Tina came in well before the other girls, went upstairs, and was sick in their bathroom. Betsy followed her up the stairs and stood by while Tina knelt in front of the toilet.

"You *py-yied* again?" Betsy pulled off Tina's headband and pulled a handful of blonde hair back.

"No, I didn't drink hardly anything, I'm just sick to my stomach. Haven't had much appetite lately."

Betsy wrung out a cold wash cloth and put it on the back of Tina's neck.

"Maybe you just sick, then. You been sleepin' a lot."

And as soon as Betsy heard herself say it, she realized, she knew.

Chapter 25

It was a Monday at noon. Betsy emerged from the room she shared with Tina. The breakfast dishes were done and put away, and the laundry was caught up.

Upstairs on the landing, a girl was talking on the house phone.

"No! You're kidding me. You're lying! You. Are. Lying. Really? She said that?"

Betsy pulled a sweater over her shoulders and pattered down the stairs. On the television in the downstairs parlor, a soap opera doctor and nurse held hands at a cafeteria table as they discussed something serious in shades of gray. Several of the girls were sitting in front of it, a couple of them with curlers in their hair.

On free afternoons she wandered the campus and the town, her eyes open and searching. For once she had money and nice pockets to put it in. She looked in the windows of the storefronts around the Courthouse square, waving to the salespeople inside. Men in linen suits and bowties walked along tethered together by conversation. Then the days came with cooler weather, and the men wore wool suits and neck ties. The men spoke of lawsuits and cotton orders and football.

On the Courthouse square, cigarette smoke scented the air. It was the incense of her childhood, and it made Betsy think about her daddy. He had favored hand-rolled *perique*, the tobacco grown in St. James Parish, the tobacco with the strong, sweet, peppery aroma. Few men could smoke it by itself, unblended, without getting sick. Her daddy had been one of them.

She thought about sitting next to him in Mass when she was a girl. She would fidget and tie her ponytails under her chin or make a moustache of them and then tap him on the shoulder. He would look over from clasped hands on the back of the pew and smile and shake his head and close his eyes again, still smiling. She would grin and crouch onto the kneeler next to him. Later, she would sleep nestled into his side, the drone of Latin vague and distant.

Afterward, she would ride home on his shoulders, his hands holding firm on the cuffed ankle socks, the same big hands that had shined her black patent leather shoes the night before. Her hands clasped over his forehead as she giggled and ducked tree limbs. A cigarette perched in his smile let out smoke like a locomotive. He had carried her home like this until she began to blossom, and it was no longer proper for him to do so. She had cried then.

Not long after that, his itinerant cough lingered a few days longer than normal and then produced blood. The doctor in Thibodaux took a picture and saw a white cloud above his heart. In a month the doctor took another one, and the cloud had advanced like slow cottony smoke from a house fire. Her daddy began to dwindle, his massive upper arms loose without muscle under the sun browned skin. He became a leafless winter branch of a man. His sallow cheeks pulled for air that his lungs had no use for.

The undertaker, Mr. Gravois, fashioned a smile on her daddy and draped a Rosary in his hands. He dressed him in a shirt and tie; Betsy had never seen a tie on her daddy in his life.

"Don't cry," her mother scolded her before the funeral. "It won' change nuttin', so don' even start, no."

Sammy's daddy had come by to pay his respects to Betsy's mama. He held his hat in his hand with the big Masonic ring. His nickel gray eyes wore sadness.

"I'm sorry for your loss."

Her mama just snorted.

"Nobody knew more about Mount Teague than Alcide. When to plant, when to cut. He was the best." He shifted from one foot to the other like he was standing barefoot on hot coals and trying not to show it.

"The hands, the hands, they, they all loved him, called him *Monsieur Chef d'equipe.* For the longest time I thought they were saying, Chef-to-keep." He chuckled wryly, but it came out as awkward and uncomfortable.

A silence followed, and then he added, trying to smile, "Means Mr. Foreman."

"I know what it means," she said quickly, bluntly.

At last Trey Teague looked down and mumbled, "Hard to replace."

Betsy's mama twisted her mouth into a pucker and lifted her chin, but remained silent.

"That all?" She finally said.

Mr. Teague looked around nervously and put his hat back on his head and left.

Later, at the cemetery after the priest sprinkled the casket and gave an intonation, all but Betsy and her mama left. Betsy wailed like a lost soul. It was a cry so deep and feral that most of her family stopped and turned around.

Her mother popped her leg and said, "Stop it. Hear me? Stop it. The last thing this family needs now is a side show."

He was gone, but each waft of smoke brought the promise of it belonging to Sammy. Her head would jerk up and around each time she smelled it, and then she was disappointed again. The baby inside her would only know its *papere* by stories. It was beginning to look like her baby would only know Sammy that way, too.

But she kept hoping she would see him, or at least some trace of him. She drifted through the Grove down to the stadium, marveling how big it was. A whole church would fit inside of it, a whole cathedral maybe. The sound of a band wafted through the air, and Betsy followed it. The Ole Miss band was practicing.

She took off her shoes, scrambled up an oak tree, and sat on a limb. The brassy notes of the band were thunderous and majestic. They played Dixie and then a show tune she had heard on the radio but couldn't name. The band director dismissed the band after another run-through of Dixie.

The rest of the band drifted away, but a tuba player and a trombone player stayed behind on the edge of the grassy practice field to cut up. The tuba player was a tall boy with dark brown hair and a bucket hat. He gathered big mouthfuls of air and pushed them through the tuba into elephantine notes like the footsteps of a hippo. The much shorter trumpet player joined in, the horn erupting into a brassy, blaring shriek like a bird. They played Johnny Cash, "I Walk the Line," the sound of the tuba waddling up and down the melody. After a couple of dozen bars, they began laughing and stopped playing, bending over with their instruments in their merriment. In the tree, Betsy laughed silently along with them, her chin propped on her hands, which rested on a limb as she sat. They regained their composure and played another song: Love-love-me-do, you-know-I-love-you. Betsy stopped laughing and laid her cheek on the back of her hand.

Chapter 26

By the fall of 1965, the city of Oxford, Mississippi had grown large enough to support half a dozen town drunks, a fact the Chamber of Commerce could have boasted of, if it had wanted to. There were as many town drunks as Baptist churches, although most people thought that this was sheer coincidence.

One of those drunks was Tom Euless, a former professor at the university who lost his position for reasons that were known and accepted by everyone except him. His whispered nickname among the faculty was Useless Tom Euless.

These days he sat on a bench in the part of campus known as the Circle and drank while he watched people feed the squirrels and birds. He always brought an empty 7Up bottle and a paper bag with a Mason jar in it. Into the green glass bottle he would transfer a liquid that was made by two bachelor brothers in the woods down around Senatobia. It was sold in Mason jars, a clear liquid that could run an automobile, strip wax off a floor, or be combined with lemonade and bitters for a pretty nice cocktail. He still dressed like a professor in loafers, slacks, and a corduroy jacket with patches on the elbows, and introduced himself to new benchmates as Professor Euless. His face was crimson tinted with a network of tiny veins like lightning flashes and a nose that was bumpy like a red avocado. His ghost blue eyes lurked under a shock of hair that was whiter than it should be for his age, as if it had been bleached from within by the liquor.

Betsy was feeding peanuts to the squirrels, watching the way their wiry little hands took the shell from her, then how they bounded a short retreat and admired it, rotating it while cracking it with their teeth. They moved suddenly, bounding, looking, bounding, checking, bounding, gray plumed tails undulating, flickering.

"Three years ago last month, do you believe it?" Euless said.

"What's that?"

"Three years last month, Meredith enrolled."

"Mare-dit'? Who's she?"

"He. He was a he. James Meredith, a negro who came to school here. The first." Tom Euless took a sip from the green glass bottle. "You're not from around here are you?"

"No sir."

"Had a big riot, National Guard, tear gas, people shot, couple of 'em killed. One over there at that building, the Lyceum." He pointed with his 7Up bottle. "French journalist and a jukebox repairman. Shot in the head, both of 'em."

"Why's that? Betsy asked.

113

"Who knows why? They were in the wrong place at the wrong time, I suppose. Some of these buildings still have bullet holes. It was bedlam." He belched quietly into his lower lip.

Squirrels hopped in the grass, peering down into it. Betsy rattled in a paper bag for another peanut. A squirrel grasped it and retreated.

"You know, I used to teach here, Southern History," Euless said. "Damn administration threw me out like a week-old newspaper, though. *They said* because I had a drinking problem. Now I'll admit that I like to have a toddy every now and again, but it's never been a problem, ever." He took a sip from the 7Up bottle and made a face and sniffed. "Ludicrous."

"You ever have a student name Sammy Teague?" Betsy asked hopefully.

"No, never," the professor parried away the question and moved to another topic.

"Some people thought it was the 3 Cs, Coloreds, Communists, and Catholics."

"You gettin' farred?"

"No, the riot. They said the Communists and the Catholics came in from outside of Oxford to stir up the Coloreds, the Negroes. Course, those who said it were from outside Oxford, too. I've always said that the fourth C could've been Crackers."

Betsy smiled politely. She didn't know what a Cracker was. Maybe it was like a cracklin'. She knew what that was, a *gratton*, the roasted fatty skin of a pig.

Euless eased into a discourse on the emigration of the Scots-Irish and the American Revolution as it pertained to the southern colonies and the administration of Andrew Jackson and the Missouri Compromise and that was just the beginning. The Mason jar was diminishing, until he turned it almost completely upside down and the last drops trickled out into the 7Up bottle. Euless' tremor rattled the edge of the jar on the bottle.

And still he continued to talk, taking the South into the twentieth century and demonstrating the fact that history may or may not repeat itself, but history professors most certainly do.

Betsy was out of peanuts, and the squirrels had no interest in Southern History and wandered away. She yawned big, her mouth stretching.

114

"Well, gotta go. Gotta get supper started." She stood up and brushed the wrinkles out of her dress, a lightweight cotton hand-me-down from Tina. The bench had left impressions in the backs of her legs.

"Oh? What's for supper?" Euless said. He was more than a little buzzed and always got hungry when he was drunk, probably because he was always drunk by suppertime.

"Roze beef, rice an' gravy. Nice talkin' to you."

Professor Euless watched her go, admiring the way her dress fell over her hips, and wishing he were twenty again and could start over. The lids were beginning to droop down over his blue pupils.

The sun was setting, and Tom was getting sleepy. Soon, he would be asleep on the bench, and the city police would wake him up and tell him to go home and he would do it and his wife would yell and then cry and he would stand there weaving and stunned, tilting and dumbfounded, blowing out hiccups like bubbles and she would go to bed disgusted again and he would sleep on the couch again and she would get up in the morning and go to work and he would get up around noon and come down to the Circle.

Chapter 27

The ten gallon tub was filled with empty brown beer bottles. The hands that had put them there had departed to the cherished seventh of their lives. It was one of the first mild days of the year, and the work had almost been pleasant. A day that makes people who work indoors wish that they worked outdoors, not understanding what outdoor work can be like.

Without having much of a seventh to cherish, Jude and Sammy were the only two left in the mill yard. Even Mr. Finley had locked up and driven off in his bulbous old Dodge pickup.

"How do you get home every day?" Sammy asked

"I walk," Jude said. "Through the woods. Shorter. I'd drive, if the state'd give a driver's license to a man got one hand. Must be some pol'cy. Then I'd have to get a car, and all at."

"Where you live?" Sammy asked.

"Oh, I got a place," Jude said evasively. "You hungry? Man, I sure am."

"Yeah. First Rate work pulls a big appetite," Sammy joked.

"No doubt, brother," Jude said. "Well, let's get us somethin'. I know a place we can eat at the same table, if you ain't ashamed to eat with a one armed, colored Harpo Marx."

"And if you ain't ashamed to eat with somebody who looks like Jesus smokin' a cigarette," Sammy said.

Jude laughed, "You do look like him, if he smoked. Who knows, maybe he did for a while, till his mama made 'im quit."

Sammy pulled the top of the Mustang back and down.

"I hear it's hell for three days," Jude said as he helped with the top from the other side of the car.

"What is?"

"Quittin' smokin'." Jude patted the front pocket of his overalls and found it empty.

Sammy offered Jude a cigarette, and he took it. "You thinkin' about quittin'?"

"Nah. I'll probably quit smokin' the day I die."

They pulled out of the mill yard and onto the highway. They drove in and out of autumn shadows, the air chilly but the sun warm. Sammy was scanning the road. Jude watched him.

"You always look like you're lookin' fer somethin'," Jude said.

"Aren't we all lookin' for somethin'?" Sammy asked as he checked traffic at a four-way stop and palmed the steering wheel into a turn.

"Hmmp," Jude smiled and snorted. "I ain't lookin' fer nothin'. Nothin' at all." He turned quiet and smiled as his hand rode the currents coming off the side view mirror, diving and rising with a small change in the plane of his hand. The air currents jiggled his blonde curls. He wasn't out of touch with reality, it just didn't interest him. His leg jiggled, oscillating with energy.

The B&B Café was in an alley just off the square in Oxford. On the left was a counter with barstools and on the right were booths. In the back was a jukebox, blinking and silent. A black man in a sweater vest was counting money at the register.

"Well hey now Butch," Jude said.

"Well, looky here! The one ommed bandit!"

Then he looked at Sammy and said with a scowl, "We don't serve no white people here."

When he got the look he wanted on Sammy's face, he laughed big at the joke.

Ha-HA! And he pointed at Sammy, "Got ya, now! Das a popeyed lie, dere! We serve black people, white people," his eyebrows went up and his eyes got big, "*blue* people, see through peoples. Long as dey got green money, we serve 'em." He laughed again and said, "Have seat."

They sat down at a booth and Butch gave them two menus, but Jude gave them right back and said, "Two specials."

From inside the kitchen, a black man smiled out through a toothless grin and said, "Hey deh, Jude! Was poppin'?"

The waitress, Georgette, a woman with mountainous shoulders and a multitude of chins, brought them two plates with collards, ham hocks and hoppin' john. She set a basket full of towel-wrapped cornbread on the table with two Mason jars of ice tea. They thanked her and set into it all. They talked of the mill and the weather.

"You ever go see your folks?" Sammy asked.

"Ain't got none," Jude said. He was stretched out lengthwise on the bench seat of the booth. His plate was clean.

Sammy's hands were on his head in repose as he wondered. He couldn't hold another bite. Two bowls of peach cobbler had been scoured cleaned and sat with spoons in them.

"You boys show went through dese groceries," Georgette said as she picked up the plates and bowls and left the tab.

"Yes ma'am," Sammy said, and he shut his eyes. "What now?" he asked Jude.

"How bout the drive in?" Jude asked, picking his teeth with a toothpick. "The Rebel's got that new Elvis picture showin', *Tickle Me* or somethin' like that."

"Nah, let's just drive around and look at all the pretty girls," Sammy said. "Especially brunettes with big brown eyes." One in particular, Sammy thought.

They began in the town square, driving around the courthouse. Night was falling, and their faces were yellow-green in the dashboard light. In front of an ice cream shop there was a small knot of girls exchanging glances with a small knot of boys.

117

"Oh, looky here, Jude said. "Here's one."

Sammy hit the brakes, almost squealing the tires, and the girls and boys looked over to the Mustang.

"There in the sweater," Jude said.

Sammy recognized her as Glenda, one of Tina's sorority sisters. Her grandmother was a Lambda, which made Glenda a Lambda legacy, but her father had married an Italian woman, and that automatically excluded their daughter from being a Lambda. But it didn't exclude Glenda from her mother's good looks. She kept chatting in her group, and didn't seem to recognize Sammy.

"Oh yeah," Sammy said, trying not to sound disappointed. "She's a beauty all right."

"Well you oughta stop and talk to 'er," Jude said, incredulous at Sammy's inaction.

"With this beard? And this long hair?"

"Your hair ain't that long. And maybe she likes the wild type," Jude said, baring his teeth and growling like a panther.

"Maybe she don't," Sammy chuckled and shook his head.

They continued on down to the corner and then up and down every street in Oxford, driving past the icons of Sammy's past life. For some it would have inspired nostalgia, but he didn't want the last two years of it back, just the last two months. At each new turn his heart rose like a prospector's, each new street a shovel full of hopeful earth that fell through the sieve leaving a bare screen with a mound full of meaningless dirt beneath it.

As night encroached, he gave up and offered to drive Jude home.

"Where do you live exactly?" he asked Jude.

"I take a room from some people just this side aThaxton."

They were quiet, the radio was turned down to a murmuring hum, the Shirelles asking, "Will You Still Love Me Tomorrow?" When they reached a remote section of Hurricane Road, Jude said, "You can let me out here. I'll walk the rest of the way."

Sammy pulled up to a simple country road without a marker. He let Jude out and watched him go, a shadow disappearing into shadows.

Sammy waited at the junction for a time, but curiosity made him turn down the weedy, red gravel lane. Within a quarter mile he came to a ragged house with green tar-papered sides. Outside was a gray propane tank that looked like a submarine and sat outside like an undetonated bomb. A young black man in a sleeveless undershirt leaned his chiseled torso against one of the spindly posts of the house. On a couch at the other end of the porch was an old black man who had the floppy gums of the toothless. He passed a paper bag to a middle-aged man in dirt-smeared overalls who sat on the couch with him. A mongrel dog was tied to the post of the house, and a kerosene lantern threw a meager light over all of them.

Sammy continued on a quarter mile more until the road ended in little more than a logging road and then a trail and then no road at all, just woods. He backed up until the road was wide enough to turn around in. He passed the house again, and the porch was empty, the dog untied and on the porch. It lifted its muzzle to the sky and shouted a solitary bark through wrinkled black lips as Sammy passed on his way up to the main road.

As he turned onto the highway, he switched the radio to a station where announcers were wrapping up the Ole Miss football game. Ole Miss had defeated LSU 23-0 in a game played in Jackson. It used to be one of the highlights of the year, a red-letter date on the social calendar, especially for him. But he had had no idea that it was today.

Chapter 28

All the toilets were scrubbed, up and down the halls, and the bathtubs, too, all left gleaming white and waiting to be used again. She had dusted around the daily mayhem of books and notes and clothes, trying not to disturb the arrangement of school items anymore than she needed to. Betsy wondered if she were a housekeeper or a zookeeper.

The pledges, the freshmen, were the worst. Half-eaten things, blouses, bras, underwear, unmatched socks all lurked under beds and in between sheets. Clean clothes were never put away, they just waited in stacks on dressers or on the floor to be worn again. She sniffed the clothes as she picked them up from the floor, and if they were clean, she folded them, and if they weren't, she tossed them into a basket.

She paused and looked into some of the books. *College Geometry. Western Civilization. Principles of Economics.* And then she resumed dusting.

She had been an enthusiastic student, until her daddy died, and then everything involuted, imploding as the world of happiness and gentle encouragement came to an end.

"You go to school, Bess. You a smart girl, you. You can do anything, anything you want," her daddy would say as he narrowed his eyes with a cigarette on his lip, his large index finger, sun-browned and leathery, admonishing her. But the cigarettes took him and sometime during her freshman year she stopped going to St. Matthew High School so she could take care of her mama who struggled with grief and her Mimi who struggled with age.

Betsy worked down the halls of the Kappa house, changing sheets and pillow cases, and wondering if any of the girls had ever made a bed or picked up after themselves. She gathered up glass after half filled glass on nightstands and bookshelves, emptying the contents into a bucket which filled into a nameless brown slurry. She made two trips downstairs with handfuls of empties until she just brought up a wicker laundry basket to put the rest in.

She brought the basket of glasses downstairs to the kitchen and set it down on the counter. It was heavy, and when she eased it onto the hexagonal tiles it gave a muted tinkle like the nudge of a glass chandelier. Tina was giving one of the pledges a haircut. Frances, the sweet girl with the unfortunately long, slender face, was sitting on a kitchen stool with her back to the sink. Mary Nell and Loretta were there, leaning against the kitchen counter across from her and watching. Mary Nell had her hands on the edge of the counter. Loretta stood next to her, her arms folded under her large breasts. Tina bent over looking into Frances' face, looking for something to go with, a small spark of opportunity.

"Okay," Tina said resolutely.

Frances looked at Tina fearfully, "Have you cut hair before?"

"Sure, lots of times," Tina said, oblivious to the sound of her voice stretching the truth. Her calm blue eyes could talk a girl into crossing Niagara Falls on a tightrope. "Relax."

She washed Frances' straw colored hair, the girl's beautiful figure rippling under her blouse and jeans as she leaned her head back into the sink. The tiny needle jets of the sprayer rinsed out the white foam, and the girl smiled. Tina sat her up again and then combed through the long blonde hair, working out tangles as Frances winced and sagged. Tina pushed in on Frances' chest and lower back. The girl straightened and drew taller.

"Good posture!" Tina chided quietly. "A Kappa has good posture!" And then she measured lengths of hair between her fingers, pulled them up, observed them from different angles.

"I've got it," Tina said as her face lit up. "This long hair needs to be about...shoulder length." Scissors snipped, and straw colored hair fell to the floor, gleaming in the bright midday autumn light that streamed through the kitchen windows. Frances looked down at it and bit her lower lip. Her brow was knitted in apprehension.

When the sink was free, Betsy stood next to them and washed the dishes she had collected, looking up between them to check the progress. Tina's face was determined, pursing her lips as the comb pulled furrows through Frances' hair like rows in a wheat field.

When a rack full of dishes was washed and rinsed, Betsy leaned against the counter drying them with a dish towel and watching. Frances was relaxed now, resigned to change and enjoying the tender pull of the comb and the light crunching *shick, shick* of the scissors.

Loretta leaned back against the kitchen counter as Mary Nell sat behind her on the hexagonal white tiles of the counter, her knees on either side of the big girl as she made braids in Loretta's auburn hair. Loretta's forearms rested on Mary Nell's knees.

"What's your major now, Tina? This semester?" Loretta said with her eyes closed under the small forest of auburn braids.

"This semester?" Tina said as she concentrated on Frances' hair. "This semester it's Elementary Ed. What's yours?"

"Still undeclared," Loretta said. "My folks are gettin' antsy." Mary Nell handed her a pinch of a braid, and Loretta held it with her thumb and forefinger while Mary Nell got a rubber band for it.

Tina pulled the comb down and through. Frances' eyes were hidden under a straw-yellow curtain. Tina put her fingers across Frances' eyes as if she were saluting for the girl. *Shick, shick.* Hair fluttered down like hay falling from a loft.

121

"Was a mayjah?" Betsy asked.

"The main thing you study. My parents think mine is Kappa Chi," Mary Nell said. She was looking for unbraided hair on Loretta's head and beginning to run out. Loretta looked like the hydra from the Greek myth, except with a kind, round face.

"Your major is what you want to do with your life," Tina said. Her fingers pulled evenly to Frances' shoulders as she gauged the length. "I change mine about every other semester. Can't help it, I like everything."

Loretta spoke up, her eyes shut as Mary Nell doubled a rubber band around a braid-let of auburn hair. "My daddy says my major is husbandry with a minor in pre-wed." They all laughed.

"My daddy can't complain, because my grades are all A's and B's," Tina said. "He's got a sticker on his car that says, 'My Daughter and My Money Go to Ole Miss.'"

"What you wanna do with ya life, then?" Betsy asked. The sink gurgled as the dishwater drained, and Betsy dried her hands.

"Oh, I don't know. Maybe I'll just cut hair," Tina's voice trailed away as she admired her work.

She was finished cutting. She put down the scissors and towel dried Frances' hair. The brush worked again, and Tina swept the ends of the new bangs to the side with her fingertips.

"Don't look yet," Tina told her. Frances sat still while her eyes roved as if she were watching a bee buzz around her head.

Mary Nell looked up from Loretta's hair and saw Frances' new hairstyle. "Okay. Okay, I'm startin' to see it." A few remaining strands of unbraided auburn hair streamed between Mary Nell's fingers.

Loretta opened up one eye, looked at Frances, and said, "Oh, yeah!" Then she closed it again and told Mary Nell, "Don't stop-keep goin'."

Tina ran upstairs and came back down with a makeup bag and a hand mirror. She scratched around in the blue canvass bag and pulled out eye shadow, eye liner, and mascara and lined them up on a counter.

"Close your eyes," she said, and Frances closed them. Tina put her fingers on Frances' chin and lifted the girl's face up and out. Tina put a small sweep of dusky blue across each eyelid, traced eye liner around each eye, and then teased out lashes with the little tubular brush. The tip of Tina's tongue pushed out to the side as she concentrated.

"Now, push out your lips," Tina said, and Frances did it. Tina twisted the metal cylinder and applied a peach color. "Now press your lips together, like this." Tina folded her lips in and together, and released them with a quiet smack. The girl repeated it.

Betsy turned from putting the last glass in the cupboard, and her jaw dropped, then her upper lip embraced her lower lip.

"A moobie star!" she said.

Loretta opened her eyes. Her hair was solidly in little braids like a little black child might wear them.

"Oh. My goodness," she quietly exclaimed as her face fell in amazement.

Tina gave Frances the mirror, and the girl saw someone she had never seen before. Her fingertips went to her chin, her face, her hair as she verified that it was really her, and her eyes dampened.

"Don't cry now, you'll make your mascara run," Tina said. "Now go up to my closet and pick somethin' out. Something with a high hemline and a low neck line. Should be plenty to choose from."

Frances got up and threw herself around Tina. Tina smiled and put her hands on Frances' waist and drew the girl back. Her hips flared gracefully, pleasantly under Tina's hands.

"I knew you were in there," Tina smiled with her eyes. She kissed Frances' forehead and then pulled stray hairs off her lips.

Frances trotted through the house. In the parlor a chorus of oohs and shrieks arose. "Frances, you're beautiful!" someone exclaimed, and then another voice, "The next Miss Mississippi!"

Tina swept blonde hair off the kitchen stool and patted it.

"Okay, Bessie. Now you."

Chapter 29

The patrol car wandered silently through the streets of Napoleonville, turning left on one street, right on another, then left on the next, like a shark cruising a reef. Finally, it pulled up outside of Aucoin's. The little orange dog was there, and when the deputy got out the dog rolled on his back to have his belly scratched. Everyone else did it these days, most adding a kind, cooing word in English or French. The deputy used the side of his boot to brush the dog out of the way.

"Bonjour, deputy," Aucoin called nervously.

"You know I don't speak that crap," Parris scowled. Behind his thick glasses, Aucoin's eyes wandered as if they were looking for the spoken words there in the air in front of his face.

"Look here," the deputy put his forearms on the counter and leaned in as he got right down to it. "I'm looking for that Duplechain girl. Ain't seen her for some time. Any ideas?"

"I ain't seen her neither," Aucoin said. It wasn't a lie, but it wasn't the truth that Parris was looking for, either.

"You ain't?" The ceiling fan over the single plank cypress counter swayed and beat the air. He looked into Aucoin's eyes. The old man's thick glasses made them large and unfocused. "Maybe I oughta take that little dog of yours to refresh your memory. Make a great bait animal for the boys trainin' they fightin' dogs."

Aucoin looked at the little dog and swallowed.

"She got on the bus for up north come now three weeks."

"That so?"

"That's so." Mr. Aucoin swallowed again and waited to see if that was enough information.

"And?" The deputy asked. "Where was this bus headed?"

"Mississippi somewheres." Aucoin said.

He waited for the deputy to speak, feeling like Judas waiting for thirty pieces of silver. Instead, Parris just smiled and patted Aucoin's cheek. The old man's glasses slipped to the side. Without them, his eyes were small and sharp. Aucoin pushed the black rims back in place with his finger, and his eyes were magnified again.

On the way out, the deputy helped himself to a carton of milk and a honey bun. The screen door slapped closed, and there was a thud and Chanceux yelped. Mr. Aucoin ran to the door in time to see the patrol car slide down the street. The little dog put his front paws on Aucoin's leg, and the old man rubbed the dog's head.

The patrol car was headed north.

Chapter 30

The Greater Starlight Temple AME Church stood on a curve in the county highway between Oxford and New Albany. It was formerly the Providence Road Baptist Church, but a split in the congregation over an issue long ago and now remembered by no one had led to the dissolution of the church. The church house stood vacant for a time and then was sold to the present congregation, shepherded by the Rev. Octavius Robinson, seminary classmate of Dr. King. The marquis in front of the church recommended to passersby to "Cast Your Burdens on the Lord."

Behind the church, past the shady lawn where countless church suppers had been held, the ground sloped gently down to the Tallahatchie, a fact convenient for baptisms, which were now held the first Sunday of every month. A path led down the grassy bank through knee high weeds to a beach that reached out and under the clear, rust colored water. The current threw lines on the surface that drifted downstream, coiling and uncoiling.

On this particular day, a blue Mustang was the only car parked in the gravel parking lot. Down in back of the church, two young men swam in the water that was the rusty color of the brown one.

"You're not afraid somebody's gonna walk up on us?" Sammy asked. He was waist deep in the water. His neck and arms were sunburned red like his daddy's neck and arms got from playing golf at the country club, the club with the blue-trimmed, clear-water pool.

"Not really. We'll hear a car on the gravel. Sides, I'm sure the good ladies of the congregation have seen a pecker or two in their day." Jude's hand and his stump were behind his head as he lay naked on the sandbar. "Fact, I'd be surprised if they wouldn't mind seein' one more. Heh heh." He reached down and shook himself.

Sammy chuckled, turned and went under the water that was now churned turbid brown. His arms dug through the water as he went down into the deeper, cooler current. When he surfaced, Jude was measuring the sun with his thumb and forefinger. Two piles of clothes were on either side of him in the sand. The remaining two beers from the six-pack were cooling in the water, pressed into the sand to keep them from floating off. The other four cans were empty on their sides in the sand by Jude. In the sky an egret flew high, its wings blinking white with each flap.

Sammy belched the last of Mr. Finley's Saturday noon beer and went under again. It would take at least one more plunge to get a week's worth of sweat and sawdust off. In the rusty brownness, the current tugged on him playfully and let him go. When he came up again, Jude was up and knee deep in the water. He scrubbed himself with a bar of Ivory soap until he was white with lather. He tossed the soap to Sammy.

Sammy soaped up, and then he and Jude for a brief moment were identical white. They dipped into the brown current together and waded up to the bank in their original colors, pushing water off their skin. They sat on their clothes, and Jude gave one of the last two beers to Sammy, and they opened them. Neither said anything as they listened for the silent current. The turbid water was clearing again.

"So you wouldn't be embarrassed about one of the ladies in your church seein' you?" Sammy asked.

"Oh, this not my church. I'm Catholic."

"Catholic?" It hadn't occurred to Sammy that a colored person anywhere other than Louisiana would be Catholic.

"Yep." Jude pulled at his beer. "Raised by the good Sisters in Memphis at the orf-nidge."

"You still go? To church?" Sammy asked, his gaze turning from the river to Jude.

"Go to Mass bout ever Sunday, almost," Jude said without a hint of pride as he reclined on an elbow and faced Sammy. "Whether I need to or not."

"Pontotoc or Oxford?"

"Oxford. St. John's."

The Catholic Church, Sammy thought. Why hadn't he thought of it before?

Chapter 31

They filed into the cool quietness of the church and sat on the back pew. Jude eased the kneeler down and got on it while Sammy stayed seated and scanned the church. Most of the heads were ancient and white headed, not the one he was looking for. From time to time a cough from somewhere near the front fluttered out into the quiet. Jude sat back on the pew and pulled up the kneeler.

Above the altar was a large painting of Christ in a crimson robe trimmed in gold and a shining gold crown on his head. The painter saw to it that his subject's eyes looked at everyone, that his face was soft and thoughtful, his beard neatly trimmed. Two fingers on one hand were stretched in a benediction. In one corner of the front of the church was an altar to the Blessed Mother, rows and columns of flickering candles before her. In the other corner, St. Joseph bided his time.

'Father said you could sit on the back row, but he can't give you the Eucharist," Jude whispered. "Or he said you could wait in the rectory across the way. Door's unlocked." Jude had on the nicer of his two shirts, a pair of faded dungarees, and his work boots.

Sammy had been raised with a stuffy Episcopalian God, a God that was only modestly interested in him, a God who only wished he would be a little nicer to his sisters and maybe not masturbate so much. Growing up, going to church was just something you did once a week as a prelude to the Sunday brunch at the country club, part of a package. The Episcopalian God was in sharp contrast to what he felt was the intense and largely unpleasable Catholic God, the God that made you to suffer, because suffering was redemptive and He wanted you redeemed, by God.

Some people feel lost without church. Some people feel lost with it. Sammy was neither.

Jude, on the other hand, rarely missed. No matter how hungover he was or what bed he woke up in, he almost always found a way to come in. It was his only connection to his past and his only family besides the men of the mill.

Sammy sat in the back with Jude and listened and watched the pageantry of the Catholic mass, the Latin that would soon be supplanted in favor of English after the Second Vatican Council. His eyes scanned the people who came in, but there was no sign of her. He waited until the second reading, Paul's letter to the Ephesians, and then slipped out when everyone stood for the Gospel. She wasn't there.

*   *   *

Across the way from the Kappa house, the Lambdas were getting ready for church. They emerged chatting, holding the door for each other with white gloved hands and carrying clutch purses. They clicked down the steps of the massively columned porch in white heels and got into their cars, where they tied scarves around their perfectly done hair and touched up their perfectly done lips in pocket mirrors. Then they were off to exercise the freedom of religion by attending the Baptist, Episcopalian, or Presbyterian churches. Methodist was also an acceptable choice.

The Lambdas were girls who never drank from the bottle, always a glass. They were girls who preferred martinis because that was what movie stars drank. They were girls who went to France in the summers and came back with trunks full of new clothes and a few words of French tortured by a Mississippi accent. Seee-voooo-plaaaay.

In the Kappa house, Betsy threw a dress over herself and fluffed out her hair. She was glad that she'd let Tina cut it into a bob. It gave her an air of Parisian glamour, but mostly it was easier to keep. She grabbed the handkerchief she used as a mantilla and left Tina sprawled out in the sheets. Tina's head was tilted back and her mouth was open, the edges of her two front teeth just below her upper lip. Betsy was grateful for a place to sleep, and it no longer bothered her as much to wonder if Sammy had slept there. In some strange way it was a comfort to think he might have been there. Tina never gave her an indication whether he had been there or not.

Betsy hurried across the landing and then tiptoed quickly down the stairs, weaving around sleeping girls. The photos of nearly a century of Kappas looked off and away as if embarrassed.

Down in the parlor on the couches there were more crumpled forms. A girl named Winnie from Yazoo was serving as the "sweeper," the pledge who was appointed to rise early or just stay up late and gather all traces of alcohol in a bag or bags and drive them to the dump, in case there was a search by the university. Winnie was a cherub-faced girl, whose own headache manifested as a frown

128

under her bloodshot eyes. She looked up at Betsy, and the frown straightened a little, and Betsy smiled and tilted her head in sympathy. Winnie returned to picking up. Coming upon a boy sleeping on the floor, Winnie poked him with her toe and said, "Hey, you gotta go." The boy grunted.

Betsy glanced at the grandfather clock in the foyer and went out the door. The air was cooler now, and the dash to church hopefully wouldn't raise a sweat. She had stayed up late again, kneeling with girls at the toilet and pulling their hair out of the spray, mopping brows with cool cloths and saying soothing words. She endured her own morning sickness through the haze of sweet, cheap perfume and vomit. Now she would say a prayer for them, asking for the assistance of the unknown patron saint of hangovers, the intercessor for the dry and nauseated.

At three in the morning, she'd finally gotten to sleep. In the last few weeks her sleep had gotten unpredictable, veering between insomnia and insatiable slumber. She debated even going to Mass, but felt that if she were ever to find Sammy, she would need divine help. Her plan was to petition St. Anthony, the patron saint of lost things, with a novena to help her find him. She would recite the rhyming prayer that her Tante Lucille had taught her:

St. Anthony, St. Anthony, please come around, something is lost and cannot be found.

At the door of St. John, a tidal wave of fatigue fell on her as she opened it. She leaned behind the door and yawned so deep and long that she recalled her father's saying: "Sha, yawn dat big you gonna swallow your face." Someone passed through the door and past her, and she straightened up and went in.

The gospel was being read as she entered, and she blended in while everyone was standing. She eased in to the last pew next to a mulatto man with curly blonde hair. They exchanged smiles.

They all sat and listened to the homily and then took their Lord on the tongue and drank his precious blood. The priest rose for the benediction, and she and the little caramel man stood with all the others.

"Peace be with you," the priest said.

"And also with you," the man and Betsy said to each other along with the congregation. He reminded her of the mulattoes that lived in St. James Parish. He rested his hand and his stump on the back of the pew, and she wondered what had happened to him.

After the priest and his attendants recessed out of the back of the church, the man seemed to pause for her. She smiled and kneeled again. He genuflected to the altar and followed the crowd out.

She stayed on the kneeler until the church was empty and then began her prayer of supplication, ending with a Hail, Holy Queen:

Hail, Holy Queen, Mother of mercy, our life, our sweetness and our *hope.*
To thee do we cry, poor banished children of Eve.

The phrase struck her and a sob arose, but she gulped it back.

To thee do we send up our sighs, mourning and weeping in this valley of tears. Turn then, most gracious Advocate,

A distant sound made her pause. She thought she heard a piano playing.

Thine eyes of mercy toward us, and after this our exile, show unto us the blessed fruit of thy womb, Jesus. O clement, O loving, O sweet Virgin Mary. Amen.

When she had completed her Rosary, she got up and wiped her eyes. Getting up was beginning to hurt now as her secret continued to grow within her. She lifted the kneeler back under the pew and tottered a little wide legged to the light of the doorway. She hoped St. Anthony had been listening.

At the doorway she thought she heard the bass riff of "Twist and Shout." She looked around but it was silent, so she smiled at her hopefulness and let the door close. Perhaps St. Anthony was working on her prayer.

She turned up University Avenue, back to the Kappa Chi house to start Sunday dinner. Her dress flowing around her curves, her handkerchief mantilla over her black bob of hair, and the smallest kernel, a mustard seed, of hope in her heart.

*   *   *

The entrance to the rectory had an outer screen door ornamented with aluminum scrolls. He opened it and found the rectory unlocked as promised. There was a large living room with a small kitchen, a bathroom, and a bedroom attached. Every doorway had a crucifix above it, the sagging, muscular, pierced body of Jesus sliding down toward each portal. In the center of the room, there were a couch and two armchairs with green and brown crocheted blankets over the backs of them. A floor lamp stood between the armchairs, and under it there was a small side table with a half filled cup of coffee and a detective novel opened in its middle and turned down.

On one wall was a bookcase with a statue of the Infant of Prague on the center shelf, a small child with a crown twice the size of his little head and the robes of a king. Adjacent to the bookcase on the adjoining wall was a picture of Pope Paul VI, the pope who had recently been the first ever to visit the United States and who had just declared that the Jews weren't collectively responsible for Christ's death, just a few of them were. Around the pontiff's portrait were picture upon picture of church events past.

Sammy paused and looked through them, especially the ones of the young first communicants. The boys were invariably in dark blazers and neckties, wearing them uncomfortably as if they were made of cardboard. The girls wore lacy white dresses and veils, knee socks and gloves. All of the children smiled sheepishly and posed with Father Eichert like he was a celebrity. He bent down to smile an identical smile in each picture. Sammy lingered on one picture of a little dark-haired, dark-eyed girl who looked very much like he remembered Betsy, the little bride-girl from his childhood. The memory of it came flying home suddenly and landed on a perch in his heart.

On the mantel above the fireplace was an elaborate Bavarian clock in dark walnut and brass. The long and short arrow hands on the time-beiged face swept over the Roman numerals at its circumference, and the ticking accompanied the memories of the photographs on the wall adjacent to it. The arrow hands both reached XII, and the clock chimed solemnly.

He turned to the wall across from the fireplace and saw an old upright piano. He hadn't played or thought about playing in weeks, months. He lightly touched middle C, and it resonated deliciously. The steady tone soothed him, and he yearned to play but was afraid he would disturb Mass. So instead he pulled down an old copy of *Lives of the Saints* and sat down with it in an armchair.

A multicolored cat jumped up onto the arm of the chair and startled him. The cat nestled in beside him, flipping over on his back and flattening out his ears with a little cat grin on his face. Sammy scratched the downy fur under the cat's chin, and the cat closed his eyes and pushed the side of his mouth against Sammy's fingers.

Sammy flipped through the book studying the pictures and the descriptions. Saint Sebastian, pierced with arrows until he was a porcupine of a man. Saint Denis, who the book said walked six miles holding his severed head which miraculously gave a sermon the whole way before he finally fell over. Saint Anthony, patron of lost things.

Lost things.

All right, St. Anthony, he thought, here's one for you. Help me find Betsy Duplechain. Last known address Hwy. 308, St. Matthew Parish, Louisiana. Believed to be in Lafayette County, Mississippi. Now, go get 'em. Sic 'em, boy.

Sammy turned the page.

St. Jude, patron of hopeless causes. Even though he was skeptical of the whole saint business, his heart sank a little.

The aluminum screen door squeaked open, and Sammy shut the book and stood up. Father Eichert and Jude came in from Mass.

"Father, this is Sammy Teague," Jude gestured with his stump. "Sammy, Father Eichert."

"Hello, Sammy," Father Eichert said. Eichert was a tall man with a white hairline that had receded to the top of his head, leaving the front half of his scalp a smooth, glossy extension of his forehead. He took off his black coat, put it on the coat rack by the door, and then shook Sammy's hand. Sammy felt the priest's soft, warm hand and gaze, a gaze that followed Sammy's eyes to the piano behind him.

"You play?"

"A little."

"Well, it's a little out of tune, but help yourself," the priest said.

Sammy sat and initially just played chords. His fingers felt bigger and meatier, and less nimble than the last time he played. He compensated by playing slower.

Jude and the priest appeared on either side of Sammy's back. Father Eichert had made himself a highball, clear, smooth stones of ice in honey-colored bourbon. He loosened his collar, and the white strip at his throat hung loose.

"Thing's like a noose sometimes," he said. "Play something, then. Don't be shy. Anything at all."

The first thing that came to mind was "Twist and Shout." Sammy's fingers stumbled over it but then fell into the groove, his left hand finding the bass line, his right hand finding the melody. A sour note crept in from time to time where the piano stepped on an out-of-tune key, but it felt wonderful to play and sounded passable. Sammy felt a hand on his shoulder and looked over it to see Father Eichert smiling with his eyes closed. Over Sammy's other shoulder, Jude was astonished.

"Where'd you learn to do that?"

"My mama made me learn," Sammy said tersely as he continued playing and concentrating on his hands.

He finished "Twist and Shout" in a quick succession of chords.

"Splendid!" Father Eichert exclaimed.

"Do another'n," Jude said.

Sammy launched into "All My Lovin'," and Jude recognized it and sang softly and tentatively,

Today I will kiss you
Tomorrow I'll miss you

Sammy mumbled along with him. Father Eichert waved his glass with the music and closed his eyes. The honey-colored liquid tilted merrily. He opened them again in mock exasperation.

"Sing loud, boys, make God sorry for the voice He gave you!" His hand made a rolling motion like he was trying to extract their voices out of them.

Their voices rose and pulled almost even with the music.

"That's it," he said, and he teased again, "I'm sure He's very sorry indeed! Splendid!"

When the song ended Father Eichert fastened his collar and said, "Well, I hate to run you lads off, but one of my old widows is expecting me for Sunday dinner, and I don't want to disappoint her. You know, of course, I'm the most eligible *ineligible* bachelor in all of Lafayette County, Mississippi." He winked at them and continued.

"You boys do come again, won't you? Perhaps I'll dust off these old vocal chords, and then we'll *really* make God sorry."

They left, and the priest locked the rectory behind them. The church lot was empty except for Father's old Plymouth and the blue Mustang. The Plymouth pulled out, Father Eichert clutching the wheel at ten and two and peering over it carefully.

Sammy pulled out of the parking lot, onto South Fifth Street and to the stop sign at University Avenue. He looked down toward campus and saw the remote shimmer of a young woman walking away, three or four blocks distant. Her walk was familiar, her form fading as she made her way past the front gates of the university. There was something white on her head, like a handkerchief. He checked traffic in the other direction as his memory chewed on the vision. He looked again, and she was gone.

Sammy drove where he saw the woman last, not sure if it was Betsy or not. But it didn't matter. There was no sign of whoever it had been.

Chapter 32

The air was sharp and sulfurous. The smoldering fires that burned the cane stubble in the fields were dying out, and scattered embers throbbed in the furrows under the darkness of the cool autumn sky. Through the window of the little bungalow, the lights of Mount Teague glowed grandly under the bows of the live oaks and taunted him from across the distance. The solitary live oak in the Parris yard was dying, limbs sawed close to the trunk in an effort to delay the death of the old tree. The taken limbs left a blackened O on the trunk as if the tree were howling silently.

Parris was dressed in khaki trousers and a sleeveless undershirt. A lamp behind him backlit his figure and hid his face. His cowboy boots were to the side of his feet, the white socks on them brown on the bottom from grime, both from within and without. The room had the smell of his socks and his feet, as well as the smell of stale cigarette smoke, infrequently washed clothing, and days-old food in the kitchen sink, the odor of chronic, indolent bachelorhood. He sat in a ragged armchair and poured a couple of fingers of Johnny Walker into a glass as he talked on the phone. A soiled kitchen towel was over the receiver to disguise his voice.

"Looka here," he said. "Dis shairf Lebeau. Me 'n Parris gotta head norf foe while. Gotta...gotta...big shairf convention up yonda...Chicagah. Need you'n Olivier to watch dis side da Parish. Now don't go fillin' up da jail now. Only 'rest da sumbitches fo' rape 'n muhda, and then only if is white, heah?"

A voice buzzed on the other end.

"Cause he da bess depty I got, das why." Parris smirked to himself, trying hard to contain his laughter. "Mebbee you do gooda job as he do, den I take you to convention up Chicagah or some ways up yonda."

"Awright den. I call when I...when we get back."

He hung up the phone and then laughed and shook his head. "Dumbasses," he murmured.

He leaned forward and took a bite of the frozen dinner on the TV tray, only halfway warm due to his appetite and impatience. Ice settled in his glass as he washed the bite down with a sip of whiskey. His eyes narrowed as he looked out the window to the orange glowing squares of Mount Teague. Sometimes he thought it would be easier and quicker to just burn the whole place to the ground. This time of year would be perfect. The burning cane might just get out of hand and get a hold of all that old cypress. It wouldn't take long. It would look just like an accident.

No, he thought. I want the house and everything, not just the land under it. He took another bite and chewed vacantly. His eyes were shadowed by the glow of the solitary lamp at his back. The side of his fork hacked a small violence against the plug of meat in the foil compartment of the TV dinner. He smacked mechanically and looked at the outer package.

135

What is this shit anyway? he thought. Ever since granny died, he couldn't get a good meal. At first, no housekeeper would work for more than a week, and then none would even work a day when word got out how much he paid and the things he expected them to do, in the kitchen and in the bedroom.

The ice jingled as his lower lip seemed to lift the glass. Well, he heard that Duplechain girl was a mighty good cook. He'd figure out a way to keep her. In the kitchen and in the bedroom. Money or brute force.

A match scuffed across the strip on the cover of its booklet and snapped into a tiny bright blaze. The flame illuminated his cold blue eyes as his mouth pumped air through the cigarette. Smoke curled up and around his head as he shook out the match.

He got up from the arm chair, his movement in the dark shadows marked by the orange ember of his cigarette. The back door wheezed open, and the ember lowered as he sat in a metal chair on his back porch. A downed water oak, still unremoved weeks after the hurricane, took up most of his backyard. The brown, brittle leaves made a dry, sizzling sound whenever there was a breeze. Far across the fields, the lights were going out one by one in the big house. He was watching it.

Chapter 33

Betsy arrived early for church. She was losing heart and had stopped asking for help from St. Anthony. Today she would petition St. Jude, the patron saint of the Impossible and intercessor for the hopeless and despairing. She set the kneeler down quietly and put her knees on it. She produced a Rosary from her purse and genuflected fluidly and began her prayer. The sleeveless yellow polka dot dress still smelled new; Tina couldn't have worn it more than a couple of times. Over it Betsy wore a white sweater. It was cold outside, and besides, it was immodest to leave one's shoulders bare in Mass. The white heels pinched her feet, but she was just now getting used to walking in them. Tina would have dissuaded her from wearing white or yellow this far after Labor Day, but Tina was fast asleep in their bed. It was just as well; the yellow dress was looser in the waist and more comfortable.

Jude slipped into Mass right before the entrance procession. Sammy had let him out, parked and went straight for the rectory. He was glad for a soft couch to nap on, an indoor restroom to use and, after Mass, a piano to play.

Mass was about to start when Betsy felt the pew creak next to her. She looked up from the tangle of brown and white beads in her fingers to see the one-handed mulatto boy. They exchanged smiles. He kneeled down next to her, and she went back to her prayer. Her fingers moved down the line of beads as her lips bounced lightly with the prayer of supplication.

As the entrance procession began, she hurriedly finished her petition, genuflected and stood up with the rest of the congregation. They sang "Holy God, We Praise Thy Name," Father Eichert's terrible voice receding as he paced up the aisle with the altar servers, boys in black and white lace albs. He ascended the altar and bent down and kissed it.

In the pew ahead of Betsy and Jude was a family of six. The mother and father sat on either side of their four children. The oldest was a bespectacled and bookish young man of about ten, who sat dutiful and erect next to his father. Next to him was his younger brother, about eight, who fidgeted, standing on the kneeler and twisting while he looked up at the light fixtures. Next to him was the older sister, about six or so. She colored in a book about ponies, all of them with flowing manes and large, long lashed eyes. She carefully kept the crayons in the lines.

On the end was the baby sister who spent the whole of Mass crawling in and out of her mother's lap and making hand puppets over her sister's coloring. The big sister calmly pushed away her little sister's pincher grasp creatures and kept coloring. At one point the four year old crawled under the pew and gazed up at Jude and Betsy. Jude made a face at the little girl, and she made one back at him and giggled. Betsy smiled at her and looked back up and forward to get re-engaged in the liturgy.

Mass dragged on, and the children began to wilt like flowers in the heat. The big sister had colored all she cared for and was reading in a book entitled *My First Book of Saints*. She turned one page after another without really looking at any of them. The book was for children and left out all the saints that had been beheaded, burned, or shot with arrows.

The older boy struggled but sat up straight next to his father, valiantly kneeling and standing at all the appropriate times. Meanwhile his younger brother had stopped trying altogether and was slumped down in the pew watching how his fingers could interlock and unlock. The little sister was asleep, her eyes like a lamb's.

Father Eichert's homily droned distantly like a bee in a glass jar, like the whisper of a dry west Texas wind: *today's reading tells us that if our eye offends us, we should pluck it out, and if our hand offends us, we should cut it off, rather than be thrown into Gehenna with two good eyes and two good hands. But does it mean we should literally cut off our hands?*

As much as Betsy tried not to, she glanced at Jude. He saw her and looked down at his stump and made a whimsical face. Betsy snorted suddenly and uncontrollably, and put her fingers over her mouth. She quivered red-faced with insistent church laughter, delicious and forbidden. He egged her on, pretending a chop with his hand on his stump. She feigned a coughing fit and exited the pew and the church. Outside the door, she bent over and laughed until tears ran down on her face. She caught her breath, embarrassed to have laughed at the misfortune of another, and in church of all places. She leaned against the wall and exhaled loudly, her composure returning. When she returned, she sat in another pew and kept her gaze straight ahead.

When Mass was finished, Jude rushed to intercept her.

"Look, I'm sorry to get you so tickled in Mass."

"You so bad, you!" Betsy scolded him with a smile.

Jude offered his hand. "Jude Hawkins. Sawmill accident, in case you're wondering."

"Betsy Duplechain," she said, putting her hand in his. She withdrew it slowly and said, "Did you say Jude?"

"Yeah, Jude. Listen," he said. "My friend is waiting in the rectory for me. One of father's church ladies has got dinner for us, him and me and Father Eichert. Join us?"

"Thanks, but I gotta get Sunday supper started at the house."

"You got a family?"

"Oh, no. I keep house for some of the girls on campus. The Kappas."

"Oh. Oh well. Maybe next time, then."

"Maybe so."

She turned and went down the steps to the sidewalk on University Avenue. Her walk was still a little awkward in the heels. Jude watched her go.

Mrs. Murray was one of Father Eichert's widows. She had an angular face with a sharp chin and nose which she rouged, and it made her look like the puppets from Punch and Judy. She had glazed a ham, made a carrot dish she called copper pennies, and green beans and rolls. They sat down, the four of them.

Bless us O Lord, and these thy gifts which we are about to receive through the bounty of Christ our Lord, Amen, the three Catholics said and then genuflected together. Sammy just smiled politely with his hands clasped at the edge of the table.

Father Eichert rubbed his hands together and surveyed the spread of food. "And as my father used to say, hot diggity dam, slice up the ham." He waited for Mrs. Murray's certain response.

"Michael," she chided.

"I didn't get any piety from him, that's for sure."

Plates and serving spoons were set in motion, clicking against each other.

"Well, Sammy, I see you met Mags," Father said.

"Mags?" Sammy asked.

"Mags is short for MagnifiCat," Mrs. Murray said as she poured them ice tea. "Lemon?"

"No ma'am," Sammy said. The cat sat primly waiting for a handout.

"That cat is about every possible color a cat could be," Jude said before he took a long sip of iced tea.

Sammy scratched the cat's head with his shoe, and Mags droned out a loud, coarse purr. He rubbed across Sammy's pants leg and strutted back and forth, dipping and turning his head.

"The cat of many colors, I call him. A parishioner gave him to me. I've been offered all kinds of animals, cats, dogs, raccoon and possum pups, birds. People must think I'm some kind of St. Francis of Assisi," the priest said, and he took a bite of a roll.

St. Francis of Assisi. Sammy drifted away to the image of St. Francis on the wall of the kitchen in the tenant house, the image that was underscored with the black waterline of flood water. St. Francis in his brown robe with the tassel tie, and sandals and a sparrow on his finger and his hair bowl-cut around a shaven bald spot and animals clustered at his feet and Sammy's mind was there in the kitchen waiting, waiting for Betsy in an aluminum chair in the kitchen that smelled like mud, the kitchen with the waterline marked on the wall. He thought he heard her call his name from the back of the little house and he sat there and waited, waited for her to come through the door of the little kitchen and she called his name again and it was closer and seemed to be from the next room of the little house.

Sammy?

"Sammy?" Mrs. Murray said. Her rouge-spotted chin and nose and cheeks were pointed at him. "Jude just told you something you might find interesting."

"What? Ma'am? Oh, sorry, just drifted off, sorry." He had stopped chewing in the middle of a bite. He resumed and said to Mrs. Murray, "I do that sometimes when the food's really good."

"Oh, you flatterer!" She shined.

"It's my experience that a young man drifts off like that when he's in love," Father Eichert teased. "Can you tell him again, Jude?"

"I was just sayin', you shoulda seen the gal I sat next to in church today," Jude said. "Dark hair, big brown eyes. Just your type."

"That right?" Sammy said. False leads were beginning to grate on him, like a child on the playground being incessantly teased with the promise of a surprise, only to have it denied.

"Oh yeah. About your age, too."

"You get her name?"

"She told me," Jude said, but it was apparent that that detail had given him the slip. "Somethin' with an S or a C in it. Somethin' like that."

"Well that narrows it down," Father Eichert said sarcastically. "I think I know the one you're talking about, though. Always comes early or stays late, saying the Rosary. A very lovely looking girl indeed. And devout."

Mrs. Murray brought an apple pie to the table with four plates. She unstacked them methodically and sank a serving fork into the brown crust of the pie. She gave the men large slices and then gave herself a small slice.

"Well, Sammy, you'll have to come to Mass to meet her," she said.

"Maybe so," he mumbled. He'd tried that already.

After the apple pie, Mrs. Murray backed away and began collecting dishes.

"Don't bother, my dear, I'll take care of the dishes after such a wonderful meal," Father Eichert said as he leaned back with his hands on his belly.

"Thank you, love," she said. "Well, excuse me but some ladies and I play cards at three every Sunday."

"Bridge?" Sammy asked.

"Oh, no, certainly not," Mrs. Murray said, her gray bun shaking no. "Poker, five card stud. Bridge is for sissies and old ladies."

Father Eichert stood up as Mrs. Murray gathered her purse and gloves. She gave him her cheek and he kissed it.

"Why don't you ever invite me to play," Father asked in a voice that was playfully petulant.

"Oh, Father, it's a rough crowd. Those old biddies would eat you alive."

Father raised his eyebrows to Sammy and Jude. "Can you believe that?"

She left, and Father Eichert made himself a highball. He seemed to be thinking as he poured the bourbon.

"Tell you boys a secret?" he asked as his swizzle stick churned among the rocks of ice in his whiskey.

Sammy's arm hung over the back of his chair.

"I'm retiring."

Jude's face dropped.

"Retiring?"

"I'm an old man, Jude. Don't know how much more good health God's gonna give me."

"What are you gonna do?" Jude asked.

"Travel! Never been to the Vatican, France or anywhere, really. Probably spend six months or a year in Europe, then if my health is still good, maybe mission work in Central America."

"When?"

141

"End of the year. Give the diocese a chance to get a new priest in."

Jude was silent the rest of the afternoon.

Chapter 34

Sammy sat on the hood of his car, his elbows on his knees as he looked at the ground. The morning was full and bright, the tree line orange and brown and green under a crystalline sky. It had turned cool again in the night, the kind of night he loved as a child when he burrowed under the covers until the morning when he listened to Della Mae bump around in the kitchen downstairs. But last night he had not slept well, tossing and turning in the back seat of the Mustang, and twice going out to throw up but, in the end, only staring at the ground instead.

At lunch the day before he had eaten very little, and the men exchanged glances at his sudden lack of appetite. He had managed a half a stick of cornbread with a little water, but it swam around in his stomach aimlessly like a goldfish in a bowl. At the end of the day he crawled into the back seat of his car as soon as Mr. Finley left for home.

When Tillie arrived, she gave him a long look and monotoned, "You don't look so good."

She made him a cup of coffee that he threw up, and then he noticed the first pain, a boring ache around the middle of his stomach. Tillie made biscuits and fried up a slice of ham. He had three or four bites, eating slow and forcing them down, but they came up, too. When Mr. Finley came in he asked, "You gonna be able to work today, son?"

"I'll be fine once I get started," Sammy said, filling his chest with a deep breath. He got up from the table and grabbed his coat, a blue and black plaid flannel cast-off from one of the other men's sons. He steadied himself and walked out to Shed Number Two. There was a massive bin of pine logs he had been working on the day before, and he wanted to finish cutting them into planks. He ascended the steps to the cutting platform; they felt steeper today. Using all his strength, he pried a log, a twelve footer, up onto the ramp, and it crashed down onto the carriage.

It was hot again, and Sammy took off his coat and put it on the peg by the switch. He flipped the switch, and at the end of the carriage the teeth of the saw hesitated for a split second and blurred into a circle, whirring and whining. He checked the line of cut down the length of the log and leaned into the lever to engage the carriage. It took his whole weight to do it. The whine of the saw crescendoed as the log moved into the blade.

Sammy watched the plume of saw dust fly up and out of the kerf in the log, arching like the tail of an off-white bird. The sharp smell of pine was on everything, and the air was not air but the ripping sound of wood being separated. The dust settled on the carriage of the saw and the ground under it, and his mind wandered away like a small child at a county fair.

He saw the sawdust piled on the ground and thought of the live oak limb on his old Tbird and thought of Betsy and how they had sweated at the ends of the hand saw and then his mind thought of them sweating naked together with their hands clutching on the bare skin on each other's backs and then.

He was cold again, trembling from it, and he reached for his coat.

His arm stuck in the sleeve, and he struggled to work it through. The whole mill teetered around him and he fell. The log hit his stomach like a punch to his gut, and he grunted like a prizefighter. He tried to push himself back up, and he thought that his strength had left him completely until he saw that a stub of a limb, not an inch around and two inches long, had snagged his coat. His right hand was stuck in his sleeve, and his left hand couldn't reach around to free his coat.

He looked back and saw the carriage lever. He tried to reach it with his foot, flailing with the toe outstretched, but the carriage advanced with him on it and the lever receded away.

Pain howled in his gut, but he struggled against it, flapping helplessly like a fish on a boat deck. Each slap against his stomach was like a mallet blow on a stake. The carriage was advancing slowly, working methodically through the twenty inches of pine. Sammy began to feel the breath of the saw, distant but approaching. He relaxed for a second, saw dust accumulating on his back. He

143

reached for the last of his strength, but his efforts were feeble. The saw was louder now, blowing a line in the sawdust on his back where it planned to take him. Sammy closed his eyes. Everything went quiet.

When he opened them, there were the men of the mill, standing around in a semicircle. One of them stepped forward to jerk the coat out of the snag.

He broke from his trance to see Mr. Finley's face, the chaw of tobacco in his cheek misshaping his face and making him look like he had the mumps on one side. His lips moved around the lump, and Sammy studied them like a traveler trying to make out a foreign language.

You gotta pay tension, boy, Mr. Finley's lips said. *Yer gonna get yer ass smashed or ripped one butt cheek from tuther if ya don't pay tension.*

The men rolled Sammy over, and he sat on the log. He reached out to steady himself, and his hand recoiled from the hot teeth of the resting saw. Instead, he put his palms onto the flaky purple-gray bark of the pine log and leaned forward. He looked up, and there was Jude, with the lever nestled in his armpit. Jude's eyes were narrowed onto his hand as it lit a cigarette. He shook the match out and tossed it under the carriage. He smiled and exhaled at Sammy all at once.

Two men lifted Sammy off the log. When his feet hit the platform, he winced as pain shot through his stomach. It was lower now, and like a rat gnawing, and more constant. He leaned forward with his hands on his knees and retched again, but the retching brought up nothing and only intensified the pain.

"This boy's hot as a goddammed far cracker," one of the men exclaimed.

"Sweatin' buckshot," another said.

Mr. Finley worked the chaw in his mouth as he thought and looked at the ground. Finally, he spat an amber stream and said, "All right, then. Let's git him to town."

They loaded Sammy into the back of a truck as gently as men used to transferring lumber could. Jude jumped in the back with him, and slapped the driver's door to signal ready. The faded red pickup pulled out of the weeds of the mill yard. Sammy moaned with each shaking lurch in and out of the ruts and potholes.

The intense blue sky was deep and cloudless. The rushing wind flattened Jude's blonde curls as a thin stream of smoke trailed from his lips like the plume of a jet. He sat next to Sammy, his forearms propped on his knees, looking off into the distance as the cigarette burned in his caramel fingers. The ragged breeze rushed by.

At the hospital in Oxford, an orderly in white came out and began looking over Sammy.

There was the slam of the passenger side door of the truck and then Mr. Finley's voice: "This'n ain't cut, just sick."

Someone who smelled like dirt and sweat and tree sap picked Sammy up and put him on a stretcher. He felt heavy like a log going down the ramp at the mill. The big electric blue sky was above him and then it gave way to a ceiling. There was a succession of lights above him that passed one after another as he moved down a hallway. The stretcher turned and then the jingle of a pulled curtain chain. A doctor looking thoughtfully as he pressed and agitated the pain again. He called for something in a voice that sounded underwater. Moving again, a sting in his wrist. Three identical faces, masked and upside down. A black rubber mask smell, and sweet air. *Count backerds from a hunnert, Mr. Taygue.* Ninety seven, ninety six, and then the sleep of the dead.

Chapter 35

The blue lights swirled in neon, painting the trunks and branches of the trees sapphire, while the white lights paired two by two and stretched down the highway and around the curve. The rain had slowed down to a mist and beaded itself on the bill of the policeman's cap, the black crescent that protruded from under the hood of his slicker. The drivers slowed to satisfy their morbid curiosity, the ones near the rear of the slowdown cursing the ones at the head for it, until it was their turn and they themselves had to slow down and look.

The policeman was directing traffic with a flashlight and waiting for the ambulance. One of the girls still needed it, but it was too late for the other two. The Cadillac was jammed into a tree, half its original length.   Nearby, a sheet covered one of the two girls. The other one was still in the car, they were pretty sure. They would load it on the back of a truck with a tarp over it and cut her out at the city garage. The one who had survived, so far, was lying down on the backseat of the squad car in the care of another officer, out of the rain. The backseat would have to be wiped down from all the blood.

The ambulance arrived with another set of revolving lights, these red, scouring the trunks and the undersides of the branches of the trees around the spot on the highway. It lurched backwards, jostling and sliding in the red mud. And the rain came down heavy again.

The phone on the landing rang at two in the morning. It woke Betsy, who patted the sheets and realized that Tina wasn't there. One of the girls answered it and there was a brief conversation and the girl shrieked. A door opened and another girl's voice said, What? What is it?

The second girl's voice said, Hello? And she started crying and then there were doors opening and girls crying and shrieking and more crying.

Betsy sat up as one of the girls opened the door abruptly, a wedge of light piercing Betsy's eyes. She threw her hand over them and saw the silhouette of the girl against the hall light.

The shadow girl tried to say something and just bawled.

Crying girls tumbled into cars that filled randomly and sped away, their lights reflecting white and red on the wet streets. They all arrived at the hospital within two minutes of each other, most in pajamas, housecoats, and curlers. In the waiting room, they sat in the molded plastic chairs, pastel green, orange and blue, and leaned against each other, gazing into blankness, or holding their heads in their hands until a doctor in scrubs and an Oxford city policeman opened a door.

The group of girls closest to the door stood up and gathered around it first, and then the wave propagated across the waiting room, and then the doctor said something, and there was a wave of turning and crying. Red faces contorted grotesquely in grief. The whole room wailed.

"Is there a Bessie here?" the doctor asked above the noise. The crowd quieted a little and parted to reveal her.

"She asked for you," said the doctor.

146

They walked briskly down a hall together.

"I wanna prepare you," he said. "She's really banged up, she's gonna look rough." And then something about an engine block, a floor board, and a blow to the head.

They walked by doorways, names and room numbers flashing by, a blur clouded by chaos, unreadable.

One of them said, Room 328, Samuel Teague. They strode right by it.

Chapter 36

The Sunflower Motel and Tourist Court's unkempt marquis promised kitchenettes, air conditioning and private baths. In the office, the Vacancy sign glowed in red. The 'No' part of the sign no longer worked or had to. There was always vacancy.

The St. Matthew Parish Sheriff's Department cruiser was parked outside Room No. 6. The misshapen outline of the parish adorned the car door, a shape a psychiatrist might use to test for mental disorders.

Inside, the room was dominated by oranges and browns, and a noisy window air conditioning unit that spewed out icy air. On the night stand under the sixty watt bulb, the paper wrapping of the motel tumbler was wadded up next to the ice bucket and the bottom half-amber, upper half-clear Johnny Walker bottle. He had looked for a whorehouse, but no one would tell him where it was so instead he pleasured himself and took a shower. His wet hair stuck out where he had just dried it with a towel.

He was relaxed again, enjoying a cigarette and his favorite nonsexual fantasy: the destruction of the Teagues, those Teagues with their gentile manners and their cotillions and their country club and their dinner parties beneath the oaks. Pretenders and swindlers, all of them.

Old man Teague, who had cheated his father out of his home and his land, he was old and would die soon enough on his own. And Trey Teague, he was weak. A simple set of legal maneuvers would settle him. The two daughters had no interest in the place. They were married and moved off. They would sell for a song.

The issue was that playboy, Sammy. Parris knew the boy was smart and good looking, though he had the reputation of being lazy. The safest thing in his case would be to eliminate him altogether. And that was what he was on his way to doing now. The plan was taking wings.

Yes, Bulldog old boy, he told himself, you'll have Mount Teague one day. And after he removed the old portraits from the walls, he'd make a big bonfire and throw them in. Then he would put Parrises up there, except he would have to have some done up of his daddy and his granddaddy. Don't they have artists who'll do that from photographs down in Jackson Square in New Orleans? Then he would sit up on the balcony and watch the sun and rain feed the sugarcane, *his* sugarcane. The leaves would grow like hundred dollar bills out of the black earth.

And that Duplechain girl. Her daddy was gone and couldn't keep Parris away anymore. He would bed her one day, of that he was sure. He would hold her throat while he grunted on top of her, pushing her jaw up while she screamed in pleasure or just screamed. And then he would lie in bed wet from her and wait while she cooked up something for him downstairs.

He took another sip of his whiskey while he imagined the grandeur of it. Would he rename it Mount Parris or New Verona plantation? He smiled and tapped a cinder into the glass of the ashtray. A tiny orange chunk of flame glowed as his jutting lower lip pulled on his cigarette. He scratched himself under his towel and his gut.

Maybe the next town up the road would have a whorehouse.

Chapter 37

The stippled gray bark of the trunk ascended into the cloud of green leaves. The limbs began to shake and rotate, becoming snakes like the Hydra in mythology, the one he had read about, the one that

Hercules fought. They were as big around as regular live oak limbs, but the scaly gray bark became bronze with copperhead ends, and black with moccasin-headed ends. The limbs rotated around like that ride at the state fair, the Cobra, the one that he and his sister Charlotte had gotten so sick on. The snake head ends rotated around advancing and opening toward him, showing the hooked fangs and soft white flesh on the inside of their mouths, then receding to let another head wheel and advance. The next head surged forward and nudged his midsection. He felt the sharpness of the bite and tried to shrink back but couldn't.

Sammy awoke clutching the mattress to a world that was out of focus. His stomach itched, and he put his hand there and felt silk tape and bandages. He looked up to the stranger at the foot of his bed.

The doctor was a middle aged man with small, squinty eyes and hair and long sideburns the color of a fox. His grin was perpetual, always there whether he was giving good news or bad. He wore a navy blue jacket, and white and black plaid pants. His bottom lip worked side to side rubbing his top lip as he looked at Sammy's chart.

"Well, there he is." The doctor looked up from the chart and smiled. "How you feel, son?"

Sammy's dry lips were stuck together, and so the doctor continued on.

"Appendix! That's what it was. Normally it's kinda floppy, but yours was swole up like a little pecker! Belly full of pus!" The doctor held the chart close to his chest and beamed like a farmer with a blue ribbon.

"Nurses'll get you up today, walk you around. It'll hurt like a sumbitch, gotta tell you. Had to give you the big cut, up and down." The doctor nonchalantly wiggled his index and middle finger vertically. "Sorry, but they're not gonna take you for *Playgirl* now." He chuckled at his favorite joke.

A static-borne voice called over the intercom. *Dr. Gilders, you're needed on the colored ward.* The doctor turned his ear to it and smiled knowingly.

"You'll be here close to a week. No mill work for six weeks, maybe eight with that cut. I'll see you again in the morning."

149

The doctor left. Sammy struggled to the side of the bed, sitting up in time to look out the window and see the doctor open the trunk of his car and put his coat there beside his golf clubs. The doctor got in and sped off.

Sammy stood up slowly, the cold air grazing his backside. He pulled the gown closed.

On the other side of the curtain, an old man mumbled something.

"Daddy?" a middle-aged woman's voice said. "What do you need, daddy? You want some water? Oh, looky here at this puddin'! Don't you want some?"

"I wanna go home," the old man's voice croaked. "Just wanna go home."

"You can't go home till you git bit-ter," she crooned. "Now here, try some of this puddin'."

Sammy only vaguely remembered the night before. He heard the commotion of a dozen or more voices, young distressed feminine voices that were shushed by the nurses.

He teetered to the doorway of his room. Behind the curtain, the woman said, "Did you see these flowers? They're from Aunt Sissy. Aren't they purty? *Hydrangeas.*"

"Your mama shore loved hydrangeas," the old man's voice said, his mood sounding brighter.

In the hall, every step was a challenge, the muscles of Sammy's stomach feeling like they would pull apart. His IV pole felt flimsy, like he was helping hold it up, not it helping him. The breeze brushed against his bare cheeks, and he pulled the gown around again. He tottered down the hall, past the desk where nurses with caps pinned down on their thick hair wrote thoughtfully in charts. He made it as far as the dayroom, where skewed rectangles of light littered the floor, and two patients, older women in hospital robes, watched the black and white television.

He turned and paced down the hall, looking at the names. Harriet Wright, 312. Bernice Sutton, 310. He stopped when he saw the next name.

Tina Sullivan, 308.

The room was filled with flowers and cards and stuffed animals. He didn't recognize the patient in the bed. He turned, thinking it must be a different Tina Sullivan.

"Sammy?" The voice was barely a whisper.

150

Tina's face was a solid bruise. Her eyes were swollen like plums.

"Sammy." Her labored voice trickled out.

"Mary Nell and Loretta are dead. Nobody'll tell me, but I know they're dead. I saw them. Why won't they just tell me?" The skin of her plum-eyes tightened, and a tear crawled down the eggplant bruise on her face. "Why won't they just tell me, Sammy?

"They took me to Memphis, to a clinic. I was pregnant so they took me. Now Mary Nell and Loretta and my baby are all dead." She stopped crying, and a small, feeble snore fell between her lips. Sammy was grateful for it and turned to leave. Then he heard her again.

"Sammy? Is this a dream? Am I dreaming? Go get Bessie for me, will you Sammy? Go get Bessie. *BESSIE!*" She shouted in a voice that carried this time, and her body shook.

The slits in her plum-eyes closed completely, and she slept.

A nurse came in, a large woman whose uniform struggled to contain her.

"You get back to your room, Mr. Teague, and let her rest. Poor dear. The doctor says she may never be the same."

Chapter 38

A few men from the mill, Jude Hawkins, Archie Wilson and an almost chinless white man named Curtis Wingo came to get Sammy when he was discharged. The nurse wheeled him to the front and eased him into Archie's car, a big red and black Buick as long and wide as a boxcar.

"You want anything Sammy?" Archie asked.

"A hamburger. A great big hamburger," Sammy said.

Archie smiled broadly and said, "Now, das my boy!"

The four of them went to Angelo and Steve's. Jude, Archie and Curtis watched with satisfaction as Sammy sat in the backseat and ate his burger and his fries and then ordered a second milkshake.

"Looks like the young feller's back in fightin' trim," Curtis said, picking his teeth with a toothpick.

They drove to the mill and arrived just in time for Saturday beer. The men all patted Sammy on the back and asked to see his scar. He lifted his shirt to a chorus of 'Looka that!' and 'Hot damn, boy!'

"That's a good'n," Mr. Finley said.

A ruddy faced man with red crew-cut hair spoke. "I seen ol' Sammy from acrossa yard and I said damn, he looks bad. Ain't that right, Archie?"

"Show nuff. I tol' Bobby Ray, I said now that's the whitest boy I ever seen, an' I seen some whitens."

They all laughed, a big circle of men, and then one by one, they put their bottles in the bucket and left. Only Jude and Sammy remained.

"You headed home?" Jude asked with a look on his face like he already knew the answer and was about to get it.

Sammy was silent and looked off over the tree line. It was now solidly orange and brown.

"You ain't got no place to stay, do you?" Jude looked down at the cigarette burning in his hand, twisting his hand to see the burning end and then the filter tip end. Then he looked at Sammy who let the truth slip.

"Been sleepin' in my car," Sammy admitted.

"This whole time? Boy, you jess had a fuckin' operation! You can't go sleepin' in yer car!"

"Where else am I gonna stay?" Sammy asked.

Jude threw his cigarette down and stepped on it.

"C'mon," he said.

They emerged into the town of Pontotoc, past the domed octagonal roof of the First Baptist Church and the limestone columns and red roof of the Pontotoc County Courthouse. On the red brick side of the Corner Grocery on Washington Street a brightly painted carton of milk cascaded into a glass and gaily suggested, 'See if you don't like Barber's best.'

They turned north onto Main Street, out of Pontotoc then through the sleepy town of Ecru, and then into the woods again. Wood smoke and the buttery smell of cotton seed hung in the cool, crisp air. The ribbon of highway, speckled gray and yellow striped, cut through the countryside. Barbed wire lined the road in three parallel strands that went around and through trees and posts, where pine straw had collected at their bases. They passed through a long straightaway of picked-over cotton fields, gray stalks and desiccated brown leaves speckled with snowy remnants. Big barn red cotton pickers and cotton wagons with tufts of stray cotton adherent to their sides stood idle near the tree line in the failing sunlight. Then in another stretch of dense pine and hardwoods, there was a broad sweeping turn in the highway.

"Right here, right here," Jude said suddenly.

Sammy cringed as he applied the brake, his stomach muscles demonstrating to him another previously unknown function. You never know what your stomach muscles do for you until you have them cut. Sammy's reminded him as the Mustang decelerated and turned.

On the outside edge of the arc of highway, there was a small indentation, a dimple in the line of brown, orange and yellow leaves. In a month, the leaves would be gone and the roadhouse would only be obscured by the gray winter trunks and branches. A fiery red limb of a sweetgum tree hung low over the double rutted lane. Along the fence line at the entrance, a sign with a smiling hooded elf advertised for Brownie Chocolate Drink and announced in shotgun pellet pocked letters the name of the roadhouse.

The County Line Inn was either in Pontotoc or Union County. Each one claimed it was in the other, not wanting the headache of patrolling it. So the County Line Inn was essentially in neither, a no man's land. Sammy had thought he knew about every den of iniquity and cradle of sin in three states, but somehow he had missed this one.

A rust colored dog, lupine and feral, strained against its leash. The dog's lip rose and quivered in a snarl, its jaws snapping repeatedly. With each lunge, the loop of the rope thumped against the porch post it was tethered to. Pointed teeth and pink gums flashed as warning after canine warning gurgled up from its throat. Jude cooed to the animal, who recognized him then. It lowered its head and immediately switched to begging forgiveness, smacking its lips, and blinking its eyes.

"Good girl, Sheba," Jude whispered as he rubbed her ears. Sammy offered her the back of his hand, and she sniffed it and then licked it like she would a puppy. She was every color on the spectrum between orange and brown, like a coyote.

"Don't give her no mind," a voice behind the screen called. A woman's face was behind the blackened screen of the door, vague like the upturned face of the drowned in murky water. "She's real pertective a me when it's just us two hyar. Come on in, kind sirs."

Opalina looked up from her sweeping and pushed a strand of hair back from her forehead.

"That who I think it is?" She shielded her eyes to see who the shadow visitors were.

"Evenin', Miss Opalina." Jude saluted her with a raised stump.

"Well, Mr. Hawkins, then," she said and smiled as she recognized the voice. They had a natural affinity for each other, sharing the weightless, uncertain origin of the parentless.

The late afternoon sun came in low over the opposite tree line and highlighted the woman. Opalina Hardy was a woman in her sixties who dressed like a woman in her forties and spoke like a woman in her twenties. Her small, freckled hands held a broom tightly between thick, round palms and stubby fingers as she swept the plank floors. Her hair was a platinum blonde, two shades from being white, courtesy of the Pontotoc Drug and Sundries. She wore it in a great sweeping tornado, though when she worked, a stray silvery blonde strand would fall, and she had a habit of sweeping it away from her face with the back of her hand. At the corner of her mouth was a Peggy Lee mole, right where she had put it. Her eyes were the color of the Gulf water in Pensacola, a luminous emerald green, especially soft and intense in the direct beam of sunlight. Skin was beginning to hang from the angles of her jaw, and a magenta-red birthmark fanned out across her left cheek like the lingering imprint of a long ago slap. She wore a plaid orange and white dress that was the pale color of sherbet, though she preferred black at night when the inn entertained customers. Her bare feet and calves were as freckled as her face and hands, and there was a roughness about her that came from being raised without the tenderness of a mother, a frankness that put the face value of things as the non-negotiable price.

On one side of the barroom, presumably the Pontotoc County side, was a Coca-Cola cooler with a slide top. Inside was beer, the brown bottles lurking in the cold depths under shiny, spurred caps. On the wall behind the varnished plywood bar, the second hand swept over the glowing face of the *Falstaff* clock. There were two or three bottles of cheap whiskey on a shelf beside it. The head of a deer and the head of a boar were on opposite walls as if conferring over some question together, maybe, *did you just hear a gunshot?* A box fan in a front window rotated like an airplane propeller, throwing a flickering shadow of evening light across the length of the barroom floor. A glass jar of yellow-brown rubbers was placed at the end of the bar with a sign that read *Lollipops, 5 cents,* someone's idea of a joke.

"This here's Sammy Teague. You still lookin' fer a night watchman, ain't ya?" Jude said. "Position ain't been filled, has it?"

"Ha!" she snapped like it was a joke. "Nary an applicant," she said as she leaned the broom against the bar and fished a pair of glasses out of her apron pocket. Her lips pulled on one limb of them, and they opened and she put them on. Sammy came into focus. She smiled and then it diminished.

"You got relations with the law?"

"No ma'am."

"You swear?"

"No ma'am,   I mean, yes ma'am. I swear, no relations with the law."

"He just had his 'pendix out," Jude said pointing to Sammy's midsection, and then he put his stump to his own stomach and said, "A little gimpy."

"All right. All right, then." She paused while she looked him over some more and scratched the dewlap of flesh at the angle of her jaw below the birthmark. "You know what this job entails?"

"No ma'am, not exactly."

"Okay, then, I'll be straight with you, Mr. Teague. We entertain men here, not gentlemen, men. This may not be a fine and fancy Yer-peen brothel, but I keep it clean and deal fair with my customers and my girls."

Opalina Hardy taught her girls the ancient art from an ancient land, from all ancient lands. A gesture to make a man feel cherished: a hand on the side of his chest, just around from his heart. A gesture to make a man feel admired: a hand on his chest, just over his heart. And after all, the men came here as much to feel cherished and admired as to be laid, though the men themselves were unaware of their need for those two things.

There were things that were not permissible: no violence, no bondage, and no threesomes. A prophylactic was to be worn at all times. All men would be inspected by their girl before services were rendered. A rash, a bump or anything else out of the ordinary would result in the return of the patron's money without a transaction taking place. In the event of a dispute, Miss Hardy and her Colt revolver would be the final arbiter.

"So here's the deal," she continued. "I give you a place to stay up in that shack on the ridge." Her head tilted toward wherever it was. "You keep an eye on the road comin' and goin' and if need be, give the signal. Here, I'll show ya."

They went out a side door that slapped behind them. Trash was burning in a barrel in the yard by a picnic table. Sheba whined and strained at her tether, her tail wagging low as her ears pulled back and her mouth opened wide in a sigh like the squeal of an air brake. They followed a trail up onto a ridge where a shed blended in like a purple and gray chameleon. Sheba barked at them from below as they ascended the hill. Chickens chuckled quietly in a coop at the back edge of the clearing.

Pine straw was piled in copper drifts against the side of the shed. The vertical boards of the shed were gray, though a couple of them were black from impending rot. Inside a wheezing door, there was a wood plank floor that Sammy judged to be dry and solid. A frame single bed was against a wall with a moldy cotton ticked mattress supported by a lattice of ropes.

"Better'n your car, ain't it?" Jude said cheerfully.

"Hmmp," Sammy snorted and raised his eyebrows. Even the Teague duck camp down in the marsh in Cocodrie was nicer than this, ten times nicer. The camp on stilts in the field of yellow marsh grass where the man got up in the dark to make you breakfast and the smell of the coffee woke you up, and then another man paddled you out to your duck blind. And then midmorning he paddled you back to the camp and cleaned your ducks or your fish and your gun. Meanwhile you listened to your grandpappy's stories of how the rest of the world wanted to take away what you had worked so hard for, oft told stories that invariably preceded his cocktail and his nap.

Was it still there in the marsh after the storm? Sammy thought.

Miss Opalina said, "Last feller we had watchin' turned out to like to go with men, run off to Memphis with another feller that was thataway. You ain't like that, now are you?"

"No ma'am."

"If you were, it'd not be my binness. Keep you away from the girls, I guess." She clucked out a wry chuckle.

"You's to stay up here, keep a lookout down that way," she turned to the other direction, "and that way. You see somethin with lights atop it, you pull this cord here."

A black cord ricocheted off pine trees, running over nails sunk into their trunks, down the hillside to the roadhouse. Opalina's stubby pink freckled hand snatched the cord and yanked. Back down the hill at the Inn, a bell tinkled. Sheba barked.

"Can't have no smoking or nothin' up here to give away that you's up here. No lights. Gotta be dark. Dark as a tomb, hear?"

"Yes ma'am," Sammy said.

"I'll give ya sheets and quilts 'n such fer the bed, and a meal before the start of the evening. We start at sundown ever day except Sunday."

Sammy was relieved to have Sunday off. It would give him a chance to look for Betsy. Then Opalina Hardy added one more thing.

"On Sunday we start bout two. The after church crowd."

The women arrived first, driven in from somewhere and dropped off. They were a nondescript bunch, not pretty, not ugly, not fat, not thin. They disappeared inside where they sat on barstools and lounged around the pool table as the purple light hummed in the bar. After a while, they fetched water in basins and carried them to the rooms outback with cheap linen towels draped over their forearms.

And then as the cold evening air nestled in on the County Line Inn, the men came. They came in their pulpwood trucks and pickups with their bellies full of the supper their wives had prepared, the supper they had blessed together with bowed heads and they had eaten with their families. They had slipped out afterward on the pretense of some errand, or with no excuse at all. Some of the wives knew where they were going and were glad to be relieved of their conjugal duty. The rest pretended not to know.

157

From inside, the jukebox played George Jones and Hank Williams. Harsh voices and coarse laughter rumbled off the walls and out the windows, windows that were darkened by monstrous shadows. Iridescent blue light oozed around them. One by one the men paired with the women, who led them by the hand down the long common porch of the line of rooms in the back of the County Line Inn, rooms that were numbered one through six. The couples disappeared into them, and soon the sounds of exaggerated passion erupted to crescendos. Then the doors opened, one and then the other and then the next, the visits varying very little in time. The women smoked, their cigarettes glowing orange like fireflies, intensifying and fading. The men staggered to their vehicles under a mantle of relief, refreshment, and self-disgust. The women finished their smoke, then flicked their cigarettes away and went back to the inn. Sammy sat outside his shack on the ridge and saw it all.

At the end of the night, when the last customer pulled out, one of the women ascended the hill to the shack. Sammy saw the shape of her dress glow in the moonlit darkness, a white shift with small pink flowers. She knocked on his door.

"Miss Hardy sent me up here to see 'bout you," she said. The girl was barely a woman.

Sammy said, "I'm all right."

"Sit down yonder on yer bed," she said.

Dumbfounded and still not fully understanding, he sat down. She sat down next to him and started kissing his neck and rubbing her hands on his chest. She smelled like lye soap scented with gardenias. He winced when her hand slid over his stomach and his scar.

"Sorry," she grinned into his ear. "I fergot." Her hand slid down further, and she palmed him, but her caresses failed. She got down on her knees before him and lifted up his shirt, kissing gingerly around his scar.

"No," he said. "You don't have to. You're very pretty," he said, though he hadn't really taken a good look at her, "But you really don't have to."

"You ain't queer like our last feller are you?" she asked. She kissed his stomach one last time and looked up for his answer with a grin.

158

His lip quivered, and he put his face in his hands.

"Hey," she said with her hands on his knees. She brushed her hair back over her ear and sat next to him. "Hey," she said again softly as she put her arm around him. "We don't have to. Miss Hardy just thought you might like some."

He leaned his side into her, sobbing. She put her arms around him and shushed him tenderly and whispered.

"It's all right. There, now, it's all right. All right, all right."

She helped him into the rickety bed, and pulled the bare covers and the tattered quilt over him. She left for a few minutes, the pale cloud of her dress floating down to the inn for a moment and then floating back up with the smell of something to eat, soup maybe. She left it on the nightstand, an overturned crate, and kissed him on his forehead and left again. Her dress luminesced in the moonlight, where she approached the headlights of a pickup, her ride home. The door slammed in the night, and Sammy heard it make the highway and fade off into the night.

Chapter 39

Betsy walked down the hall of the hospital, a corridor filled with the sounds of carts with squeaking wheels and the purposeful questions of nurses. A bulletin board was decorated with cut out pilgrims and Indians, their paper images stapled to it within an orange, red, and brown border, and a smiling, unsuspecting turkey between them.

The young man in room 328 had just been discharged and wheeled out, given over to a group of black and white pine-scented men. A housekeeper was stripping the bed and putting the sheets in a rolling hamper. She hummed a gospel song low and sweet as she tucked in the new clean sheets over the plastic mattress.

Betsy found Tina in the dayroom. The bruises on Tina's face were yellowing, though her eyes were still swollen to the point that she couldn't see well. She was sitting in a wheelchair and listening to a woman read aloud to her. The woman was older, a retired English teacher admitted to the hospital for a stomach ailment that she was reluctant to talk about. She was of such an era that asked that a lady not discuss such things. She was a tall woman with a helmet of brown hair, a dyed shade of brown that did not occur in nature. Tina sat in a chair across from her as the woman held a book, Faulkner's *As I Lay Dying,* just in front of her face to accommodate her aging vision.

Betsy put her hand on Tina's shoulder, and Tina put hers on it. She looked up and strained to see through the slits in her eyes. And then she kissed Betsy's hand and put it to her cheek. Betsy knelt down, and Tina leaned over in her wheelchair and grabbed on to her. She kissed Betsy on her cheek, and Betsy heard Tina sniffle, all the crying Tina could do now after almost a week of it.

"We can stop here, if you like," the woman said.

"No, no, keep reading if you don't mind, if you're not too tired," Tina murmured.

"Oh, my dear, I could read all day. It makes me feel like I'm a young mother again and my children are little. Pull up a chair," she said to Betsy.

Betsy pulled over a chair, an old donated armchair in blue toile with trees and birds and frayed piping. She helped Tina up, and they both sat down into it, embraced by it. They snuggled tightly, side by side, their heads next to each other.

The old English teacher read to them, animated and looking up from the book to recite the lines of the characters as if she was reading for a play. A light, cold rain fell and streaked the windows outside, and the dank scenery was obscured and muted like it was behind frosted glass. The woman's voice lifted and fell and danced through the story, the characters living and breathing. Tina and Betsy sat nestled together like sisters, like small girls being read to.

They listened as the retired teacher read the story of a woman who dies wishing to be buried with her people, and the swollen river, and her survivors who have to contend with it. The girls sat and listened and watched the rain and snuggled close, and Betsy ran her fingers through Tina's hair. And the rain-streaked windows shielded them from a cold world.

Finally, the teacher reached the end of a chapter and said, "I never thought I'd say this, and my late husband *certainly* never thought I'd say this, but my voice is about exhausted." She smiled and slipped a bookmark almost in the middle of the book. She stood up and pulled her housecoat around herself and nosed her bunion-gnarled feet into her house shoes.

"I do so hope you both finish Mr. Faulkner's lovely book." She showed them the title again and slipped it into one of the large pockets of her housecoat before easing down the hallway. Her slippers scratched down the hallway across the floors that had been buffed to a gloss.

The rain picked up outside and became audible, a light, pleasant patter. An aide brought them two paper cups of tea without them asking, and they sat together, close enough to hear each other's breath blow wrinkles across the honey colored surface of their cups, close enough to hear each other's rippling sips.

"I can see," Tina said finally.

"You can see?"

"They were afraid I wouldn't be able to. But I can see."

"That's good. Is good to see."

Tina smiled and leaned away. Her eyes squinted at Betsy. Tina's face was the color of a beautiful sunset. Her smile faded, and she said evenly, "Mary Nell and Loretta are dead." It was the first time Tina could say it without crying.

"I know."

The rain rattled on the glass and rode down the surface of it in streaks.

"I was pregnant. Now I'm not."

"I know that, too."

They joined hands and watched the rain. Outside, gray puddles were forming here and there.

"Mama and daddy are comin' up from Laurel to bring me home. It'll probably be the spring before I come back. If I come back."

Betsy pulled Tina to her and stroked Tina's blonde hair. It was no longer silky, and needed to be washed. Betsy kissed the top of Tina's head and kept stroking her hair.

An aide woke them. It was dark outside, and the light in the dayroom was artificially bright, a powerful, sharp light. In the window reflection, two girls, one dark haired and one light haired looked back with sleepy faces. The aide in the window leaned over the girls and whispered to the dark haired one.

"Visitin' hours is over, now. You gone have to head on, baby. "

They helped Tina out of the armchair. The aide pulled over the wheelchair and locked the wheels.

"I believe I can make it on my own now," Tina said.

"Awright, den," the aide said. "Jess let us hepya."

Tina walked down the glossy floor between the aid and Betsy, her hands held by a soft brown hand and a rough white hand. They eased her into bed and pulled the sheets up and over her chest. The aide glanced at all the stuffed animals and potted plants in Tina's room. It looked like a toy truck had collided with a florist delivery van.

"You gone go home fo' too long," the aide said as she pulled up the covers. "What you gonna do wit all dese plants 'n stuffed animals?"

"The stuffed animals, take what you want and give them to your grandchildren. Save the rest for children who have to come into the hospital, and the plants, give to all the old people, especially the ones who don't have many visitors. Save the ginger lily, though, I like how it smells."

"Awright, den. Jess a few mo minutes, now," the aide said, and she left the room.

Betsy leaned in and hugged Tina one more time, and Tina told her the thing that one Kappa told another as an expression of admiration.

"When I grow up, I wanna be just like you."

Betsy smiled and kissed Tina's forehead, yellowed and bruised-brown, and turned and left.

It would be years before they saw each other again.

Chapter 40

The grass was still green and growing, but at a slower pace now. A black man in a blue shirt with his name over the pocket mowed the grass of the Circle with a big wheeled mower. Brittle brown leaves disappeared under the red metal deck and were ejected as coarse brown mulch into the air that was aromatic and green with the scent of cut grass and exhaust. Small engines chugged in every corner as the campus was put to bed for a long winter nap.

Professor Tom Euless sat on a bench and watched the man finish up. Euless held a green glass 7Up bottle in his right hand like a scepter. In the paper bag beside him was a Mason jar, a reservoir of Senatobia's finest. He sat on the park bench in white seersucker even though it was well after Labor Day, and the rest of the town's men had put theirs away and taken on darker colors. It was still reasonably clean, even though it was what he had woken up in. He sat and peered over his red avocado nose, contemplating the battle of Shiloh and wishing Beauregard had pressed his advantage after the first day instead of holding up for the night. Leaves continued to parachute to the ground on the freshly mowed grass of the Circle. He took a sip from his scepter.

A man in khaki suddenly appeared on the other end of the bench, and it startled Euless. The man was a sheriff, but the patch on his shoulder was an odd shape, not the shape of Lafayette County or any other shape he had seen before. Euless warily shifted the paper bag of liquor from one side to the other. The sheriff was quiet, and it made Euless nervous. Policemen never sat on this bench; they only told him to wake up and get off it and go home.

The sheriff struck a match and cupped his hands over the cigarette in his mouth. He shook the match out and threw it on the ground. Euless looked at it and felt like his temple had been defiled. The smoke of the Lucky Strike wafted in the air as the sheriff looked at Euless and said nothing. The blue-eyed stare made the professor slump a little more.

"How's the football team doin'?" Parris asked as he looked around. His jaw worked as his tongue tried to pry a piece of food from between his back teeth.

"How's that?" Euless asked.

"The football team, Ole Miss Rebels? Hoddy-toddy, all that, how they doin'?"

"Oh, I don't really keep up with all that," Euless said. *Just a bunch of Neanderthals, no more interested in scholarly endeavor than a housecat*, he thought to himself. The mowers puttered

163

somewhere else on campus. Then Euless felt badly for refusing the overture for a conversation and decided to strike one up of his own.

"Well, it's finished."

"What's finished?"

"The arch. In St. Louis. They finished it."

Parris' eyes were still, vacant, and blue.

"The Gateway Arch. Gateway to the West," Euless said as if everyone's daily schedule had been hinging on it.

Parris answered by raising his eyebrows. Euless took this as interest.

"Can't go up in it, yet, but they say you will, in time."

"Wasn't plannin' on it," Parris said.

"Priest and a rabbi prayed over the capstone." Euless held his hands up like he was warming them over a fire.

Parris grunted.

Euless presented his hand to Parris. "Professor Tom Euless, Southern History."

Parris looked at the hand like it was a squirrel. He moved not an inch, sitting with one leg crossed over another. Euless slowly withdrew his hand.

"Perfessor, is it? Say, you ever have a student name a Sammy Teague?"

"You're the second person to ask me that."

"That so? Who was the first?"

"This pretty young woman."

"Saw her down here?"

"Why yes, this very bench."

"How long ago?"

"Oh, I can't remember. Can't judge time like I used to."

Parris disappeared for a moment and then reappeared with a bottle of Johnny Walker. He handed it to Euless. Euless was rendered speechless, a small feat, and held the bottle like one would hold a newborn baby. He immediately brought the 7Up bottle to his lips and drained it of the remaining clear liquid from the Senatobia brothers. Then he opened the Johnny Walker and poured some into the green glass bottle. As an afterthought, he offered some to Parris, but the deputy smiled and held up a hand.

"You remember now?" Parris smiled at Euless like he was a dear friend.

The professor still couldn't remember, but he made up a number out of gratitude.

"Oh, about two weeks, I guess."

"That right? Say where she was stayin'?" Parris re-crossed his legs and put his arm on the back of the bench between them.

"No, I'm sure she didn't say," Euless said, and he took a swig from the green bottle.

"I see," Parris said. He watched a mockingbird harass a squirrel. White stripes on gray wings fluttered around the squirrel until the animal found shelter under the limbs of an azalea bush. The bird withdrew, coasting through the air in a series of sweeping arcs. There was quiet for a while as Euless nursed from the green glass teat.

"Looka here, Perfessor," Parris said. "Which a these buildings is the Agger-culture 'n Economics buildin'?"

Euless pointed with the bottle through the Circle. "Brevard Hall, that brown brick building with the columns right there." He poured a little Johnny Walker into the 7UP bottle and was about to give a discourse on the Democratic Party and the Solid South. He looked up from capping the whiskey bottle, and the bench was empty. Only the smoke of the Lucky Strike was left hanging in the air.

Chapter 41

Plunk.

Thunder and lightning had boomed and flashed all morning, and then the rain, cold and dense, had fallen all afternoon. The hole in the roof had sent a pattering trickle into the bucket. Now just an hour or two before sunset, the rain had moved on, east and south to Tuscaloosa and Meridian. The leak in the roof elongated into fat clear drops that cleaved away and fell into the bucket. Sammy sat watching it. Just a little more and the bucket would need to be emptied.

Plunk.

He lay on the bed in his shack, fighting the urge to light up a cigarette. Instead he looked at his stomach and the scar that stretched up and sidestepped his navel. He used to take such pride in his midsection, toned and tanned in the summer, a grand excuse to go shirtless.

Plunk.

There was a knock on the door of his shack, the hard double knock that was familiar now.

"Come in, Jude," Sammy said to the door.

"How'd you know it was me?" He didn't wait for an answer, instead scanning the shack. "Love what you've done with the place. Nice slop jar."

"Oh, my mama would've called that an accent piece," Sammy said, getting up. It was getting easier. He picked up the Mason jar with golden urine in it. "I was waiting on the rain to slack up to empty this." He opened the door and threw its contents out onto the carpet of pine straw and replaced it on the overturned crate by his bed.

"What's new at the mill?"

"Same old. Makin' little ones outta big ones. Sheriff came by today."

"Lafayette County or Pontotoc?"

"Neither. Saint...." Jude squinted and scratched his head for the answer.

"Saint Matthew?" Sammy asked as his faint smile faded completely.

"Yeah. That's right. Saint Matthew."

"Let me guess. Square head? Big lower jaw? Red hair?"

"That's him. Somebody you know?"

"I'm afraid so. What did he want?"

"He came to talk to you, brother."

"Me, huh?" Sammy said as he opened the belly of the stove. The fire was dying down, and it was too close to nightfall to rekindle it. "What about?"

"Somethin' about you ain't turned in for the draft."

"The draft?" Sammy eased back from the stove and sat down on his bed.

"You know. US Army, Vietnam. That draft."

"So what happened?"

166

"Well, cruiser pulls up, sheriff gets out. Finley comes out on the porch and says 'help you?' They get to talkin'. And pretty soon they look like they's gonna get into it. Tillie rang the bell, and then we all stopped what we was doin' and gathered around and then Finley says, 'He ain't here so I suggest you get the hell on your way, deppity.' I swear I think he'd a shot ol' Finley if we hadn't been there."

There was a pause and a plunk. "So then?" Sammy asked.

"Fella left. Pulled onto the highway back towards Oxford."

"Did Finley tell him where I was?"

"I don't believe he did."

They sat in silence. Sammy put his top lip in his lower lip and his hand on his forehead as he thought. The leak plunked one last time in the bucket. Outside, a gust of wind blew rain out of the trees, and it pattered on the roof. Finally Jude spoke.

"Brother, I don't care whether you go to Vietnam or not. They sure ain't takin' me." He waved his stump in a small circle. "If you ain't got a mind to go, then don't."

"It's not that I don't want to go. Maybe I oughta go. It's just that I haven't thought about it. I've been in school until now."

Jude got up and picked up the tin rain bucket with his hand and put it in the crook of his stump. He opened the door and emptied the bucket outside, and then brought it back in again.

Sammy got up and shut the door after Jude came inside. "That deputy doesn't want me to just go to Vietnam. He wants me to go to Vietnam and not come back."

Jude turned the bucket upside down and sat on it. "Why's that?"

"Our families back home have been at odds for years. If I'm out of the picture, he has a better chance of taking our place." It felt odd to refer to Mount Teague as 'our place,' after what had happened between Sammy and his parents. "His jealousy is no secret back home. Once he ran me off the road, I saw his face, I'm sure it wasn't an accident. Barely missed a big live oak."

"Well, Finley sent him on his way, but I don't expect he's gone fer good."

A drop of rain cleaved from the hole in the roof and hit the floor.

Chapter 42

It was November, and weeks of searching had turned up no sign of Betsy. The days were getting shorter, the sun collapsing in the western sky like a marathon runner at the finish line.

They sat together on the bank of the Tallahatchie. Jude deftly cracked peanuts in his one hand, emptied them in his mouth, and then threw the shells into the river where the current bore them away.

Sammy didn't trust the brown water with the scar from his surgery, and besides, it was too cold to bathe in the river. He had taken to bathing in a washtub in the storeroom at the County Line Inn. Some of the girls would take turns watching him through a tiny hole in the wall and giggle and whisper to each other, "Miss Opalina's new watchman is a mighty purty feller. Too bad he's *thataway*."

Sammy and Jude's shadows stretched across the river and landed on the opposite bank. Sammy was frustrated with not working and not finding Betsy. Hope was slipping way elsewhere, following the current to a sea somewhere while the world wobbled on its axis. It was regular and predictable, but it was still a wobble.

"What did Finley say, when you told him?"

"He said just to know what you're gettin' into," Jude said. "And that if you knew what you were gettin' into, you wouldn't go."

Jude flicked the shells in, his middle finger launching them off his thumb. They floated through the air in an arc, landing lightly on the surface and barely making a single circular ripple that quickly dissipated as the current moved.

"Why do you stay around here, anyway?" Jude asked, emptying a peanut shell into his mouth and then throwing the rest in the river. He chewed and brushed his fingers rapidly on his pants leg. "You plannin' to go back to school in the spring?"

That was a good question, and Sammy pondered it. Perhaps it was the right thing to do, to enlist. The men of the Teague family had a long history with the military, for as far back as oral tradition held. He had seen them in uniform, in old daguerreotypes and yellowed pictures with the edges tattered, and in his mind from family stories.

John Malcolm Teague was a man who seemed to have coalesced from nothing out of the Appalachian wilderness. He claimed to be a veteran of the Seminole Wars and scraped together a modest living trading horses, making quick money and then drifting westward until he arrived in newly formed Tunica County, Mississippi. He was smitten with the daughter of a planter named Tunstall, and in wooing Miss Tunstall, John Teague concealed his illiteracy with bluster and charm. It was more than enough, and her father consented to the union. John Teague proved that you could marry more money in five minutes than you could make in a lifetime.

Sam was born in 1838, the year that the xenophobic and anti-Catholic painter and inventor Samuel Morse first demonstrated the telegraph, and the year that the Cherokee were removed from their lands in the east and put on the Trail of Tears. At sixteen, his father sent him to Oxford to get an education and become the gentleman farmer that a lack of education had kept him from being.

On a trip to New Orleans between terms, young Sam Teague saw a Notice of Sale for a plantation in St. Matthew Parish, Louisiana. The family that had owned it had been eradicated over the space of two weeks by yellow fever. He borrowed money from his father and bought it, and never returned to school. Irrigated with the sweat of other men and the mules they whipped, the place flourished.

Then, in the midst of prosperity, civil war broke out. Sam Teague joined the Home Guard, a unit that patrolled St. Matthew Parish and the surrounding areas in charge of rounding up deserters, shirkers, scrawny stray chickens and fat hogs. When he came back, though he never really went far, he bought the neighboring plantation, Hollyfield, from the estate of a man who went to fight in Virginia with his sons. None of them had come back, which left his widow and her daughters suddenly and profoundly destitute. It was easy pickings. Grandpappy liked to quote his father, Sam Sr.: When the cards are shuffled and cut, and the hands are dealt, some lucky bastards get the face cards, and the other poor bastards don't.

Sam Teague, Sr. went through three wives who bore him five daughters before the fourth wife bore him a son, Sam Teague, Jr. That was Grandpappy, born in 1881 on the day that President Garfield was shot by the office seeker Charles Guiteau.

"What an auspicious day!" Sam Sr. exclaimed. "The world purges itself of a Yankee and replenishes itself with a southern gentleman!" In the downstairs parlor there were Havana cigars and glasses of port all around while upstairs his young wife recuperated, having been bled almost as pale as President Garfield by her ordeal.

Junior grew into the shoes of his father. In 1898, the *Maine* sank in Havana harbor, and the newspapers said it was the Spanish who had done it. The country was eager to believe it, and the populace was in an uproar. Even though he had just turned seventeen, Grandpappy persuaded his father to let him join up. His mother, who looked more like Sam Sr.'s daughter than his wife, waved Junior off at the train station in Thibodaux as he waved back from the railcar that bristled with the eager heads of all the other young soldiers. He got as far as Tampa before the whole thing in Cuba was settled. He spent two months drinking rum, smoking Ybor cigars, and paying for the company of the Five Dollar Girls in the Sporting District. Nevertheless, he came home strutting like a hero. The following fall, he went off to college in Oxford like his father had done.

In 1910, Samuel Teague, III, Trey, was born to Junior's wife, a taciturn young lady from Bolivar County with pasty skin and sunken eyes, whose parents had sent her to study in Oxford for the purpose of meeting and marrying someone exactly like Junior Teague.

Trey Teague left for Oxford in a seersucker suit, wingtip shoes, and a boater hat. At the train depot in Hattiesburg he met beautiful young Mamie Collingsworth, who was also on her way to study at Ole Miss. In 1933, Trey Teague came home from Oxford with a fresh degree and a young bride to find that Mount Teague had doubled in size with the acquisition of Verona, the old Parris place. Mount Teague absorbed the blows of the Depression, shaking them off with sheer size. When the Second World War began, the army decided Samuel Teague, III with his degree in Agriculture & Economics would be best utilized in the Office of the Quartermaster in Washington. He and his lovely young wife Mamie, *née Collingsworth,* from Ewell County, moved to the capital, where Sammy's sisters were born. Trey had captain's bars and a position in an office at the War Department where telephones rang and typewriters clacked all day. At night there were parties with men in dress uniform, and women in long dresses and evening length gloves.

Whether it was the Confederate States of America or the United States of America, the Teague men always did their bit, or at least gave the appearance of doing it. The fighting and bleeding and dying were invariably left to others.

Sammy watched his shadow stretch across the Tallahatchie, long and narrow, a different angle than the week before and the week before that. Back at his shack on the ridge above the County Line Inn, the sun was setting further south on the horizon every day. It had nestled in behind the tall pine, and then the next sunset had moved incrementally to the left of it. It was beginning to encroach on the big red oak, which was dropping her leaves a little more with each flurry of autumn wind, shaking and swaying and teasing like a burlesque dancer shedding clothes.

Sammy sat and examined the cold, bitter facts. He had no picture of Betsy and was beginning to forget what she looked like, his memory straining to latch onto some small detail, a facial feature, a gesture, something. He only remembered how she felt against his skin, her voice, her scent. These things were indelible and would be remembered forever.

Futility had finally overtaken Hope. The search for her was returning empty every time; she may well have gone back to Louisiana. His name had been put on the long roll of those who had been seduced and then betrayed by intense longing, and now action was needed, any action. He stood up and brushed sand from his backside. Jude flicked a shell and looked up at him.

"Will you go down there with me?" Sammy asked him.

"Where?"

"The recruiting station in Oxford."

"Sure," Jude said.

*   *   *

The grandfather clock in the parlor ticked patiently and obstinately. The television was just a convex gray glass, soundless and pictureless as the girls studied around it. No one wanted canned laughter or implausible plotlines or bass-noted drama. Drama had unfolded itself unannounced from two dimensions into three, from

171

black and white to living color, right there in the Kappa house. And then death had visited them in living color. No one wanted any more drama, not even two dimensional or black and white. All any of them wanted was each other's silent company. No one said anything.

The semester was well into its second half, and the girls were quiet and focused for that reason as well. Sylvia tapped the eraser end of her pencil on her Trigonometry book as she stared into it, either baffled or bored. She was prone on the floor, her legs in an A except when the top of one foot moved over to rub the back of the opposite calf. Frances, the ugly duckling who had become a beautiful swan of a girl, slumped down on the couch with a handful of loose leaf paper notes at arm's length between her face and the ceiling. She looked up at them as if she were waiting for the contents of the notes to fall into her. Another girl played with her gum, stretching it out with her thumb and forefinger like the pod of an amoeba before chewing it up again and popping a small bubble with a clack. Another girl twirled a small lock of her hair around and around with her finger. They were all in their usual study poses, all trying to buckle down for the homestretch.

Betsy folded clothes quietly. She kept fishing in the basket, hoping she would come across something of Tina's. A couple of times she had, but now the laundry was caught up and every stray piece of Tina's was folded and put in a cardboard box to be shipped to Meridian. Betsy had reverently folded clothes that had belonged to Mary Nell and Loretta and put them in a box, and put the box in the cabinet above the laundry. She didn't want to send them to the girls' grieving parents, but she didn't want to throw them away, either. Slowly she had come across them and then there were just a few, and now Betsy was pretty sure she had gotten all of them. She continued folding as the girls around her studied. And the clock tapped, placid and indifferent.

The front door opened, and the girls all jerked their heads and recoiled at the prospect of some other sudden, unfortunate news, but it was just Glenda, the dark haired girl with the Italian mother. She set her notebook on the foyer table and on it a textbook, *Three Hundred Years of Southern History,* by Thomas J. Euless, PhD.

Glenda took off her pink cashmere sweater and put it on her books.

172

"You will never guess who I saw at the enlistment office. Not in a million years. Remember that boy that Tina was dating before Freddy? Sammy Teague?"

"Yeah, that real handsome one?"

"Yeah, him. Well, I was going by the recruiting station and I saw him. His hair was long and he had a beard, but it was him, same gray eyes. Isn't that ironic? Tina looked for him all semester."

"What was he doing in the recruiting station?" one of the girls asked.

"What does anyone do in the recruiting station? Joining the army, silly."

Betsy felt the world collapse to a pinpoint, and there was a surging escape of quarantined emotions like a balloon deflating. She began shaking, crying silently for Tina and Mary Nell and Loretta. She cried for the boy with one hand, and she cried for Sammy bleeding in the jungle somewhere, and for the baby floating inside her destined to be fatherless. She shook and cried for everyone who had ever lost anything irreplaceable.

She felt arms around her, many arms and soft heads of hair against her cheek, and then she couldn't cry anymore. She sensed movement, scurrying and purposeful, like the movement of ants on a disturbed mound. The girls felt their pillar of strength had crumbled, and they scrambled around like they were trying to rebuild it. Each felt that if Betsy fell, they would all fall.

Someone rubbed Betsy's shoulders while another brushed her hair. She stared forward, catatonic and helpless under the pressing weight of her tragedy. Nellie, a French major from Biloxi who had cultivated a lithe, refined Parisian accent and a penchant for berets, put on a record by Edith Piaf, the Little Sparrow. It was their comfort music, played every Sunday afternoon after dinner. At first some of the girls mocked it, warbling a falsetto of nasal, nonsense French sounding syllables along to Miss Piaf's plaintive songs, but it had become as much a part of Sunday afternoons as the soft autumn breezes that stirred the curtains as it played and the lingering smell of Betsy's cooking. They would listen to Edith Piaf as they studied, and Betsy would hum along and sing quietly as she cleaned the kitchen. The Little Sparrow's face looked up from the album cover, sad eyed and pained, as if asking the heavens, *why me?*

"La Vie En Rose" played, and Nellie sang along softly as the girls sat around their Bessie, the girl with the accent, a rare and beautiful bird that had appeared as if blown by a storm into their house. The door opened, and a girl came in with a chocolate milkshake from the square. They put the straw in Betsy's lips, and it went from white to brown as she gave a feeble pull.

"Non, Je Ne Regrette Riens" played. They all huddled together around Betsy, by her side and at her feet.

"What does this mean, again?" one of the girls asked quietly.

"It means, *I don't regret nothin'*," Betsy murmured.

Chapter 43

Veterans' Day, which Mr. Finley still called Armistice Day, had already come and gone, and the recruiting station in Oxford had handled the influx of inductees inspired by patriotic fervor. It was quiet again, and the recruiting sergeant sat in a chair behind the desk with his fingers locked over his head, staring at Uncle Sam's pointed finger. He and Uncle Sam contemplated each other as they waited for the end of the fall semester when grades would come out, and underperforming male students would flunk out and be raked off into their bin.

The sergeant's knees pushed out into the knife edge pleats of his khaki pants, and his muscular elbows pushed out from his short sleeve khaki shirt. His dress shoes were polished to a glossy black, the shoelaces tied to even lengths. Outside the window, the sky was lumpy gray from horizon to horizon, as traffic headed down to the square in Oxford in irregular intervals. The sergeant closed his eyes for a minute. His hair was in a crew cut, short black bristles arising from his scalp. The bell on the door dinged, and he opened his eyes.

Two young men came in, a light skinned black man with blonde curls and a white boy with long hair and a beard.

Sammy's head was splitting. Opalina had allowed him the night off to celebrate with Jude and a few of the younger men of the mill. A girl who was expecting a visit from someone named Aunt Flo had stayed on lookout from the shack on the ridge. Sammy and Jude were curious about the kind of aunt that would visit her niece at the whorehouse where she worked. They had kept an eye out for the woman but never got a glimpse of her.

Sammy and Jude and the rest of the men had drunk heavily while Opalina looked after them like a den mother would look over a group of unruly scouts. They drank until the world spun wildly, and strange conversations seemed sensible:

Hey-hey-Jude-you think I oughta get my haircut 'fore I go? –No, Sammy, I believe they'll do it for you, iffen you ask 'em real nice, what you think, Curtis? - Oh, them sumbitches'll give you a haircut, awright, a mighty fine haircut-yeah, you right, Curtis, a-fine-ass-A-number one haircut-hey-Opalina-two-more-wait-three-more-wait-Curtis you want one?-Fuggit-make it four a them whiskey dranks-Gimme a cigarette, man- Hey-hey-hey-turn-this-song-up-this'n is fer my friend-my brother-Sammy-Teague-goin' off to Vietnam, muff-huggin' Viet-fuggin'-Nam-raise-yer-glass-raise-yer got-damn glass I said-here's to lil' white Sambo-Sammy Teague!

Gradually the cigarette smoke had cleared, and the bar had emptied. The girls who had laughed and flirted with them in between patrons were picked up and then there were just men left and then it was just Sammy and Jude. They woke up with their heads on the same table like two Thanksgiving turkeys that had gobbled their all and were waiting for the axe. The ride into Oxford had been a silent one.

When they entered the recruiting office, the sergeant sat up and said, "Good morning. What can I do for you two?"

"Here to join up," Sammy heard his own voice say. His mouth was dry. Nausea was close by, and vomiting was a real possibility.

"Outstanding! Fill this out." The sergeant pushed a form forward with a pen. Sammy looked at the pen as if trying to figure out which end wrote.

"You a student at the university?"

"I was."

"What makes you want to be a warrior?"

"Serve my country."

It sounded like the right answer. Sammy studied the form. His hangover made it seem much more complicated than it was. The sergeant watched Sammy ponder it and then looked up at Jude. Jude stood with his arms behind his back like he was at parade rest.

"How about you, young man? Are you a warrior?"

Jude pulled his handless arm from behind his back.

"Oh," the sergeant said.

On the line that said *person to notify in case of emergency*, Sammy put *Betsy Duplechain* and in the blank that said address, *USA*. He finished the form and laid the pen on it. It rolled off the desk, and he squatted to pick it up. His ears felt as if they would blow out in different directions, and he winced.

"Come in the back with me, soldier," the recruiter said. He and Sammy went down a hallway and into a back room.

When they were gone, Jude imitated the poster on the wall, narrowing his eyes at Uncle Sam and pointing his stump at him. Then he sat on the green imitation leather couch and looked at brochures with all the wonderful opportunities a career in the service could offer a young man, almost like a travel agency. The faces of the soldiers in the laminated pictures were upturned and admiring a flag that fluttered and waved in a still-life of patriotism.

Then he watched the traffic go by. The stoplight turned red, and a police car stopped in front of the recruiting station to wait on it. In the glass, Jude saw the reflection of the odd shape on the door. Then he looked at the driver, the square head and the wavy red hair. The man's finger probed a nostril, pulling the tip of his nose forward. The light changed, and the cruiser moved through the light.

"Sorry, son, come back later, you hear?" Jude heard the voice coming from the back room. Sammy and the sergeant emerged from the back room. Sammy moved to the door and pressed on the handle. Jude followed him onto the cold sidewalk. It hadn't warmed a degree.

"Well, what happened?" Jude asked as he lit a cigarette. He exhaled and shook out the match.

"Well, I took a test, real simple, about presidents and the branches of government, and some math and then they had me fill out a health questionnaire. The sergeant looked it over and said I'll never pass the physical so soon after an operation like that, and to come back when the doctor clears me."

"What now?" Jude asked.

Sammy turned the key, and the Mustang cranked.

"Back to Opalina's I guess."

Chapter 44

It had been a long week at the Kappa house. Mary Nell's parents had come up from Natchez to clean out her room, and the next day Loretta's had come up from Hattiesburg to get her things. Betsy had helped each couple, standing by patiently as each set of parents had paused to endure a breakdown together, each mother crying and each red-faced, red-eyed father rubbing his wife's shoulder in an almost identical fashion, each pausing at the door with a cardboard box of now unneeded belongings and each taking one last look into the room before turning and leaving.

The day awoke frosty and bright and took its time in warming up. Betsy had gone down to the Jitney Jungle to get the ingredients for a cake for the girls, a special treat for the trauma they had endured, and now the comparatively inconsequential trauma of midterms. She had used her own money; she wanted it to be from her personally.

The autumn morning sun was shining, and Betsy's spirits were trying to shine with it. The air was clean and cool, and she was looking forward to filling the house with the rich, warm smell of a cake baking. She wore a sage green dress with three quarter length sleeves and a pair of old black flats of Tina's that once were a size too big and now with her advancing state were almost a size too small. She carried a paper sack with the red *JJ* on it.

She crossed the courthouse square past the Confederate soldier perched atop the granite obelisk. As the weeks had passed, people were beginning to recognize her, and she waved and smiled back at them. Under the red and white vertical striped awning outside of Neilson's, an old man with a big barrel gut and a panama hat again called to her like he always did, 'Hey, Miss Pretty,' and she pursed her lips and blushed at the compliment like she always did.

In the glass of a shop window, she saw a police cruiser and a shape she recognized at once, the irregularly irregular shape of St. Matthew Parish, a shape with not one straight line to it. She froze. The reflection stopped, and the driver said in a familiar voice, "Excuse me, miss."

Her heart was pounding as she stood completely still like a frightened animal. She lifted the paper bag of groceries unnaturally high to conceal her face and slunk down the row of shops, pretending she didn't hear him. The reflection followed her in the windows, appearing in each successive one.

At the end of the line of stores, she ducked down an alley and began running, the butter and eggs and flour and cocoa jostling together in the bag, her flats slapping on the pavement. Her tall, thin shadow and then she herself ran past a black man who was sweeping behind a shop. The black man turned and saw the sheriff's car following her, no lights, just following her.

She turned onto South Eleventh Street and then onto Tyler. At the Presbyterian Church on South Tenth Street, she paused to take off her flats, hopping on one foot and then on the other in her haste to get them off and get running again. She held them in her free hand and took off down the hill toward South Ninth Street, her breasts shaking under her dress with each lunging stride, air rushing in and out across her lips, the brown paper shopping bag rattling. She looked over her shoulder, and the cruiser was still there. At the end of Tyler there was a vacant lot and her feet dug into the dirt of it and she ignored the sting of the stickers in the grass. Her feet threw out flecks of morning dew. Across the lot was the old depot and past that, the train tracks. She heard the grind and squeal of the wheels of an approaching train and the throaty puff of its engine. She scrambled up through the large chunks of blue-gray gravel, the soles of her feet feeling the rocky coolness and then the cold smoothness of the twin silver rails and then the rocks again. She realized she had dropped one of her shoes between the rails and turned to get it. The engine scolded her with a blast of its horn, and she left it. She turned; up ahead were Sorority Row and the Kappa House. The train rumbled closely at her back.

She scrambled across the backyard and into the back door. Her chest heaved and her hands shook as she sorted through the contents of the paper bag. She opened the cardboard carton of eggs, and her shoulders slumped. They were all broken.

She threw them away, put the rest of the ingredients in the pantry, and went upstairs holding a single shoe. Her door closed in defeat.

A little later, there was a knock on the door downstairs. One of the girls opened it, and there was a sheriff's deputy. The girl put her hand over her mouth, expecting more bad news.

"Good aftanoon, ma'am," Parris said as he touched the brim of his cowboy hat.

"Please say there's nothing wrong, is there, officer?" the girl lowered her hand and asked.

"Oh, no, no, no. Just need your help lookin' for somebody. That's all, no need for alarm."

"Oh, thank goodness," the girl exhaled. "We've had an awful month around here."

"Well, I'm so very sorry to hear that," Parris gushed.

Relief spread through the parlor and another girl, an upper classman, said, "Girls aren't we forgetting something?"

About five of the girls, all pledges, stood up and cheered together, "Hey-hey-ho-hi-gotta say it's great! *Clap!* To be a Kappa Chi!"

Parris pretended the clap startled him, and he quickly drew his revolver like a gunfighter. The girls squealed, the mirth in their eyes suddenly replaced by subdued terror. A couple of them started upstairs before he laughed. But he kept the revolver drawn; he was enamored with the authority and the sheer power the thing brought. He relished the look of fear and helplessness that it put on the face of the person on the other end of it, and he was enjoying it now.

"Look here, ladies, I'm looking for a girl name a Betsy, Betsy Duplechain." He talked with the gun as if it were a conductor's baton.

The girls looked confused.

"There's a lady named Bessie," one of them said sheepishly, trying to be helpful.

"Talk funny, got an accent?" Parris said amiably.

"Yeah, that's her," another girl nodded so hard that her ponytail shook.

Betsy appeared on the landing. Her eyes were cold and unblinking, but her knees felt weak.

"Can I help you, sir?" she said flatly.

"Well, Miss Duplechain, good aftanoon." Parris took his hat off with his free hand and put it back on again.

179

"I'm lookin' for somebody, I don't believe I need to tell you who, now do I?"

"I ain' seen 'im." She shook her head no in small movements. Her jaw was set.

He canted his head and smiled. "You can go to hell for lyin', now."

"Das for true, I ain't seen him, *depty*," she said the word like it would slime her lips.

"Hell you ain't," Parris said. He raised the revolver, the girls cringed, and then Parris simply used it to gesture with.

"Come down these stairs, *Bessie*, and we'll discuss it."

A couple of the girls cast their glances to the back of the house toward the kitchen, but nobody moved.

Then an older woman's voice came from behind them, from the kitchen, and said, "Excuse me?"

"Miss Pearlina!" one of the girls exclaimed.

All eyes turned to see a woman standing at the door to the kitchen and holding a pump shotgun diagonally across her chest. On her head was a carefully sculpted tornado of hair that was dyed to a black so deep it was blue. It made her fair skin seem porcelain and her green eyes the translucent color of the sea. Her face was as defiant as Betsy's.

"Get upstairs, girls," she said without breaking her stare at Parris. The girls filtered upstairs uneasily, their footsteps drumming on the carpet. Betsy stayed on the landing as the rest of the girls disappeared into their rooms.

"Can I help you deputy?" Miss Pearlina said.

Parris stood motionless, his eyes on the shotgun. His gun hand lowered like a failing erection.

"I just have a little business to conduct here…" he said. She cut him off.

"These girls have seen enough tragedy this semester to last them a lifetime. Let's not add a dead body in their parlor to it."

"You wouldn't," Parris said, his smile fading. "Not in the house with these girls here."

"You don't know that for sure," she said. She pumped a shell into the chamber and added, "But I do."

Parris' eyes widened.

She continued. "My daddy drank. He drank quite a bit. Used to come home late, get all handsy with me and my sister. We lived way out in the country, by ourselves without no mama, y' see, and we thought every family was like that, so we just bore it. It's when he started hittin' us that we figured we were different.

"He worked at a creosote plant, my daddy, when he worked. One Monday morning, he didn't show, and nobody ever saw him again. Just disappeared." She smiled and gave a mock look of wonder at the small miracle of his disappearance.

"See, deputy, I've always kept this shotgun locked up in the pantry for a situation just like that one, and this one. To protect these girls." She leveled the gun at Parris.

"Now, good sir, will you kindly leave, and not come back?"

Parris kept his eyes on Miss Pearlina, trying to nose his revolver back into its holster without looking, and reaching back for the door knob. He eased himself through. Cowboy boots clunked rapidly on the porch, and then the cruiser roared to life outside and silently drifted away.

One of the girls ran down the stairs and locked the door behind him, then closed her eyes and slid down the door to the floor. The rest of the girls came down the stairs and mobbed around Miss Pearlina, hugging her. She smiled and lifted the shotgun out of the way of the hugs. She kissed the tops of the heads nearest to her.

"Now back up to your rooms, girls. I suspect the campus police will need to know about this, and I need to collect my thoughts."

Betsy turned to go into her room.

"Not you," Miss Pearlina said. "You're my fill-in, Bessie, aren't you?"

"Yes ma'am."

"Come with me, Bessie." Betsy came downstairs, and they entered the kitchen. Miss Perlina's suitcases were still on the floor where she had come in the back door.

"The kitchen's even cleaner than when I left it. Laundry's caught up. Girls look well fed, maybe too well fed," she gave a wry smile. "You've done a good job taking care of my girls, and I thank you for it."

She pumped the shells out of the side of the shotgun and into her small freckled hand. Opening the pantry, she set the shotgun back inside and the shells on a shelf above it.

"The last time I unlocked this cabinet was three years ago, when they enrolled Meredith. Shoulda seen the chaos then," she said shaking her head.

She locked the door and dropped the key into her bra next to her tremendous bosom. She sat down at the kitchen table and pulled out a chair for Betsy. Betsy sat down nervously with her knees together and her hands on them.

"That true? What you said about your daddy?"

"Ever word," Miss Pearlina said. Upstairs the girls were talking excitedly, rehashing the experience.

"Did y'all kill 'im?" Betsy asked after a moment of deliberation.

Miss Pearlina looked into Betsy's face and was silent for a time before she smiled and said, "I suppose he musta just ran off, dear," and then she changed the subject.

"Bessie, I think it's best for your safety and the safety of these girls that you leave. My sister has a little tavern out in the country near here. It's not much to look at, but at least it's a place to stay and something to do, and a little money in your pocket. I'll get one of the KA boys to drive you out there."

Miss Pearlina squeezed Betsy's hand and said, "I'm sorry. I would've liked to have gotten to know you better."

Betsy pursed her lips together, looked down and nodded.

"Here're the directions, and a recommendation to sister." Her hand scrawled out the message in looping left-handed script. She handed it to Betsy.

"Ask for Opalina Hardy."

Chapter 45

Mr. Finley sat at his desk. He had just come in from Pontotoc where he had eaten breakfast at the diner and attended to some business at the courthouse. He had belched all the way home and wondered if his breakfast wasn't setting well. It was cold outside, and inside the office the gas space heater glowed blue and orange as it radiated a powerful heat into the office.

He felt a mild pressure in his chest and scratched the graying hair under his shirt, his gaze never leaving the ledger sheet on his desk. The tightness intensified, and he loosened his collar, revealing the boundary of the ruddy redness of his neck and the pale white skin below it. Suddenly he realized that he was sweating and his breath was shortening. His hand fumbled around in the wide desk drawer, his fingers feeling around shakily. They found the envelope and flipped it onto his desk. He took off his straw fedora, his hands still quivering, hesitating as he placed it on the desktop calendar, November 1965. On the space that was the 11[th,] he had written in his tight, jagged handwriting 'forty seven years.'

His scalp sweated under the thick gray hair. He leaned back in his chair and turned his face to the ceiling like a fish in a diminishing puddle of water. His hand flicked at whatever was on his chest; it was as heavy as a log, and he expected his hand to feel scaly bark, but there was only shirt and chest hair. From somewhere, it seemed another log was added, and he closed his eyes.

He saw men with saucers on their heads and behind his heavy closed lids, his eyes focused and then he saw the olive drab and the calves clad in puttees and the rifles. His lips staggered around the words, "The hunnert fifty-fifth. That church. Fraynce." He hadn't thought of the little church in years, not since the nightmares had finally stopped. One of its white walls was collapsed, and an army mule was tethered to the trunk of a branchless tree outside. US was stamped on the mule's flank.

One of the men, Chester Simmons, offered a drink from a canteen.

Why old Chet, Finley said, I ain't seen you since…

…Since my section of the trench caved in, and yours didn't, Chester said laughing. Nosir, I've been a-sleepin' since then.

Chet Simmons laughed like it had been a well played practical joke. Finley laughed because Chet Simmons was laughing.

Finley's mind looked around. Norris Crosby, John Perkins, and say, there's George Evans and Tom Hendry. Each shook his hand and Chester Simmons offered another drink. The liquid in the canteen smelled like liquor this time.

No, Chet, I, I don't drink no more, Finley said.

Well, you can now. Hows bout a drink for old-time-sake, there, Finley?

Well, all right, Finley said. His lips touched the metal rim of the canteen as they all began singing, a chorus of dozens and then hundreds and then thousands of male voices. They sang, "I'm Gonna Hang Out the Washing on the Siegfried Line," and then "Keep Your Head Down, Fritzie Boy."

Sitting on a stump at the edge of the clearing was a tall, thin figure, a familiar frame who rested his forearms on his knees. The eyes of his gas mask were perfectly round and opaque under the metal brim of his helmet. A ribbed hose hung down from the eyes like an elephant trunk to a canvas box strapped to his chest. The figure stood up, and then Finley knew who it was from the man's sheer height.

Whoop Caraway, Finley said to himself. The thin man's real name was Horace, but he looked so much like a whooping crane that the nickname quickly took hold and stuck. He had had a handsome blue eyed face until a shell took it off and replaced it with a mash of blood and protruding bone like a china plate of smashed tomatoes. Finley and Norris Crosby were there when it happened, and had watched air surge in and out of the bloody hole that moments earlier was a mouth. Kneeling beside Caraway, they had prayed for a swift and merciful end. The prayer was answered almost six hours later.

Caraway moved to a muddy lane that wound away from the clearing and out into a pocked gray-brown landscape that looked like a fireless hell that had nothing left to consume. He was like some strange and unknown Egyptian god, the body of a bird, the face of an elephant. He led the mule, whose sides swayed with each step and whose ears lay back behind his black rimmed eyes.

The men followed Caraway singing, and Finley fell in with them, following them as he had those forty, fifty years before. The canteen was passed up and down the line as night fell on the churchyard and the cool, mud-scented air. As he handed the canteen to the man in front on him, Finley saw his own hands. The skin on them was tight and fresh and young and unblemished.

Where we goin'? Finley asked.

Home, someone said. We takin' you home.

Finley's heart rose. It had been so long, he couldn't remember what home looked like. He only knew that he had once had one.

Caraway stopped as the men filed past him, and he turned to Finley. In the big, round opaque glass eyes Finley saw the reflection of a man whose hair was black and full again. He was motioned past by Caraway. Shells whizzed and whined over the horizon that was quickly fading from shades of light blue to midnight blue to black. It pulsed with light that was timed with the explosions.

Night fell on the sawmill, too, though it was only ten o'clock in the morning.

Jude was stacking boards when he looked up to see Tillie there.

"Believe he's dead." She said it without any salutation or preamble. Her expression was as flat as always.

"What?" Jude asked. He stopped and turned, still holding the board in his hand and on his stump.

"He dead in his office."

"Who is?"

"He is."

Jude threw down the board he was holding. It made a hard, rattling slap against the others, and he ran to the office. He knew that the Choctaw were reluctant to utter the names of the dead.

Mr. Finley was reclining back in his chair with his arms dangling at his side. His face was turned to the ceiling and to the sky above it and to heaven above that. There was a trace of a grin on his lips.

On his desk was an envelope, and written on the outside was "To the men of the mill."

Jude opened it.

If you're reading this then it means I've up and died. I was never good at saying it but I hope you men know that you've been one damn fine crew. I appreciate all the hard work you've done to keep this mill afloat and the lights on and money in our pockets all these years. Now that I'm gone I want Archie Wilson running the mill. I know I don't have to say it, but to be sure I don't want no grumbling about the color of Archie's skin. There's not a better man for the job and you all should know it. He can get a hundred extra board feet out of a log better than any man I know. If it's a problem for some of you whites to be working for a colored man then you best get on your way, or else my ghost will come back and scare all the hell out of you in your sleep and make you piss the bed. Ha ha.

You men and Tillie if she chooses can take equal shares in the mill, as I have no heirs.

Mr. Yates is my lawyer down in Pontotoc and he has all the papers ready. So long, good knowing y'all and I hope to see you over there.

Finley

P.S. Take what's left of me and bury me next to mama and daddy in the Mount Olivet Cemetery over in Panola County. Mr. Yates knows the details.

And then added without a postscript:

I done the best I could for you.

Chapter 46

A black and white Alcide Duplechain looked out though the tarnished brass frame. He was wearing a khaki work shirt and pants which were separated by a black belt. In the furrows at his feet were leather boots, and the rounded toes of them were obviously well worn even though it was a black and white photograph. He was bareheaded, his hair slicked back, and above his square jaw a smile beamed back at the camera, though with a certain unease. His hands rested at thigh level, one of them holding a cigarette. Behind him was a dense jungle of sugarcane stalks rising well above his head and sprouting into leafy ends.

Besides the clothes on her back, the picture was the only thing she had from home. After an argument with her mother, half in English, half in French, her mother told her, *"Vivre avec ma loi ou sorte d'ici!"* Live by my rules or get out.

Betsy hastily packed her suitcase. Almost as an afterthought, Betsy had snatched the picture of her daddy from the corner of her mirror and tucked it in her sweater pocket. Then she had shouted to her mother, "You don't know what it's like to love somebody this way, mama!" And then the door slammed, a portrait of the irony of her last words to her mama in her sweater pocket.

The picture had ridden in there with her on that long, lonely night, and when she was finally established in the Kappa house, she found a frame for it. Everything else had been in her valise.

Betsy reverently laid the picture so that it rested on top of her neatly folded clothes in the small overnight case. She had looked through the pictures of long-ago Sammy that Tina had finally put away, and Betsy debated taking one. At last she did, a candid shot of Sammy with the month, May-65, stamped in black in the white margin. Sammy stood with his shirttail out over his jeans and a beer in his hand, leaning against the red Tbird with a smile that suggested that it wasn't the first beer of the day. Certainly Tina wouldn't miss the picture. She may never even come back for it.

Betsy sat on the bed she and Tina had shared and looked at the walls of their room. It had been a safe haven, an island that she had washed up on, and now she was preparing to head back out into a sea of pine and cotton. Colonel Reb and the belligerent Laurel Golden Tornado looked down at her. She rubbed her tears with the back of her hand, got up and latched the overnight case shut. She brushed out her dress to make the wrinkles fall. It was her nicest, a hand-me-down from Tina like almost all of her clothes. She wanted to present her best appearance for her new employer.

Through the closed door sweet sublime voices rose, cooing a song about friendship and memory and sisterhood. It was a song originated in the last century by the daughter of a Civil War veteran, first sung by women now long gone from the campus and the earth, their pictures now on the wall of the Kappa house.

She opened the door to her room and found the lights off in the house, the drapes drawn, and the landing and the downstairs as dark as they could get in the afternoon sun. Girls in white dresses lined the landing and down the stairs, their voices soft and angelic as they sang the song usually reserved for graduating seniors. Suitcase in hand, she walked through them, all of their faces shining with tears in the candlelight. She looked into the face above each candle and paused to remember each name that went with it and a kindness that had passed between them. Some would pause from singing as she neared, and they would wish her well, thank her for her help with French, or tell her that her cooking was the best. All said they would miss her and remember her forever and it was true, they would.

187

Miss Pearlina leaned in the darkened doorway of the kitchen with her arms folded across her chest and smiled wistfully. At the bottom of the stairs, Glenda was there. She hugged Betsy's neck and kissed her cheek before presenting her to a young man who would be her ceremonial escort into the world. The girls on the stairs sang a different song, "God Be with You Till We Meet Again," the old Methodist benediction hymn. The escort offered her his arm, and she hesitated so Glenda put Betsy's hand on the inside of the young man's elbow. Normally there would be a parlor-full of young men in tuxedoes, all waiting for the seniors, but this time it was for Betsy alone, and the young man simply wore a jacket and tie. He opened the door, and the afternoon light and chill rushed in, and Betsy squinted and turned her face down.

She barely remembered the ride out. The town was empty to her now because she knew that Sammy wasn't there or wouldn't be there for long. It was the backdrop of a ghost story, the story of two lonely souls who couldn't occupy the same dimension, but somehow knew the other was nearby, as if each were behind a sheet of one-way glass.

The campus and then the square and then the city of Oxford all slipped away one by one.

Chapter 47

The uniform of the St. Matthew Parish Sheriff's Department, khaki pants and shirt, was thrown over the back of the motel room's only chair. The big man with the wavy red hair was trying on his new clothes.

Course ain't nobody gonna tell a law man where the whorehouse is, he thought to himself. Shoulda figgered that'n out there, Bulldog ol' boy.

He buttoned up his shirt in the mirror. The top button wouldn't reach around his neck, so he left it undone. He pulled on the end of the tie he was going to wear, and it slithered out, around and under his collar. His hand scratched around in the paper bag, *J. E.*

Neilson's printed on the front. He pulled out a pair of gray slacks, snapped the tags off them, and pulled them on.

He sat on the side of the bed, reached for the phone and dialed a number. While he waited he lit a cigarette and shook out the match. The phone gave a series of guttural rings and then clicked, and there was a small voice on the other end of the phone.

"Operator, Vacherie, Louisiana, Sheriff's Office." He waited again. "Olivier? This Parris. Sheriff Lebeau asked me to call and say we gonna be a little while longer up here in St. Louie."

A question mumbled and hummed on the other end of the phone.

"Oh, did I say St. Louie? Chicago, I mean."

Another hum on the phone. Parris listened with the cigarette on his lip and the phone cradled between his ear and his shoulder while he jammed on his cowboy boots. He grinned, and the cigarette tilted upward. He put the phone and the cigarette in the same hand, and it looked like smoke was coming out of his ear.

"Well, then, I suggest you take that up with him when he gets back. But I bleeve he'd just get a new deputy, is all. All right."

He hung up the phone and tapped out an ash into the glass ashtray. He raked the room key off the dresser and put it in his pocket. And then he left to make some inquiries.

Within a few hours, he returned with the information he needed. He looked at the directions he got from some of the boys on campus:

Head out on the State Highway toward Pontotoc, left at the Sinclair station, then about three miles up the road. It'll be there in a bend, kinda hard to see. Look for the Brownie Advertisement, with the little man on it.

The name of the place is The County Line Inn.

Chapter 48

"I think you oughta know, just 'cause I know where this place is, it doesn't mean I've necessarily *patronized* it," the boy said. His name was Billy, a tall, athletic boy from McComb whose eyes squinted under his thick black lashes when he laughed, and he laughed a lot.

"Okay," Betsy said, and she smiled politely. She wasn't sure she knew what patronized meant, but she thought it was some way of cleaning, like sanitized.

The road out of town went through cotton and pine and hardwood, past farmhouses set off from the road and surrounded by the dry brown leafy stalks of cornfields. She imagined the corn to be sugarcane.

"Smell the cottonseed?" Billy asked. "Always smells like fall to me."

"Smell a cane burnin' all-wheeze smell like fall to me," she said as she looked out the window.

They passed a brown field flecked with white, like spotty snow, where a red cotton picker sat at the edge of the tree line. There were woods again, and the car swerved suddenly and dove into the woods on a rutted lane. The smiling face of an elf holding up a brown bottle flashed by. The car bumped in and out of potholes and puddles. The inn loomed gray-brown in the woods.

Billy got out and got Betsy's things from the trunk. On the porch, a dog, obviously part wolf or coyote, barked and snarled. Billy stopped short of the porch as it strained at its chain leash. A voice inside said, "Who is it, Sheba? Who, girl?"

The screen door squeaked open, and Opalina stepped out.

"Hello, Billy. Where ya been hidin'? Ain't seen ya fer a time."

"Uh, around," he answered Opalina, and then to Betsy, "Gotta go. Good luck, now."

He jumped back in the car, backed up abruptly and swung around toward the highway.

Opalina watched in amusement as he retreated down the lane, and then directed her gaze to Betsy.

"Looks like yer ride's done left ya. I help you, miss?"

Betsy gave her the note from Miss Pearlina. Opalina dug in her apron pocket for her glasses. She put them on, then read the note and folded it up again. She put the note and the glasses in her apron pocket.

"Well, Miss Bessie...." Opalina's voice trailed off as she looked up.

Betsy had set down her overnight case and approached the dog. It thumped its bushy reddish brown tail on the boards of the porch.

"Sha, be bee," she cooed at the animal.

Sheba didn't growl at all and wagged her wolf-like tail and licked her lips at the anticipation of Betsy's hand stroking her head. The dog rolled over and gave her belly to Betsy. Sheba's rust-colored tail swept over the same spot on the porch like a broom.

"Well I never," Miss Opalina said in amazement.

Betsy squatted down to pet the dog and looked up to Opalina.

Opalina asked her, "You just here to cook, or are you innerstid in entertainin' men too?"

"I don't think I could entertain 'em too good, no. I can't sing or nothin' like that."

Opalina guffawed and shook her head. "Babe in the woods," she said. "Let me show you the kitchen, then."

Opalina held the door for Betsy. Their footsteps thudded hollowly on the floorboards and jingled the rows of clean glasses over the bar. They passed through the gray swinging door to the kitchen. It was smaller than the one in the Kappa House. Opalina showed Betsy everything, opening and closing cabinets and the refrigerator. They exited through a screen door in the back and rounded the corner to a side yard.

"Cluckers in the back," Opalina gestured toward the edge of the woods and a chicken coop there. "Can you git a live chicken ready fer the pot?"

"Yessum."

"Generally it'll be just me and you here during the day. At night when we have customers, if there's any trouble, you'll hear this here bell. It rangs, you take off fer the woods, hear?" She tapped it, and it dinged. At the front corner of the inn, Sheba's ears lifted, and she tilted her head in canine wonder.

Opalina pointed to the ridge above the inn. "I got a watchman stays up in at cabin yonder on the ridge. He's off at a funeral today."

Chapter 49

Autumn rains were beginning to wash the color out of the tree line and raise the smell of decaying leaves from the earth. A few skinny sprays of flowers on wire stands stood guard over a rectangular mound of red clay clods. A preacher in a navy blue suit with a wide striped tie read from a Bible. A breeze, unfelt by anyone there, teased the pages. He finished reading and closed the black leather cover and raised his hands and prayed. And when the prayer was finished, Mr. Finley and his coffin were lowered into the earth by two black men in overalls. The men of the mill each took a clod of earth and tossed it into the hole. There would be no reception in the church hall afterwards, no covered dishes, no laughter or reminiscing. Everyone would just go home.

Tillie wailed a primal, primitive wail, a brisk tailwind for the soul of Mr. Finley, speeding him off to the afterlife. The men stood around her, all wanting to put a hand on her shoulder, or an arm around her, but all unsure. She dropped to her knees on the red soil and fell forward onto her square black bangs and rose weeping again, her forehead marked with the red clay. The men stood around nervously until her wailing diminished, and then Archie Wilson reached down with his strong brown hand and gently pulled her up. They all walked off together as the two black men began filling the hole in earnest, shovels shuffling through the dirt that fell and thumped off the pine.

Chapter 50

"Take this up to the watchman," Miss Opalina said.

Betsy had been bringing meals to the mysterious occupant for a week now, setting down the basket with the blue checkered towel in it, knocking on the door of the shack on the ridge, and turning to pick her way down the trail back to the inn. She was usually half way down the slope and obscured by the pines when she heard the distant click of the door and the scrape of the bottom of it against the floorboards.

She had witnessed the nightly show for a week now, and she knew what kind of inn this was. The girls were more reserved than the Kappas, and had a quiet, hopeless resignation. They all smoked as they draped themselves over the barstools, the jukebox blaring out country tunes and emitting a purple light that mixed with the blue and yellow light of the neon beer signs. Misshapen men came and courted them quickly, the outcome of their romantic efforts certain from the outset, like winning a prize at the fair. Success was guaranteed, a winner every time. Within half an hour, the girls were smoking on the barstools again.

During the days, Betsy slept in and then woke and played with Sheba. Then, in the cold fall sunlight, she lounged on an Adirondack chair and read through Miss Opalina's old trashy paperbacks. One was *The Lieutenant's Wife,* another, *The Naughty Maid,* and another, *Is That Package for Me, Mr. Postman?* Each had a variation of the same illustration on the front: a woman in sexy lingerie in the foreground and her pensive lover or lovers, male or female, in the background.

She had never read much before and certainly would never have read books like these at home. There was always too much else to do, but now there wasn't near enough. The hours crept, and Betsy would do anything to pass the time.

"Why don't you take some a that up to the watchman?" Miss Opalina said.

Betsy had taken some of last night's cornbread and crumpled it into a bowl with Pet milk and sprinkled sugar on it. There was still a little left over, so she put some into a smaller bowl. She put the blue checked kitchen towel over it, loaded it into a basket with a spoon, and headed up the ridge again.

Today her curiosity was up. She was bored and had explored every other corner of the inn. She had imagined the watchman as an old grizzled man, seventy or eighty at least. Today she would meet him.

She knocked on the door and waited with the basket and a smile, like a new neighbor coming to visit. The door opened, and her smile faded.

And then there he was, and they looked at each other. Their first thoughts were complete disbelief:

Miss Opalina's watchman looks just like Sammy Teague.
Miss Opalina's new cook looks just like Betsy Duplechain.

It took a brief moment, and then they let themselves believe it. They were together, they fell together, they were together grasping each other's face, together kissing each other all over their faces, everywhere but on the mouth. They stood together as if on a trap door, but it was the world that fell and not them. Neither said anything, afraid that any talk would break the spell, or awake them from the dream. So they just held onto each other, crying, laughing, sobbing, smiling, but not saying anything. There was no language to express how they felt anyway.

Instead, they fell to the bed, staying as close as possible to each other, pressed together like they were one person. A light rain began, and they listened to it. Their breath became a chilly vapor, but it was too late in the day for a fire. The air was moldy and musty, and the leak in the roof dripped when it acquired enough moisture for it. But they were under this roof together, and that made it home. A big truck, a logging truck from the sound of it, rumbled off and away down the cold and distant highway. Smoke scented the air from the barrel of trash that Opalina was burning down at the inn.

Betsy whispered, "Im afraid that if I close my eyes and open them again, you gonna be gone."

"Hold on to me then, and I'll keep watch on myself so that I don't slip away."

She smiled and very deliberately closed her eyes for a brief second and opened them again.

"You still here."

"I'm still here. And so are you."

She shivered, and Sammy said "You cold?" She nodded and nestled into him, but he got up and she looked perplexed. In the corner of the tiny shack, was the battered old valise. He laid it down and popped open the clasps. He took out the red Ole Miss t-shirt, and she smiled again. She sat up, and he put it on her, but she kept her arms inside it. They settled back down on the bed again. Down the hill, there was a bark, and then a metal pot rattled as Opalina put scraps out for Sheba.

Betsy dozed, lightly covered in slumber. There was a scratching sound, and she was barely aware of the faintest jostling of the bed.

She finally awoke enough and sat up beside Sammy. She snaked her arms through the sleeves of the shirt.

He had a pocketknife, one that Mr. Finley gave him because every good mill man needed one to peel away layers of gray patina from a board to check its grain, its scent, its identity. Sammy had carved out a message on the window sill:

I, Samuel Teague, IV, resolve never again to leave behind the love of my life, Betsy Duplechain, so help me God.

He would have put the date, but he had no idea what day it was.

Betsy twisted her head, read the message and smiled, and they kissed on the lips this time. She held out her hand for the knife, and he gave it to her. She worked silently for a few minutes and added at the bottom:

Forever and ever.

She folded up the knife and gave it back to him. He put it in his pocket, and they nestled back into the bed again. He spooned her and drew on her back with his finger and then dragged his fingernails lightly up and down her spine. He put his nose to the nape of her neck and lightly pressed his lips there. She sighed not in the anticipation of sexual excitement but in relief at finally being home, under this leaky roof with this imperfect man who had become everything she would ever want or need.

His hand snuck under the t-shirt and unbuttoned the back of her dress. He traced messages to her, on the bare skin of her back, his finger moving over her bra. She reached back under the red t-shirt, inside her dress, and unclasped her bra. His palm moved over her back, and she waited to see if passion or the peace of sleep overtook her first. Behind her, his breathing deepened and his hand moved under her bra and cupped her breast. She opened her eyes and then closed them with a shudder, a light exhalation of air escaping between her parted lips.

She turned to him on the simple, creaky mattress that was warm now from their bodies. Her hand found him, and he was firm along the length of her palm. He made a small sound, and she studied his face, quietly amused at how such a rugged looking man could whimper like that.

They kissed slowly and deeply, and the room seemed to glow in the chill of the afternoon. They looked at each other, and in her dark eyes Sammy caught a glimpse of that part of him that had fallen into her that first time, a time that seemed years ago but was only a few months. It was there, and had been there the whole time.

The sound of her breathing was as unique as a finger print, the scent of his arousal something forgotten and suddenly remembered. The rain raised a rich brown and green aroma from the fecund earth. She took his hand and laced her fingers with his and put them together between her thighs where she was damp. They felt like they were circling something, like they were in the outer rings of a whirlpool and being drawn toward the center.

Outside on the path, there was the crunch of feet trudging up the hill, and then a light knock on the door.

"Betsy?" Opalina's voice called out through the door. "Betsy? Yer gonna need to come down and start cookin', hear? We expectin' visitors soon."

The County Line Inn was always expecting visitors.

Sammy kissed Betsy's neck. She raised her chin and put her eyes to the door.

"Yes ma'am."

She kissed him again, hard on the lips.

"Don't work too hard," Sammy said, "I'm gonna be all over you tonight."

"Don't go to sleep, then," she narrowed her eyes, "You betta be awake, or I'm gonna wake you up."

She kissed him one last time and said, "This the perfect weather for gumbo. I bring you some later."

She stood up, and he smiled and admired her as she reached up under the shirt and inside her dress to refasten her bra. He got up and buttoned her dress for her, but then palmed her breasts through her clothes. They felt bigger than he remembered them to be. She smiled, and closed her eyes and leaned her head back. Then she took his hands and kissed them.

He walked her down to the inn, her hand in his, and sat with her in the kitchen. She moved around it as before, efficient and in control, stray black hair falling around her face as she worked. He left her reluctantly to assume his post on the ridge as night began to fall.

And it would fall hard.

Chapter 51

Opalina was polishing glasses as Johnny Cash sang from the jukebox, "Ring of Fire." At the counter, a redheaded girl named Florence was flirting with a greasy haired, heavily cologned man whose gut pushed his overalls into a great sweeping convex mound. Her finger ran up and down the neck of his beer bottle as she smiled coyly, and they got up. As they walked past the end of the counter, she reached into the lollipop jar for a condom.

Going out through the side door, they passed a girl named Maggie Lynn as she was coming in from the rooms. She was a fair haired girl, her eyebrows and eyelashes barely darker than her skin. She was holding her lower stomach and trying to smile.

"That big block-headed feller is rough," she said.

"Got a biggun, then, does he?" Miss Opalina smiled as she set down a glass and grabbed another.

"No ma'am, not atall, really purty small, act-shly. Guess he was tryin' to make up fer it. Didn't wanna wear the rubber, neither."

Alarmed, Opalina looked up from drying the glass in her hand.

"But he did, didn't he?"

"Yessum, finally. I was this close to kneein' 'im in his vittles like you said to, iffen they don't."

Parris came through the side door past the purple light of the jukebox. He was smiling big and rubbing his stomach. His paid-for paramour saw him and exited through the kitchen.

"Y'all got somethin' a nutha to eat?"

"Yessir," Opalina said, coaxing her look of concern into a happier, more hospitable expression. "We got this soup our new cook made. Do have a seat and I'll get you some."

"Well, all righty. And have one them girls get ready fo' round numba two." He lit a cigarette.

Miss Opalina went in the kitchen, ladled out a bowl and put the rice in the middle like Betsy had showed her. She pushed back-first through the gray metal door and presented it to Parris.

"Cook says we can serve it to ya with tater salad if ya druther."

Parris looked down into the deep brown gumbo with the island of white rice in it. He took a spoonful.

"Well I'll be. This here's gumbo. Great night fo' it. Tastes just like back home. "

"And where you from, may I ask?"

"Louisiana."

"Do tell! Our new cook's from there. "

Parris' eyes narrowed as his mind worked suspiciously. He put another spoonful to his lips, and his eyes narrowed even further.

Sammy was finding it hard to stay up on the ridge knowing that Betsy was down in the kitchen. He and Jude stood among the cars and trucks parked in the lot. Their hands were stuffed in their pockets in the intermittent cold drizzle, any colder would be sleet. One of Jude's cuffs hung empty.

The parking lot held cars with Mississippi plates, except for one with Tennessee plates and one with Alabama plates.

And the one with Louisiana plates. The one that said 'police.'

Sammy's heart sank. He looked in the back seat and saw the lights that had been removed from the top. Under white hotel towels hung over the doors was the splotchy shape of St. Matthew Parish.

"It's him," Jude said over Sammy's shoulder. "Run up yonder to yer cabin 'n git you 'n Betsy's thangs. I'll run 'n fetch her. Time fer you two to scoot." There was a seriousness in Jude's face, a gravity in his voice that Sammy had never seen or heard. Sammy turned to him, and Jude extended his hand.

"Take care, brother," Jude said. Their hands pulled away for a moment, and then they embraced, patting backs awkwardly while their hands remained clasped. Jude's stump thumped on Sammy's back.

They withdrew, and Jude shooed him with his hand, "Now, git, go on, now. North, east, west, don't matter, jess go!"

Sammy ran up the path to the shack on the ridge, the pain from his scar small and ignorable now.

Meanwhile, at the counter, a false smile spread over Parris' face.

"Well, this is certainly damn fine gumbo, ma'am, if you'll excuse my language. May I give my compliments to the cook?"

Before Opalina could answer, he was off his stool, dabbing the corner of his mouth with a napkin and heading to the kitchen. He poked his head through the kitchen door. The hand with the napkin fell slowly.

The girl looked different now, her hair was shorter, and she looked like she had gained a little weight, but the big, black pupils of her eyes were unmistakable. She was wearing an Ole Miss t-shirt over her dress and rolling out dough with a pin. His voice startled her.

"Well, Miss *Bessie* Duplechain, what a delight it is to see you again. And wouldn't yo mama like to know you workin' in a whorehouse? I'll most certainly have to tell her, next time I see her. Course, it may be a while. She moved off to Opelousas or Jeff Davis Parish or somewhere, since that playboy's daddy evicted her 'n that ol' woman and bulldozed that old tenant shack down, all the way the ground. Can't even tell it was there."

Something inside Betsy imploded and fell into a heap, but her façade rose with the rolling pin in her hand.

They stood contemplating each other for a moment, and then she threw the rolling pin at Parris and ran. He ducked, and it rattled the pots hanging behind him. The screen door at the back of the kitchen slapped against the jamb. She hurriedly untied her apron and tossed it to the ground in the puddle of light at the backdoor, and ran into the shadows.

Parris took off after her, following the instinct of a predator to chase a thing that's fleeing. He stopped at the back door and looked both ways into the night.

She ran out to the back near the edge of the woods where Sheba stayed tied at night. The chickens whooped a startled, fluttering cackle as she rushed up on them. The dog strained at her leash, wagging her tail and moaning for Betsy's attention.

Parris had lost sight of Betsy and suspected she had ducked into one of the rooms. He went down the row, opening doors where men in boxers shouted and women with sheets wrapped around them squealed. One by one he emptied the rooms, until the last room. He smiled to himself and rammed his shoulder into the door, and it gave way with a hollow thump. A tall, skinny man ran past him, his erection bouncing as he clutched his pants and shoes. The girl slipped under the covers, trying to disappear. Parris smiled and whipped the sheets back, and an uncomfortable, irregular smile met his. It wasn't the face he was expecting, and he felt like slapping the girl's snaggle-toothed face, and he almost did. His hand paused in midair.

He ran back out into the yard and scanned the trees at the edge of the light. The sudden exertion of the chase left Parris panting, his hands clenched at his sides. He reached up and wiped drizzle and sweat from his face with his palm. He turned and went back into the inn.

Sammy was putting their things in the back of the Mustang when he heard the commotion. Men in various states of undress ran past him for the parking lot and sped off in their vehicles, tires digging into the gravel and slinging it as the drivers thought of excuses for missing pants, shirts, and shoes. At the edge of the clearing that was suffused with light from the open doors of the rooms, several of the girls were standing together, covering themselves in the drizzle. Their hair dripped with moisture, and their makeup ran blue-black onto their cheeks as they hid behind trees.

Suddenly, there was a rustle in the underbrush by the chicken coop and a flurry of red and white, and then Betsy came running, holding the hem of her dress in one hand and her shoes in the other. She darted across the yard of the inn through the light, between the girls hiding in the woods and the rooms where they had worked. She rushed to Sammy, and they embraced and kissed. The girls in the woods saw them and thought, well, I guess Miss Opalina's purty watch-feller ain't atall *thataway*.

"We gotta go, baby," Sammy said. He opened the door as he imagined the chase that would ensue. The call on the police radio for help in apprehending the fugitives for some trumped up offense, the lights reattached and twirling red and blue with the siren shrieking and whining through the night.

He shut the door and rounded to the driver side of the Mustang, pausing to look at the police cruiser parked across the lot.

All four tires were flat. The hotel towels had been pulled off the doors and tied to the long whip of radio antenna. The amoeba shape of St. Matthew Parish stretched across the door.   Under the rear bumper, the cruiser's battery sat as if the car had passed a shiny black cube of a turd.

"C'mon, Sammy!" Betsy's voice was muffled through the glass of the driver's window. She rapped on it with her fingernail. "We gotta go!"

He got in and cranked the Mustang. The headlights shot across the yard of the inn and caught the dragon-face and blonde curls of his friend, his brother, Jude Hawkins, among the screen of brown leaves at the back edge of the yard. He was bending over Sheba, deftly using one hand to undo her leash. With the effortless gait of her ancestors, the dog loped across the yard toward the inn, her head low, ears back, teeth bared. Jude stood and watched her go. Then he raised his stump in farewell, turned, and evaporated into the woods.

The purple and blue lights were off, and the bright, white lights were on inside the County Line Inn. Parris stood in the empty room and looked to the side door, and then the back. Chairs and tables had been hastily overturned, and on the bar sat his bowl of gumbo. His blank eyes stared at it as his mind plotted.   He heard a click and turned around.

Now, with the gun in her hand, Opalina looked familiar to him, her platinum blonde tornado of hair like the reverse image of something he had seen before, the negative of a photograph of someone he had met under similar circumstances. And the tone of her voice was familiar as well.

"This should go without sayin' to all but the most *dense* of individuals, but you 'n yer business are no longer welcomed here, kind sir."

He turned and stepped onto the porch. There, pulling out of the parking lot was what he had come to Mississippi for all along.

Sammy Teague and Betsy Duplechain.

Behind him he heard a canine snarl, watery and dripping. He turned and saw the coyote-dog there, the full length of its teeth exposed down to the gums. Parris trotted to his car, keeping his eyes over his shoulder at the dog. Sheba eased forward, hackles up, but Opalina said *stay* in a low voice, and the dog sat and whined.

"Stay right there, Mr. Dick Little. Keep yer hands on yer car, pleasir."

"That ain't my name."

"From what I hear, it oughta be." She held the gun and blew out a mouthful of smoke as nonchalantly as if she were waiting on the bus.

"Can't I at least have my suppa?"

"I believe you got enough winter fat on ya to miss a meal, *I said hands on yer car.* Man'll be here shortly to get yer tars aired up. Ain't slashed, just got the air let out of 'em."

Parris shivered in the cold night air, dense with mist. Opalina and Sheba sat comfortably on the steps of the porch under the overhang.

"Can I have a cigarette?" Parris asked.

"No."

Parris was soaked to the bone when, at last, a man with a compressor in the bed of his pickup arrived and put air in each tire. When they were inflated, Miss Opalina allowed Parris to take his hands off the car to pay the man. The man left as soon as he was paid, and Parris warily eased into the car and turned the key. Nothing happened.

Opalina sat on the steps in the dark with her legs parted, and the folds of her dress hanging between them. Her backlit tornado of hair made her head look oblong like a pharaoh's. She smoked with one hand and held the gun with the other. Sheba lay with her head on her paws.

Parris got out. His hands came out of the crack in the door first.

"Won't start," he said.

"Your problem."

"Will you least let me see why?"

"All right. Better hurry, though. I'm catchin' a cramp in my trigger finger." She fired a shot at his feet, and it sprayed mud on his trousers and echoed in the cold and wet night woods. He shuddered and pushed his face into his upper arm with the shot.

"See? Can't hold out much longer. Might seize up again."

He scrambled to the front of the car. His hands went up higher in the air as if he were praising Jesus in a revival tent.

"Just gonna look under the hood," he called out with his hands still high.

"Can't hold out much longer," she said casually, and she blew out another cloud of smoke.

He opened the hood, fumbling with the latch.

202

"Battery's gone," he yelled into the engine, his breath wafted as a cold vapor that the porch light illuminated.

She was unmoved. "Yer gonna hafta think fast then."

He circled around the car with his hands up. Opalina threw her cigarette to the ground and stood up. Sheba stood up too. Her tail wagged in expectation.

Parris was contemplating just running off into the woods when he saw the battery under the back bumper. His arms had drooped, and he raised them higher.

"Here it is." he said with his eyes on it.

She stepped inside the door and hid behind the edge of it. As he emerged from behind the car, she cocked the hammer of the revolver. He had the battery in his hands and was lugging it forward.

"Just gotta git it hooked up," he shouted to her.

He dropped it in place under the hood, and it pinched his finger.

"Shit!" he mumbled and shook his finger. Opalina fired another shot in the ground at his feet, and he hit his head on the raised hood. His shaky hands tightened the connections and then went up in the air again.

"Goin' now, ma'am," he said as he stood at the door of his cruiser.

Opalina lit another cigarette with her free hand and took a drag of it as she dropped her lighter into a pocket of her dress. She blew the smoke out, raised the gun and aimed straight at him.

"Don't you *ever* come round her again disturbin' my girls and my customers. As God is my witness you'll never make it out a here! And don't get any ideers a sneakin' up here, neither," she said. "I got half dozen men up in these woods at any one time a-watchin' the place." That part wasn't true, but Parris was in no position to question her. In fact, it seemed quite possible.

Then she pulled her hands back, the gun hand and the cigarette hand, as she leaned into her final shouted taunt. "*And sorry bout yer tiny pecker. Hope you find it one day!*"

He pulled back from the parking lot expecting another shot. Tires squealed, and the long whippy antenna sagged limply under the weight of the hotel towels. His taillights jostled down the dark lane and quickly vanished on the highway.

Chapter 52

Sammy chose north. The headlights of the Mustang bore a hole in the night, following the road doggedly, patiently. The night was as dark and quiet as a hundred years ago, a thousand years ago, when people lived with mounds shaped like their gods, and fire was the only answer against darkness. The air was cold and wet, and two deer were moving. The headlights caught the pinpoint reflections of their eyes in the woods at the edge of the road.

Betsy's face glowed beautifully in the glow of the dash, and it was surreal that she was there. Sammy realized that they had never driven in a car together. She leaned over and kissed his shoulder. He drove for a while and then looked over to see that she was asleep.

New Albany, Ripley, and across the Tennessee line, through Bolivar. Past Jackson, Tennessee they entered Milan. Sammy had gone to boarding school with a boy from there and knew that it wasn't pronounced like the Italian city, it was pronounced 'My Lan'. Thirty minutes later My Lan' was followed by another Tennessee town with a European name.

Paris.

They passed through it and over the Tennessee River and then the Cumberland. In Clarksville, Tennessee, they stopped to get gas. Sammy kept his head low and his hand on his forehead concealing his face, his hair swept down over his forehead and neck as the pump gulped gas into the car. An olive drab bus with *Fort Campbell, Kentucky* written on the side lumbered up to the opposite pump and stopped with a short yelp of its brake. Inside it, new recruits looked out into the night. Their faces wore every possible mask, the entire spectrum between comedy and tragedy, faces ready for adventure and glory and doom and slaughter.

As Sammy and Betsy pulled away, one face caught Sammy's attention. In the very backseat was a freckled face boy who looked twelve but certainly was older, eighteen at least. Their eyes met. The boy's face was one of such terror and despair that it made Sammy pull out more slowly than he wanted to. And then they were back into the darkness. It was just after midnight.

They passed into Kentucky, through Russellville, Bowling Green, Horse Cave. At two in the morning they stopped at a traffic light in Elizabethtown. Sammy's finger tapped the steering wheel impatiently. In the rearview mirror, a police cruiser appeared. Sammy's ringed, exhausted eyes appeared in the mirror with it. He glanced at the sign that said Harrodsburg, next right, and when the light turned green, he turned left. The police car turned and followed. Sammy drove purposefully, just under the limit, hands at ten and two. The police car turned on its lights, and Sammy slowed, his mind too tired to think. Then, it turned onto a side street on its way to some other errand. *City of Elizabethtown* was written across its door. Sammy was too exhausted to be elated.

He rewarded the good luck and providence of that road and continued down it, more west now, until he began drifting across the center line, once narrowly missing a bridge rail. Betsy woke and looked at him with concern. At four in the morning, he couldn't go any longer and saw a sign that his fatigue took for an omen:

Just Drive In.

Part III: Kentucky

Chapter 53

When Johnny Bettis came home from Chicago, his parents could tell at once that he hadn't had a haircut or a shave since he'd left. His hair hung down a greasy camel color, with a beard slightly darker. As they scanned the bus at the depot in Owensboro, there was a ring of unoccupied seats around him. Several of the other passengers got off the bus waving their hands under their noses, and one said, "Whew, at last."

The driver told the Bettises through the door after Johnny got off, "I'm glad y'all are here, one more stop and I would have had to put him off."

Their boy, their only child, was the valedictorian at County Consolidated High, and had won a scholarship to the University of Chicago. They had sent him off with proud tears and waited for news of his progress. His first letter described his classes, his dorm room, and the food in the dining hall. His second letter detailed his conversion to Catholicism and his third his conversion to Judaism. The next one concerned the agents from the government who had a special interest in his thoughts due to the fact that he had been a member of the Pentecostal, Catholic, and Jewish faiths. The last letter they got from him was a rambling one, written in scrawling script, three entire pages with no punctuation, and then there were no more letters. The Bettises called someone at the university, who told them that John had not gone to class since three weeks into the semester. A professor went out looking for him and found him sleeping in a doorway on Wabash Street. Pigeons strutted around the crumpled form under the cardboard and newspapers. He put the young man on the next bus home.

Alta and Dewey took their son to their family doctor who sent them to the doctor in Louisville, who made the diagnosis.

"Skitzer-frenyer?" Dewey Bettis said quizzically. "What the hell is that?"

"Dewey! Your language! You oughten talk like that," Alta said.

The doctor in Louisville gave Johnny a medicine that made him sleep for long stretches, and when he was awake he shuffled when he walked, his thumbs rubbing his index fingers in small circles. He began refusing the pills, at first spitting them out when his mother wasn't looking and then refusing to take them at all. They brought him to church regularly, furtively hoping in the higher power, but even a mother's pure and earnest prayer would not work.

Then one Sunday Johnny exclaimed loudly in the middle of silent meditation, "Someone has taken my Lord, and I do not know where they have laid him!" The preacher kept his face to the top of the pulpit but opened his eyes and cut them to the source of the exclamation. Johnny was standing now, and the preacher cut his eyes to the usher, a white-headed man in a gray, ill-fitting suit, the sleeves too long and the pants too short. The preacher twitched his head in the direction of the noise, and the usher waded past Johnny's pew mates and gently took his arm.

"Why do you seek the living among the dead?" Johnny shouted over his shoulder on his way out. Mr. and Mrs. Bettis followed behind him into the spring air.

Mrs. King, the pianist, squinted into the sheet music as if to jump start her eyes and then nervously began "What a Friend We Have in Jesus." The congregation and the preacher were relieved to have the uncomfortable silence broken and began singing. The door squeaked and shut, and the Bettises had not been back to church together since.

Another trip to the doctor in Louisville was made. This time he recommended the State Home in Hopkinsville.

"I'm not leavin' my boy there," Alta said, folding her arms across her chest.

"But Mrs. Bettis, it's for his own protection. The world is a difficult place for someone like John," the doctor explained.

"We can't handle him, Alta, you know that," Dewey implored his wife.

"I'm not leaving him," she repeated, and she looked up and away.

They brought him home where he spent his days doing only the most simple tasks, a long fall for a boy who had gone from brilliant to bizarre. Often, his father would find him waist deep in the Ohio, just beyond the reeds swaying in the wind with the distant opposite bank billowing green behind him, preaching to the few people gathered there.   They smirked and chuckled to themselves, and whispered to each other behind their hands. Dewey usually would have to wade out into the water to retrieve him.

Or, more often, he would find his son sitting on a stump in the side yard talking with unseen angels who would protect him from the government agents, also unseen. His hands gestured wildly as he debated the government men, occasionally walking around the side yard like a lawyer giving closing arguments. Even the rain wouldn't bring him in. His mother would go out with an umbrella and throw a coat over him, persuading him to come inside.

Just before Johnny had gone to college, Dewey Bettis had sold most of his farm. He reasoned that he couldn't work it by himself. His hope was that a drive-in movie theater would be more lucrative with less effort. Perhaps Johnny would make it big in engineering and get hired on with President Kennedy's new space program, and help them out as they aged. Only ten acres or so of the farm was left, and it would lie fallow most years. But Dewey could work late nights and sleep-in in the mornings.

The strangers appeared on a Sunday morning. It was cold and overcast, and a chilly mist alternated with near silent showers. A line of gray trees, studded with rare yellow holdover leaves, was outlined against the gray skies on the far edge of the field that once grew corn but now held cars on the nights that the Just Drive In showed features. A few miles away, a diesel engine droned as a tugboat pushed a barge up the Ohio, and big cement trucks grumbled faintly as they lumbered up each end of the bridge being built across the river.

The mailbox once said Bettis, but summer heat and winter cold and spring rain and autumn winds had worn away one of the Ts, and it now read 'Bet is.' The draft of stray passing cars pulled and pushed at the tops of the dried weeds sprouting from the base of the weathered gray post. Winter nights fell harder here than anywhere else, and winter mornings labored under the inertia of the cold.

Inside the little farmhouse, the orange tinted yellow lights glowed on the three of them. The radio murmured that corn was up one and a quarter, hog prices down one and a half. There would be more rain today, and tomorrow sleet and snow were possible.

"Anything's possible," Johnny blurted out as he mopped up a puddle of honey with a biscuit. Hairs in his camel-colored beard were stuck together around his mouth in small clumps of petrified amber.

"Yep." Mr. Bettis said. He wore a white undershirt and trousers. His eyes continued to watch his fork as it scooped into a cloud of grits. "Yes it is, son."

A man with a rich voice announced, *we now bring you the Sunday morning services from the First Baptist Church of Louisville.* An organ fanfare flowered suddenly.

Johnny put down his knife and fork on his half-finished plate and went outside without a word to his mother or father. Across the way at the barn there was something new, a blue Mustang convertible was parked there. He eyed it silently, his face expressionless. Then he marched toward it with his hands at his sides. In the raspy, dry cornfield beyond the barn, a headless scarecrow sagged on a post. When Johnny got to the barn, he reached out and rigidly pushed the door open.

The two strangers were under an old tack blanket in the barn, a nest of yellow straw around them. The man, who had a beard himself though scragglier, was spooning the woman, whose dark hair fell over her face. The man's head jerked up when Johnny spoke.

"Are you the ones who were sent, or should I wait for another?"

The woman continued to sleep. The man spoke.

"We don't want any trouble. We were just tired, see? Tired."

"Tired, hired, mired," Johnny said.

He returned to the house, not bothering to pick around the shallow puddles of cold water in the yard. The screen door slammed, and he barged into the kitchen. Alta was scraping plates and running dishwater.

"Mother, there are people in the barn. Angels."

Alta eased the plates into the dishwater. "Oh, isn't that nice, son. Angels in the barn. Isn't that nice, Dewey?"

"Oh, it certainly is," Dewey said into his paper, and then he leaned his head back and looked down his nose at the page as he turned it. "Can't never have too many angels in your barn, *I* say."

Johnny left again, retracing his beeline to the barn. The two were up now, the woman brushing straw out of her black hair. Their breath clouded into vapor in the cold.

"I hope there's no trouble," the man said. "We'll move on, if you want."

"No, come with me. Come with me and I will make you fishers of men."

The man stepped in front of the woman, and canted his head at Johnny like a dog trying to figure out a new sound.

Johnny gestured for the two to follow him, and then he got involved in a conversation with some unseen someone.

"No, no, no. That's what *you* say. Oh, no, that's what *you* say," he paused short pauses between his sentences like he was trying to get a word in, his head shaking vigorously, his hands fluttering like two mockingbirds attacking a garden snake. Then he put his fingers in his ears and yelled, *SHUT UP!* He opened the barn door and another gust of cold air tumbled in.

The man looked at the woman, who put her hands on his back. They followed Johnny out the door toward the house, going around the puddles instead of through them. They whispered to each other from the sides of their mouths.

Chapter 54

The kitchen smelled of bacon grease and lemon scented dish soap, and was decorated in platitudes and scripture. They occurred on towels, figurines, framed on the wall and on throw pillows.

As For Me and My House, We Will Serve the Lord.

If Life Hands You Lemons, Squeeze Them and Make Lemonade.

Just as You Sow You Shall Reap

Gossip is the Devil's Radio

Your word is a lamp unto my feet and a light for my path.

Orange-brown shellacked cedar planks lined the walls vertically with dark knots scattered within them. At the kitchen table, a man read the *Hancock County News, Sunday Edition*. Only his two hands, once rough but now getting softer and mottled with age spots, were visible. A woman was at the kitchen sink, her belted dress, white and worn with small pink printed flowers and thin blue stripes, hung helplessly from her thin frame. Her hair was straight and wiry, black and streaked evenly with gray. The water in the sink sloshed and dripped around the dishes that clinked together in it. The radio on the kitchen counter was playing. A church service, small scattered coughs somewhere in the congregation as the preacher spoke.

Suddenly the door flung open, seemingly by itself, and then Johnny was there with two others. The door bounced lightly off the doorstop. He said what he had to say boldly, but his eyes were ambivalent.

"Here, Father," he said. "Here, angels."

"Uh-huh," Dewey said behind the paper, and then he turned the page.

Johnny snatched the paper and pulled it down, and Dewey looked up. It had happened so many times before that he wasn't startled by it anymore. What startled him were the two strangers that were behind his son. The puffy eyes in his hair-rimmed balding head snapped open.

"Alta," he said as he stood up with the paper in one hand. He was six inches shorter than his wife. Either he was unusually short, or she was unusually tall.

She shook water off her hands into the sink and dried them on a kitchen towel that said, *God Bless This Kitchen*. She turned and straightened up when she saw them. Now she was a almost a foot taller.

"Angels," Johnny said again.

The man shook his head. His long sandy brown hair hung past his chin, and above his scraggly brown beard, his nickel colored eyes looked tired.

"Uh, morning. We're, we're not really angels," Sammy stated the obvious. "I'm Sammy, this Betsy." He lifted his hand in a greeting.

211

"We're travelin' and we were tired, so we slept in your barn." He shifted and pushed the hair out of his face. "Would you mind if we slept there another night?"

"Nonsense," Alta said. "Animals sleep in barns. You're guests, and you'll sleep in the house. You two look famished."

She didn't ask if they were hungry, she simply dried off the skillet she had just washed and put it on the stove. With a turn of her wrist, a blue ring of flame leaped into a circle under the black iron. From the refrigerator, she produced leftover bacon, grits, biscuits, and a carton of eggs. She took two eggs out and cracked them into the skillet. Then she stacked the coffee pot.

While Betsy and Sammy ate, the church service played on the radio. Alta listened to it while she cleaned the kitchen again, and Dewey pretended to listen to it, nodding occasionally and humming with the hymns while he read the paper. Johnny had wandered outside somewhere and left the door open again. Alta paused from cleaning and closed it, barely looking up.

Betsy and Sammy ate voraciously. There was no small talk as the radio service continued, Alta pausing to pray when the radio said pray, and singing along with the hymns in a high pitched, birdlike warble.

Dewey got up and adjourned to an easy chair with the last of the Sunday paper. On the radio, the preacher delivered his sermon, railing like he was running for office, his voice adding extra syllables to words for emphasis. The organ bellowed two notes like a foghorn and a steamboat whistle as the choir sang the concluding song in a soaring whirlwind.

As the song on the radio rose, Dewey napped open-mouthed, his lower lip quivering as it was pulled in and out by the tide of his breathing. In his lap the paper was open to an ad, stylish women in pointy cupped brassieres gathered together like they were in some strangely progressive Junior League or PTA meeting, discussing service projects or children's grades. At the kitchen table, Sammy's head nodded, and Betsy's rested on her hand like they had caught sleeping sickness from Dewey. Their plates were cleaned.

Betsy woke with a start to Alta's voice and touch on her shoulder. "Let's us go change the sheets on the boy's bed."

They removed the old ones and put them in a pile that reeked of the unwashed. Even when the sheets were removed, the smell of them clung to everything in the room in small invisible clumps. Alta and Betsy snapped sheets and let them float to the bed and stuffed pillows into clean cases. Books and piles of papers stood in towering stacks of clutter, and Betsy had to sidestep them.

"Just so's you know," Alta said as she and Betsy tucked in corners, "the unmarried don't lie together under this roof."

"Yes ma'am," Betsy said as cheerfully as she could, though a tinge of disappointment crept in.

The walls of Johnny's room were a shrine to a boy who had once been, a museum to an era of Hope and Possibility. There was a child's drawing of the solar system. Science fair and spelling bee awards. A picture of Johnny in baseball, football, basketball uniforms. Certificates and trophies. Second team All-District football. Honorable Mention All-Kentucky baseball.

There was a picture of Stan Musial, the St. Louis Cardinal great. Musial had autographed it, but someone had later added a crown drawn in ballpoint pen around his head.

As soon as the bed was made, Betsy fell on it and slept all afternoon on top of the sheets.

*   *   *

Sammy napped on the couch all afternoon while Dewey listened to a football game on the radio, either the St. Louis Cardinals or the Chicago Bears, Sammy could never tell. He would wake from time to time with the roar of the crowd like a great exhalation as the announcer's voice flared in excitement, and then he would drift back to sleep again.

At supper, Alta opened mason jars of squash and green beans with new potatoes, the contents in the jars like specimens in a biology lab. She spooned out the contents, the spoon rattling around inside the jars to empty them completely into the pots on the stove. Then she brought out a foil-covered ham and sliced off thin, even slices and laid them out on plates. The food was bland, more fuel than food, but they were grateful.

Dewey gave a perfunctory blessing that Alta added to in case God was displeased with its brevity. Johnny had come in and sat rigidly at the table between Sammy and Betsy. They had wanted to sit together, to hold hands during the blessing, to rest their legs together under the table, but they were afraid of stirring him up. After supper, Betsy took Sammy by the hand and pulled him up from the table.

"Let's do the dishes." They worked side by side, hip to hip, hands in warm soapy water, Betsy scrubbing, Sammy rinsing.

Later, Alta knitted and read the Bible, occasionally quoting aloud, while Dewey did the crossword puzzle and muttered *Praise God* every time she did. Johnny sat on the couch and looked straight ahead, his lips moving silently as he nodded and shook his head. Betsy and Sammy sat on the couch and fought sleep.

At bed time, Alta made a pallet for Johnny on the floor and set out blankets for Sammy on the couch. Betsy slept in Johnny's room.

Sammy fell asleep on the couch to the sounds of soft music on the radio, barely remembering Alta coming in her housecoat to turn it off. Johnny slept on the floor in the living room on his pallet of quilts and mumbled incoherently. Sammy couldn't tell if he was talking in his sleep or just talking.

He woke in the middle of the night to find Johnny gone from the pallet on the floor. Someone mumbled outside, and at first Sammy thought it was the radio. He looked out the window to find Johnny standing on a stump, facing the blank, unanimated movie screen. His head hung down, chin to his chest, as if in humble supplication. Snow was falling thick, around him and on him, collecting on him as if he were a graveyard monument.

Chapter 55

It was early in the morning. Johnny had come in sometime in the night and was sleeping on the pallet of blankets and quilts on the floor. Alta was in the kitchen making breakfast. Coffee scented the air a deep brown. Voices spoke low over the radio.

"We have here in the studio Clyde Perkins, the man that caught that enormous blue cat, what was it Mr. Perkins? One hundred and two pounds?"

The microphone yawned with feedback for a moment as Clyde Perkins said, *"That's right, hunnert-n-two pounds."*

"One hundred and two pound blue cat in the Ohio below the Cannelton locks. Tell us about that, Clyde."

"Well..." the microphone whined with feedback again, and the announcer said in a distant voice, *not so close, Mr. Perkins.* Clyde began again.

"Well, we been a-fishin' on the near side, the Kentucky side, fer a while and my boy says, says, Diddy, why don't we try t'other side, the Indianner side and I said well why don't we and so's we cross over yonder and set lines, normally we use stank bait, night crawlers-n-such...."

The radio man followed with a trail of *uh-huhs* with an occasional *hmmm* and a rare *is that right?* Clyde rambled on.

"....well, anyways that mornin' we used some cut up shad on grit big treble hooks, bout yea long, eased 'em into the water..."

More *uh-huhs* and *hmms* followed until the announcer could stand it no longer. Mr. Perkins' microphone went silent in mid-sentence, and the announcer said, *"Well, we thank you Mr. Clyde Perkins of Hawesville with what is truly a big fish story. Now the weather for Paducah, Owensboro and Tell City..."*

The radio faded, and Sammy woke again with Betsy's face right in his.

"Baby, wake up, look outside."

Sammy sat up. The world was white, six inches of soft, angelic snow.

"So beautiful," Betsy said as she admired it. "Like everything's got sugar on it."

Chapter 56

On the screen, John Wayne's face spoke, but what he was saying was only heard by the people in their cars who had paid for speakers. Johnny Bettis stood on his stump in the side yard silhouetted against the screen over the fence. The hubcaps in his outstretched hands and the kettle overturned on his head made his outline that of a Celtic cross, superimposed over the light of the screen. The night was black and cold, and Johnny exhaled clouds.

"Says he can hear God when he does that." The voice startled Sammy. Next to him with the flashing reflection of the screen in his face was Dewey. He wore a heavy coat and a black sock cap.

"That so?" Sammy said.

Johnny raised one arm and lowered the other, searching for the signal and skewing the cross.

"Says sometimes he hears the devil, too," Dewey said. Johnny raised one foot and put the sole of it on the inside of his opposite knee.

"His mama thinks he's got a demon. Been tryin' to pray it out of 'im. Course, she believes ever other person she can't figger out's got one. Doctor in Lou-vull says he's got a case a that skits-o-frena-yer. I studied on it and I believe he's right. Ain't no damn demon. Angels, devils, hell, when yer child starts actin' crazy an' talkin nonsense it don't matter what he's got. All I know is that it takes a little bit of yer heart ever time they do it. Like you hurt for 'em because they don't know to hurt for themselves."

He wrapped his arms around himself to hold out the cold and to hold in the pain. He pulled the sock cap down over his ears. His face squeezed out toad-like from under it, the light from the screen turning it purple and then blue. They stood watching Johnny's shape change on the backdrop of the screen.

"Glad the snow moved through," Dewey said, sensing Sammy's discomfort with the previous subject. "Hard to sell tickets when it's snowin'. Better if it's already on the ground. Well, this reel's almost up. Gotta get back to the projection shed to put on the second one."

Mr. Bettis shook his head and turned. His footsteps crunched over the frozen ground. Johnny Bettis was now a Y with his arms stretched up and out.

Chapter 57

"Yessir, come through here about midnight, right when the Fort Campbell Bus come through. Two of 'em, man and a woman in a blue Mustang like you said."

"See which way they went?"

"Went up the highway yonder towards Bowlin' Green."

"Well I thank you," the sheriff said as his face heaved out a smile. It took great effort to be cordial with the bitter anger that burned in him. Parris put one hand in the coat pocket with the honey bun he had helped himself to, and put two fingers of the other to the brim of his hat. Then he put that hand in the other coat pocket with the carton of chocolate milk and he left.

The cruiser droned down the road hungrily. He unwrapped the honey bun and threw the wrapper out the window. His mind chewed over the events of the night, but could not swallow them:

The man that woman called to put air in my tires charged twenty dollars, just to come out and blow air in the tires. Twenty dollars. I don't care if it is cold and rainin' and out in the sticks. And then he don't even stay, just takes back off into the night. Car wouldn't start, turn the key, nothin', even the radio wouldn't work. Look under the hood, battery's gone and sittin' under the back end the whole time. Clever.

And all the while that woman standin' in the doorway with a gun in her hand, smokin, and that wolf-dog at her feet. And my supper gettin' cold on the bar behind 'em.

But I know who it was what done it.

Follow them simple-minded tarts home and show 'em you know where they live, and they'll tell you ever thing you want to know. Threaten their families and their pets, oh especially their pets, and they'll squeal like a pig with a knife at its throat.

That yella boy, same one works at that mill.

No time to settle up with him right now. My business is headed north in that blue Mustang.

He took a big half moon bite of honey bun, chewed a few times and threw the pieces back down his gullet like a reptile. Then he chugged the entire carton of chocolate milk, and wiped his mouth on his sleeve. The draft of the cruiser nudged the yellow weeds at the base of the sign that read:

Welcome to Kentucky

The Bluegrass State

An empty chocolate milk carton bounced off the ground near the weeds.

Chapter 58

Her shoe tapped lightly on the flimsy, flaky white surface, and she withdrew it with a giggle. Sammy held her hand, already one step ahead of her and ankle deep in the snow. She stepped again, and her foot sank down into it with a slushy whoosh. She giggled again.

"What it taste like?" she asked and stooped down to scoop up a little, still holding Sammy's hand. She put her tongue to the snow, and then her lips took a small nibble. She seemed a little disappointed.

"Taste like watta."

They walked out into the yard, up toward the barn hand in hand to get their bags out of the car. Betsy's cheeks were red from the cold, her white smile in between. As they got to the barn, Sammy said, "Look at this." He got on his back in the snow and waved his arms and legs. He got up and brushed snow off his back.

"Snow angel," Sammy said.

"Lemme try," Betsy said. She carefully got onto the ground and waved her arms next to Sammy's snow angel. She got up, and Sammy brushed snow from her back, his hand lingering on her backside.

"That's me an' you," Betsy said, and she put her arms around Sammy's neck.

He kissed her, and she put her hand on his beard.

"Boy, you got a beard like an ole pa-pa."

He smiled. His hands crept down from her waist, and they kissed again. Betsy smiled and gestured with her eyes to the top of the barn.

"She didn't say nothin' bout *this* roof."

They rolled through the barn door. Against the far wall of the barn was an old red tractor, the paint mottled and faded. The big back tires were chest high and the front tires knee high. On the molded metal seat and the ground were nuts, bolts, belts, tools, and spare parts where someone, either Johnny or Dewey, had embarked on a project and gotten distracted, overwhelmed, or disinterested.

Betsy and Sammy kissed again. He pointed up and whispered, "The loft."

She ascended the ladder first, and he followed. They reclined in the hay. Her hand crept inside his black and blue plaid coat, and she felt his body through his shirt.

"Mais, where you got these muscles?"

"Those are courtesy of Finley's Mill."

His hands moved behind her and undid the buttons of her dress between her shoulders. She kissed his neck and unbuttoned his shirt hurriedly. She looked at his stomach.

"Sammy. Baby. What's this?"

"Appendix."

"*Pauvre bête*. It hurt?" He flinched as she traced her finger lightly over his scar. It was raised and pink.

"Not anymore. Maybe just a little, mostly tickles."

They kissed again, and he pulled her dress down off her shoulders. She reached behind herself and undid her bra. Her breasts fell forward, under the cups of the bra, and he took them gently in his hands, surprised at their fullness. He pulled back from their kissing and lifted up the cups. He looked at her breasts, fuller and the nipples brown now, and then looked at her. She smiled; he had noticed.

They kissed again, their hands roving.

"Don't tell me you're on your period," Sammy whispered breathlessly. "Just wouldn't that be our luck?"

"Don't worry," she said as she closed her eyes and leaned her head back to give him her neck. He kissed it, his beard tickling her skin. "Ain't had none, not since August."

Sammy thought, now why in the world would a girl not have a period?

He stopped kissing her, and they looked at each other. She smiled and nodded her head.

"We gonna have a baby, Sammy."

The news that a year ago would inspire pacing and ringing of hands and making plans, now was good news, worthy of a herald of trumpets. He fell back in the hay and laughed, the great laughter of the hopelessly and happily overwhelmed. Then he ran his fingers through his hair and kept laughing. Finally, he rolled onto his elbow above her and kissed her a peck, a snapping kiss. The kisses escalated into breathing, and the breathing escalated into panting.

Suddenly the door wheezed open, and Sammy and Betsy froze. They pulled the clothes that had been undone back over themselves and peered over the edge of the loft.

Down below, Johnny was looking through tools and talking to himself, his hands swatting the thoughts and voices that buzzed around his head like gnats. A tool scraped off the wall from its hanger, and he said, *this will do the work.* And then the door creaked open again, letting even colder air into the barn.

They sighed exasperated sighs, pulled their clothes over themselves and began rebuttoning buttons. The passion had leaked out of the moment.

Chapter 59

Finally, through the hazy web of internal static, he received the message. The devil was coming, coming for the angel people. Johnny put down the hubcaps and took the kettle off his head. He followed the footprints in the snow and paused at the barn door to look at the two snow angels there. Inside the barn, the angels were laughing. He nodded at the sign, an affirmation.

To fight the devil, you must think like the devil and fight like the devil fights. He went to the barn and retrieved a long handled, three tined hayfork. This will do the work, Johnny said. Yes, said the voices, Yes, it will. Strike with courage, they said, strike the devil with courage. He will come from the south, wearing the light colored clothing of southern folk, here in the midst of winter. *Strike him.*

Johnny put the hayfork over his shoulder and marched to the side yard and hid it just under the edge of the house where the snow had not fallen. And then he waited while the sun fell in the west and the darkness loomed over it, first blue, and then cold black and studded with stars.

Dewey invited Sammy and Betsy to sit in the projection booth with him while Alta went to prayer meeting. The movie was a double feature, first *The Sons of Katie Elder*, starring John Wayne, and then *The Greatest Story Ever Told*, starring Max Von Sydow as Christ. Dewey was in the habit of first playing the movie that he thought Alta would object to most, while she was at prayer meeting. She particularly frowned on the James Bond movies with their scantily clad jezebels and Bond himself, waking up bare-chested with a different one in each scene. Dewey saved these and showed them marathon style on the weeks she went to the revival in Paducah with her sister.

As the sky blue sky deepened to midnight blue, the movie previews invited patrons to visit the concession stand, which on the screen was spacious, well stocked, and clean but at the Just Drive In was a converted deer stand with only a handful of items to sell. Betsy and Sammy shared one of those items, popcorn served up by Dewey's hired girl, a small breasted, heavy set teen with an acne pocked face.

In the projection booth, Mr. Bettis was looking over his glasses, checking the reels and getting them in order. Betsy and Sammy sat next to each other on a tattered plaid couch, happily munching, the lights of the screen flashing in their faces as their hands went from the bag to their mouths and back again. Betsy leaned into Sammy's shoulder. Dewey smiled and found a blanket in a cabinet and draped it over them.

The first feature began, John Wayne playing one of the four sons of a mother who had died lamenting the fact that her sons were all ne'er-do-wells, including John Wayne, who was a gunfighter. Sammy had never been a fan of westerns, but he would sit on a pan of hot coals through a movie in Chinese if it meant Betsy was beside him.

He scanned the cars in the drive in. There were at best a couple of dozen. The couple in the Chrysler who had already fogged up the windows. Next to it, a mother and father and their station wagon full of children. Then Sammy came across a police cruiser. His eyes focused, and he saw the Louisiana plates. He squinted harder trying to discern the occupant but there wasn't one.

An hour earlier Parris had seen the blue Mustang parked by the barn. His plan was to wait until dark and then find that Teague boy and put an end to all this foolishness. Parris was bigger, and, if he could get Sammy alone, he could probably snap his neck. That Teague boy was soft and weak from never having done an honest day's work in his life. Snap his neck and it would look like he fell out of the loft.

The Just Drive In would be the perfect cover. Just wait for the movie show to start, slip out like it was a trip to the restroom, take care of things, and then return. If he was in the barn, then they probably wouldn't find the body for at least a day. By then he would be halfway to St. Matthew Parish, and with any luck he'd have that Duplechain girl with him. He was glad he'd remembered the duct tape. If things worked out right, he would have her while that Teague boy watched, just before his neck snapped.

A jumble of Psalms ran through Johnny's head, bits and pieces of a dozen or more, all in the wrong combinations. The voices discussed the action in feverish commentary like the St. Louis Cardinals play-by-play men on the radio. Johnny waited.

And then there he was, the devil. He's not near as thin as I thought, Johnny said, less like a snake or a lizard or a goat and more like a hog, and the voices answered back, the devil can take many forms to confuse the righteous. Fear not.

Parris stood on his toes and looked in the dark house. It was empty, not a soul. Good, no witnesses, he thought. Likely they're in the barn, so much easier. He eased back, his cowboy boots crunching in the snow and leaving pointed footprints. Across the fence on the drive-in screen, men were gearing up for a gunfight, terse silent dialogue with palms on holstered guns.

The voices flared frantically, the devil is here, here in the side yard. Heavenly light illuminated the hayfork, the tines sharp and gleaming. Strike him, strike him, strike him the voices said, the voices of the angels and the government agents and the play-by-play men, all yelling in disjointed unison. Their voices shrieking, groaning and then trailing down to the prolonged hiss of a single feminine voice whispering seductively, *Strike him*.

The hayfork flashed in the glow of the silver screen, then made the sound of a dart hitting a board. *Caught the outside corner,* the play-by-play men said, *strike one.*

"God. *Dammit,*" Parris moaned a second after one of the tines impaled his upper right arm against the house. His left hand fumbled across his body for the gun on his right hip. Johnny's bearded face was placid, his eyes heavy lidded, ambivalent, bored looking. His long brown hair shook as he wiggled the hayfork, trying to dislodge it for another thrust. Each small movement made the deputy grimace.

The deputy's left hand finally found the pearl handle of his revolver. He unsheathed it, his hand trembling in pain as he tried to reverse it in his hand. He almost dropped it when Johnny succeeded in dislodging the hayfork.

Johnny pulled it back like a javelin ready for launch. The pale throat of the devil reflected a red light.

At the Just Drive In, John Wayne and his movie brothers were involved in a gunfight. Shots rang out as the brothers on the screen found themselves pinned down under a bridge. One of the shots seemed particularly realistic and caused the couple necking in the Chrysler to stop and wipe the condensation from the window and then resume their necking.

Sammy saw the familiar form return to the cruiser. Parris leaned into the car where he pulled out a white box with a red cross on it and lumbered off to the restroom. Sammy watched as Parris stayed there until the first movie was finished, and Dewey had the first reel of *The Greatest Story Ever Told* running. Sammy pulled the blanket over himself and Betsy.

Mr. Bettis had just settled into his chair when there was a knock on the door of the projection booth. He looked at Sammy who peeked from under the blanket. Betsy had fallen asleep during the first feature, only briefly raising her head during the gunfight. Dewey opened the door a crack, and Sammy heard a familiar voice outside.

"You the owner?

"I am, sir."

"Listen, what kind of a death trap is this? That outhouse you call a restroom had a nail stickin' out bout yea long." Through the crack in the door Sammy saw a thumb and middle finger stretched far apart. "Liked to impaled me."

"I'm sorry sir," Mr. Bettis said. "I'll see to it."

"That's all right, I already pulled it out the wall myself. Just make sure there ain't no more, hear?"

"Certainly," Mr. Bettis said, "Thank you kindly for bringing it to my attention." He shut the crack in the door.

Sammy watched as Parris went back to his car with his first aid kit and waited for the sirens to appear next door.

Alta came home from Women's Fellowship, pleased to see Dewey's choice of movie. Through the dining room window, the screen flashed across the fence as the apostles mouthed silent dialogue. She kicked off her shoes, her bunions were killing her, and checked the house for Johnny but couldn't find him. She assumed he was in the side yard, talking to himself, watching the movie, or both. When she looked out the window, she saw him lying in the snow, and at first she thought he was napping and went to get him a blanket in case she couldn't persuade him to come in.

When she returned from the linen closet, she checked again to make sure he hadn't already gotten up. The light from the big screen flooded the side yard, and she dropped the blanket.

She left the door open and let the screen door slam. Through the screen, the cold crept into the house. She rounded into the side yard, her bare feet kicking up small tuffs of snow. She plowed into the snow on her knees and examined her son, his head resting on one of the hubcaps as if it were a platter. She reached under him and pulled him up.

She looked into his vacant eyes and ran her fingers through his hair to straighten it like she used to do on so many of those school mornings when he was young and a rising star and anything was possible. Then she shook with grief and sobbed.

"My boy, my boy, my poor, broken boy," she wailed and shuddered as she rocked his cooling body. His blood was freezing on her hands and her dress. His face was peaceful as the voices quieted and a pleasant silence took their place, a stillness like the first day of spring when even the birds are quietly in awe at the beauty of it.

Behind him, the big screen flashed a sad-faced, thorn-crowned, blue-eyed Max Von Sydow.

Chapter 60

When the sirens of the local law got there, Parris eased out of his car and walked over to the side yard, on the pretense of offering help. He stayed long enough to leave plausible footprints, and when the county sheriff said, 'We've got it from here,' Parris even comforted Alta Bettis.

"We'll find who did this. They can't be far away," he said as his hand squeezed Alta's shoulder.

Then he returned to his car in the drive in, pulled out, and went straight to the local emergency room.

"What happened to you?" the doctor said. He had a crew cut and thick black rimmed glasses.

"Ran into a nail out that drive in."

The young doctor examined the wound, pushing his glasses up on the top of his head, looking closely from one puncture wound to the other and back.

"Well you must've hit it pretty hard, then," he said, trying to imagine how it could've happen.

"Damn straight. Am I gonna need stitches or anythin'?"

"No, don't believe. Pretty clean through and through." The doctor dabbed at one of the two wounds, and Parris winced.

"You're lucky," the doctor said as he wrapped gauze around Parris' upper arm, "Nail missed everything important. Say, what happened over there tonight?"

"Boy got shot. Somebody saw a yella boy with one hand run off is what I heard."

The doctor looked over his glasses at Parris. "Funny, I take care of just about everybody on this stretch of the river, and I don't know anybody like that," he said. "Seems like I would, is all."

"That's just what I heard," Parris said.

Chapter 61

The Hancock County sheriff was a young man, lanky with a cowboy hat and a bomber jacket. He looked over the body and the scene, including a trail of blood on the side of the house. It most likely was the boy's, he concluded. There were sets of footprints from that sheriff who had shown up to help. The Hancock sheriff went inside, brushing the snow off his shoes at the welcome mat, and found Sammy and Betsy sitting side by side on the couch in the living room.

"Now who are you two?" The sheriff asked them.

"Those are our guests," Dewey answered for them. "They been with me in the projection booth the whole time."

"All right, then. Now Dewey, do you know anybody who would've wanted your son dead?"

"No. Ever-body liked Johnny," and then he lowered his head and said bitterly, "Kept 'em entertained, I guess."

Alta couldn't be persuaded to let them take her son without her, so the ambulance crew let her ride to the morgue with his body. The women from her prayer group arrived there and kept a vigil with her, waiting for a Lazarus-like miracle that never came. In the wee hours of the morning, they drove her home and put her to bed for an hour or two of fitful sleep.

The lights in the kitchen burned all night. Dewey sat at the kitchen table with his head in his hands. Occasionally a thunderstorm of grief would boil up inside of him, and he would shake with it and then rub the tears from his face. Sammy lay under the blankets on the couch, his eyes wide and watching. In Johnny's room, Betsy said the Sorrowful mysteries.

An hour before daybreak, Sammy and Betsy gathered their things and told Dewey, "Guess we'll need to head on now." Alta was in the bedroom down the hall where she had just dozed off again, after a solid hour of sobbing that gusted into an occasional soul-scraping howl.

Dewey looked up from the spot on the floor where his stare had faltered and nodded at Sammy.

"If you're headed north, the bridge down at Hawesville's not ready yet. Spose to be next few months. Hafta go further down towards Owensboro."

They started for the door, and Dewey raised his head again and asked, "Do you believe there's a heaven? Tell me there is."

Betsy leaned forward and put her cheek to his balding forehead. It smelled like popcorn.

"Trust me, there is."

Chapter 62

It was first light, and the hidden sun was struggling to make the world become less dark and only managing a dull gray. Sammy carefully eased down the Tar Springs Road as he and Betsy watched for signs of Parris. The fuel needle sagged toward E. The car needed gas.

On the outskirts of Hawesville, they pulled into a service station. The majestic winged horse on the Mobil sign rose out of a weedy yard of rusting engines set up on cinder blocks, and transmissions hung from swing sets like curing hams. A boy of about twelve in a blue jumpsuit a couple of sizes too big came out, rubbing his hands together like he'd seen his father do and said, "Hep you?"

"Fill it with regular, please sir." Sammy said. The boy used two hands to wrangle the nozzle off the pump and put it in the Mustang. As the pump whirred and thumped, Sammy went inside to use the restroom.

On the wall above the urinal was a dispenser for condoms and something called Horny Goat Weed. In the foreground was a picture of a Nanny goat with big eyes and long lashes, and in the background was a Billy goat in a fog of red hearts. The smell of bleach was losing its battle against the smell of mold and urine. The fan in the ceiling hummed as it tried unsuccessfully to pull all of the smells away.

Sammy came out zipping up his pants when he heard, "Packa Lucky Strikes." The voice and the back of the khaki uniform were massive and familiar. There was a brown blood stain and a tear in the shirt sleeve. Sammy quietly crossed behind Parris and went out the door.

Sammy walked as quickly as he could without running, took the nozzle from the boy, and replaced it on the pump. He gave the boy a ten and said quietly, "Keep the change."

He pulled out of the service station carefully and eased onto the main road. He made it a quarter mile and was congratulating himself on slipping away when he saw the cruiser in his rearview. Sammy pulled on a side street and it followed. He took a left and it took a left. He took a right and it took a right. He found the main drag again and slowly accelerated. The cruiser stayed behind him, running without lights, just following. Sammy kept it just under the limit, the cruiser shadowing. In the rearview mirror, there was no mistaking who was behind them.

He panicked when he got to the turn off for the bridge, and instead of passing it up and going further downstream, he turned. Up onto the approach, he saw the Ohio River and the tiers of gray bristled tree lines marching off into the distance on the other side. Halfway up the ramp he came to the Under Construction sign and swerved around it with squealing tires. Parris went through it, scraps of wood flying through the air. The top of the bridge was icy, and both cars fell in and out of fishtails. They approached the square arch of rivet-studded girders. Betsy looked back and then forward. She grabbed the dashboard and began praying:

Je vous salue, Marie, pleine de grâce. Le Seigneur est avec vous. Vous êtes bénie entre toutes les femmes,

The cruiser was getting closer, and Sammy sped up, the speedometer needle passing over the seventy like a hand over a card in a parlor trick. There was still concrete on the road deck under them and up ahead, but he had no idea how much of the bridge was unfinished past that. In the rearview, the cruiser was getting even larger. Betsy rocked back and forth as her prayer quickened into breathlessness:

Et Jésus, le fruit de vos entrailles, est béni. Sainte Marie, Mère de Dieu, Priez pour nous, pauvres pécheurs, maintenant et à l'heure de notre mort.

The needle passed over the ninety mark and began to lean into the hundred when Sammy saw it, the gap in the pavement yawning up ahead. He pushed the accelerator and the needle fell forward, and it sounded as if the Mustang would explode. Girders flashed by in a strobe of shadows, flickering rapidly into a crescendo. Betsy continued to hurriedly whimper the *Hail, Mary* in French, rocking, rocking, and Sammy was sobbing I-love-you-baby in English, his hands squeezing the steering wheel.

Suddenly the hum of the tires stopped, and they were airborne. It felt like forever, like they were flying, and then the Mustang bottomed out hard, bouncing twice on the concrete of the other side. The hum of the road resumed. There was distant whump behind them and then the rattle of metal. They looked back and saw the undercarriage of the cruiser tilted into the air, front tires spinning helplessly. A hubcap rolled off the cruiser and onto its edge and then into a distant circular crescendo.

The hand of the Mustang's speedometer passed back over the eighty, the seventy, the sixty, the fifty, and they were on the decline of the bridge approach. Behind them, the cruiser teetered on the pavement edge, just hanging there, rocking gingerly like a seesaw.

Sammy eased on the brake as the Mustang hit a patch of ice. The Mustang swung around, revolving on the ice. The scenery whirled around them. The guard rail and the gray downstream bank, the gray girders of the bridge against the white sky, the guard rail and the gray bristled upstream bank, the base of the bridge with the barricade, and again, and then a whirling blur of gray and white and the flash of the barricade growing larger, larger with each revolution. Betsy's eyes closed, her hands clutching the dashboard, Sammy's eyes closed, his hands clutching the steering wheel. The car nudged softly into the barricade and stopped, and they opened their eyes.

The first arrivals of the construction crew were gathered there, their faces agape in the oval openings of their balaclavas under the silver hard hats. They had moved to the side of the road to watch the spectacle. Behind them was a newly minted sign greeting its very first visitors:

Welcome to Indiana

Crossroads of America

Two of the workers scrambled up the ice covered incline. A third came over to the Mustang with his hand on his silver hardhat. Sammy opened the door and fell out at the man's feet. The man helped him up and exclaimed in admiration, "Hot damn! That was some daredevil show! The governors of Kentucky and Indiana were supposed to be the first ones to cross, to cut the ribbon in the spring, but I believe you guys beat 'em!"

Sammy staggered over to the edge of the road and was sick. Betsy stayed on the front seat, curled in a ball with her head still tucked down. He heard the worker again.

"Hate to interrupt yer puke, but the project man should be here any minute, and he'll sure's hell call the police. Best you get on way from here now."

Sammy rested with his knees on the ice and his hands on his knees. He wiped his mouth on the back of his hand, inhaled deeply, nodded and rose, and got back in the car. The keys rattled in his shaking hand as he put the key in the ignition and started the car.

They eased down the bridge abutment and turned left at the sign that said "To Tell City." The road circled around and back to the highway near the water's edge. By the riverside just under the bridge, Sammy pulled the car off to the side of the road. He got out on wobbly legs and could barely manage to get a cigarette out of the pack. His hand jiggled as he tried to light it and finally he gave up and threw it to the ground. Betsy was in the front seat with her legs drawn up and her head buried under her arms muttering. *Merci, mon dieu, merci, merci, merci.*

They looked up together as they heard the groan of metal twisting from the road deck of the bridge above them. The cruiser was still up there, teetering, each motion rocking wider. Finally, the car dislodged, the front tires striking the edge of the gap in the pavement, and then it fell, back end first into the water, a fall that seemed to take minutes but was only a few seconds.

When it hit the surface, the Ohio inhaled it and sent up a geyser of water that leaped up and then fell and shattered into big circular waves. One of the headlights of the cruiser broke the surface from below and then went under again. The water flattened and bubbles filtered to the top. A cowboy hat floated up, its crown submerged in the water. The current took it downstream for a few yards and then dropped it into the depths of the cold Ohio.

Sammy got back into the car, and they held each other for a minute until he stopped shaking and could drive again. The fog covered sign said Tell City 3.

Chapter 63

His sweaty hair was matted to his bare head. At the top of the bridge, Parris and the two highway workers watched as the cruiser rocked on its underbelly. He had managed to ease out of the window and crawl over the hood and onto the pavement.

When it slipped with a shearing, scraping, popping noise, the three of them retreated a few steps back. The front tires bumped off the edge where the pavement stopped, and the car bounced into the gap and disappeared. They approached the edge again to peer over and watch the splash below.

"Man," one of the highway workers said. Across the way on the other side of the chasm, a group of the Kentucky workers stood in the wet, steel-cold air and looked down into the abyss with them.

The winter wind whistled, and then the other Indiana man said, "You all right, officer? You need a ride?"

"No." Parris grunted.

The other one picked up the lost hubcap and said, "Don't fergit yer hubcap."

"Kiss my ass," Parris said, and he staggered down the approach ramp of the bridge and then slipped on the ice onto his backside. He struggled to get to his feet and then resumed walking. There was a brown stain in his khaki trousers, the same color as the dried blood on his sleeve.

"I believe the good sheriff done *soiled* himself," one of the men chuckled quietly.

"I believe you're right," the other said.

They were two men who had no special love of the law, two men who bounced between employed and imprisoned. They spent the rest of the gray-domed day in the cold swirling wind carrying heavy shoulder loads of rebar and using shovels to rake concrete out of the mixer chute. Far below them the flat, dark beast of a river waited patiently for one of them to fall so that it could swallow them. Whirlpools dimpled the water around the bridge pilings like mouths opening for them. Their burden was made light, however, as they enjoyed the recurring joke of the day.

"The shittin' sheriff! Off to catch another poop-atrator!" one would exclaim randomly. Their wool gloved hands would pull cigarettes off their lips and fire imaginary shots from their right and left hands, *Pow! Pow!* before bending slightly at the waist and making a farting noise. And each time they would laugh like the joke was fresh.

Parris walked the three miles into Tell City, the fog making it seem farther away than that. The town was beginning to wake up, the rush of cars stirring the chilly air. Some of the shop windows had been painted up for the town basketball team. *'Go Marksmen!'* was spelled out in crimson and white, along with *'Sink the Commodores!'* A hapless, big-eyed admiral was drawn in green going down with his ship.

Parris walked along Twelfth Street. The sun struggled against the clouds and failed, and the air remained wet and cold. He came upon a Pontiac dealership and ducked inside.

"Mornin', sir," the salesman said. His hair was slick, and he wore a white shirt and striped tie with crisply pressed slacks.

"Need a new car," Parris said as he scanned the showroom.

"Lookin' to finance?"

"Cash."

"Well, then," the salesman licked his lips and smiled. He regarded Parris' uniform. "Looks like you got into a scrape. You with the law?"

"Yeah," Parris said flatly as he bent over to look at the sticker of a black Pontiac GTO. The salesman sniffed the air and wrinkled up his nose.

"This'n," Parris said. "How much?"

"That one's..." the salesman checked the sticker "...thirty four hunnert."

"Take a check?"

"Sure, but I'll need to call 'n verify it."

Parris' meaty hand wrote out the check and handed it to the man, who held it up as if he wanted to see through it. Then he picked up the phone, still eyeing the check and clutching it in case it tried to get away.

"Operator, Thabo-Ducks, Loozy-anner. Planters State Bank."

"Tibba-doe," Parris said

"Uh, that's Tibber-doe," the salesman corrected himself for the operator. He smiled awkwardly at Parris as they waited.

Parris went over to the window and saw a clothing store across the street. The town was emerging like a moth from a cocoon, getting to its business as cars began to pass with more frequency. He noticed his reflection in the showroom window. His khaki shirt was speckled brown with the dried blood of that crazy boy. He started to pull his sheriff's jacket over the spattered stain, but realized it was at the bottom of the Ohio.

Two teenage boys walked down the street outside. One was bouncing a basketball, the other had his hands in the pockets of a crimson letterman's jacket. The salesman called from across the showroom.

"Well, she says 'Plenty of money. It don't even scratch the surface,'" he said proudly.

They filled out the papers, and the salesman handed Parris the keys to a brand new black Pontiac GTO.

"I'll come back for it."

He walked across the street, pausing to let a car pass. On the opposite sidewalk was Braustein's Menswear, the glass enclosure of a display window out front. A woman was changing manikins out of pilgrim and Indian costumes and into Christmas clothes. On the sidewalk in front of Braustein's, there was a red metal newspaper vending machine. Through the wire lattice the Perry County News proclaimed:

Hawesville Man Shot and Killed

And in smaller print:

Police Seeking Light Skinned, One Armed Negro

Parris smirked at the headlines and went in Braustein's. He gathered up three pairs of pants, some shirts, undershirts, underwear, socks, and a new leather coat. He laid them on the counter and picked up a black wool suit and a tie. The lady who had been dressing the window display went through his items, methodically entering the prices as the adding machine whirred and dinged. Behind Parris, a woman and her small daughter waited with a few things. The little girl held her mother's skirt in one hand and her nose in the other. Her small voice was nasal.

"Mama," she said, "That man made a..."

"Shhh," her mother said across her index finger.

Parris went back across the street and collected his new car. He drove into town and rented a room at the Schweizerland Motel. The marquis of the Schweizerland was adorned with a man in a black jacket with a brightly embroidered lapel. He was blowing into an immense alphorn as an amiable-looking mountain goat stood by him.

After Parris had showered and changed into clean clothes, he walked down to the Ohio and threw his old khaki uniform into the black water. It lingered for a moment, flailing slowly and dreamlike, like seaweed. Then the river swallowed it, engulfing the blood on the shirt and the fright in the trousers, down into its blackness.

He returned to his motel room and sat down with a map. The big finger of his big hand moved over the map, a net of lines speckled with circles and place names. It traced out the most direct route to the Canadian border.

Detroit.

Part IV: Indiana

Chapter 64

The fog had thinned a little, and, at the advancing edge of it, farmhouses with barns and silos appeared as the road lifted and fell and curved around them. The Mustang had developed a rattle somewhere underneath it.

"We need to get married," Sammy said suddenly. He had always imagined the moment so differently, on bended knee with a gem-topped ring in a velvet box, at the country club after a candlelight dinner with a violinist ready to play.

"Okay," Betsy smiled, and she leaned over to kiss him. Her lips felt warm and dry to him.

"We need to get you set up with a doctor," Sammy said, "When we get where we're goin'."

"Where we goin'?" Betsy asked.

"I don't know," Sammy said as his eyes nervously scanned the road.

The road hummed beneath them as they held hands. She curled up on her side in the front seat and put Sammy's black and blue plaid jacket over herself. Sammy felt her hand loosen and looked over to see her eyes closed with two comma brushes of thick eyelashes in their place.

After half an hour, Betsy woke, and they stopped at a little roadside diner and ate breakfast. Outside the diner, intermittent traffic made wet rushing tracks on the rain soaked road. In front of the diner by the side of the road, a sycamore had shed its big leaves into a dry brown carpet that rustled and tossed itself with each passing car. Inside the diner were the smells of stale coffee and fried food and damp clothing and cigarette smoke. People muttered conversations in the unnaturally low watt light.

Sammy was ravenous, but Betsy ate very little. She rested her elbows on the table and cradled her chin in her hands. Her plate was undisturbed except for a few bites.

"You not hungry, baby?" Sammy asked Betsy. His mouth was full, and he put his hand over it as he chewed.

"Just got a little chill, that's all."

The waitress, a dark haired young woman in a brown polyester uniform and a yellow apron, floated from booth to booth with a coffee pot. Her hips were the size and shape of a church bell, and her legs made a scratching noise from her thick white hose when she walked.

She approached Sammy and Betsy's table and asked, "Anything wrong?"

"No ma'am, just not hungry like I thought."

"Want some tea or something?"

"Yes ma'am, that'd be good."

"Okay, hun," the waitress said. Her legs scratched out a rhythm as she went behind the counter. A truck driver in the opposite booth looked up from his paper and watched the waitress go.

She returned with the tea, the strings draped over the side of the enamel ware cup. Betsy blew on the surface and took a sip.

"My throat is sore. The tea feels good on it." She took a few sips of it and laid her head down on the smooth red Formica of the counter. Sammy looked at the tab and carefully counted out the money to cover it.

They got back in the car just as a rain came down that quickly turned to sleet, and Betsy fell asleep again. The thin canvas roof of the Mustang was all that separated them from the elements, but for Sammy any roof that Betsy was under was home.

The sound under the Mustang was getting louder, a metal on metal sound, a guttural grinding. Another few miles down the highway it began lurching in a way that would delight children on a carnival ride but terrified Sammy. He was beginning to take on worries, worries that clouded his mind, the worries of a family man. How will I feed them? How will I clothe them? How will I keep them safe? The worries of a shepherd, a man who looked after not only himself but those around him.

Betsy woke up and looked out the window at the sleet. She looked at Sammy who stared down the road and stated the obvious.

"Something's wrong."

The car began to slow, failing to respond to the accelerator. It emitted a groan, creeping along as other cars passed them, even old farmers in dilapidated pickups. Sammy pulled over on the side of the road.

He stepped out into the weather, the sleet tapping on the car and the ground. He pulled the black and blue flannel jacket around him and got down to take a look. His knees crunched into a thin sheet of ice on the ground. The underside of the Mustang was a dark jumble of metal he couldn't even begin to make heads or tails of.

His cheeks were reddened under his beard, and he got back in and said, "Next town, we stop to get this looked at." He started the car, and it went about ten feet when something fell below it. He got out again and saw something protruding from the bottom of the car that hadn't been there moments before. He got back in.

"Well, here we are," he said, trying to make light of it. "Alone at last."

"What we gonna do?" Betsy asked. Her voice was raspy. She rattled out a cough and put her hand to her throat. "Ooh," she winced.

He got out and looked up and down the empty highway, his breath misting in the cold. He put his fingers to the pack of cigarettes in his shirt pocket, but then left the pack there. The sleet tapped on his head, and the ends of his hair and beard began to pick up frozen droplets of it. It fritted the windshield glass and blurred Betsy's image. Sammy found it oddly distressing.

From around a bend in the highway, a car whose color had faded to a salmon pink appeared, its driver a bespectacled middle-aged man with hands at ten and two, carefully surveying the road. He pulled even with them and stopped, then leaned over to crank down the passenger side window. He wore brass-rimmed spectacles, a corduroy coat, and a plaid hat with ear flaps.

"Sweet Jesus!" he said. His voice had the frank, flat honesty of the Midwest. Behind the lenses of his glasses, his eyes were hazel, bright and sincere. "What are you doing standing out in this weather?"

"Car broke down."

"Well, get in! Might as well get your bags, too. Nothing'll be open with this weather. More snow coming in, maybe a foot, they're saying."

"You take us to a hotel, we'd be grateful."

"Oh, I can take you to a hotel. You'll have it all to yourself."

Sammy opened the trunk of the Mustang and got their suitcases, the expensive leather one his mother had bought him when he started Ole Miss and Betsy's old flaking red-brown one and her overnight case. He put them in the trunk of the man's car, an old Nash Rambler. The backseat was filled with cardboard boxes, so the three of them sat on the front seat, Betsy in the middle.

The man's knees protruded up near the wheel. He extended his hand to Sammy. "Anthony Keary. Call me Tony."

"Sammy Teague. And this is Betsy," and then he added, "My wife." The words felt strange in his mouth. Betsy looked at Sammy, smiling in wonder at the sound of it for the first time. She took his hand, and Sammy felt how warm she was.

"Nice to meet you, Mrs. Teague." She blushed at the sound of it and tried not to smile. The car accelerated out of its puttering.

"Yes, indeed, more snow tonight they say. You'll see up ahead, it's already accumulated some. Where are you two headed?"

"Up north."

"Up north from Louisiana? Well, Sammy, that's exactly opposite of the birds. This time of year, they're nesting down south, and the foxes are all in their dens. No time to be headed north."

"How did you know we were from Louisiana?"

"Your license plate." He looked from the road and raised his eyebrows at Sammy. "'Sportsman's Paradise?'"

There was a Rosary hanging from the rearview mirror and a Miraculous Medal.

"You catlic'?" Betsy asked.

"Am I? I should say so," he laughed as he pulled his coat open a bit to show his black shirt and white collar. "I'm a priest! Society of Jesus, a Jesuit. God's Marines!"

In the passenger side view mirror, the blue Mustang became a small gray object, and then it was gone.

Chapter 65

They drove under the double arch, West Baden Springs, Carlsbad of America, and past a smaller sign by the drive, West Baden College, Society of Jesus. A light snow was on the ground, mottled with brown patches of bare earth. Through the gray spikes of winter trees there it was, a six story, pale yellow brick colossus with a brick red dome.

"One of my old aunts used to come here for her rheumatism," Sammy said looking up at it from under the rearview mirror. "I recognize it from the postcard."

"This was quite a destination back in the day," Keary said as he pushed up the bridge of his glasses with his finger. "People came here to 'take the cure.' Train brought them in at the station back behind us. The hotel had the best of everything. Pro baseball teams trained here, White Sox, Cubs, St. Louis, when they were the Browns, Pirates, Phillies. Joe Louis, the boxer, trained here, but he couldn't stay at the hotel because he was a Negro. Had a two tier bicycle track, right over there. Beautiful gardens, and of course, the baths. Some place. The stock market crash knocked it out, or rather, knocked out the patrons, and the owner, a Mr. Ballard, sold it to the Jesuits for one dollar."

"One dollar?"

"One dollar. You believe that? All this. I hear he'd paid a million for it."

The base of the steps was flanked by dark green cast iron lampposts with clusters of white globes on top of them. They got out and climbed up the steps, Keary carrying their bags. Betsy lagged behind them, looking up at the great yellow building, and Sammy took her hand and they looked up together. They followed Keary onto the main porch. The railings were painted dark green like the lampposts. Sammy paused to study a curious detail in them.

"See the swastikas in the railing?" Keary gestured with his head. "When they built the hotel in 1902, they had no idea what those would come to mean. It was just decoration. A case of the Nazis stealing art, I guess, art that can never be recovered. It'll always be associated with evil now."

They entered through a chapel, large and ornate with thick round columns and a floor covered in tiny tiles. Behind the altar was a picture of Christ with two other men at his feet, all with halos above their heads.

"This used to be the lobby. The check-in desk was over there," Keary said as he nodded in its direction.

They exited the chapel through a side door, and then they moved into the atrium. It was enormous.

Keary's voice echoed in the large central space. "Two hundred feet across here, a hundred feet up to the roof in the center. When it was opened in 1902, they called it the eighth wonder of the world. Largest free standing dome at the time. That new one down in Houston, the Astrodome I think they call it, is the biggest now."

Betsy and Sammy stood in the middle of it and gazed up in wonder. It was grander than Mount Teague, it was grander than ten Mount Teagues. Six story columns, topped with sculptured capitals, twenty four of them, marched around the perimeter with balconies in between, skylights in the roof, and a floor that was intricately tiled. The white painted girders soared upward to a circular medallion, a canopy that had presided over spectacle after grand spectacle.

Under that roof men in bowlers, boaters, and top hats had waited for women to meet them, women in long skirts and shoes that buttoned up the side, long sleeved blouses with puffs at the shoulders and swept up hair. A measure of the mirth and enchantment of it all had seeped into the tiles, a bit of the grandeur had been absorbed by the walls and columns. Now in a small corner of it, two couches and an end table had been placed at the edges of an area rug, just a few yards square, to form a small living area. The atrium dwarfed it.

Keary set the suitcases down on the rug and examined his hands and shook them out. "I was coming back from Illinois, went to help out my dad. I've been shoveling snow for two days." Keary seemed delighted and deeply honored to have parents to do for. He held out his hands to reveal two round red blisters on his palms.

"No doubt, I'm not as used to honest work as I thought, I suppose." He laughed, and it echoed out into the immense space.

"I'll make us a fire on such a cold, cold day," he said, and then he disappeared from the atrium through a door.

Betsy leaned into Sammy, and he could feel her breathe and smell the sweet breath of the sick. She put her forehead on his shoulder and shut her eyes. The couches were drawn up near a huge fireplace with a stone mosaic of a tree with fruit, a brook rushing over rocks, and an elf with some sort of cup. Betsy and Sammy sat tentatively on the edge of the couch.

Keary came in with an armload of firewood and arranged it with kindling. From the mantle he produced a match and struck it, and it snapped and flared. Keary placed the small flame under the logs, and a glow began under them. He took off his hat, the plaid one with the flaps, and put it on the hearth. He recited a poem as he tinkered with the fire.

Sundays too my father got up early
and put his clothes on in the blueblack cold,
Then with cracked hands that ached
from labor in the weekday weather made
banked fires blaze. No one ever thanked him.

Tony looked over his shoulder at Sammy and smiled with the words, "No one ever thanked him," and then he brushed his hands into the fire and continued reciting:

I'd wake and hear the cold splintering, breaking,
When the rooms were warm, he'd call
and slowly I would rise and dress,
fearing the chronic angers of that house,

He took the poker and pried a space between the logs for the fire to explore and finished:

Speaking indifferently to him,
who had driven out the cold
and polished my good shoes as well.
What did I know, what did I know
Of love's austere and lonely offices?

He brushed his hands again and turned around with a smile. Behind his back, his hands enjoyed the warmth of the fire. His blonde hair was thick and fell over his head like the crest of a bird.

241

"Robert Frost?" Sammy asked. It was the only name of a poet he remembered. He had known others for English tests, but they had been crammed, regurgitated for the exam, and forgotten.

"No, Robert S. Hayden. A black man, poet from Detroit." He smiled as the fire warmed his back. "You know, when I first saw you guys from way off on the highway, I thought maybe you were the couple from Michigan, come to see about buying the place."

"It's for sale?"

"Yep, the Jesuits can't keep it any longer, dwindling enrollment closed the college. I'm up here tending it until it's sold. I fill in for the diocese here as well. I've been saying Mass down in French Lick the last few Sundays."

"What will you do when it's sold?"

"Whatever the Lord and Chicago need me to." He said it matter-of-factly, as if whatever it was would be the greatest adventure ever.

Sammy looked back in the fire glow to watch the firelight play off the immense dome. Through the skylights, the curtain was falling on the day.

"I've sat through many a dry commencement speech in this place. Slept through a couple," Keary snickered. He saw Sammy looking up into the dome.

"There are angels up there, you know."

"Up where?"

"In the dome. There's a little room, circular, about sixteen feet in diameter. You have to take stairs, on the outside, on the roof, and then go down a ladder. But there are angels painted on the inside walls."

Betsy coughed, and it echoed in the atrium.

"My goodness, Betsy. You sound like a sea lion, just awful. I'll have to make you a toddy after dinner."

He turned and rubbed his hands to the fire.

"The dining hall used to be on the main floor, just off the atrium, but since I eat alone, I like to take supper in my quarters on the second floor. Cozier. Easier to heat."

*   *   *

Keary's quarters were Spartan compared to the opulent atrium and dome. It was essentially an efficiency apartment. A neatly

242

made bed with a royal blue blanket folded over carefully at the foot, with a crucifix on the wall over it. A desk with cabriole legs stacked with books, ecclesiastical and non-ecclesiastical, and papers. Pictures of a white haired couple who must have been his parents. Pictures of Keary with his brothers and sisters, all with arms around each other, all smiling.

Across from the bed was a small kitchen set against the wall. On the white refrigerator with the rounded corners were pictures of children, his nieces and nephews, and their artwork.

Outside the window, the Indiana night had fallen quickly, and Keary stood at the stove with a black iron skillet frothing with hot grease.

"Walleye and bass! The fruits of Lake Patoka," he said. His blonde hair rose and fell from his head like a small tidal wave in a straw colored sea. He was wearing a flowered apron over his black pants and shirt, a very womanly apron, but it didn't seem to bother him in the least. His glasses were perched on the end of his nose as he dredged the fillets in meal. He eased them into the grease, which made a shushing sound. He took a loaf of brown bread, homemade in the kitchen of a parishioner in French Lick, and cut it in two.

"You need help?" Betsy said. She felt odd having someone else cook for her.

"You're not use to being cooked for, are you?" He read her mind. "Chop some of that cabbage then." His hands were in flour, and he gestured with his head.

When the meal was prepared they sat, and he gave thanks for the food with a short, simple blessing. They dug in.

"How did you come to be a priest?" Sammy asked. The idea of it, especially the celibacy aspect, seemed unnatural to Sammy.

"Well," he finished his bite and swallowed. "In two words? Susie McNamara." He laughed, though there was a sense that there had been a time that he couldn't. "I was in love with that girl, and we dated for a time, but she ran off with someone else. So I bounced around, floundered, really, and eventually married a different bride, the church."

Betsy found herself feeling sorry not for Tony Keary, but for Susie McNamara.

"Have you every regretted it? Becoming a priest?"

"Oh, it would have been nice to have had a family, you know, a family of my own. But the people you take care of become your family, no different than the two of you will become family, mostly because you take care of each other. You need three things in this world to be happy: someone to love, something to live for, and something to do. The church gives me all three."

After supper, they went downstairs and sat by the fire and talked. Keary was a prodigious story teller. He seemed to have been everywhere, to have met everyone. From time to time, he would leave and return with wood and add it to the fire. They sat looking into the flames as it grew late. He hadn't run out of stories and probably wouldn't.

"Do you want me to get you a room ready upstairs?"

The fire was so hospitable, crackling, leaping, dancing merrily, and they were so transfixed by it. Above the skylights in the dome, the night sky was releasing a flurry of snow. Neither could imagine being more content than right at that very place.

"We fine," Betsy said.

"Well, then, I'm headed up to bed," Keary said. "You know where I'll be, right upstairs. Don't hesitate."

Sammy and Betsy snuggled together on the couch in the glow, with the immense dome flashing dimly behind them. Their faces were side by side, the light from the fire changing them from yellow to orange to white to dark and back through the spectrum. The flames curled up from under the logs and moved into liquid orange and yellow tips.

"Where'd you get that picture of me?" Sammy finally asked. "The one by my old Tbird. I saw it when you opened your suitcase."

In the firelight, she told him everything, everywhere she had been. About the longest, loneliest night of her life, on the highway, about the salesman, Deacon John and Rosaline Laurence, and about Tina, and about the Kappas. Sammy held her.

"Tina," Sammy said. "A great girl, and sweet, but a child, not a woman. Not like you."

Betsy wondered about the depth of their relationship, but she let it go. It didn't matter now.

"So I guess it *was* you, in the upstairs window," Sammy said.

"It was. I tried to catch you, to yell at you through the window, but it wouldn't open. I even ran down the street in my nightgown."

"You know, I thought it might be you by the way your shadow moved. Or at least I had hoped it was you." His voice was tinged with awe at being able to do such a thing, that you could know someone so well to distinguish her by a gesture of her shadow.

They smiled. The flames shimmied and swayed. "You played the piano in the rectory didn't you?"

"With Father Eichert," Sammy said.

The elf on the fireplace vibrated in the firelight. Keary sang somewhere in the building, his fine tenor distant and mellow, rendering "Just a Closer Walk with Thee." It filled the dome and soothed the couple on the couch into a contented slumber.

Chapter 66

Betsy awoke to bright sunlight streaming in through the skylights. Sammy was still asleep behind her. During the night, a blanket had been draped over them, a soft royal blue blanket with SJ and a cross embroidered on it.

The columns around the perimeter of the atrium stood silently. She rubbed her eyes and looked up and around at them. She had not slept so well in months, but her throat was still sore.

She lifted Sammy's arm and rose quietly. Sitting down on the other couch, she looked back at him. He seemed different now. He took up most of the length of the couch, taller it seemed, gentler, more thoughtful. More manly.

There was a charred log in the fireplace, and the smell of smoke was faint at most. In the stone mantle the elf raised his glass to something.

She rose and went to find a bathroom. She wandered the circular hallway, found one, and then walked through the entire circle and back to where she started. A door led out to a circular balcony that curved around the building that was bordered by the swastika-pocked green iron railing. Beyond it, evergreen trees held burdens of snow in their dark green boughs. Through them she saw Keary seated under a gazebo on the hillside.

He had set down the load of firewood he was carrying and was resting under the roof where the priests before him had years ago, for some reason, cemented over one of the springs. This one was once called Jacobs Spring. The flaps of his plaid cap were down over his ears, and he had mittens on. The firewood was a collection of three logs about ten to twelve feet long, just short enough to fit in the big fireplace. He sat smiling and admiring the valley through his brass rimmed spectacles, listening to the sound of dogs barking and children playing in the town across it. The town's black and brown roofs, now hidden under white, had crept up the hillside over the years, advancing in fits and starts of prosperity and decline and then rebound. Smoke curled from chimneys as life was happening under the snow-covered roofs, slowly for some, quickly for others, happiness, sadness, but life was happening and there was joy at the very root of it.

She went back and got Sammy's black and blue plaid coat and came up the hill. The snowy grounds were intensely white in the sunlight. She called to Keary as she neared, watching her feet sink into the snow.

"It's so pretty. We don't have this back home."

"No, but you have beauty of your own. Every place does. Come join me, my dear. Keep an old man company for a minute."

"Aw, you not that ole." She put her hands to her eyes to shield them from the sun that was reflecting off the snow.

"I'm older than you think, and a little older now than when I picked up that load of firewood a few minutes ago, and I feel it." Smiling, he pointed to the wood and leaned back against a column of the gazebo. Over across the valley in the town, a dog barked. A car went by on the highway.

She approached, and he said, "How are you feeling today? Better, I hope."

"A little better. Just a little."

"I'm glad. I think you were about to worry Sammy sick." He paused and tilted his head as he looked her in the eye. "You and Sammy aren't really married, are you?"

Her smile faded. "No sir, we're not, not yet. Sorry we lied."

"Oh, that's all right, people get ashamed and frightened sometimes. Mary wasn't married when she found out she was with child. Your baby must be due in May, right?"

Betsy felt her jaw drop. She wasn't even showing yet.

"How, how you know about that?"

"I've just got a gift for things like that. My dad's like that too, I must've gotten it from him. We're just..." He closed his eyes, and his finger scratched the air for the word, then he opened his eyes and pointed when he found it, "...intuitive, I think they call it. Back home, he always knew when the Illinois would flood, and he would get the flock out of the lower pasture, move 'em to higher ground. We kept sheep, see. Neighbors would always follow his lead."

Betsy was still incredulous. She looked down at her stomach and put a hand there.

"You know what it's gonna be?"

"Your baby? Oh yeah, I know, but I don't want to spoil your surprise."

"No, tell me."

"It's gonna be either a boy or a girl," he said, and he winked at her as he got to his feet and brushed dirt off his backside. He stooped down and picked up the logs of firewood putting two of them over his shoulder. He couldn't get the last one, a dogwood six inches around with a small green leaf attached.

"Can you get that one, my dear?"

Betsy picked it up and put it on his shoulder with the other two.

"Well," he said, "Pick up your burdens with singing, I always say." He started down the hillside to the big round building, his tenor voice carrying:

Were I the perfect child of God
Whose faith was deep, and whose love was broad,
Not guilty, doubtful, worn or flawed,
I'd gladly follow Jesus.

He broke his song and shouted back to her. The logs on his shoulder moved with the turn.

"You're sick, Betsy. Come inside and get well first. We have snow most of the winter here. You can enjoy it when you're well."

She followed him down the hill.

247

Chapter 67

The night landscape whirred and bent in the wind-blown snow. The big square headed man stood in it by the side of the road. The headlights of the black GTO illuminated the flakes like motes of dust. The highway was empty.

The headlights also caught the square tail lights and Louisiana plates of the Mustang. A Thibodaux dealership, it had to be them. Parris squatted low to peer under it and saw the problem. If it was what he thought it was, probably a universal joint or a drive shaft, then it was fixable. It would require the price of a tow and three days labor or so, but then they would be mobile again. He stood and thought it out, snow collecting on the brim of his gray fedora.

He left and went into town and returned again. He took a screwdriver and removed the two screws from the license plate, pausing every few turns to look up the road and then down it. He threw the license plate into the trunk of the GTO and took out two cans of gasoline. He used a pocket knife to slit the canvas top of the Mustang, making a flap. Checking the highway again, one direction and then the other, he turned the can up, shook gasoline around the interior of the car, and then dropped the empty can in the flap.

He took the other can and dowsed the outside of the car, soaking each wheel and then dropping the second can in the flap with the first. He looked up and down the road again and saw the empty highway. He took the pack of Lucky Strikes from his pocket and shook one out. He held it in his teeth as he struck a match and fired the cigarette. He exhaled, his smoky breath enveloping snowflakes, and he threw the match on the Mustang. The flame hesitated and then raced out in all directions, over and then into the car which in a fleeting second went from blue to brilliant, fluid orange. The flames danced in Parris' eyes, much like the cold night in 1931 when he was a child. The car quickly became a solid block of flames. He sat on the hood of the GTO and smoked in the snow and watched it. The only way he could have been more satisfied would be if those two had been in it.

A pair of headlights approached from the opposite direction and slowed. It was a Plymouth Satellite with a group of four teenagers, two couples on a double date. The driver rolled down his window. The window right behind him had two faces in it, a slick-haired, freckled-faced boy and a ponytailed girl with buck teeth. Both were mesmerized by the blaze.

"Hey mister," the driver said, "You need us to go get the fire department down in Tell City? We're headed that away."

"No need. It's my brother-in-law's car. I believe it's too late to save it, don't you? Just let it burn. I'll stay here and tend it."

"Awright," the boy said. The Plymouth pulled away, the boy and the girl in the backseat now twisted back in their seats, still watching the blaze.

Parris stayed there until the fire went out, and there was little more than twisted metal. Whirlwinds of flimsy ash and cinders floated up while snow fell down. Around the charred remains there was a ring of bare earth and highway where the heat had melted the snow. He threw the butt of his cigarette onto the black and gray heap of ashes and got in the GTO. It flared to life sounding like the Mustang had when it went up in flames, and he pulled around on the highway and went back into town, back to the warmth of his room at the Schweizerland Motel. The Mustang emitted a smoky glow in the rearview mirror.

Chapter 68

The whispers tried to take off into the dome of the atrium, which caused Betsy to lower her head in attempt to keep her voice down. Her tan had faded, and her smooth skin was more creamy and her freckles more noticeable.

"He knows, Sammy, he knows we gonna have a baby."

"You told him?"

"I *didn't* tell 'im. He just knew, knew without me sayin' nothin'. And he knows we not married." Her voice was quietly distressed.

They were interrupted by the sound of the outside door in the chapel opening. The echo squeezed through the chapel and into the atrium and was still big. Keary walked into the atrium looking through a stack of mail. He was wearing the traditional black outfit with a white collar, but he still had on the plaid cap with the ear flaps. He looked up from the letters and smiled like he was genuinely glad to see them.

"Well, good morning. Went to visit a few *shut-ins* at the county jail in Paoli." He held a brown-papered package under his arm as he continued to look through the mail. "Every one of them innocent when they talk to the judge but guilty as sin when they talk to me."

He set the mail down on a table at the base of a marble urn. He pulled the package from under his arm.

"From my parents." His expression was bemused as he held it up and looked over his glasses.

Sammy could see the address, handwritten on the brown paper in a flawless script:

Rex & Mary Keary,
423 South Orange Street,
Havana, Illinois

"Bet it's for my birthday later this month. Another birthday! Where does time go?"

"How old, then?" Betsy asked.

"Thirty three, again," he looked over his glasses at Betsy and added, "In fact, I think I'll stay at thirty three from here on out." He looked at the name on the package and said, "Dear Old Dad. Never slows down."

Sammy asked him, "What does your father do?"

"Farmed for a long time. He's always had sheep, but he's older now, so he moved to town and lets my brothers take care of them. Now he makes things. He's real creative. Makes furniture, welds, does carpentry, paints, you name it. He never slows down. An *artiste*." Keary put the package down with the letters.

"You not gonna open it?"

"Not-until-my-birthday." He waved a finger in a playful admonition. "I've been trying to get them to come visit, but they don't like to travel if they can help it. Shame. This is such a grand place."

"You think it's ever gonna be a hotel again?"

"I'm afraid the days of the big destination hotels are done. This place being open again as a hotel is about as likely as having a Jesuit pope."

He took off his cap and fell back onto one of the couches. As he leaned back, he caught sight of the dome.

"I told you we have angels at the top of the dome, didn't I? Do you want to see them?"

"Yeah," they said.

"It's up on the roof, cold up there. You'll both need a jacket."

"Really don't have one," Betsy said. All she had was her old brown sweater.

"Well, I have one for you, if you don't mind army surplus. Wait one minute and I'll grab it."

He disappeared upstairs. Sammy and Betsy laid back on the couches and looked up to the ceiling. They both wondered if he was exaggerating the angels or outright making them up.

He came back downstairs and into the atrium holding an olive drab army jacket. He held it up. *Keary, A.* was over the pocket.

"You were in the army?" Sammy asked.

"Yes I was. Forty eight to fifty three, after the McNamara years. Guess I was running away, and the Army's got plenty of places to run to."

"Korea?"

"Everywhere but. Germany, France. Atomic testing in the Pacific. We blew up an island in an atoll in the Pacific called Eniwetok, Operation Ivy Mike. Came home, joined the order." He said it like it was the logical sequence of events, like it was exactly how it was supposed to happen.

They rode the elevator to the sixth floor and then went outside through a door to the eaves of the roof. They ascended a metal staircase on the outside of the roof to a small room. Betsy paused to get her breath, and Keary and Sammy paused with her. A ladder led down into a small circular room like an oversized drum.

"This is called the compression room. It's where the big girders you see below push against each other," Keary said as he descended the ladder. They followed him down.

In the room there were angels painted over the metal panels studded with rivets. Sammy and Betsy contemplated the angels, and the angels contemplated them. The angels looked like something out of a Byzantine church, their faces peering through halos of pale yellow dots and tilting thoughtfully as they played instruments, horns and tambourines. There were seven of them with a blank area where an eighth had been, now only flecks and chips of brightly colored paint. Graffiti had been scrawled over some of the paintings.

"Some of that graffiti's fifty years old. The angels are probably from the Italian craftsmen who helped build the place, though nobody's sure. An eighth one was right here, but it's weathered away, I guess. We used to sit around the fire downstairs and speculate on them. Someone suggested that they're the seven archangels, and the eighth represented Lucifer. He envied God and desired equality with Him but fell into hell, remember?"

Outside a large tree branch snapped under the weight of snow and ice and plummeted to the ground with a brushy smack. They floated from painting to painting like patrons in an art gallery. The angels seemed to want to talk, to tell some story, to reveal some truth. Finally, Keary spoke.

"Let's get this young lady back downstairs. This has been a lot of exertion for someone who's sick. Follow me," Keary said. He put a foot on the second rung and was halfway up the ladder when Sammy called up to him.

"Tony?"

Keary stopped and looked down at him, "Yes?"

"Will you marry us?"

"When? Right now?"

"As soon as possible."

He smiled and nodded his head.

"Well, I'd be honored. How about tomorrow?"

Chapter 69

Keary prepared a guest room for Betsy. It had been one of the choicest ones in the glory days of the hotel, one with a fireplace, a small sitting area, and a large bed. The lamp cast a halo of orange light over her sleeping face, freckled cheeks, black brush eyelashes, lips slightly parted, dry and cracked. Keary smiled as Sammy kissed her forehead.

"Well, I'm not in the habit of throwing wild bachelor parties, but how's about a beer, then? Place across the street."

The idea of a beer appealed to Sammy.

"She'll be okay here?"

"Surely. Remember," he pointed to the dome. "There are angels watching over her, archangels." He smiled and clapped a hand on Sammy's shoulder. "One beer, won't be long."

They bundled up and walked down the brick lane and under the double arches. Snow coated the pavement. The main highway was a mash of icy ruts where the snow had been compressed by tires. They crossed it.

The windows of the Dead Rat Saloon glowed hospitably. Keary held the door for Sammy.

Hey! The cry went up when Keary himself entered. He waved at everyone and gave a small bow.

They made their way to the bar as Keary gave a series of handshakes to men and cheek kisses to women. A heavenly panoramic mountain scene courtesy of Hamm's beer decorated one end of the bar and at the other was one for Falstaff beer. Next to that was a picture of Al Capone in a light colored, double breasted suit, white fedora, and five o'clock shadow. As a joke, *Do not serve this man* was written at the bottom.

Near the bar, a short man with bug eyes and jowls like a Boston Terrier approached Keary.

"Hey, father, I got one for you."

"Okay, Stanley, let's hear it."

"All right, this priest and this nun are headed to a religious retreat."

"I like it already, go on."

"Well, they have car trouble in this little town with one hotel, and wouldn't you know it, there's only one room with one bed left. So they have to take it.

"They get settled in for the night, the nun in the bed, the priest in the chair and she says, 'Father, I'm cold.'

"So he gets up and gets a blanket out of the closet, puts it on her and gets settled back in the chair. He's almost asleep, she says 'I'm still cold.' So he gets up, puts on his shoes, goes to the night office, gets a blanket, comes back, puts it on her, gets settled back in his chair. She says, 'I'm still cold.' So he says, 'Sister, you want to play like we're husband and wife?' 'Yeah!' she says.

"So he says, 'well, then get up and *get your own goddam blanket.*'"

Keary bent over and laughed until he cried. Stanley and Sammy watched him laugh, laughing themselves. Then Keary stood up red-faced and wiped tears from his eyes and said, "Stanley, You may be Methodist, but you owe me a confession for that one."

"Tell ya what, father," Stanley said. "Let me gather up some other sins and I'll just make one trip."

They laughed again, then they shook hands and Keary said, "Tell Gertie I said hello."

Stanley patted Keary on the shoulder and said, "Sure thing."

Sammy followed Keary up to the bar and they sat down. The barmaid pulled a beer from a tap without him even asking. Keary held up two fingers, and she pulled one for Sammy. She held a cigarette in the hand that pulled down on the tap. Her hand had crude tattoos on them.

She said, "Hey, Father. How you been?"

He took a sip of his beer.

"Never better! I was thirsty, and you gave me drink," he said. "What about you? How's your sister?"

"Ha!" She laughed without concealing her disgust. "St. Nelda of Paoli? Indiana's only living martyr?"

"Now, sweetheart," Keary admonished her with a smile. "A little charity."

"I know, I know," she said as she turned her head with his gentle accusation. The tattooed hand tapped an ash into a glass ashtray.

In the mirror behind the bar Keary recognized someone. He took a quick sip of his beer and excused himself to have a word with him. In the mirror, Sammy watched Keary and the man clasp hands and smile. The man said something and Keary laughed, and then as Keary returned to the bar, he said something else to the man.

"That's Neil," Keary said as he sat down again. "He's got a tow truck. He said the roads should be good tomorrow, county had the salt and gravel boys out all day, so we can see about your car. Said he'll take us tomorrow."

They sat and had a beer. Keary pointed to the picture of Al Capone and said that in the twenties, Capone was seen in town frequently, including right here in the Dead Rat. Then he went into other stories of local interest. For someone who wasn't a local, he had a wealth of knowledge about the place.

One beer was enough for Sammy, and he sat preoccupied with leaving Betsy alone. They finished their beers and after what seemed a half hour of hellos and goodbyes, they were able to leave the bar and cross the street.

"My kinda people," Keary said. "No pretense about them whatsoever."

Their feet crunched on the packed snow as they went under the double arch. Their breath made clouds, and their hands were clenched tightly in the pockets of their jackets.

As they approached the hotel, Keary said, "I'll get you some blankets for the couch. You two ought to sleep separately one more night. It's a tradition if nothing else."

As Keary went to get blankets and start a fire for Sammy, Sammy went upstairs to check on Betsy. She had shifted to the edge of the orange spot of light. He kissed her forehead and pushed her hair out of her face. It was wet with sweat.

Chapter 70

Sammy woke to shafts of bright cold sunshine slanting through the skylights in the dome. From a room somewhere came the hesitant clack of a typewriter and the creaking, unzipping sound of the cylinder knob and the clack again. He rose from the couch and looked at the charred log in the fireplace and then followed the sound.

Keary was seated at a typewriter in the former dean's office, his hazel eyes peering over brass-rimmed glasses at the document curling around and out of the cylinder.

"Good morning, Samuel," he said without looking up. "Thank goodness I saw you. This typing has got my goat and I was on the verge of some decidedly *unchristian* language." He turned the knob and advanced the paper a little

Officiant, he mumbled, *okay*, *that's me*. His index finger hunted down the letters and pecked them out. *A-n-t-h-o-n-y-K-e-a-r-y-comma-S-period-J-* his fingertip swirled above the keys, and then he typed the last character-*period*. He twirled the paper out.

"Okay, that's the one for the church. When Betsy gets up we'll head into Paoli to the courthouse for the one from the state of Indiana."

They heard a coarse, honking cough down the corridor, and then Betsy appeared at the door behind them. She was dressed but her hair was tousled. There were circles under her eyes, and she smiled weakly.

Keary took one look at her and said, "We can put this off until another day, if you'd rather."

"No," they said together.

"Very well," he said.

They rode into Paoli in the old Rambler. The back seat had been cleared of the boxes, but they still sat three abreast across the front seat. Betsy was bundled up, protected from the elements by Keary's army coat as she leaned into Sammy. In Paoli the square was much like the one in Oxford, with a courthouse in the middle and a cupola atop it, but with more massive white columns. They went inside and registered their names and the clerk produced the document, *Certificate of Marriage, State of Indiana*. On the way back to West Baden, they held it up and admired it, tracing their fingers over the golden embossed seal. Keary glanced at them, then watched the road and smiled.

They passed back through West Baden and then into French Lick. The French Lick Hotel, made of the same pale yellow brick as the West Baden Hotel, loomed on a hill to the right. Further down on the left there was a group of red brick buildings. All the way, Keary told Sammy and Betsy what each had been in the past. On a corner was a two story building. On the side a sign was painted in green and white:

Stay at
Luxurious
French Lick Springs

Resort Hotel
Come Take the
Healing Waters

And on the building next to it another painted sign promised 'results':

Pluto Water
When nature won't, Pluto will

Keary parked the car, and they got out. He gestured to the hill opposite the main street from them. The white-steepled church rose there, seemingly up and out of the earth.

"Our Lady of Springs. Where I've been saying Mass."

They went into a building that read across the front in big letters: *Terhune Sisters*. The window was trimmed in blue tinsel, and there was a white aluminum Christmas tree with spherical blue metallic ornaments on it.

Mary and Martha, the Terhune sisters, weren't sisters at all, but sisters-in-law who had married and then been widowed by brothers. Mary Bryan Terhune ran a women's clothing boutique, which had the biggest selection of wedding and bridesmaid's dresses in Orange County. It had been there for decades, during the heyday of the valley when young couples would come, relax, drink, gamble, and then want to get married suddenly. *Terhune Sisters* had even kept the same hours as the casinos and nightclubs to accommodate the impulsive couples. A clergyman was also kept on call.

The shop's men's and women's sections were separated by a wall that was incomplete, giving a common area in the front. On the women's side, headless and armless manikins wore different sewing projects in different stages of completion. A rack of spools of thread in an advancing rainbow of colors slanted near a wall next to bolts of fabric and a wooden display case of buttons and clasps.

Mary Terhune was feeding material through a sewing machine. She looked up over half moon reading glasses, pulled a pin from between her lips and said, "Hello, Tony."

"Hello, Mary. Hard at it, I see."

"Yes, gotta make hay while the sun shines, as they say." She straightened up from the sewing machine and made a face while she

257

stretched her back. She was completely gray headed with glasses that rose to points at the upper corners. Betsy smelled something strong and sweet, and when the woman got up from the machine, Betsy realized it was Mary's perfume. It wafted around her like an aura. The woman was old and plump, but with the lightness in her step of a woman half her age.

"We have a bride here," Keary said.

"Oh, do we!" Mary said, putting her glasses in her pocket. She grasped Betsy's hands with both of hers and said, "Congratulations, dear! Mary Bryan Terhune."

"Betsy Duplechain." Then she realized it would be probably be the last time she would say her old name.

"Now, Betsy, what kind of dress are you looking for? We have these," she gestured to several manikins, "And those. This is *peau de soie,*" she ran the back of her hand over the silky white fabric. "It's French for 'silky skin.'" Her eyes flashed lustily as if the term were the most erotic thing possible.

"Yes ma'am," Betsy said.

Mary showed Betsy every dress, low necklines, medium necklines, silk, satin, beaded lace, big trains, no train, puff sleeves, even some with bare shoulders.

Never in Mass, Betsy thought.

"You don't care for these, do you?" at last Mary said. "Tell you what, I've got one more. It's what we like to call *vintage.*"

She disappeared to the back and came carrying a silky, satiny, lacy pile of fabric over her arm. She lifted it up, unfurling it like a flag on a windy day. Betsy's eyes lit up in amazement.

If it wasn't an exact replica of the dress her Mimi had made, the one that was ruined in the flood, it was very, very close. The neck was high, and the dress was elaborately made in satin and silk with lace overlays that ran down on all sides of it.

"This one, this is it," Betsy said, and then she asked, "But how much?"

"Tell you what, since you're a friend of Tony's, I'll just let you borrow it. I wouldn't sell it to you anyway. It was mine, y'see, I was married in it myself." She winked at Betsy. "Let's take it back to the fitting room. Wouldn't want the groom walking in on you. Bad luck."

They went to the back to a fitting room with a white, tufted settee and a full length mirror. Betsy undressed and then got into the dress. It rustled as she pulled it up, and Mary fastened it in the back, looking over her glasses. Betsy saw herself in the mirror, and despite the tired look on her face, she was radiant. She put her fingers over her mouth.

"Yes, Betsy, it's true, you're beautiful," Mary said around the pin in her mouth. "The thing's a bit loose though, now isn't it?" She reached over and got a pin cushion bristling with pins and began to take in the extra fabric. She put her palm on Betsy's stomach and smiled up at her. It wasn't the first time she'd had to work around a slight swelling in a bride's lower stomach.

"Brides were bigger back then." She raised her eyebrows, lowered her eyelids and purred, "It was *sexy*."

"When you were married in this dress?" Betsy was holding up her arms as Mary continued to place pins.

"January first, 1910," Mary said as she placed a pin. "I was sixteen years old, how it was back then. People whispered if you weren't married by eighteen and pregnant by twenty."

Meanwhile in the men's side of the old brick building, Sammy was conferring with Vance, Martha Logan Terhune's nephew. At forty seven he was a confirmed bachelor, though quiet talk circulated that he was fond of taking trips on the train with other confirmed bachelors to Chicago and New York, where they liked to shop the latest fashions and attend the theater.

"So you're getting married! That's fabulous. Is Aunt Mary assisting the lucky girl?" Vance gushed.

"Yessir," Sammy said.

"Oh don't call me sir, young man," he scolded playfully. He turned to a rack of tuxedo jackets. "Here are the latest. You must be..." Vance put two fingers to his chin and shut one eye as he contemplated Sammy's shoulders, "A forty regular, am I right?"

"I think so, I mean, I used to be a thirty eight regular, but I've gained some muscle."

"I can see that," Vance said. He paused in some sort of private reverie and then shuffled through jackets on a rack between a set of markers that said '38' and '42.' He pulled one out, one with a shiny black lapel.

"This one," Vance said. He found the matching trousers. "And these. There's a changing room back by that sock display."

Sammy emerged with the black trousers puddled around his sock feet. Vance knelt before him with pins in his mouth. Sammy shifted uncomfortably. Vance turned the cuff under and took the pins out of his mouth one by one and skewered the cuff into place.

"There," he said, and he rose. He examined the shoulders across the jacket and checked the snugness of the trouser waist with two thumbs.

"You are going to be a simply *dashing* groom, young man," Vance said.

"I believe he will," a voice said. Keary had reappeared, having gone around to the barber shop to visit. He leaned against a wooden desk piled with fashion plates. The alterations were made on the spot, and the dress and the tuxedo were put in separate boxes and loaded onto the back seat of the Rambler.

All this time, Martha Logan Terhune had sat and slaved over the books while her nephew and sister-in-law helped the young couple. She was a worrywart, always fretting over details, and no detail was too small. The sky was always teetering over Martha and about to fall if she didn't take measures to prevent it.

They were back at West Baden by noon. Betsy was exhausted, and they put her to bed. Sammy and Keary waited in rocking chairs on the porch, and after a little time, Neil arrived in his tow truck. It thundered and rumbled down the brick lane, and the brakes yelped a hiccup in front of the hotel. They got in and the tow truck growled back through French Lick again, Sammy looking past Neil into the Terhune Sister's shop. Mary was assisting another bride, Vance another groom, and Martha was still riveted to the books. They passed out of town and back down the road toward Tell City. After a while, Keary spoke.

"I think that was it back there, we passed it," he said. "Go back, Neil."

Neil stopped the tow truck, turned around in the highway, and went back. The tow truck crooned deeply like the bellow of a dinosaur and shook its occupants with each gear change. The chains on the back swung from the iron booms and rattled heavily.

"Right here," Keary said. The truck lurched to a halt.

Keary opened the door and stepped down. He approached a small mound of snow, and then Sammy could see it, a slight rectangular shape. He got out, too. His feet crunched over the snow on the shoulder of the road, and he stood next to Tony.

Keary used the instep of his foot to sweep away the covering of snow. The blackened remnants of something were there. The ornamental galloping Mustang had been melted into a shape more like a mule. Keary picked it up. He was uncustomarily quiet. His manner had lost all buoyancy. He stood there with his lips pressed together, and his teeth grinding.

Sammy heard a door of the tow truck slam and crunching footsteps. Neil joined them.

"Somethin' must've caught fire under it," Neil said. "Maybe the bottom just got hot and caught the grass afire."

"Maybe," Keary said staring into the mess. Finally he spoke again.

"Someone did this on purpose."

There was nothing left to scoop up. They headed back into town in the tow truck. Silence hung in the cab. Keary stared straight ahead.

By the time they returned to West Baden, Keary was himself again. After they checked on Betsy, who was still napping, Keary whispered to Sammy.

"Come with me," he said.

They went to Keary's quarters. He dug in a drawer and produced a velvet covered box. He opened it at Sammy.

"It was for Susie McNamara, but I never got a chance to give it to her."

"I can't take your ring."

"Nor can you afford one right now. Here's a good rule of thumb, Samuel: if you keep something for more than a year and don't use it, it's hoarding, and it's a sin. That means that I've had this sin on me since 1948. Take it, it should belong to someone who's in love, not squirreled away in a box somewhere."

He pressed it into Sammy's palm.

"Trust me, girls love diamonds. Now let's go get you trimmed up a little. You look like St. Joseph with that beard."

Chapter 71

Betsy stood in a room off the back of the church. She felt feverish and a little lightheaded. She had to move slowly, or else she thought she would pass out. She felt like she was underwater and being swayed back and forth by ocean currents.

"I hope you don't mind, but I invited a few people who would know a thing or two about marriage. And I've arranged for someone to walk you down the aisle," Keary said.

A man appeared in the doorway, as old as the rest of the white heads in the congregation, but he looked strangely familiar to Betsy. Her fever blunted everything and wouldn't let her mind make any connection. It was troublesome because, if she had been well, it would have been obviously simple.

"Betsy, this is Mr. Foreman," Keary said.

Mr. Foreman smiled, and when he did, he was even more familiar to her. He smelled of tobacco smoke and had the coarse, weathered features of a man who had worked outdoors all his life. He was dressed in a suit and a tie, but pulled at the tie like he had seldom, if ever, worn one before.

Betsy was feeling another surge of fever welling up in her, and it made her eyes glassy and unfocused. The old man took her hand in his, their forearms side by side. Through the white linen of her glove, his hand was large and gnarled, but had a gentleness to it, and her hand seemed to fit in it like she had held it before.

"You gonna need a ring," he said.

"Sir?" Her eyes were swimming. It was hard to see, and the veil didn't help matters.

"Here, baby, take mine, I don't need it no more," he said, and he took the gold band off his thick finger, pressed it into the palm of her white gloved hand, and folded her fingers around it.

"You so beautiful," he said, and she blushed, and her fever made the blush feel even warmer. Her pulse throbbed in her ears, and she thought he said, "Sha."

Mary played the wedding march on the cello, the only cello in Orange County. Everyone stood and turned, ancient, kind faces,

faces that admired them and wished them well without saying a word. At the altar was Father Keary, suddenly transfigured in a white cassock with a golden stole. Sammy was waiting next to him in a black tux, his hair pulled back and his beard neatly trimmed.

She and her escort promenaded down the aisle, and at the end of it, Sammy stepped forward. Mr. Foreman shook Sammy's hand and congratulated him. Turning from Sammy, he kissed Betsy on both cheeks. And then he hugged her tight and whispered into her ear. The smell of perique was sweet and strong.

"Mais, I'm so proud of you. You made a good choice, Bess."

Her eyes teared up, and the congregation sighed, aah. Betsy turned to get a good look at the man, but he had blended in with the congregation.

Everyone sat down, and Sammy and Betsy stooped down onto the kneeler. She glanced over her shoulder one last time to look for the man, Mr. Foreman. All she saw was a sea of ancient faces, thoughtful and beatific. Sammy felt her arm above the white linen glove and gave her a small look of alarm. She was burning up.

There were the customary readings and a beautifully rendered *Ave Maria* on the cello. They remained kneeling while at their backs the pews creaked slowly with the cycle of standing, sitting and kneeling as the elderly followed the liturgy.

Then everyone sat down, and Keary began his homily. He thanked everyone for coming out on such a cold night to celebrate with this young couple. He spoke of their story, Sammy and Betsy, how they had grown up together, separately, each in the World Next Door, and isn't that how love and goodness and beauty are sometimes, hidden in plain sight? Then he cited the second reading, Paul's words to the Corinthians about how love is patient and kind, and admonished the young couple to always try to put their names where love is: Sammy is patient, Betsy is kind, Sammy hopes all things, Betsy believes all things.

He looked right at Sammy and said, "when I was a child, I spoke like a child and had the thoughts of a child. When I became a man, I put away childish things."

And then he said, "Sammy, if I could give you a present, it would be Gratitude and Humility, and I would wrap it in a package shaped like Betsy. And Betsy, if I could give you a present, it would be Kindness, Forbearance and Compassion, and I would wrap it in a package shaped like Sammy. And then I would ask that you share your gifts with one another."

He blessed the rings, and they stood and faced each other and exchanged vows. Neither would remember much of it. They knelt again.

Then Communion was given. The old people tottered up. Father Keary held up the host to each person, the disk pale and round like a moon, right between his eyes as he said, "The body of Christ."

"Amen," each said.

Finally, Sammy and Betsy rose and Father Keary said, "I now pronounce you man and wife. What God has joined, let no man put asunder. Sammy, you may kiss your bride."

They stood and faced each other, and Betsy whispered, "Boy, you sure you want my code?"

Sammy smiled and whispered back, "What's yours is mine and mine is yours. From now on we share everything, even colds."

They kissed, and Keary motioned for them to face the congregation.

"Ladies and gentlemen, Mr. and Mrs. Samuel Teague!"

The old bodies in the congregation rose, pulling themselves up, using canes and the backs of pews. They applauded, the old women dabbing away tears and the old men giving them a thumbs up. Keary motioned for them to walk down the aisle and out of the chapel as Mary played the wedding recessional on the cello. Both Sammy and Betsy smiled broadly as they waved to everyone. Each one of them looked like they had just made the deal of a lifetime.

Towards the back of church, Betsy looked at the ring on her hand. Under the applause she whispered to Sammy, "It's beautiful, where you got this?"

Sammy just smiled, and they exited the chapel and went to the reception.

The band, Ivy Jarrell and the Easynotes, had been a staple of the Springs Valley nightclub and casino scene in the twenties and thirties. In the decades since, Ivy had put on the weight of an additional woman within her silky, light brown skin but her voice was still smooth and buttery.

"Ladies and gentlemen," her husky voice purred into the microphone as the couple entered, "Mr. and Mrs. Sammy Teague."

264

All the ancient liver-spotted hands applauded, all the denture-perfect mouths smiled. One old man whistled with his thumb and middle finger in his mouth, and his old wife shot him a disapproving glance.

And then they danced their first dance, Ivy Jarrell covering Etta James' "At Last." The saxophone crooned along mellowly. Just as soon as it was over, the tempo was dialed up with "Little Bitty Pretty One." Some of the old people danced rigidly to it, most of them moving slower than Sammy and Betsy had during the previous slow number.

There were finger sandwiches, little bowls of rhubarb pie with ice cream, and a simple white wedding cake, round with three layers.

A receiving line was formed. As the band played, the old people shuffled down past them, telling stories of how they met, how they married, and how they stayed married. There were stories of chance and whimsy and difficulty and perseverance. And there was a lot of advice.

"Only strangers are perfect," an old man said.

"And the more you get to know someone the stranger and less perfect they get," his wife leaned in and interjected.

He took her hand and said, "Speak for yourself, old gal."

She kissed his shoulder with her aged lips and then wiped at the faint trace of lipstick it left on the sleeve of his suit jacket. They moved down the line, and another couple took their place.

This old husband shook Sammy's hand and shouted so he could hear himself through his poor hearing, "MY ADVICE TO YOU TO BE A GOOD HUSBAND IS DO AS YOU'RE TOLD AND NOBODY GETS HURT." He grinned with one of his favorite witty aphorisms of the last half century. It no longer got his wife's goat, and she spoke in a normal tone of voice.

"All I can say is it's too late to stop and train another one."

She patted his shoulder, and her husband smiled at what he assumed had been a compliment. His hearing aid was turned down.

The last of the well-wishers, perhaps the most ancient couple of them all, approached. The old woman was being pushed in a wheelchair by her husband, who seemed to be held up by it more than he was pushing it. His voice was leathery.

"Young man," he addressed Sammy, "When I was a boy I had an old uncle who told me 'you could marry more money in five minutes than you could make in a lifetime,'" he said. "It sounded like good advice to me. When I told my father what my uncle had told me, he said, 'that's true, son. But it would be the hardest money you ever made. He said marry someone kind and industrious. It's the best any of us can hope for.' And he was right."

Keary appeared at the other end of the room with several bottles of wine and an array of glasses. He beckoned for Sammy and Betsy to join him. He poured wine into the glasses much like he would on the altar.

"This is what we used to make from our vineyards," he said quietly to Sammy and Betsy as he showed them the label, then he showed them another. "Now this is the good stuff, a vineyard we had down in Canaan, Indiana, closer to Louisville. Soil must be better."

When he was finished pouring and everyone had a glass, he made the toast.

"To Mr. and Mrs. Sammy Teague!"

"Hear, hear! Long happy life!" they said as they raised their glasses together.

Sammy wanted a picture of the two of them with Keary, and Keary said he needed to 'see a man about a horse' and that he would be right back. Meanwhile, Betsy gamely smiled and posed with Sammy though she was exhausted to the point of delirium. When Keary returned, he was caught up in small eddies of conversation. Finally, Mr. Barnes, the photographer, said he had waited as long as he could and packed up his camera.

"Well," Keary returned just after Mr. Barnes left and said, as buoyant as ever, "We'll just have to remember it with a *mental* picture, won't we? Those kinds are better, anyway. Closer to the heart."

Finally, Betsy sat back in a wingback chair and fell asleep with her chin on the high lace collar. Sammy scooped her up and took her upstairs to put her to bed. Several of the old women blushed, and one cooed, "So *romantic.*"

He ascended the stairs with her, and she opened her eyes. They were glassy, the lids partially over them.

"Wish I felt betta. I'd be all over you, boy," she said. And she nestled her head into his neck.

He let her down gently on the bed they were to share at last, the one that a couple of the ladies had snuck in and scattered rose petals on. He smiled and swept them off with his hand. He pulled off her shoes, noticing that she had worn white stockings and a lace garter. He kissed her forehead and shut the door behind himself.

When Sammy returned downstairs, the Easynotes were packing up, and the last guests were leaving, Keary wishing them a safe trip home. Keary and Sammy adjourned to the atrium where Keary made a fire in the fireplace and they sat silently and watched it.

Sammy kept taking off the ring and looking at it. For some reason, A. D. had been engraved on the inside of it. Maybe it was a partial designation of a year that was unfinished or had worn off. He was pondering this when Keary spoke.

"The closest spot to cross into Canada is gonna be Detroit," Keary said into the vastness of the atrium.

"You knew."

"Of course I knew. I knew when I picked you two up on the road. But you're still torn about going, aren't you?"

"Yes."

"What makes you want to enlist, then?"

"Duty to country. Duty in general. What a man does, faces up to things."

"All right. What makes you want to skip the army, and go to Canada?"

"Duty to Betsy, to my baby."

"Now, where do you think you can do the most good?"

The question hung in the air.

"But Tony, there are men with wives and babies who are going to Vietnam." Sammy stopped fidgeting with his wedding band and slipped it onto his finger.

"There are, most certainly. If you're waiting for me to decide for you, I'm not going to," Keary said. "What I will say to you, however, is to examine your conscience. If you go to Vietnam, have a good reason. You already know the reason you wouldn't."

The fire crackled, and the light jiggled with the movement of the flames.

"The Ambassador Bridge is the crossing in Detroit. The guys at the border may give you trouble or they may not, it's case by case. They may let you cross if you're an objector, and they almost certainly won't if you're a deserter. You're not a deserter, are you? You haven't already enlisted and are on the lam, are you?"

"No."

"I thought not." He took off his glasses to polish the lenses.

"Did I ever tell you about Eniwetok?"

"Eniwetok?"

"An atoll in the pacific. Well, when we went there, with the army, there were a couple hundred people living in the atoll. The army wanted it, to test the H bomb. So the citizens of Eniwetok were resettled."

"Willingly?"

Keary shook his head no as if he couldn't admit to it out loud, and then he exhaled a breath onto each lens. He looked through them and worked at a speck with his handkerchief.

"No," he sighed, "They didn't ask us to come, and we didn't ask them if we could come. Now, from what I can tell, the South Vietnamese don't want us there as much as we *want* them to want us there.

"And now Eniwetok is tainted with radiation, and no one knows when the former residents will be able to go back to it, the home of their ancestors, if ever," he said to his glasses as he polished them once more. He held them up and looked through them at the dome where the angels were, and then he put them back on.

"Well, young man, it's your wedding night, not the time for discussion of these kinds of things." He stood up and stretched. "Off to bed, see you in the morning."

Sammy looked back into the cavernous atrium and saw Anthony's firelight shadow projected big across it. Sammy watched the fire dip and weave around the logs in it. And then he got up and went upstairs.

Betsy was sound asleep on top of the sheets in her wedding dress. Sammy kicked off his shoes, took off his jacket, and curled up next to her, and they slept as man and wife.

Chapter 72

When Keary got to his quarters, he took a minute to outline next Sunday's homily. His head had begun to hurt, and he attributed it to the wine, but then it began to worsen. He had not had a migraine in years, not since he was stationed in Holland. He rubbed his eyes, got up and kneeled at the predieu by his bed. He closed his eyes and even though he didn't want it to, the memory played itself and he was forced to watch it:

A body in a red dress, bloated, floating face down in a canal, blonde hair hovering, suspended in the water and swept up like it was standing on end, and still frightened.

Local Dutch police and military police together on the bank, conferring.

His younger self, even more spindly then, helping retrieve the girl with a pole, everyone with hands over their noses.

Then there he was in another scene, in army fatigues in the military courtroom.

The red-haired, blue-eyed PFC, brought into the courtroom with hands cuffed in front of him, cigarette in his smile, MPs on either side of him.

Questions about the missing girl.

Did you know Miss de Graaf?

You could say we knew one anotha.

Were you ever alone with her?

Reckon we were alone sometimes.

Did you ever meet Miss de Graaf for a sexual encounter?

Yeah, she couldn't keep her hands off me. A smirk.

When did you see her last, Private?

Examining his fingernails.

Can't remember that.

Private, did you kill Miss Heidi de Graaf by strangulation after a sexual encounter?

No I did not kill that woman by strangulation after a sexual encounter.

And then reading the red-haired man's next thought, as clear as skywriting on a bold blue sky, *I suffocated her with a pillow.*

The red haired smirk, answers flippant, laden with contempt, bordering on insubordination.

Have you reached a verdict regarding this soldier?

We find the defendant, *Not* guilty due to insufficient evidence.

The quiet uproar of the Dutch citizens, profound disappointment in the failure of their liberators' justice.

And the smirk again.

Keary held his head like it hurt, like he was being poked all around his scalp. He put his fingers in his blonde hair as he wrestled with his agony. He got up and put on his coat and the cap with the flaps over his ears. He put his hands in his coat pockets and walked to the Dead Rat.

The crowd was thin, just a few stragglers leaving right before closing time. But there the man was through the window, decidedly heavier now than in those postwar years, nursing a whiskey on the rocks.

PFC Percy Parris.

Keary went in and sat at the bar down from him. Sally, the barmaid, was engaged in a heated conversation with Parris. It was just the three of them in the bar.

"Not if you were the last man on the whole fuckin' earth," her voice rose.

Parris grabbed her forearm and stared into her eyes, but she shook herself loose. Parris laughed like the rebuff was a temporary setback and took a sip of his whiskey. In mid-sip, he glanced down the bar at Keary. Parris set down his drink.

"What you lookin' at?"

Keary said nothing and just kept his gaze on Parris, a gaze that was intense and thoughtful, almost sympathetic. Finally, Parris rose as if he felt a lingering discomfort, put on his fedora and left.

Keary rose when the GTO pulled away.

"Go ahead and lock up, and when you get back to Paoli, stop at the police station and get them to follow you home, okay?"

"Why?" Sally asked.

"Just do it," he said.

He followed her out to her car, saw her into it and shut the door for her. He watched her pull out and head down the street. He looked around and then headed through the double arches and back to his quarters.

When he got there, he got back on the predieu and stayed there until daybreak.

Chapter 73

Betsy got sicker.

Her throat hurt, and her eyes burned. Her cough plowed air over the back of her weeping throat, and then she sneezed which made her cough again.

And then she got sicker.

Her fever soared, and her body shook to rid itself of it, but it just crept back inside of her. Her voice was husky, then raspy, then gone. Her body felt achy and lifeless and hollow. Outside the frosted windows, the hills rested under the gray and white shades of an Indiana winter.

Keary kept the fire going in the fireplace and brought Sammy lunch and Betsy tea and toast, which she ate very little of. Keary would pick up the food he had brought, the toast either uneaten or just missing a small half circle bite with tiny scalloped edges, the tea barely touched. Sammy slept in a chair at her bedside. On good days she would open an eye and manage a smile at him.

hey boy, what you did all day? she squeezed out in a hoarse whisper, and then she went to sleep again. Her lips bounced off each other lightly as she muttered a narrative of things that only she could see.

don't fuss me mama, you see that moccasin, daddy? half way up that cypress, see him? look, there he goes, Mary Nell, how you know my daddy? hey, Loretta

Often Keary would find Sammy kneeling at the bedside asleep with Betsy's hand on his head. Once or twice a day, Sammy escorted her to the bathroom, waiting outside the door listening for the tinkle and flush and then escorting her back to bed.

Sammy awoke in the chair one afternoon to see Betsy's brown eyes staring at him. He smiled at her, but she didn't return the smile. Her eyes were heavy lidded and vacant. He struggled against the blanket that was over him as if it had been trying to attack him, finally getting out from under it and throwing it to the floor.

"Betsy? Baby?" He was right in her face and on the verge of panic when she blinked. That's when Keary called the doctor.

Talitha Cumie had the upright posture of someone who was told from an early age that how you carried yourself advertised you instantly to others. She was the great granddaughter of Jeremiah Cumie, a runaway slave so headstrong and intelligent and, consequently, hard to handle, that his former master was secretly glad to see him go and didn't send out a pursuit party on the moonless antebellum night that he slipped away.

There was a merry obstinacy to Dr. Cumie, an air that said that she knew what was best for you and was waiting patiently for you to realize it yourself. Her stubbornness had driven her professors at Case Western in Cleveland mad. When she had graduated near the top of her class, they were both proud and relieved.

As she listened to Betsy' chest, Dr. Cumie's face contorted through a range of expressions as if it, and not her brain, would make the diagnosis. She pinched Betsy's wrist to feel her pulse, looking up at her own forehead as if the answer were there. Then she closed her eyes as if the answer might be written there behind her eyelids. She rolled up her stethoscope and put it in her bag.

"Influenza. Not pneumonia yet, but close."

Sammy asked the question. It almost seemed like the question asked itself.

"Will they be okay? Betsy and the baby?"

He waited for the answer he wanted: Why sure, by tomorrow good as new, you'll see. What he got was another answer:

"We'll see."

She snapped the flowered canvas bag shut and stood up. Her eyes were sharp and inquisitive. Her hair was gathered in a headband, and it pushed out backward like a makeup brush or the tail feathers of a bird.

"Fluids, more rest tonight, I'll be back in the morning, and if she's no better, we'll take her into Bloomington to the hospital. We'd go there now if it wasn't so late."

She stood tall with her bag by her side. Her legs were clad in thick tights under her wool skirt. She wore a corduroy coat over a thick white cotton blouse. She had gotten right down to business and had never taken it off.

"Thank you, Talitha," Keary said.

"Thank you, doctor," Sammy said. His eyes were liquid with gratitude, gratitude and hope and fear for his wife and baby.

Keary walked Dr. Cumie out.

Later, Betsy awoke to feel a pressure at her side, on the bed. She patted the covers expecting to feel Chanceux curled up and sleeping there. It was Keary. The lamp was to the side of his head, which was tilted thoughtfully. He spoke in a low, even voice, the sound of a smile, if a smile could make a sound. Snow fell outside the window like dust in a sunbeam. Sammy was sound asleep next to her.

"When I was growing up, my little sister was sick with something, I think it was diphtheria, though I can't remember exactly." He took a small cloth and submerged it in a basin on the bedside table. Steam was coming out of the basin. He wrung it out.

"Mother was *in a state*, as they used to say back then." He opened up the top buttons of Betsy's gown and laid the cloth there. He put his palm on her chest. She felt warm, cherished.

"Anyway, Callie, my sister, we called her Callie, was real sick. I remember that our old aunts came and prayed the Rosary in the sitting room. She was that sick." He adjusted the cloth up onto Betsy's throat. It smelled aromatic, like tar or camphor, or like lemons.

"Now, we had this neighbor, Mr. Lam. From China, he was. Originally came to work on the railroad. Real, real old. Well, he knew about a poultice, something from the old country, where he came from. He made one, put it on her."

Keary straightened up. The lamp was squarely behind him. The fire in the fireplace crackled. His glasses reflected it.

"Well, anyway, the very next morning, we found her at the kitchen table. Eating cornbread with an enormous slab of butter on it." His hazel eyes crinkled as he chuckled.

Betsy felt her throat burn under the cloth. Something was happening in her chest.

"The strange thing is, Mr. Lam died that same night. Must've been a hundred years old."

He stood up and stretched his arms high above his head and then out to his sides before putting his hands on his hips.

"Well, that's just some old story about my little sister and a man from China. Sleep tight. We'll see if this does the trick."

Dr. Cumie arrived the next morning fully prepared to make arrangements to transport the patient to the hospital in Bloomington if she was no better. She found her sitting up in bed eating bread and butter, and sipping the last of her tea.

"Miraculous," Cumie said.

She put her stethoscope and listened. Her face was resolute like a child taking something apart.

"Clearing," she said. She put away the stethoscope and pulled a different one out of her bag.

"Fetoscope," she said, showing it to Sammy.

She unbuttoned Betsy's gown to expose the low rounded swell of stomach, and then put the bell of the stethoscope to Betsy's skin. Cumie listened for a moment and gave a thumbs up.

"You want to listen?" she asked Sammy as she took the earpieces out of her ears. "It'll be a light, quick tap. You'll feel it in your forehead as much as hear it. Very faint."

Sammy concentrated as he put his forehead to the fetoscope.

And then there it was, a light drumming tap just like she said it would be. His face lit up, and he smiled at Betsy.

"You hear it?" Betsy asked hopefully.

"Yeah. Yeah, it's there. Our baby. It's our baby."

Dr. Cumie collected her instruments and joked, "Well Tony, you've done it again, beat me to the cure. How am I ever going to make a living?"

They walked out the door and down the hall tethered together in a halo of conversation that receded with them. They talked like old friends, like old school chums, inquiring about family and things until there was the distant sound of a door opening and closing.

Betsy shifted to her side and propped herself up on an elbow.

"You know what I'd like right now? A banana moon pie and a Pop Rouge. A long bath, a banana moon pie, and a Pop Rouge."

Sammy smiled and wordlessly began lacing up his boots to go across the street to the store. He put on his blue and black plaid jacket just as Keary appeared at the door with a Nehi Red for her.

Chapter 74

That day, Betsy was able to sit up for short stretches and even get up to the bathroom without assistance. Keary brought her northern treats like snow ice cream, made with evaporated milk and sugar, and rhubarb pie.

He also brought her books to read. The first was *My Antonia* by Willa Cather, the story of an immigrant girl who loses her father at a young age. Betsy kept a list of words she wasn't sure about, and each day the list got smaller and smaller until there was no list. She moved onto *The Adventures of Tom Sawyer*, a book she would have read if she had stayed in school. She finished it in a day.

She stayed nestled under a quilt dressed in pajama bottoms and the Ole Miss t-shirt that Sammy had now happily ceded to her. She read until she fell asleep, the book overturned on her stomach, and then woke and picked up the book again. She read with one hand while eating with the other. She read on the toilet, and would have read in the shower if she could have figured out how. She felt like Columbus discovering the New World.

Sammy had developed a need for physical labor. He felt slovenly and useless without it. He shoveled snow and cut firewood, and Keary sat with Betsy and wrote letters and prepared homilies while she read. In the evening, Sammy sat with his wife, and they read side by side in bed, the lamps on either side glowing patiently, waiting for them to tire. The fire was the only sound in the comfortable, immaculate silence.

She read Dickens' *Great Expectations*, and Steinbeck's *East of Eden*. The story of Cain and Abel, if you look closely, Keary said. Betsy reread it in a morning, and it was true. He left her *To Kill a Mockingbird*, and she devoured it in almost one sitting. That evening Keary came in and asked her how she had liked it. Sammy was sitting up and reading it after her. He had never heard of it and felt that a year earlier in his life he might have found it to be subversive.

"I liked it a lot," she said, and she started to elaborate on it, but Sammy shushed her.

"Don't spoil it," Sammy said as he pointed to the book in his lap and then put the finger across his lips.

"Don't fuss me boy," she smiled and knitted her eyebrows.

"En francais, alors," Keary said.

"Parlez francais?"

"Bien sur," he said, and then in English,   "I've always loved languages. Interesting, language can both unite and separate people. I speak eight of them, though I'll have to admit my Portuguese and Swahili are a little rusty. Not too many native speakers in southern Indiana," he looked over his glasses and smiled.

And then they switched back to French, discussing *To Kill a Mockingbird*, the conversation peppered with the names of familiar characters in the gentle, airy lilt of French. *Atticus. Scout. Monsieur Ewell.*

When the book discussion was done, they switched back to English.

"Your accent," he said, "River parishes, sugar cane country. St. Matthew or St. James, maybe. Just a touch of the prairie perhaps?"

"My daddy was from St. Matthew Parish, my mama from St. Landry. How you know about all that?"

He just smiled and produced a blue, cloth-bound book.

"Here's one you might enjoy. And it's in French."

Tandis Que J'agonise, William Faulkner, was written on the front.

Betsy picked it up and flipped to the middle, trying to find where the teacher in the dayroom had stopped on that rainy afternoon that she had read to her and Tina. Her finger found the point, and she started again, on her own. She read slowly now, because though she had spoken French all her life, she had never read much of it, except for advertisements.

Keary stood up. He looked pleased with himself.

"Well, I'm going into French Lick, the high school is playing Loogootee tonight. Big game. They usually get clergy to give an invocation."

He left them reading.

Chapter 75

"Samuel!" the voice cried out to every corner of the circular atrium. Sammy looked up and then around the circumference of columns.

"Samuel!" The voice called out again.

"Here I am," Sammy answered, his voice filling the big space. "Where are you?"

"Here, in a side room."

Sammy started along the perimeter, looking into the spaces off the atrium until he came upon Keary in one of them. He was trying to push a grand piano.

"Oh, good. There you are. I knew you liked to play, and I remembered that this old gem was hidden in the back. It's from the hotel's glory days. Help me push it?"

Sammy looked the piano over. Above the keys, written in gold was *Steinway and Sons, NY, NY*. He was still looking at the piano as he said, "How did you know I played?"

He looked at Keary, and Keary smiled and pointed to the name on the piano.

"The best, right?"

Sammy nodded slowly and said, "Yeah, the best."

They pushed it out into the atrium, and Keary went back down from where he had come. He returned with a bench and set it down in front of the piano. Sammy hesitated.

"Go ahead," Keary said with a smile.

Sammy sat down. He was overwhelmed, afraid that such an expensive instrument would suddenly fly out from under him like tapping on the accelerator of a sports car. He opened the keyboard carefully, trying not to make a sound with the cover, and touched middle C. It was like the hallelujah chorus all by itself. It filled the atrium. Sammy looked up and around as if he thought the note might have left marks on the paint.

"Wow," was all he could say.

"Play something," Keary said.

He was suddenly overwhelmed with all he did know how to play and found it hard to choose. Finally, he decided on something he hadn't played in years. It was a song his mother had urged him to learn, something she would have him play over and over, "I Can't Give You Anything but Love." It was the only song she would ever sing along with, her raspy voice not sounding half bad as she stood over his shoulder clutching a gin and tonic. The only hitch was that she would invariably leave out the 't' in *can't* and it would come out 'I *can* give you anything but love.'

His fingers found the keys easily, the smooth surfaces pleasantly and delicately responding to each light touch. The dome seemed to change colors, a subtle shift in the shade of white with the music. Keary sang along in his fine tenor:

I can't give you anything but love
Baby
That's the only thing I've plenty of
My baby

Suddenly, it seemed like the atrium was full of people, like the Saenger in New Orleans, like Carnegie in New York, like the Royal Albert in London, an audience from the 1920's, women in cloche hats and fine dresses, men in suits and boater hats and wingtip shoes, faces transparent, just a wisp of them there in their seats, listening, enjoying. People who had been there before the stock market silently crashed, and the hotel emptied literally overnight and was sold to the Jesuits for a dollar.

Sammy played and Keary sang all afternoon. After they began a selection of Beatles tunes, Sammy felt the bench creak and Betsy lean and put her head on his shoulder. She was in her gown and robe, her hair tousled, but she was smiling. She was up and smiling, and for the first time in days she had come downstairs.

He played all afternoon, and his fingers didn't miss a key once.

Chapter 76

On Sunday, Betsy talked Sammy into going to church. They rode in Keary's old Rambler into French Lick to the church on the hill, Our Lady of Springs.

When they pulled up, there were two ladies at a table in the parking lot. One was older, one was younger, and they resembled each other enough to pass for mother and daughter. On the table were a variety of religious candles, medals and rosaries.

"Not again," Keary said under his breath.

"Good morning, ladies. You're going to have to take all this somewhere else, sweetie," he told the older woman. "This ought not be a marketplace. Have a nice day now, and God bless you." The women began packing up.

Sammy and Betsy waited on Keary to elaborate on what had happened but he didn't. On the front steps Keary shook hands with a man with graying temples and small eyes.

"Sammy, Betsy, this is Mr. Matthews, the county assessor, and his wife Myrna." Myrna was finishing a cigarette.

They exchanged greetings and entered the church, which was trimmed in green garland with red bows. Sammy and Betsy sat midway down, and Keary excused himself to get dressed for Mass.

The gospel reading was the story of John the Baptist asking Jesus, "Are you the one who is to come, or should we wait for another?" It was read, and everyone sat down. Keary stood up for his homily.

"You know," he said, "Now that we can conduct Mass in what is called vernacular languages, like English, and not Latin, I feel like we're all more connected. And frankly, there were times in the past that I felt like I was just driving the bus."

He turned his back to them and put his hands on an imaginary steering wheel. They laughed, and he looked over his shoulder at them and smiled. He droned something in Latin as he pretended to drive, and they laughed harder.

"Well, I'll just cut to the chase for you, and you can go back to worrying over holiday plans and Christmas lists. The Jews were waiting for the Messiah, and had no idea who it could be. So I tell you, people, it all boils down to this: it would be wise to believe that Christ could be anyone of us, and to treat each other as such."

He sat down. All eyes were on him, and you could hear a pin drop.

That afternoon, they were gathered around the fire upstairs. All three were reading quietly. The fire crackled and spat.

"I've been thinking," Keary said, "You two ought to call your parents."

Sammy and Betsy looked up, startled.

"Being a parent isn't easy, from what I hear," Keary said over his glasses. "My dad used to say, there's no such thing as a professional parent; we all learn on the job."

Sammy and Betsy stayed quiet. Their old lives were the last thing they wanted right now. Keary spoke again.

"Listen, you two, I don't know what they've done or haven't done, but they deserve to hear from you."

"You don't understand, Tony," Sammy said.

"Yes I do. I've seen families estranged from each other in every possible combination, and usually over trivialities. I've seen old people die alone merely because someone's feelings were hurt, and I've seen siblings estranged for the rest of their lives over inheritance money. *Inheritance money*, Samuel. Or their dearly departed mother's brooch. Believe me, I do understand."

Keary set his book down and picked up the phone. He handed it to Sammy, and Sammy took it. His voice felt strange as it crawled out of his mouth and gave the operator instructions. The phone rang twice and he wanted to hang up, but it kept ringing, just the hard trickle of the ring, and then, after ten rings there was still no answer. After twenty rings, he couldn't make himself hang up, and Keary took the phone from him. Sammy felt something wet on his cheeks and realized that he had tears in his eyes.

"Nobody's home," Keary said gently, and he took the phone from Sammy and pressed on the base to hang up.

"How about you, Betsy? Call your mother?" He offered the phone to her.

"We don't have a phone, and I'm not sure where she is."

"Well, let's write a letter then."

What do I say? she thought.

"Tell her you've been thinking about her. Remind her of something that's a secret between the two of you, maybe a memory that just the two of you shared. Thank her for something, it can be from a long time ago and small, of no consequence."

She sat and thought. And then she wrote.

Remember when we used to sing and weed the graves on All Saints' Day? We would sing, *Les Maringouins Ont Tout Mangé Ma Belle*, and *Saut, Crapaud*, and *Sur le Pont d'Avignon*. She thanked her mother for showing her how to make a roux, how to prepare a chicken, for taking care of her when she had her tonsils out. for taking her to the state fair in Baton Rouge that time, even though money was tight. For teaching her how to swim, and sew and laugh and sing and peel crawfish and pick crabs. For making her First Communion dress. For helping her take care of her daddy when he was dying. For marrying him in the first place.

Before she knew it, the letter was five pages long. Keary took it and folded it. He slid it into an envelope and licked the edge.

They mailed the letter the following day to her mother's last known address.

"The post office will forward it," Keary said, "It'll find her,"

And eventually, it did.

Chapter 77

They wore their coats and carried towels.

"This is one of the last ones, the hot springs that caused all this to get built in the first place. Most of the rest of 'em have dried up or been covered up."

He stayed on a trail that he knew was there under the soft, cold blanket of white. Their footsteps shuffled and squeaked in the snow. Keary stopped and put his hand to his ear.

"Hear it?" he said.

There was a bubbling, the sound of air popping and smacking on the surface of water. They continued on the trail, and it was louder and unmistakable. A few steps further down, Sammy saw it, a dark ring in the snow cover. When they reached it, Sammy knelt and put his fingertips in it. It was hot, barely tolerable.

"Well, last one in is a Protestant," Tony said as he kicked off his shoes. His tongue pierced his smile as he anticipated the water. He peeled his shirt off and shimmied down his trousers.

Sammy brushed snow off a log nearby and sat to wrestle off his shoes. He took off his coat, and then his pants. He looked over to Tony.

Keary was in a swath of baggy white underwear. His midsection was surprisingly athletic, the muscles segments well defined. There was a small round scar under his ribcage.

"What happened to you?"

Tony looked down and pointed to the scar.

"That? Story behind that." With Tony Keary, there was a story behind everything.

"My brother and I were bailing hay one summer day, in a quarter section right above the river. He threw a bale to me and it had, of all things, a bayonet in it. No idea how it got there, but an Illinois regiment did drill in that field in the days before the Civil War, so that's the most likely explanation. Probably down in the ground and just worked its way up, got into a bale. Anyway, the tip of it got me. Poked me pretty good and left a scar that looks worse than it really is. I see you've had an operation. Appendix?"

"Yeah, how'd you know?"

"Most common operation for someone your age."

Keary slipped out of his underwear and eased into the water, making a face that was a mixture of pleasure and pain.

"Ahhhh." he said, as he closed his eyes and leaned his head back. The spring pool was only a few feet deep, and the bottom was made up of smooth stones, slippery with a coat of algae and moss. It bubbled and popped around him like he was in a pot, the guest of honor at a cannibals' potluck. Sammy peeled off his underwear and eased in with him.

"Mr. Teague, I've been thinking," Keary said. The round lenses of his glasses were opaque, cloudy with condensation from the heat of the spring. He dipped a little further down into the spring, to the level of his ears, and tilted his face to the sky.

That was his favorite prelude, *I've been thinking.* He would say it as unexpectedly as a clap of thunder on a sunny day, as suddenly as a quick, piercing ray of sunlight through a break in a cloudy sky.

"If everyone in the world were the exact same shade of the exact same color, human beings would find something else different about themselves and divide off and fight about that. There would be great wars devoted to wiping out people with different color eyes or hair."

He took off his glasses and held them up as he dipped his head in the water. He reemerged, his hair hanging wet, and palmed water off his face. He put his glasses back on. White lenses.

"But really, there are only two kinds of people in this world, Samuel Teague. And it's not rich and poor, black and white, Jew and Muslim. It's the Kind and the Unkind. The Unkind are resentful at the contentment of the Kind, and there's a constant state of war between the two, a war of persuasion. And when the Kind become Unkind, they lose their divinity and their humanity, they lose their identity, their Christ, and they become the Unkind, and the Unkind win."

A cardinal flew onto a limb, a brilliant red exclamation mark set against a world of white. A small bit of snow was disturbed from the limb and filtered to the ground like an isolated shaft of snowfall, a column of white. The cardinal lifted and flapped its wings and coasted away.

The sun was setting in pastel magenta and orange, and gave the dome of the old college-hotel a golden-red sheen. The ridge under the sunset was a jagged line of black shadows. In the winter twilight, the snow under the trees was glowing white with the faintest hint of iridescent blue or purple.

They dried and dressed, and picked their way down the trail. The only light now was the moon reflected off the snow, a glowing, ethereal light. In the darkness, Keary sang out a sublime "Just a Closer Walk with Thee." They approached the Lost River which was making a quiet rush in the darkness. A tree had fallen across it.

"Ah! A short-cut. God provides again!" Keary said. He put his arms out and tiptoed over to the other side. Sammy hesitated, balking like a mule at an obstacle.

"A little faith, Samuel. Just go," Keary called out, and he made a rolling, beckoning gesture. The river murmured in the dark as the black water rushed downstream.

Sammy made a sudden burst down the log as if he were going to jump across the river. At the halfway point of the fallen tree, his feet slipped, gouging the decaying bark, and he fell into the icy water.

He felt his body constrict against the cold. He dangled in the water by a branch of the fallen tree, his feet still not touching the bottom. It was deeper than it looked.

He looked up in the moonlight and saw Keary's face, the pale white moon next to it, his hand reaching down for him. Sammy grasped it, and it pulled him up.

Chapter 78

The trail had gone cold, and he came home to regroup and to show his face to the parish.

The black GTO slid between the two rows of oaks and stopped in the driveway. On the front porch, Trey Teague was feeding the squirrel that had gotten in the habit of venturing there, even trying to come in the house if the screen door was left open. Trey sat in a wicker chair and handed the little fellow pecans, admiring how the creature's tiny knuckled paws held the nut, and thinking how much it looked like a little brown watermelon in its hands.

Deputy Parris got out of the GTO and pulled at his pants to straighten them. He had on a cowboy hat with his dark gray suit. Even though it was a fall day, true and cool, Parris was sweating, so he pulled off his suit jacket and tossed it in the GTO.

"Hey there, Trey."

"Hey Parris. Where's your police car?"

Parris looked back at the GTO and then at Trey. "Like to have a car like this'n for, uh, undercover work. Blends in better."

Trey gave an expression that said, *oh*, and stood up from his squat in front of the squirrel. Parris ascended the steps, and they shook hands uneasily like two rivals before an athletic contest.

"Cute little fella," Parris said looking down at the squirrel.

"Keeps wandering up here," Trey said as he continued to admire the squirrel.

"Half a dozen more and you could make yourself a stew."

"Really? Never had it." Squirrel stew was for poor people.

"Wanted to come check on things over here. Listen, ain't seen your boy for a while. Not up at school, I hear."

"No," Trey shook his head. His guilty, broken heart couldn't hold in the truth. "Not up at school."

"That so?"

"Yeah."

"Any ideas where?"

In the small silence, the squirrel's small feet and claws clicked on the boards of the porch as he flicked his tail and exited. He bounded into the yard and scrambled up into a live oak. His gray body hugged the trunk as he spiraled up and around it, finally bounding down a limb that bobbed under his small weight.

Trey reached into his shirt pocket. "This letter came from the Duplechain girl today, for her mama." He pointed to the vacant lot next door. The mailbox still stood by the highway, but without a house.

"I'm supposing that he and the girl are together." He looked at the address. "Postmarked West Baden, Indiana. My old aunt used to go up there for her health."

"When was it postmarked?" Parris asked, his voice almost overly sympathetic.

Trey looked at the letter again. "Three days ago. Just got here today."

"What'd it say?"

"I don't read other people's mail. Impolite. And against the law."

"Oh yeah," Parris said. "I knew that. Listen, Trey, I know we've had our differences through the years, but I'd be glad to make amends and help you find him. A lawman's got contacts, got some stroke, can get things done. Be glad to help, if you'd let me."

"Would you?" The desperation of a grieving father was erasing his memory and clouding his judgment.

"Sure," Parris said with a smile. Trey stood up, and they shook hands.

"In fact, I'll go right now. Can I use your phone?"

"Sure. Certainly." Trey was overwhelmed by this sudden hospitality. "Just keep your voice down. Mamie's asleep upstairs with a headache."

285

"Sure, buddy, though I have to say, she's not one who needs a lot of beauty sleep." The flattery curled out of Parris' mouth like a flowering vine. Trey opened the screen door, they slipped in, and then he eased it shut behind them. He pointed to the phone.

Parris took it, dialed the number and listened for the ring.

"Olivier? This Parris. Sheriff needs me to run and find that Teague boy. Missing person case, y'see." A pause, and then Parris' voice rose and fell again as he remembered to keep it down. "Well you just gonna have to take that up with him.

"All right, Trey. I'm on my way right now."

Parris tried not to seem in too much of a hurry. He got in his car and turned onto 308. As soon as he was past the far reaches of Mount Teague, he gunned the GTO and headed north.

He'd studied the map. He'd burned their car. Now he knew about where they were, and how and where they would be headed: to Detroit, by way of Indianapolis. On the bus.

Chapter 79

The couple from Michigan was coming to see about buying the place, so Keary sent Sammy and Betsy on a walk into French Lick, "to get you two out of my hair for a while," he joked. They couldn't see how three people could get in each other's way in a former three hundred bed hotel, but they went anyway. The day had warmed up, and the snow had melted on the streets and in small patches where the yellowed grass was exposed in the yards. Betsy was wearing a new peacoat, a rich green color, given to her by one of the old people.

Some boys were sword fighting with sticks in a front yard. Their frenzied footsteps had plowed irregular furrows and pits in the snow. A dog, a mismatched sort of dog who looked like he had been put together by a committee, sat on his haunches and watched them play. He barked occasionally as if he were giving them tips until he spotted Sammy and Betsy and ambled toward them. The boys stopped their sword fight. Their thick winter coats were wet with snow and sweaty from their little boy play.

"Careful, lady, he bites," one of them said.

She ruffled the dog's coat. "Not this sweet doggie," she said, "Not this sweet dog. Te chien." The dog worked his back leg while his black lips fell into a smile.

"Wow," the boy said. "He don't like nobody except us."

She stood up, and Sammy took her hand. He read her mind and answered her silent question.

"Aucoin's got Chanceux. Probably has him twice his size on Vienna sausages and scraps."

"Prolly," she smiled.

They made their way through the streets of French Lick. As they passed a row of houses, someone inside one of them, a child perhaps, was playing the piano, practicing the "Sunburst Waltz." The sound of it floated out an open window, the melody pausing and repeating from time to time. A woman's voice somewhere in the house said, "Vera, close that win-der. House's gittin' cold." The playing stopped and the window made a clump against the sill. The song began again, though muffled now.

They walked along further, hand in hand, the sun continuing to diminish the snow cover. From down the street came the sound of a basketball pocking on concrete and the rattle of a goal.

The blonde headed boy had a nose that was just a little too big for his face and an upper lip that was just a little too small. He hit shot after shot, long range, lay ups, turnaround jumpers. Sammy and Betsy were in awe. They sat and watched him. He seemed not to notice them.

"How old are you?" Sammy asked, convinced the boy must be about to enter high school.

"Just turned nine, sir," he said as he scooped up another made shot from under the basket and dribbled out to the perimeter for another.

They sat and watched him for over an hour, and he didn't miss five shots the whole time. It was almost on the level with art, a ballet. After a while the smell of a hundred different suppers cooking inside the houses of the town scented the air. The sun was low in the western sky.

"Larry!" a woman's voice called from up on the hill. "Come get your supper!"

The boy said "See ya" to Sammy and Betsy and dribbled a fast break up the hill.

They got up and walked back to West Baden in the failing purple gray light. The sun was setting between two layers of clouds like an orange eye as they crossed the main highway, a molten orange and pink and blue tiger striped sunset.

Keary met them at the door.

"Don't go in the atrium. I have a surprise for you. Keep your curtains to the balcony drawn until I say. Go straight up to your room, hear?"

They went up the stairs, holding hands. They sat in the darkness of their room until they heard Keary's voice in the atrium.

"Turn the lights off in your room," he said.

Sammy got up and flipped the switches on the lights. It was completely dark.

"Now," Keary shouted from the floor of the atrium. "Pull open your curtains."

Sammy and Betsy groped for the edges of them in the dark and pulled them apart. It was dark in the atrium, too, an immense, thick, absolute darkness.

And then it wasn't. Keary flipped a switch and a thirty foot Christmas tree erupted in tiny white lights. Betsy gasped in delight and took Sammy's hand and leaned into him. The lights of the tree illuminated the dome and illuminated their faces. It was like a triangular constellation, densely packed with stars.

"What do you think?" Keary called up to them.

"It's beautiful," Betsy called down to him, and then quietly to Sammy, "Beautiful." Sammy gave Keary a thumbs up.

"Thought you'd like it. I'm headed up to Christ the King in Paoli. It's bingo night."

"You play bingo?" Betsy called down.

"Oh, no, never touch the stuff. I go there to break up squabbles. I'm gonna be back late, real late. I'll lock the door. You'll have the whole place to yourself." He winked at them.

After he left, Betsy disappeared back into their room. Sammy stayed on the balcony and admired the tree, and the dome and the unseen angels at the top of it. And then Betsy appeared on the balcony.

She wore the white nightgown from their first time together, the same wash-worn gown that had been the epicenter of every erotic thought he had had since September. She pulled it by the hem, over her head, the same way she had that first time, but there were no cotton drawers. There weren't any at all. Her lower stomach pushed out in a slight swell like the undulating rise of a calm sea or the gentle lift of a rolling hill in the prairie.

"Sammy, baby, I think we got a wedding night comin'," she said with her fingertip at the edge of her smile. She closed her eyes and rubbed her hands over her upper thighs. Her eyes pleaded for him, the look of long-denied passion.

She threw the balcony doors open wider and the light from the tree fell on their bed. He pulled his shirt over his head, the sleeves clung inside out to his arms and he pulled one and then the other off. She sat naked on the bed before him, her hands trembling as she unbuttoned his pants and slid them down.

Each was aching for the other. The forces of Love and Magnetism and Nature played on them and they were left wonderfully helpless.

They kissed and fell to the bed with their lips together. She drew him inside her and then they were moving together, her hands roamed over his back, a back that was firm and muscular now, he put a hand to her breast, full and heavy now. And then they shared a sensation of a dam bursting, levees overtopping, and fields flooding. They panted and smiled with their eyes closed as they clutched each other.

He spooned her with the lights of the tree in their eyes. After a time, five minutes or an hour or more, or less, neither could tell, he kissed her neck and she shuddered and he pulled her on top of him. He found her again and she shuddered again. He studied her as she moved on top of him, and the rising of pleasure in her face and the small sounds that she cooed made him close his eyes and grasp the tops of her thighs and everything was building, building again and he wanted to feel her breasts as they fell in front of his face, and her buttocks soft and round, resting on his thighs, and then she flung herself down on him and her body tensed and then his did.

289

They fell asleep with the light of the tree throwing shadows over their bodies.

Chapter 80

"I'll be all right. Just me and the Man." Keary pointed up. "We're used to keeping company together. Look on the backseat," he said. "I got you a gift."

Sammy reached over the seat behind Betsy and got the present and put it in her lap.

"What is it?" She asked.

"Something for the baby," Keary said. "But you can't open it until the baby's here."

He drove them into French Lick, and they waited for the bus. The three of them sat on a bench, each in thought. The bus appeared down the road and rumbled into the parking lot, and they all three got up. The brakes of the bus belched, and the door opened.

"This is it," Sammy said. Betsy's eyes were misty. She couldn't say anything. "Tony, how do you tell someone thank you, and have them know that you really mean it?"

Keary smiled. "You just say it, then it takes care of itself."

"Thank you, then," Sammy said.

Sammy shook Keary's hand, and Keary kissed Betsy's cheek, and then Keary made the sign of the cross over Betsy's belly. They ascended the steps of the bus and found a seat halfway down. They put away their suitcases and sat down as Keary stood and watched them. He suddenly looked preoccupied, like he had a headache. His thumbs massaged his temples.

The doors to the bus closed, and the bus lurched forward and pulled out. Betsy looked out the window.

Keary was running alongside the bus, the ear flaps of his cap bouncing. He pounded on the door with his palm. The driver stopped the bus and opened the door. He chewed a piece of gum lazily and looked at his watch. The bus panted idly, the tailpipe chugging out an acrid steam into the cold, wet gray.

"Yeah?" he said.

"This is the wrong bus," Keary said breathlessly.

"What do you mean? This is the bus to Indianapolis."

"They need Cincinnati," Keary said.

The driver looked at his watch and shrugged his shoulders. Keary vaulted up the steps of the bus, past the confused expression of the passengers, some of them irritated, to Sammy and Betsy.

"Change of plans," he said as he gathered their bags.

They bumped down the center aisle of the bus, easing their suitcases between the seats. The other riders looked at them in confusion, and Sammy and Betsy themselves looked confused. They stepped into the cold parking lot, and sat on a bench as Keary went to the window to exchange the tickets.

In a few minutes he returned with new tickets.

"Through Cincinnati to Detroit. Now that's the ticket," he said smiling.

What was wrong with Indianapolis? Sammy thought.

"Cincinnati's better," Keary said out loud. "You'll make a transfer in Cincinnati, then to Detroit."

In fifteen minutes the bus to Cincinnati rounded the corner and crept into the parking lot. The three of them stood from the bench, each with a bag. The door to the bus opened and passengers began filing out.

Keary hugged Betsy's neck and kissed her cheek and hugged her again. Sammy extended his hand, but Keary hugged his neck and kissed his cheek, too. Betsy and Sammy filed onto the bus about midway to the back, put their luggage in overhead bins, and took seats.

Keary was standing outside the window. He waved to them, smiling beatifically with what seemed to be a tear in his eye. They waved back to him, and then scanned the bus to see who else would be making the journey with them. When they looked back, Keary was gone.

The bus rumbled back through West Baden on its way to Cincinnati. Sammy watched as the West Baden Hotel slipped away in the cold fog. He felt Betsy lean into him. She was watching it go, too. It looked lifeless, deserted, and he was reminded of one of Miss Della Mae's expressions when a jar or box or canister in the kitchen had been depleted.

Empty as the garden tomb, she would say.

He and Betsy turned and looked until they couldn't see it anymore, and then they nestled in next to each other.

Past Paoli, Betsy couldn't wait any longer and opened the gift from Keary. It was a light blue baby blanket. She held it up to admire it and then quickly folded it and put it back in the box. She opened the card, and she and Sammy read it together, their faces close:

My dear girl, I knew you wouldn't wait until that boy was born. My own mother knitted this blanket when I told her about you. Take it and swaddle him tight in it, and then read to him and sing to him and smile at him so he will see your faces and hear your voices and know that there is a God who loves him.

Tony

The bus rumbled through Indiana farm country. It was snowing again.

Chapter 81

The man sat in the waiting area of the station all day watching for the bus from French Lick and Paoli. From time to time his blue eyes appeared over the *Indianapolis Star*, framed coldly between the top edge of the newspaper and the lines of his red eyebrows and his hairline. Each fruitless glance at an emptying bus sent them back behind the paper like an alligator dipping below the surface.

He waited for most of the morning, drinking black coffee and chain smoking cigarettes, watching bus after bus unload. Finally, realizing his hunch had betrayed him, he folded the newspaper and threw it down. They may still be headed to Detroit, but they weren't going through Indianapolis.

He barged through the door of the bus station, almost knocking down an old woman who was coming in. She stood there, her gloved hands holding her purse and a shawl over her shoulders, waiting for an apology. He stalked away, throwing down a cigarette. The GTO roared to life. She stood watching it, flinching as it squealed its tires and sped down the street, a ribbon of black pavement flanked by icy cloud banks of plowed-high snow.

Part V: Detroit

Chapter 82

Detroit was a gray-black city on a gray white day, brutally, bitterly, utterly cold, especially for two people from Louisiana. Just around the corner from the bus station on Kercheval Avenue was a little convenience store called Zadeh's.

The store smelled intensely of cigarette smoke. On the wall was a sign in the squiggles and dots of Arabic, a picture of Christ on one side and the prophet Mohammed on the other. The man behind the counter was small and bald with a white beard that looked like his hair had slid down and was clinging to his chin. He sat reading a paper in Arabic, the sports page with a photo of action from the Detroit Redwings hockey game the previous night. His eyes looked up from the paper to see two teenagers around the candy display. One had a comb stuck in his hair, a short, trim afro. The other one was putting candy, quite a bit of candy, in his pocket. They walked shoulder-to-shoulder toward the door. The little man exploded from his aluminum and plywood stool. The paper fell to the floor.

"Hey-hey-hey that is stealink! Put that down, my friend. I call cops!"

The one with the comb in his hair stopped and approached the counter.

"You think I give a shit," he leaned in close and tilted his face, "Then you muss be ouch yo ball-headed mind. Go head on, call the cops. You know they don't come down this part o' town no mo." He unwrapped a piece of candy from his pocket and put it his mouth right in front of the man, and threw the wrapper in the old man's face.

The boy turned and wandered out the door casually with his friend. The bell dinged.

"Hey-hey, that is stealink, my friend. You are doing the reap off!" the man said to the closed door.

He sat down in exasperation on his stool and rubbed his dome of a head. Then he began talking with his hands as if they held the problem, to Sammy and Betsy and whoever would listen.

"Twenty, ten years go even things so much better. Ev'body kind, evbody working, evbody respect. Black, white, Arab, Jew, no problem. All to getter, all happy. All make cars to getter. Now? Beh!

"Now I say focket! Focket, my friend! I move out to Dearborn weet my sister, her family. Theece son of beaches can hivvit. Done with East Side, I am. One day theece town, up in flames, you will see it." His finger stabbed the air in emphasis.

He sat rubbing the gloss of his head and his shaggy beard, looking down in despair.

He looked up to see Betsy there holding a twenty.

"All we goss a twenny. You cheenge dat?"

The man's mood brightened, and he smiled a great toothy smile.

"Su-re. Where you are from, my friend so low-vely? You have accent, berry theek."

"Louisiana."

"Oh, Loose-yana, yes. A berry be-you-tea-full place, yes," he said, though he had no idea where Louisiana was. He was concentrating on his index finger tapping the keys of the cash register. He gave Betsy her change and said, "There you hivvit. Have the nice day, then."

Chapter 83

The man in the fedora bought some magazines from a newsstand and checked into the Algiers Motel. He was feeling tense, and after all, he thought, a man has needs. City as big as Detroit ought to have some pretty nice strip clubs. The good people of St. Matthew Parish surely wouldn't mind springin' for a few cocktails and lap dances, not that they would find out about it or that it was any of their business.

He may have been wrong about Indianapolis but he was sure about the crossing point. There were two choices, the Windsor Tunnel and the Ambassador Bridge. It would definitely be the bridge. His hunches were seldom wrong twice.

The bridge would be perfect. Wait at the top in the snow and fog. Throw them off one at a time, oh hell, at the same time if he could manage it. The girl wasn't worth the effort to wrestle back home. Long way down to the water. Impact alone would kill 'em. And then head back down the bridge for cocktails and lap dances.

The Algiers Motel on Woodward Avenue at Virginia Park had televisions in every room, though they were black and white and chained to the wall. Parris sat and watched it. A coyote painted the opening of a tunnel on a rock face, and then a bird ran into it and disappeared. The coyote chased after him and crashed into the painted rock face, shattering into pieces to the plunk of violin strings.

He sat slouched and slack jawed on the corner of the bed watching it. On the cover of one of the magazines on the bed, a blonde woman in black stockings and a push up bra brandished a riding crop.

Now on the television, the coyote launched an anvil with a giant slingshot and then somehow it fell on him, shortening the coyote into a corrugated version of himself, and he walked off dejectedly as an accordion played the same two notes over and over. The big red haired man laughed to himself. He clicked the television off and stepped out into the Michigan winter. He lit a cigarette, as much for the warmth as for the flavor. He paused on the landing of the motel. His cold blue eyes leaped like a gas flame.

The black GTO was up on blocks, and all four tires were gone. He walked down the stairs. On the landing, he paused and surveyed his car, calmly smoking the cigarette. The wheels were only the small nut-studded disks, set up on cement squares. He vowed to get even; getting even was the most important thing, because it was the step before getting ahead. His blue eyes smoldered in the cold.

He walked down to the bus stop and waited in the shelter with some women, most of them housekeepers and store clerks. He lit another cigarette.

"Man, ain't nobody wanna smell your cigarette," one of them scolded him. "Get that thing way from this baby." She waved the air between them.

He moved the lapel of his jacket back to reveal his revolver and his badge, took a big drag and blew the smoke out toward the woman. She was quiet and just turned the baby away from the smoke, still jiggling her.

He was near the end of his cigarette when the bus approached. He threw the butt under the stroller, and it smoked. He stepped in front of the woman and everyone else to get on first. He sat right up front; he felt that it was his right as a white man.

The bus rumbled through the streets, squeaking to stops, people getting on and off and then rumbling on again. At the base of the Ambassador Bridge, he got out and went to a café, got a seat near the window and waited.

He looked across the street at the spires of St. Anne. He didn't believe it was a godless world. How could it be as long as he himself was in it?

He waited for quite a while and was about to give up to go back to the Algiers Motel.

Then he saw them. They were bundled against the cold, with an uneasiness against it that the northern people didn't have.

A man in a blue and black plaid jacket, and a woman in a green peacoat.

Chapter 84

They were like two people on the end of a diving board. Snow was beginning to come down again, and the north wind picked it up and dispersed it. High atop the span in the dull smudge of winter, the words, *Ambassador* and under it, *Bridge* glowed in red. Twin lights on each side of the road rose in a sweep along the supporting cables to the tower with the letters, then down into the fog of snow toward the tower on the Canadian side. Far down below the Detroit

River wore a layer of fog. Paradoxically, the bridge led south into Canada.

They rose out of the city onto the approach ramp of the Ambassador Bridge, above St. Anne's, the Catholic church with the unusual feature of a star of David on the front over a cross. Its twin spires rose up into the murky gray cold. Betsy thought of a prayer from her childhood, a prayer for lovelorn women, another of Tante Lucille's rhymes:

St. Anne, St. Anne
Find me a man.

They ascended the long, steady incline. Far below in the fog and whirling snow, the unseen maritime sounds of the Detroit River, the deep throated pant of diesel engines, the horns and bells of ships. The stars and stripes and the maple leaf flag whipped steadily in the wind, due south. They took one last look behind them, the United States of America.

And there down at the base of the bridge, they saw him, a man ill-dressed against the cold, his bare red head picking up white from the snow.

"Don't run. Don't run. Don't run," Sammy said in a low voice. Their suitcases slapped out a rhythm against the outside of their knees. Their feet crunched over the snow. A car passed them slowly on the incline, and Sammy took the opportunity to look over his shoulder again. Parris was still a good distance away, but breaking into a trot.

"Don't run," Sammy said again, almost as a mantra. "The border agents might get suspicious." At last they arrived at the crossing.

The border kiosk on the long, ascending stretch of pavement glowed yellow in the snowy fog. Two men had drawn the miserable duty of manning it, an Ontario border agent named MacDermott and a Mountie named Levesque. As Sammy and Betsy approached, it appeared that the two Canadians were chatting and playing cards in front of a heater and trying to make the best of it. The harsh north wind blew drifts of snow past Sammy and Betsy and made them huddle together. As they neared the kiosk, MacDermott opened the sliding door.

MacDermott wore the blue uniform of the Ontario authorities, but Levesque wore the red serge jacket and Sam Browne belt with a diagonal strap. His pants were midnight blue, almost black with bags at the thighs and a yellow stripe down the side of each leg. He sat on a stool and warmed his hands at the heater. His eyes were hidden by the wide brim of his hat, There were two cups of coffee on a small stove nearby, and a table with two hands of cards dealt and interrupted.

"Good day," MacDermott said, even though it was night now, and there was no smile with it. "Passports, then?"

Sammy and Betsy looked at each other. In the kiosk, a radio cackled a message for someone else.

"Passports?" MacDermott asked again. Levesque had joined McDermott.

Betsy stepped forward, and greeted Levesque.

"Bonjour, comme ca va?"

A conversation in French ensued, Levesque looking into Betsy's face thoughtfully, then replying, then listening again. They talked for a few minutes, almost like old friends who were just catching up after an absence from each other.

"Tu me rappelles ma soeur," Levesque said.

Finally, Levesque paused, looked to McDermott, and then, with a sigh and a twitch of his head, they were admitted into Canada.

"Joyeux noel," he said.

"Joyeux noel," Betsy answered.

They ascended the sidewalk of the bridge, each glad that the magnitude of the drop over the edge was obscured. Their arms were close to their sides as the wind slapped them. They would have hugged themselves against it had they not been carrying suitcases.

"What did y'all talk about?" Sammy said as they walked.

"I told him you were my brother, and that you were a little slow in the head and that I was takin' you home to our mama."

They would laugh about that one day, a family legend, a favorite story, but they didn't just now.

"And what did he tell you?"

"That I reminded him so much of his sister. Then I told him that the man behind us is carryin' a gun that he's tryin' to smuggle in."

Two figures, clutching suitcases, ascended to the apex of the Ambassador Bridge. They walked into a whirling cloud of snow and disappeared, south into Canada.

It was Christmas Eve.

*   *   *

Moments later a red haired man with a jutting lower jaw arrived, breathless after an ascent up to the border kiosk. He approached it as if he were in a hurry and would have continued across the bridge had the Mountie not gotten out to block the road. The Ontario Provincial man joined him. Both were aggravated to be pulled away again from the warm kiosk.

"And where do you think you're goin', eh?"

Parris lips were cold and his tongue wouldn't work well.

"I a lawman," he mumbled; his face was frozen, beefy-red, and paralyzed by the cold. "Gogga cash doo fug-tives."

"Eh?" MacDermott asked. "What say?"

Meanwhile, Levesque checked Parris' jacket and found the gun.

"You can't go bringin' this across the border, don't you know? Gotta have a permit."

Levesque ushered Parris into the kiosk. Parris stole a glance down the bridge, toward the invisible quarry that was slipping away.

MacDermott opened a filing cabinet and pulled out a small sheaf of forms.

"One for the city of Windsor," he licked his thumb and pulled off the next, "One for the province of Ontario," he licked his thumb for the next, "And one for Canada."

Levesque took Parris' gun and examined it, looking down the barrel into the winter night. Then he pushed the cylinder open and emptied the bullets. They went in one cabinet, and the gun in another. Levesque locked both with a key held with a cluster of others on his belt.

"Now," MacDermott said, "Let's have a look at your passport."

Parris looked confused. His blue eyes were heavy lidded and dull like a cow's.

"No passport no enter," MacDermott said as if Parris didn't understand English. Levesque opened the sliding door and the winter wind whistled gleefully at the prospect of warm skin to chill.

They pointed Parris back down into Detroit. The use of his mouth was returning.

"Gimme my gun back then," Parris demanded.

"Can't do that," MacDermott explained. "Procedure clearly states it has to be held for a minimum of thirty days. You're lucky we don't detain you for trying to sneak it in, eh?"

Parris descended down into Detroit, wishing he had brought a heavier coat. He paused and looked around. MacDermott and Levesque had resumed their card game in the warmth of the kiosk, laughing as they laid cards down and picked them up. Behind them, the bridge ascended into white.

By the time Parris got back to the Algiers Motel, it was late and the snow had stopped. In the parking lot two men were leaning into his tire-less car through a shattered window. They were after the stereo.

Parris grabbed one by the shoulder and jerked him around, and then pushed him to the ground. The other ran around and got in Parris' face, their noses an inch apart, the man tilting his head from one side and then the other in derision. They shoved each other's shoulders, each recoiling. Parris reached for his revolver, and then remembered it was at the border crossing.

Suddenly, there was a ring of black faces, wide-eyed, feral, agitated, cold breath vaporized into a cloud above them. They buffeted him, jabbering insults as he twirled for a way out of the ring, but, with every revolution, there were more, the crowd two deep, then three deep, and then four deep. He swung out at them, and his blows were met four-fold. He felt the first dozen, and after that, he felt none of them. The glass in the remaining windows of the GTO crashed one by one, and he heard a flurry of words: *honky, peckerwood, white-ass.* He fell to the ground, only hearing the sound of shoe leather kicking against cloth and flesh and then distant sirens. He closed his eyes to the black starry heavens and then opened them again and saw dark elbows working back and forth against the sky.

He spent five days in the Henry Ford Hospital. When he was released, he took the city bus to the foot of the Ambassador Bridge and walked gingerly up the bridge to the border crossing. He filled out another set of forms to have the pearl handled revolver sent to him. Then he walked down to the bus station and bought a ticket back to St. Matthew Parish. He spent the two day journey thinking of an explanation for the bruises on his face.

Part VI: Canada

Chapter 85

The sun was coming up in the south.

He looked out over the wide St. Lawrence toward Longueil and beyond it New York and America. He always got homesick this time of year when Canada was still hungover from winter, drifts of wet granular snow stained brown and plowed to the sides of the streets, floes of ice sliding leisurely with the current of the St Lawrence. Icicles melted during the day, falling from eaves and hitting the ground with a shattering tinkle like the highest keys of a piano, and overnight they grew back like crystalline fangs. He knew the cane was knee high now and leafy green. They never discussed it, but he was sure Betsy felt it even more.

The days were getting longer now, but they were still short. The Canadian winter days were always too short, and the summer days were always too long, the sun going down close to ten o'clock at night. He glanced at his watch and realized he would be late if he didn't get a move on. He made the bus stop at the corner of Rue St. Gabriel and Rue Notre Dame just before the bus pulled away.

Inside the bus, he sat down and pulled off the sock cap Betsy had knitted for him and put it in his lap with his work gloves. His body ached from a day's work on the Quai Jacques-Cartier, loading and unloading ships. The bus turned right on Rue St. Sulpice and rumbled toward home.

In the apartment, Betsy handed him their screaming toddler.

Te couchon, Sammy said to the toddler, who opened his eyes and stopped screaming, though his bottom lip was still curled up. It was little Quint Teague's nickname, given to him by his mama for his breastfeeding prowess.

"We need to stop calling him that," she said in French, and then in English, "That's the kind of nickname that can stick to a boy."

Sammy smacked a kiss on the boy's forehead and then one on his wife's.

"There's gumbo on the stove," she said as she kissed both of them. Then she gathered up her books for her class at École des Hautes Études Commerciales de Montréal. She slipped the last one, *Principes de L'économie*, into her book sack and slipped the strap over her shoulder. They kissed again, and she went out the door. As usual, the child stopped crying when Sammy sang *Dixie* to him.

The phone rang, and Sammy picked it up. The child jiggled with his head pressed against his daddy's chest as Sammy bounced him.

"Bonjour, hi."

"Sammy?"

"Hey, daddy."

"Listen, son. I called to tell you that grandpappy passed away. Didn't come down for breakfast this morning. He was gone. Died in his sleep."

"I'm sorry, daddy."

Dutchie had looked out the kitchen window at sunset to see grandpappy wandering naked in the yard. His white skin hung from his old bones like an elephant's, shroud-white and blanched of all youth and vigor. She quickly dried her hands and ran out the back door with a sheet. He held himself, white hairs creeping over his thumb as if he were holding a baby possum to his crotch. He looked into Dutchie's face, his eyes searching for some meaning, his pale gray pupils faded to almost nothing. Then he mumbled for directions to the Sporting District. Dutchie covered him with the sheet and put her arm around him and said, "Right dis way, suh."

She took him upstairs, patiently waiting as he took one old wooden step at a time, and eased him into the low twin bed next to the big four poster bed he could no longer get up into. She pulled the comforter up around him like she would do for any of her children.

"Have 'em send up one of them Spanish gals," he muttered. His sagging face was flecked with white whiskers.

"Show will. All right, Mist' Junior. Sleep tight, now. I see you in da moanin'." She shut the door quietly behind herself. He died in the night.

Sammy and his daddy moved on to other topics, the usual ones. How does the cane look? What was the price of sugar per ton? What kind of hurricane season do they expect? What were the prospects for Ole Miss next fall? Sometimes the newsstand on Rue Saint-Jacques would have the Memphis paper, so he could keep up with them, but most of the time, not.

They told each other I love you, a thing they were doing more and more, and they hung up.

Sammy tried to think of a single kind word or piece of sage advice from his grandpappy and couldn't. So he mourned their absence.

Chapter 86

He had stayed a while on the docks to talk and joke with some French speaking African sailors from the Cote d'Ivoire. They were men with long heads, bodies skinny as branches, midnight black with yellowed eyes and smiles with yellowed teeth. They had offered him a cigarette, some eastern European brand. The day was cold, and it would have been a good day to enjoy it, but he declined with an upturned palm and a *non, merci*.

Quint was at school, Betsy was at class, and Sammy was home alone. He was content however, with a cup of coffee and today's edition of *Le Devoir*. As he sat down, the phone rang, and he reached over and answered it.

"Bonjour, hi."

"Sammy?"

His daddy's voice sounded different. Maybe it was age.

"I wanted." His daddy's voice cracked.

"I wanted." His daddy's voice sounded like it was being squeezed.

"I wanted to tell you. Your mama's. Your mama's dead." His daddy's voice shook.

The gin had finally come to collect his mama. Her small stony liver would no longer let blood pass and fluid built up in her stomach so that it looked like the gin had had its way with her and left her with a baby. She spent her last days with gaunt yellow eyes ringed gray-green, staring at nothing, rose-colored lipstick smeared clownishly around her mouth. Finally, vessels burst in her chest, and Dutchie found her delirious in a puddle of vomited blood in the dining room. Mamie Teague's last words were blood strangled: *Della Mae get back to work.*

"But I's Dutchie, Miss Mamie," she said. She called Mr. Teague at the country club and then the ambulance.

Trey Teague came straight from the putting green and saw Mamie there and said, "Oh my, oh my, oh my," frantically pacing back and forth with his palm on his forehead.

Mamie Teague was dead by the time the ambulance got her to Thibodaux.

"I wish you could've known her before," his daddy said. There was no need to say before what.

"She was a flower, a real beauty."

"I wish I could be there, daddy."

"I wish you could, too, son."

Chapter 87

Jan. 22, 1977

"*J'ai deux billets pour le match des Canadiens hocky. Voulez-vous un?*"

"*Non, merci.*"

Sammy shook hands with Jean-Pierre as a thank you, anyway, and ascended the steps of the bus. After almost twelve years, he still couldn't get use to hockey or to Canadian football, with its long field, three downs instead of four, and illegal procedure on every play. There was major league baseball now, the Expos, but, in truth, he usually was too tired to go. He was resigned to learning about hockey, however, now that Quint was showing an interest in playing. Sammy still couldn't get up on skates, though Betsy was very good and could even make a figure eight.

The bus rumbled down Rue St. Sulpice. He saw his reflection in the window of the bus and put his fingers in his hair. He felt it had thinned in recent years, though Betsy assured him that it hadn't. In his lap, the lead story in *Le Devoir* was Bill 101 and its prospects for passage. It would essentially make French the official language of Quebec. Among other things, it would give workers the right to carry on their activities in French, and consumers the right to be informed and served in French. Outside, the snow was falling heavy again.

Un autre demi-mètre de neige, someone on the bus said to someone else. Another half meter of snow.

Sammy ascended the steps to their apartment. His legs were heavy like they always were at the end of the workday. He could hear his son playing "Imagine" on the piano. He came in the door, and Quint got up, hugged him, and said, "Bonjour, papa."

"Bonjour," Sammy said, and he kissed his boy on both cheeks. "*Comment s'est passée ta journée aujourd'hui?*"

"*Bien*," Quint said, and then in English he said, "Mama called and said she'll be home from work soon."

Sammy collapsed onto the couch across from where Quint was supposed to be doing his homework on the kitchen table. Sammy unlaced his boots but was too tired to pull them off. He sat with the edition of *Le Devoir*.

He put on his reading glasses and scanned the article about Bill 101. The chance of passage was excellent, it said. Quint sat next to him, pretending to read along, but really enjoying the chance to be side by side with his hero.

The phone rang. Sammy struggled to his feet, feeling the long, cold day on the docks on the St. Lawrence in his bones and muscles. His work gloves were still wedged in the pockets of his parka.

"Son, will you get that?"

"Sure, papa."

Quint answered. "Bonjour? Alo?"

"Oh, hi Grandpere. How are things in Louise-ee-Anna? Très bien, I mean, very good. When are you coming back up to see us? Okay, here he is. Au revoir, goodbye."

Quint handed his daddy the phone.

"Hello."

"Sammy?"

"Hey daddy."

"He did it, he made good on it."

"Who did? Made good on what?"

"His campaign promise. Carter. Unconditional this time. Get a paper, turn on the news."

There was a pause as Sammy fumbled through the paper looking for the article.

"Please come home, son," his daddy said.

Sammy looked down, and there it had been all the time, at the bottom of the front page of *Le Devoir*. *Carter Accorde L'amnistie Inconditionnelle.*

Carter Grants Unconditional Amnesty.

VII. The United States

Chapter 88

The station wagon with Quebec plates was packed full. It rolled to a stop at the border crossing where snow still covered most of the ground, save for a few patches of frozen brown earth. It was spring somewhere, but not in Canada.

"Passport," the guard said as he stepped out of the warmth of the booth with the stars and stripes on it. Another guard stayed inside the border kiosk, sitting on a stool, reading the paper, and listening to the radio. There were small American flags on their shoulders. The first guard looked in the back of the station wagon and saw the telltale signs of a household being moved back after an exile. He knew it well now that amnesty had been granted.

Sammy produced the passports with the ornate Royal Coat of Arms of Canada on them. On the guard's forearm was a tattoo of a dagger and something written there, and Sammy tilted his head to read it. Without looking up from the passports, the guard said, "Khe Sanh. It's in Vietnam. I went there instead of Canada." He looked up and stared at Sammy.

The other guard reached from behind the first one, took the three passports and gave them back to Sammy.

Apologetically, he said, "Welcome to the United States." He reached inside the booth to push a button, and the arm across the road went up. They crossed the bridge over the wide, ice pocked St. Lawrence. The sign read, "Ogdensburg, New York."

It would have faster to fly, but they didn't have the money and he didn't want to ask his daddy. One grown man doesn't ask another for money, even if it is your daddy, especially if it's your daddy. It would have been faster to take the completed segments of the interstate highway system, but instead they took the back roads, following the path they had taken almost twelve years earlier in a sort of reverse pilgrimage.

Chapter 89

They moved down the highway southwest through New York and Ohio in the green station wagon with the faux wood panels, old but not yet dilapidated, a rolling monument to That Which Can Be Afforded They rode silently for the most part, heads pivoting slowly in the strange forgotten homeland.

In Toledo, they passed the turn off for Detroit and continued west instead. Sammy stopped and bought an Indiana state highway map and studied it for a moment. Quint stood next to him, and Betsy smiled at how similar their mannerisms were, knitted brows, big and little index fingers tracing over the lines on the map.

In Defiance, Ohio, they could drive no more and got a motel room. Sammy and Betsy shared one bed, and Quint took the other. He wore pajama bottoms and the Ole Miss t-shirt, faded almost to pink and more patches than original fabric.

In the morning they headed south, through Fort Wayne and Indianapolis. Just before noon they reached West Baden, and then there it was, the pale yellow building with the red top. The double arch over the drive now said Northwood Institute.

They stopped and went up the stairs, past the swastikas in the railing. The chapel was now the Springs Valley Playhouse, the altar and the painting of Christ removed. They found the atrium and the elf on the fireplace. Students were scattered around the atrium, engrossed in books and notebooks. A man who happened to be the director met them.

"May I help you?"

"We were wondering if someone might know what ever happened to Father Keary, a priest that was here ten, twelve years ago."

The man looked puzzled.

"Place was empty when we moved in, in sixty-five. Looked like it had been that way for some time."

They scanned the atrium. Quint looked up and around and quietly said, "Wow." Betsy took Sammy's hand and pointed to their balcony and smiled at Sammy, who winked at her and smiled back. He looked up to the center of the dome. In the corner of his eye he saw Betsy looking there, too, looking up where there were angels.

Across the street, the Dead Rat was boarded up, but the sign said a convenience store was planned. Sammy double checked to verify this was the place. The porch posts and molding were the same, but the door and windows were covered with plywood.

While Betsy and Quint waited in the car, Sammy went next door to a barber shop. A middle-aged man waited while his elderly father sat in the chair under a black cape. Every snip of the scissors brought down a tiny snowfall.

"Excuse me, guys," Sammy said, "When did the Dead Rat close down?"

"Huh? The what?"

"Dead Rat. Right next door."

The barber stood poised with the scissors and comb in his hands, and turned back to his customer.

The old man, who was on the verge of sleep, lifted his old gray eyes and said, "September 20th, 1928. I should know. It was the last pint pulled there and I drank it on my fortieth birthday. Capone and his bunch were in there that night."

The barber and the man's son snickered, believing that the old man's feeble mind had dove down into the murky depths and retrieved another faulty memory. Sammy sensed the laughter at the old man's expense and ignored it. He asked the old man another question.

"Do you remember a priest named Tony Keary?"

The old man was asleep. The other two men just shrugged their shoulders.

They left and went up the hill to Barnes Photography. Sammy, Betsy and Quint all got out and went in.

"We're here to pick up wedding photos," Betsy said.

The young woman looked at the couple with the ten year old boy.

"When was it?"

311

"Nineteen sixty-five."

The woman seemed confused for a moment and then said, "Oh, oh, oh. Wait. Right before daddy died he said to hold on to these." She searched in a set of cubby holes, pulled out an old eight by twelve envelope and held it up to read it. Dust fell from it.

"Teague-dupe-dupe…"

"Duplechain," Betsy said.

The woman smiled. "Well, here it is." She handed it over to Betsy.

They took them out and looked at them. They were all of just the two of them. None of any of the guests. None of Mr. Foreman. None of Tony Keary.

At the outskirts of town, two men were painting over the Terhune Sisters sign. The *Terhune* part was now obscured by a pasty mauve, and the *Sisters* part would soon be next. A banner that hung over the display windows said, "Liquidation Sale." Mauve paint from above was dripping on it.

"Sammy, stop, stop," Betsy said. He pulled over.

Betsy got out and talked to the woman who was in charge of the sale.

"I got my wedding dress here, or borrowed it," Betsy said.

"Aunt Mary would always lend people things," the woman said. "Drove mom crazy."

"Where are they now?" Betsy asked.

"Both passed away. Aunt Mary died about three months ago, and mom worried herself to death it must be five or six years ago. Uncle Vance moved to New York after that. It's just been me and Aunt Mary since. Time to let it go, I guess."

On a mannequin near the back of the store was the wedding dress. Under it, a sign said, *Best Offer.*

"It's for sale?" Betsy asked, trying not to betray her interest.

"That wedding dress? Yeah, if I can get anybody to buy it. Too old fashion for current tastes."

"How about ten bucks?" Betsy said, but she was prepared to go higher.

"How about you just take it?" The woman smiled. "It'll never sell."

Betsy gave her ten dollars anyway.

At the bridge over the Ohio, Quint looked out through the girders and over the water.

"Papa! It's as big as the St. Lawrence," he exclaimed. His mother kept her head down as she quietly prayed the Joyful Mysteries. His daddy was keeping his eyes squarely on the road as his hands squeezed the steering wheel tightly. When the car reached the Kentucky side, they seemed to exhale together.

It took them a while to find it, the house and the sign that said 'Just Drive In.' Sammy parked the car at the end of the driveway, just off the highway.

The mailbox was lying in the weeds, the other T missing and the letters reading, "Be is." The driveway was over grown, and when winter relented and spring filled in, it would be even more overgrown. At the end of the driveway, the house was encased in wisteria vines.

"This is creepy, papa," Quint said.

"Yeah it is, son," Sammy said, scanning the inside of the house. On a kitchen wall was a spray painted marijuana leaf with the words *Hi House* written under it. In the side yard, saplings were growing, but Sammy could make out two hubcaps. One was silted in, but the other held water and a mourning dove drank from it. It saw Sammy and took off with a trembling coo and a flurry of wing beats. Under the house was a rusty old hayfork.

They wandered back to the barn and found it burned down in the middle, the tractor still inside. The project that either Johnny or Dewey had begun was still unfinished.

Over in the woods that were slowly creeping skyward, the projection screen lurked like a temple overtaken by the rainforest. The projection booth's door was open, the window shattered, the projector itself long since missing. The poster on the outside was faded to almost white, but the last movies shown were still legible, *The Sons of Katie Elder,* and *The Greatest Story Ever Told.*

Chapter 90

They stayed the night in Clarksville, Tennessee, and then the next morning headed toward Mississippi. Lime green leaves were pushing out everywhere. They passed through Paris, and then Milan, My-Lan'.

Sammy pursed his lips and ground his teeth.

They got out at the County Line Inn, the Brownie Elf just a rusty, embossed shape without paint. Sammy, Betsy and Quint toured the Inn, boarded up now, the old chicken coup gone, and no sign of anyone, no sign of anyone for a long time. Chartreuse leaves filled the woods that were advancing slowly over the clearing and would overtake it completely in just a few years.

Betsy and Quint went back to the car. Sammy drifted up to the shack on the ridge. The ticking of the mattress had been removed in tuffs by field mice and birds. The pot belly stove stood cold, and the small hole in the ceiling was now a window to the deep blue spring sky. He walked in, stood under it and looked up. When he looked down, the window sill caught his eye. His finger traced the vow they had made, an impression that was as distinct as the day they had carved it:

I, Samuel Teague, IV, resolve never again to leave behind the love of my life, Betsy Duplechain, so help me God.
Forever and ever.

He took his pocketknife and worked at the sill. The board came loose, and he pried it free. He stepped out the door with the board in his hand and saw the cord ricocheting off the trees. He pulled it, and, down the hill at the ruins, a bell tinkled.

Chapter 91

Before he left to ride out to the mill, Sammy let Betsy and Quint out near the Grove and Sorority Row. She and Quint started up Sorority Row, and then she looked back and recognized the Circle. She took Quint by the hand to change his direction.

"Wait a minute, baby, let's go down here first."

They crossed the street in front of the Confederate monument. Through the trees, she saw a familiar form seated on the bench in the Circle, sitting perfectly still. As Betsy got closer, she saw why.

Seated on the bench at the Circle was a bronze statue of dearly departed Professor Tom Euless. Several years earlier, an Oxford policeman had come to wake him up at the end of the day and found him dead, his chin on his chest, both his mason jar and his 7Up bottle empty.

The university felt that some sort of a memorial was in order and commissioned a likeness of him to be displayed in his former habitat. The sculptor's aim had been to make him look handsome and scholarly, but, without his 7Up bottle, he looked lost and unnatural, and no one knew who the statue was. It soon became an icon for foolishness, turning up in odd places like seated in a lawn chair peering into sorority house windows at night, surprising people in bathroom stalls, and one year sitting in an end zone seat at the Ole Miss-Georgia football game. It had finally grown necessary to chain the Professor to the bench to prevent any further shenanigans.

What no one knew was that the Professor had died in arrears to the suppliers of his *eau de vie*. Later that year, the chain would be found severed with bolt cutters and Professor Euless would be gone for good this time, taken at last in death to satisfy a debt he had accumulated in life. No one would think to look for him in the woods down around Senatobia, sitting contentedly on the front porch of a moonshiner's shack.

For now, however, he was still chained to his bench, as he was in life. Betsy sat on the bench and contemplated him, trying to remember what he looked like in life. As she thought, she realized the only thing recognizable about the statue was a profound regret in his eyes. The sculptor had gotten that dead-on. At the base of the statue was a bronze plaque set in a round rock the size and shape of a millstone. On it was a quote, she thought it was from William Faulkner, though now she couldn't be sure, but she had written a paper on it for a literature class in Montreal:

The American South holds onto the past like a lover that is neither relinquished nor enjoyed.

"Who was he?" Quint asked. His hand was on Euless' bronze hand.

"He was a teacher here," his mama said, and then she thought of something Euless had told her once.

"There are three versions of history," he had said, "How the winners said it happened, how the losers wished it would have happened, and how it really happened."

A mockingbird, gray wings with broad white stripes like military insignia, flew out of the grove of trees and landed on the statue's head. It pumped its tail, and a white streak went down the side of the statue's head. Quint guffawed in that little boy way, and his mama shushed him. She wished she had a hosepipe or that it would rain or that they would run the sprinklers. Betsy said a quick prayer for Professor Tom and headed for sorority row.

They passed the statue of the Confederate soldier atop his pedestal, and Quint asked in French, "Who is that, mama? Was he a teacher, too?"

How do you explain something like that to a ten year old Canadian boy? That there was a war, and this is the second place trophy? If only the other statue could have awoken from his stony slumber and explained it at length.

"You'll have to ask your daddy about that," she said in English.

The Kappa House stood as it had for the last ten years, for the last hundred years, stately and hospitable. The big front door was open to let the perfect spring breeze waft in the perfect spring air. They stepped inside. Had it not been for her son next to her, Betsy would have thought she had stepped into a time machine.

Girls were moving about preparing for exams and dances and choir performances and marriage and careers and life and having a grand time in general.

Several stopped and said, "Hey-hey-ho-hi-gotta say it's great-*clap*- to be a Kappa Chi!" and then they moved onto another part of the house.

Quint smiled broadly, delighted at such an impromptu performance.

"What is this place?" he asked.

"A place for girls to live when they're going to school, baby."

She studied the pictures on the wall. Quint stood next to her, but looked all around, at everything else.

Betsy found their pictures, and her finger moved out, wishing she could touch them, to commune with them better somehow.

Loretta Hansen. Mary Nell Sawyer. Tina Sullivan. Her finger paused under the name.

"I was just a girl then, wasn't I?" a voice said. Betsy smelled a perfume, the sweet smell of ginger lily.

"Are you…is it….Bessie?"

They embraced, and, when they released the embrace, Tina Sullivan looked down to see the little boy face looking up. A face under sandy brown bangs.

"Is he yours?" Tina swept Quint's hair out of his eyes. "He's handsome. Reminds me of a boy I used to date. Just before I met you."

Quint reached his hand out to shake Tina's.

"Hello, ma'am," he said, practicing to be a southern gentleman. "Pleased to meet you, Quint Teague."

Tina knelt down and shook his hand, and then everything fell into place. She looked up at Betsy and then down at Quint. She grasped Quint and held him and he squirmed awkwardly like the little boy that he was. Tears of joy or sorrow or something else entirely were in her eyes.

"Let me look at you," Tina said, releasing him from her embrace and putting her hands on his shoulders.

"So Sammy's his…."

"Sammy's his daddy."

"I'm glad he found you," Tina looked up and said sincerely.

"What about you?" Betsy asked.

"Somewhere between still looking and stopped looking," Tina said. "I teach English here now. Southern Lit, specifically. And I'm the faculty sponsor for the Kappas."

They went through the names of girls they had known and laughed about old times, about hanging out the wash and making groceries.

"Whatever happened to Miss Pearlina?" Betsy asked.

"Her sister was some sort of business woman, very successful, apparently," Tina said. "When I came back, the spring after the

317

accident, she had left, and the two of them are still traveling the world. In fact, we just got another picture from them."

They went into the kitchen, where two of the girls were taking their turn in cleaning it. On the refrigerator was a picture of Miss Pearlina Hardy and her sister, Miss Opalina Hardy. Their towering hairdos, one almost white and the other most decidedly black, flanked the Tower of Pisa. They each were smiling broadly, their tornados of hair slanting perfectly parallel to the tower behind them.

"We got one last year of the two of them with the Eiffel Tower and, before that, Big Ben in London."

Tina laughed, the same warm, inclusive, welcoming laugh as before. In the years, she had vaulted past pretty and beautiful and was now stunning, the kind of woman that few men feel they have a chance with. Betsy thought that later she would call on St. Anne on Tina's behalf.

In the parlor, Quint was being made over by the girls, who were fascinated by his accent and that he was from a foreign country, Canada. Betsy went to retrieve him.

At the door, Tina and Betsy hugged necks and then pulled closer, swaying and kissing cheeks. They pulled away from each other with smiles and tears.

Quint met them at the door. He turned and waved to the girls in the parlor.

"Bye, now," he practiced his drawl.

Bye, now, they drawled back, and one of them added, *You sweet thang, isn't he just precious?*

Betsy and Quint walked down the walkway toward the street and toward the Grove.

"William Faulkner," Tina called out.

"William Faulkner?" Betsy turned and asked.

"The name of the man who lived in that house and wrote all those books."

Chapter 92

Finley's Mill had a new sign, larger and green with a stand of white trees painted on one side and a pallet of brown lumber painted on the other. Sammy pulled into the mill yard, the wheels crumbling through the rocky gravel. He was uneasy about leaving Betsy and Quint in town. The stars and stripes flew from the flagpole, and it was still odd for Sammy not to see the red and white maple leaf flag there. Under the sheds, men wore hard hats, safety glasses and hearing protectors that made them look like they had big mouse ears.

Sammy opened the door to the office, into the air-conditioning.

On the wall was a sepia toned picture of Mr. Finley when he was Private Finley. After he died, it was the only one the men could find of him. Under it in embossed letters was "Our Founder."

The gray headed black man at the desk shuffled through a stack of work orders. On his desk were pictures of his children, each picture with a different one of them in a graduation robe, and a few of the gray headed man himself holding grandbabies. He looked up and over his glasses.

"Dat Sammy? Sammy Teague? Come here, boy, gimme yo hand!"

A big-smiling Archie Wilson folded up his glasses and put them in his shirt pocket. The swivel chair squeaked back, and Archie rose. He shook Sammy's hand heartily like he was trying to test their shoulders for range of motion.

"Way you been, boy?" The sound of sawing machines outside was like a forgotten childhood lullaby for Sammy.

"Away," Sammy said evasively.

"Oh, I see," Archie smiled and raised his eyebrows as if that explained everything.

"How's everything here?" Sammy asked.

"Oh, jess fine. We been modernizin' the works here. You prolly seen the new machines."

"I sure did. Just a little quieter," Sammy said with a pinching gesture, "Just a little."

They sat and went down the list of men Sammy remembered.

"Still here," was the reply to most of them. "Passed," was the reply to a couple.

"What about Tillie?"

319

"Tillie married a lil' bitty white man," Archie said in a voice laden with curiosity at the absurdity of such a thing. "Moved off to Texas or somewheres."

"Still have beer on Saturdays?"

"Oh yes, mo deafly. Ain't got to drive up to Tennessee to fetch the Satty beer no mo, like Finley did. They sell it here in Miss Ippy."

"Here in the state of Mississippi?"

"Yas-suh, right cheer. Ain't that somethin'?"

Archie had left out the whereabouts of one person, the person Sammy was most looking forward to hearing from or at least about.

"Listen, Mister Archie. What about Jude? Jude Hawkins? He here today?"

Archie's smile vanished, and, after a sigh and a pause he said, "Come with me, Sammy."

They left the office and made their way through the mill, Archie limping along and not saying anything, and Sammy not asking anything.

At the fence line on the back edge of the mill yard was a neatly kept plot. The stone marker said:

Jude Hawkins
Born Apr. 23, 1942
Died Jan. 12, 1966
Cast Your Burdens on the Lord

Sammy heard his own voice far away, like someone else' voice, like shouting from the bottom of a well that becomes a whisper at the top.

"What happened?"

"Bout two or three months after you left, we found him hangin' one mornin' from one of the rafters of Shed Number Two. They's a note, said, 'God forgive me for killin' that crazy boy in Kentucky.' It didn't make no sense. Sheriff come over from Pontotoc and 'vestigated. Said he stepped up on a car battry and kicked it out from under hisself. Clear sue-side."

The mill snarled on behind them in the distance. A heavy off cut tumbled to the ground somewhere and sent out a hollow, woody note like the dropping of a huge baseball bat.

"Cat-lick church wouldn't bury 'im on account of it. Got Rev. Robinson at the AME to do it. Jess one thang I can't figure."

Sammy turned his red eyes to Archie, who turned his to Sammy. Archie's eyes bore generations of frustration.

"Tell me, Sammy. How do a man with a stump arm tie his own hand behind his back? How?"

Archie turned and started off, shaking his head, the old wound raw and weeping again. Sammy watched him limp back to the office. Archie stopped and pulled a handkerchief from his pocket and mopped his face. Turning back to the grave, Sammy imagined the events like a movie in his head:

The glint of a badge in the glow of a flashlight. The flailing stump arm, the oblong black cube of the car battery teetering to its side, dangling legs shaking. The slow twirl, white with frost on a bright winter morning, clear and still and cold.

Sammy returned later with the new priest, a young man from Memphis recently ordained. As the men of the mill stood around in the strange quiet, he blessed the grave, sprinkling holy water and conducting the rite in English, not Latin. Sammy buried his head in Betsy's shoulder, and her hand caressed it. Quint was at her side.

Quint whispered something to Betsy.

"A friend ya daddy's, baby," Betsy answered in a whisper.

"Is he still under there?" Quint looked up at his mother.

"Shhh. No, baby," she whispered. "He's in heaven."

She kissed the top of Sammy's head. "Healthy and whole."

Chapter 93

There was somewhere Sammy needed to go now, a pilgrimage to honor the dead. He was surprised to find cars filling the parking lot of the Greater Starlight Temple AME Church and spilling down the side of the highway. Sammy parked at the periphery, and he, Betsy and Quint picked their way down the shoulder to the church. The heavenly smell of wood smoke and cooking meat hung in the air like the gaze of angels. The church marquis told of this week's sermon, "What you do in the night, comes out in the light."

"I'll see if I can cut through. I just want to go down to the river. Jude and I spent a lot of time down there," Sammy said.

A lady carrying a casserole dish walked by and said, "Welcome, do jine us, won't you?"

Quint released Betsy's hand and ran. "Quint!" she said, but her son was already at the back yard of the church where he had spotted some boys his age.

The lady with the casserole dish said, "My name Sister Cleo and you's all welcome."

The back of the Greater Starlight Temple was familiar to Sammy but subtlely different with all the time that had passed and the sudden animation with all these people. A man who had shed his suit jacket for an apron turned about ten chickens' worth of chicken quarters on a big grill and sipped a grape drink between flips. The two men talking with him smiled and said good afternoon to Betsy and Sammy and then returned to their conversation with the man who was grilling. He said something, and the men guffawed, one bending down and the other backing up in the throes of something hilarious. The cook smiled as he flipped the chicken quarters.

Children played tag, while some of the older girls sang along to a hand clapping game. Women in their Sunday best talked in small knots together, holding bibles jammed with notes on scraps of paper. The older ones sat in the shade in lawn chairs with their elderly husbands, old men wearing black shoes, white socks, black trousers, white shirts and skinny black ties. A couple flirted in another splotch of shade. Three picnic tables end to end were covered with red and white checkered table cloths, the entire length a series of platters and pans of food.

Sammy left to go find Quint. Betsy stood at the periphery of the gathering and took it all in. It was like coming home.

The man at the grill shouted across the yard, "Miss Rosaline, can I make you a plate?"

"Show, chile," someone in the shade answered. "Make show you gimme summa dat nana puddin'." The voice was forgotten and familiar, a memory from a past life.

Rosaline. The name twirled Betsy's memory, and the voice stopped it like a finger on a name. She looked for the source of it.

"Miss Rosaline?" Betsy asked the man.

"Miss Rosaline Laurence? Why yes, they she go." He pointed to a cluster of old people in the shade of a tulip poplar.

There she was, enveloped in a just-too-big polyester lavender dress adorned with a dime store brooch, sitting diminutively on the webbing of a lawn chair. Her hair had gone completely gray in ten years, curly and white like the fleece of a lamb, just below her ears with a small white hat atop it. Her eyes were behind big dark sunglasses with side panels to protect them from the light.

Betsy crossed the yard, pausing to let children run by, and knelt by the chair. "Miss Rosaline? You remember me?"

Rosaline studied the white woman with the big brown eyes. "I don't rightly remember," she said, her sunglasses perched on her nose. She looked over them, her cloudy blue-gray eyes squinting like a baby when it studies a sound. Her brown hand grasped Betsy's as if it might help her tell who she was, squeezing it while her other hand joined in. They were thin hands, worn by years of love and work and joy, mostly knuckle under thin skin.

"Where's Deacon John, Miss Rosaline?" Betsy asked, looking into the woman's face.

"My John done passed; he walks witta Lawd now, show do. Now who you?" She looked into Betsy's face.

It was just a portion of one night so many years ago, Betsy thought, how could she possibly remember? She smiled and looked out at the gathering. Quint was at the river's edge with two boys about his age. They all had sticks and were prodding things in the weeds. She got up to go warn him to be careful not to fall in and to look out for snakes.

She released the old woman's hand. Betsy rose and brushed the wrinkles out of her dress.

Miss Rosaline smiled suddenly and tilted her head and said, "We prayed f'you real hard, now didn't we girl?"

"Yes ma'am, you did." Betsy smiled and knelt down again. She took Miss Rosaline's ancient brown hand, kissed it and put it to the fairness and freckles of her own cheek. "Yes ma'am you did."

Miss Rosaline raised her other hand to swear, "Praise Gawd."

Sammy ascended the hill and rejoined Betsy just as the man with the apron rattled two sets of tongs together and said in a booming voice, "Is ready! Deacon Justice, will you axe da blessin'?"

323

Everyone joined hands in a circle that encompassed the entire grounds, around trees and down to the river. Sammy and Betsy smiled when they saw Quint and his friends hurriedly throw down their sticks and join hands in the circle. Deacon Justice was a little man with a slack face and a smile with several teeth missing, but his voice was rich and resonant.

"Dear Gawd, we axe dat you bless dis food which yo gunness an' mercy have provide. When we were strangers, you met us, and when we were hungry, you fed us. And so Deh Lawd, we mose hummely besiege you...."

Reverend Brown cleared his throat, a short, quiet blast. Deacon Justice opened one eye to the reverend and shut it again.

"....to bless dis food to the norshement of our bawdies and mines. In Chrise-Jees we axe dis blessin'. Amen."

Everyone said A-men. Sister Cleo was between Sammy and Betsy and squeezed their hands. The little boys ran to the front of the line with their plates, but Reverend Robinson intervened.

"Gentlemen, gentlemen," he said to the boys in a voice that was steady and placating. "Ladies and guests first."

After dinner, Sammy wandered down to the bank and watched the river race by. The spring rains were keeping it high now, and the beach was under three feet of water, so he sat in the grass and watched the current. A twig, the size, shape and color of a peanut shell floated by, and Sammy smiled. Then a leaf, a sweetgum leaf, rode the current, looping through an eddy and continuing downstream. The five points of the leaf were upturned into a sort of floating crown. Sammy stood up and watched it as it disappeared under an overhanging tree limb, reemerging beyond it and then getting small and disappearing again.

He turned and went up the hill. He waded through the people visiting and found Reverend Robinson.

"Reverend Robinson?" Sammy asked.

"Yes?" The reverend was listening to the cook tell an animated story to a gathering of men. He stepped away from them and put a hand on Sammy's shoulder and smiled.

"I'm Sammy Teague. I used to live around here. I hear you buried a friend of mine a while back. Boy named Jude Hawkins."

"Nine, ten years ago, winter time, wasn't it?" Reverend Robinson asked.

"January '66," Sammy said.

"Oh, yes. County said it was suicide," the reverend said skeptically. "His own church wouldn't do it."

"That's right," Sammy said. "I just wanted to thank you. For doing it. For burying my friend."

"Christ said bury the dead," the reverend said. "I was glad to do my duty. As I recall, his co-workers at the mill said he was quite a character."

"That he certainly was," Sammy smiled nostalgically. "You know, he and I used to swim together, right down there."

"Oh, I know." He leveled his gaze at Sammy. "The ladies in the church told me."

Sammy blushed, years after the fact.

"Have you had some of Sister Cleo's banana puddin', Sammy?" Reverend Robinson said. He put his arm around Sammy's shoulder. "Let's go get us some."

Sammy helped clear the tables, and Betsy and Sister Cleo washed the dishes. Then they pitched horseshoes and played cards in the shade. From her chair, Rosaline's ancient voice sang for those gathered there, "Down by the Riverside."

Then it was time to leave. The congregation gathered as the Teague family got in their station wagon. The setting sun illuminated the faces of the men, women and children as they waved. The sun in their eyes made them look more hazel than brown.

An hour down the road, Quint's little voice rose from the backseat in the dark, "Papa, guess what."

"What's that?" Sammy said with his eyes on the road.

"Did you know that my friend Cornell is brown?"

Betsy put her hand over her mouth and her grin. Sammy smiled at the window, then looked into the review mirror and said, "Is that so?"

"Yeah," Quint nodded his head.

"Papa?" Quint said.

"Yeah, son?

"Can we go ice fishing when we live in Louisiana?"

"They don't have ice fishing in Louisiana like we do..." he corrected himself, "...like *they* do in Quebec. But we'll go fishing in the marsh. Me and you and grandpere."

"An' mama," Betsy added.

"And mama," Sammy smiled at Betsy.

Ten minutes later, Quint was asleep in the backseat, waves of light from the highway washing over his serene face. Under a mantle of sleep, his young mind sorted, folded and put away the events of the day so he could remember them forever.

In the green dashboard light glow, Betsy curled up on the front seat next to Sammy, his hands at twelve and six on the wheel like his daddy always had them.

"Guess what," she said.

"What? Are you gonna tell me that Sister Cleo is brown, too?" he teased.

"No," she swatted his shoulder. "I mean, yeah."

She looked in the backseat at their sleeping son and whispered in Sammy's ear. "We gonna have nutha baby."

Sammy's moist eyes glistened yellow-green in the dashboard light.

Chapter 94

The president had unconditionally pardoned all the draft dodgers, including that Teague boy. Now he was back in town, waiting to be coronated and assume the Teague throne. The sisters were in from Mississippi and Georgia, their cars parked under the oaks next to the station wagon with the Quebec plates. They had just gotten in, and then they had all left for the country club for a welcome home dinner. They wouldn't be back until well after sunset.

He would have to make it look like an accident.

The plan would be simple, and for the Teagues, it would be catastrophic.

Now, while they were away at dinner, he would turn off the gas to the house. The main valve was behind a thick patch of hydrangeas on the side. Then, get the spare key from the barn, where they kept it on a hook behind the door. Next, go inside the house and turn on the valves of all the space heaters, one in each bedroom, full blast. And then tonight, an hour after the last light goes out, turn the main valve on again. Gas'll flood the house while they all sleep. Sleep forever, gone pecan.

In the morning before their colored girl gets there, get up and go pay a call on the Teagues. Welcome home, young Sammy Teague and your beautiful wife, and your son, the next generation of swindlers!

When no one answers the knock, go around and turn off the gas, go in and start opening windows. Anyone still with a pulse gets duct tape over the mouth and nose, starting with the most able bodied and working down.

When everyone is dead, all the men, women, and children, take off the duct tape, turn off the space heaters, go outside, and turn on the main valve again.

And then call the coroner with news of the tragedy.

Parris smirked and headed to the barn for the key.

Chapter 95

He had slept in the spring sunshine most of the morning and into midday, dreaming of her kind face and voice. There had been a distant commotion from across the fields of knee high cane, the slamming of automobile doors and happy shrieks. He had lifted his head from the grass and tried to figure out the circumstances of the scene there, but he couldn't, so he had just put his head back down and tried to summon back his happy dream.

The little dog was resigned that the girl would not come back, but he still held her scent in his memory like something etched deep into rock. He had dreamed of her again, an intense dog dream that made his legs twitch, running to her in his sleep, almost feeling her stroke his head. But then he awoke and he was alone again.

He got up and wandered through the cane, the orange curl of his tail marking his movement through the rows like the periscope of a submarine submerged in a leafy green sea. Approaching the back of the barn, he paused to lap water from a puddle, and then lifted his leg on the gray cypress plank to give the possum a warning. He flicked an exclamation point of dirt on his mark.

The possum was still coming to the barn, he could smell it. If he were younger, he would set a trap for it, and when he found it he would grab it by the neck and shake it. Even though the dark woman called Dutchie now fed the mule and him, he still patrolled the barn where the mule had stayed after the water rose and then fell and the girl left.

Rounding the barn, he came across another smell, the scent of a man, the threatening odor of evil that only a dog can smell. He'd smelled it before. He paused and put his nose to the wind, blinking in thought. There was a sound that was not the wind. And then he saw the man.

The dog scampered through the weeds where the path had been when the girl's house had been there, before the water rose and then fell and the girl left. He could hear the big man's khaki pants brush across the weeds until the dog reached the empty field where the house had been. The dog's front legs and then back legs and then front legs gathered ground and threw it back in small sprays as he turned up the highway and the man followed. Chanceux could hear the man panting in that way that people do and dogs do not, slow and deep.

When the dog made the house of the dark woman called Dutchie, he went to his safe spot in the weeds behind the shed. He lay there in an orange ball and listened. His head was on its side, and his tongue lay in the weeds as he panted.

He heard the man's footsteps slow, and then he heard the man in the shed with the mule, and then the mule snorted. The dog got up and put his face in the hole that the mice had gnawed, and he saw the man and the man saw him. The man drew the gun on his hip and it shot fire and the board next to the dog splintered at the bottom. The dog returned to his safe spot and cowered with his ears low. He was exhausted and couldn't run anymore. If the man came around and found him, then that would be it.

A mule will labor for you ten years willingly and patiently, Faulkner wrote, for the privilege of kicking you once.

Or, perhaps, kicking *for* you. The blow was sudden like flicking a fly and left an imprint on Deputy Parris' forehead like the cloven hoof of the beast. His icy blue eyes stared at the roof of the barn where an early season wasp buzzed, bouncing off the underside of the tin roof with a faint tink-tink-tink. The back half of the deputy's body and head was submerged in manure, his hand still clutching the pearl handle of his revolver. His surprised face was the last expression he would ever make. The mule's whiskered mouth blithely chewed side to side.

Later, the orange dog appeared in the doorway and wandered over to the deputy's body. He cautiously sniffed it, his muzzle bouncing in the air as he surveyed it head to toe and back again. Then he lifted his leg to sign off affirmatively on the mule's work, adding a brush of dirt.

He wandered toward the big house, and that's when he picked up her scent. His muzzle scanned left and right and back and forth over the ground. He began barking, tracing the scent from the station wagon to the porch and then retracing it, reveling in it. Then he hopped up the steps waited for her, and for the boy, too. They were together, the boy and the girl. He smelled it and so it was true.

When the families all returned from dinner, the dog ran down the steps from where he had been waiting patiently under the porch light. Car doors slammed as he barked wildly and turned in circles for the girl, who knelt and hugged his squirming, trembling body. The children laughed at his antics, and the dog licked all of their faces, whining in happiness. Sammy knelt and rubbed Chanceux' jowls, and then looked up to the barn. Deputy Parris' cruiser was parked there.

He stood just as his daddy saw it, too, and they walked over to it, side by side in the cool night air, breathing small cold clouds under the boughs of the live oaks. Inside the car, the radio squawked between bursts of static. Trey craned his head around to the barn and out to the fields and to the house.

Just then, they heard Dutchie shriek, her voice distressed and small from across the field. Sammy turned and ran through the cane toward her house.

The State Police sent a couple of men down from Baton Rouge to investigate Deputy Parris' death. They ruled it an accident, and that the deputy had foolishly ignored the time honored advice of anyone who's ever been raised with horses and mules: don't walk behind them, especially a mule. And whatever you do, don't fire a gun behind one.

They went to the sheriff's office to interview Sheriff Lebeau, but couldn't find him. They scoured the parish, looking to see if anyone could tell them where he was. His time sheet was filled out; he continued to collect a paycheck as he had the last twenty years. Where could he be? With time, they found his bones under a six foot by three foot depression in the earth in an unkempt flower bed in Deputy Parris' backyard.

There are places where the dead are known to continue to vote, administering their civic duty for years after their passing, decades even. In St. Matthew Parish, a dead man had been elected sheriff for twenty years.

Chapter 96

Her Mimi had died, possibly living to a hundred, though no one knew for sure, but Betsy still went once a week to see her mama in the nursing home in Eunice, a place where the staff valiantly fought off the smell of urine and age with Pine Sol and peppermint oil. Televisions held one-sided conversations and laughed in the blank faces of the old bodies that were toppled and emptying. Her mama was becoming one of them.

On her first visit, Betsy found her mama wearing a lavender velour warm-up suit that hung loosely from her body. Now that she needed help feeding herself, her weight had plummeted to half of what it was before and her skin hung from her like a Bassett hound's. Betsy sat with her mama, who stared into the television as the soap opera characters wrangled with the same problems or variations of the same problems that they had twelve years earlier when Betsy last saw them, on the television in the Kappa house. From down the hall an old man loudly crooned out a name, like the call of a moose. No one ever knew who he was calling for.

Betsy sat patiently with her mama, who would mumble something in French from time to time. Betsy turned her ear to the muttering to help decipher it, and when she turned her head, she saw the letter she had mailed in 1965.

It was sitting in the corner of the drawer of the brown metal nightstand by her mother's bed. The postmark on the envelope said *French Lick, Ind., December 22, 1965, Season's Greetings.*

She pulled out the five pages. At the top of each page was printed, *From the desk of Anthony J. Keary, SJ.* The pages were well worn as if it had been read and reread and reread and had become something more than a letter. It had become a shrine to a missing daughter and a talisman for her return.

Also in the drawer, Betsy found a letter marked, *Return to Sender, recipient not at this address,* and a hand with a pointing finger next to it. Her mother's uneven, printed handwriting was on the envelope. It was postmarked *February 16, 1966, Eunice, La.*

It was addressed to her, so Betsy opened it.

Dearis dotta Betsy,

I hope this letta can fine you and that you come home. I no now that you the bess girl a mama can have. You mimi miss you too and if you come home I promise I ain't gonna trow you out no more. Please come home my baby I miss you somethin bad and I wont you to come home and be my girl agin. That boy daddy trew us out and bulldoze the house and now we live in Eunice wit Tante Na. You know where it is, is in Eunice, Louisiana, tween there and Church pint and Tante Na say you can stay here too wit Nonc Gabriel and you can have a dog too.

Sincerely,

Mama

In the back of the drawer were at least a dozen others, all returned. Betsy read a couple of them, all with the same heartbreaking message: I miss you, come home. She couldn't bring herself to read the others.

Betsy did keep returning, however, once a week, and, even though her mother didn't know who she or anyone else was, Betsy would read to her and pray the Rosary in French with her and tell her the story of her life, the story of a girl who married a prince, but first she had to clean him up a little.

And every week when Betsy left, her mother would ask the aid, "Sha, who dat girl, so sweet and beautiful? Mais, I wish she was *my* daughter."

Chapter 97

Easter Sunday, 1978

The sign said Mount Teague Farm, a bit of a misnomer for a ten thousand acre operation. The sign also said, Samuel and Betsy D. Teague, managers.

Tomorrow, a delegation of officials was expected from Belgium and France to tour a working sugar plantation. Mount Teague was selected due to the couple's command of French and the Place's productivity and efficiency.

On the water tower behind and above the big house, *Cane Do!* had been painted to replace the block letters MT. The front of the house was blooming in a riot of color, every azalea a chest high mound of solid blooms, the edge of the house bright with bedding plants, and the air scented with ginger lily and the banana scent of sweet magnolia.

And the smell of crawfish boiling was there, too. The roar of the gas flame under the pot competed with the murmur of conversation. A car pulled up with two familiar visitors.

Nonc Claude's wife, Tante Lucille, looked at Quint and then Sammy and exclaimed, "Sha, he looks like he made that baby wittis face, yeh! Jus' spit him out his mouth." Her fingers flew from her own mouth as she pantomimed the process. Then she smiled and gave both Sammy and Quint a big grinning kiss on the cheek. Nonc Claude shook Sammy's hand and gave his favorite niece a kiss on both cheeks. Quint shook Nonc Claude's hand, and Nonc Claude once again pretended that Quint's grip hurt his hand.

"Gaaaw! Mais das a grip!" Nonc Claude said.

Dutchie was there with her family, not as an employee, but as a guest. And Dutchie's husband and Sammy's golf partner, Ernest Favorite was there, leaning on the counter in the kitchen, he and Sammy having a beer together. Dutchie was holding Sammy and Betsy's new daughter Elizabeth on her hip. That baby rarely wanted anyone else.

"I never asked about the golf yesterday," Betsy asked.

"Man, the language!" Ernest teased, pointing at Sammy with his thumb.

"You're one to talk! Remember that shot in the water on the eighth?"

Ernest laughed. "Yeah, I guess you right."

Sammy's daddy, whom Quint called grandpere, sat in the lime green shade with Nonc Claude as the crawfish boiled. Nonc Claude got up and stirred the pot with a boat paddle as they talked about the old days of mule-drawn wagons and hand-cut cane, and they both expressed admiration for the woman who was the favorite niece of one of them and the Godsend daughter-in-law of the other. Then they bantered about the upcoming fall's LSU-Ole Miss game and about past games, especially the 1972 game and the mysterious extra seconds that appeared on the clock in Tiger Stadium. Afterwards signs appeared at the state line proclaiming, 'Now entering Louisiana, set your clock back four seconds.' They shook hands with a wager of a bottle of scotch on this fall's game. It would become a tradition, the winner making a toast to the loser, until death parted them, and maybe after that in heaven, if they could find the scotch for it.

In the barn, Quint and Charlotte's daughter Sophia milled around looking at the ancient tack on the walls and the mule who had once wore it. Quint was still in his navy blue First Communion jacket from earlier in the day.

"My mama used to let me ride him sometimes," Quint bragged. "But now he's too old."

The old gentleman's ears lay back flat against his neck like empty brown corn husks. He chewed placidly. The glossy black pupils of his big eyes had seen it all and remembered everything.

Sophia was only half listening, and gazing up into the loft.

"If you go up there, then I'll come up and give you a kiss," she said.

Samuel Teague the Fifth ascended the ladder into the Old Trick. It would be a while before his daddy found him, proudly refusing to cry out for help. The grownups had been dancing in the central hall to the old victrola.

Quint Teague's daddy set the ladder in place and gave him the advice he had heard from a man he worked with on the docks in Montreal. The man had an accent from some other country, Sammy never knew where exactly.

"Fall in love in the kitchen," Sammy said, but he left out the second half for his young son. *Not in the bedroom.* He would cover that later.

He walked with his arm draped across Quint's shoulders, back up to the house where Dutchie was dancing with Elizabeth, the baby named after the patron saint of expectant mothers. Betsy was pregnant again and sat resting her feet. If it was a boy, they would name him Jude Anthony, a double saint name, after the patron saints of lost causes and lost things.

An old fat dog lay sleeping like an orange mound on the porch.

In the end, Hurricane Betsy would be the first hurricane ever to cause over a billion dollars of damage. Billion-dollar Betsy was gone, passed north and away somewhere, leaving some lives untouched and others changed forever. No hurricane will ever be called Betsy again.

Gratitude

A big-hearted thank you to my editor, Katie Schellack, who challenged me and saw to it that this story got better. Thank you, too, to my first readers who had no idea what they were getting into, they only knew they enjoyed reading:

My very first reader, Flavia Lancon, who also happens to be my mother-in-law; Emily Aucoin, who knows all about commas; Carly Kirk, who really put a lot of effort into this; Liz Parker, the pride of Kentucky; Eileen Rome, *pauvre bête*; Emily Jones, who saw the water tower before I did; Lindsey Fontenot, Gloria Thudium, Shawn Kleinpeter, Kitzia Baxter, Steve Feigley, Jill Chenier, and Steven Sotile.

Writing a book, and any form of creative expression, really, can be lonely business, so I thank you all for making it less so. I was fortunate to have you take the time and to benefit from your honest assessments.

And thank you to my wife Catherine. I propose a new saint: Saint Catherine of Louisiana, patroness of those married to Oddballs and Knuckleheads. I can see her picture now in the next edition of *The Lives of the Saints*: seated with palms pressed together, long-suffering gaze cast heavenward, up past a glowing halo, with the author of this book in the background. Her miraculous feat: staying married to me all these years.

Tony Keary was right, there are just two kinds of people in the world, the Kind and the Unkind, and each of us has to choose which we will be, every single moment of every single day. God help us.

38770580R00202

Made in the USA
Lexington, KY
25 January 2015